Take It Like a Mom

Take It Like a Mom

Stephanie Stiles

NEW AMERICAN LIBRARY
Published by New American Library,
a division of Penguin Group (USA) Inc.,
375 Hudson Street, New York, New York 10014, USA
Penguin Group (Canada), 90 Eglinton Avenue East, Suite 700, Toronto,
Ontario M4P 2Y3, Canada (a division of Pearson Penguin Canada Inc.)
Penguin Books Ltd., 80 Strand, London WC2R 0RL, England
Penguin Ireland, 25 St. Stephen's Green, Dublin 2,
Ireland (a division of Penguin Books Ltd.)
Penguin Group (Australia), 250 Camberwell Road, Camberwell,
Victoria 3124, Australia (a division of Pearson Australia Group Pty. Ltd.)
Penguin Books India Pvt. Ltd., 11 Community Centre,
Panchsheel Park, New Delhi - 110 017, India
Penguin Group (NZ), 67 Apollo Drive, Rosedale, Auckland 0632,
New Zealand (a division of Pearson New Zealand Ltd.)
Penguin Books (South Africa) (Pty.) Ltd., 24 Sturdee Avenue,
Rosebank, Johannesburg 2196, South Africa

Penguin Books Ltd., Registered Offices:
80 Strand, London WC2R 0RL, England

First published by New American Library,
a division of Penguin Group (USA) Inc.

First Printing, July 2011
1   3   5   7   9   10   8   6   4   2

 REGISTERED TRADEMARK—MARCA REGISTRADA

LIBRARY OF CONGRESS CATALOGING-IN-PUBLICATION DATA:
Stiles, Stephanie, 1967–
Take it like a mom/Stephanie Stiles.
p.   cm.
ISBN 978-0-451-23254-0 (pbk.)
1. Stay-at-home mothers—Fiction. 2. Motherhood—Fiction. 3. Pregnant women—Fiction.
I. Title.
PS3619.T5455T35   2011
813'.6—dc22   2011005302

Set in Adobe Garamond Pro • Designed by Elke Sigal

Printed in the United States of America

For Eric, Nicholas, and Allison,
who helped me learn how to take it like a mom
(and like it)

ACKNOWLEDGMENTS

Thank you to the many people who helped, inspired, and motivated me while I was seeing this book to its completion. Without the tireless efforts of my agent, Scott Eagan, none of this could have happened; thank you to him and Greyhaus Literary Agency for taking a chance on me. Thank you to Laura Cifelli and Tracy Bernstein, my editors at NAL, who guided me, taught me, and kept me sane and dry-eyed. Thank you to everyone at NAL who supported and assisted with the project; I truly appreciate your hard work and efforts. Thank you to my mom, dad, sister, and brother, who've encouraged me all my life to like books, with a special thanks to my sister, Pam, whose stories about her boys, Michael and A.J., kept me laughing and got me thinking. Of course, I thank my own kids, Nicholas and Allison, who showed me that motherhood is better than any sitcom; without them, I simply wouldn't have written all of this. And for all the rest, I thank you, Eric.

Take It Like a Mom

Prologue

*S*ince it's always kind of awkward getting started—like a blind date, or a first date with a guy you only saw late one night in a bar—I guess I should tell you right away that my name is Annie. And my favorite TV show has always been *Bewitched*. This is significant because that show has always provided me with the defining image of stay-home motherhood. Sure, there was Lucy, but what with her always trying to break into showbiz and all, I actually think of her more as a struggling performer or unemployed vaudevillian than a wife or mother. So, Samantha Stephens is pretty much my role model. I mean, like her, I'm a stay-at-home wife and mother, only I have a son, Robby, instead of Tabitha, and my husband, Alex, doesn't work in advertising—or for Mr. Tate. Oh, and I'm not magic. Or as good-looking—although I am blond. However, that show always focused on some zany escapade that made life at home with Samantha seem exciting, with Dr. Bombay and Esmeralda and that Paul Lynde character appearing, stirring up trouble, then disappearing, and I liked that idea—I mean, not the idea of weird warlocks (or really any relatives at all) descending into my living room without forewarning or invitation or the assistance of the laws of gravity or time travel, but the idea that home could be a place where stuff, maybe even funny stuff, actually happened.

I guess that's what really inspires me—the potential joys and adventures of staying home to raise a family. In fact, if I had my own TV show, the trailer could say something along those lines—maybe something like, "Tonight, on a very special *Annie*, high jinks abound as the Forsters' Wednesday night dinner turns to mayhem. Watch as Annie serves up a healthy dose of laughter, love, and inspiration." Or something like that. Not that I've spent hours composing that or anything, but you get the idea.

And although life seemed zany enough with just Robby, when I discovered I was pregnant with number two, what I had come to think of as merely high jinks and escapades turned into a season finale–length episode of my loss of cool—assuming cool people even use the word "cool" anymore, and I'm not really sure they do. But in all honesty, pregnancy, in spite of the Angies and Heidis and Nicoles doing their best to chic it up, is still a pretty embarrassing condition to find yourself in. I mean, I hope I'm not letting out any great secret to those who are deciding to carry on the species, but pregnancy is, even if you're not blessed with stretch marks and swollen ankles, awkward. Let's be real: It's a public announcement that you've had sex—at least once and probably many more times than that. Dozens of times? Hundreds? On more than one occasion, I've found myself staring at the distended abdomen of some unsuspecting pregnant woman and wondering what kind of kinky activity led to her current state. And I don't know about you, but for the first ten years I was having sex, I was desperate to keep that information private. I couldn't even buy spermicide without pretending to the cashier that I thought it was toothpaste.

But when you're pregnant, it's somehow as if your body becomes public domain. I mean, during both my pregnancies, people I had never before spoken to reached out and touched my stomach. I'm not kidding. The guy who stocks the frozen foods at my grocery store and Alex's IT guy both did this. As I mentioned, Alex is my husband; and, given that you now know we've done it, can you please imagine that we are golden tan, fit, twenty-something, and maybe just a little sandy? We, in reality, are not. But somehow it's as if the idea that there's a baby underneath removes the social convention that strangers in our culture don't fondle each other's torsos. I would never waltz up behind a fat man at the hardware counter and caress his stomach—even if the concept appealed to me. But the thing that's stranger than their having touched me is that I didn't really care or notice how weird it was. Because, if I've learned anything, it's that pregnancy, like a good recipe or a bad mood, is meant to be shared.

One other valuable realization hit me during my second pregnancy as well. It's a lesser-known and certainly more personal consequence of pregnancy than the public proclamation of sexual activity, but it's equally noteworthy in its own right: the pregnancy superpower. Perhaps as compensation for the hemorrhoids and the sleeplessness, fate seems to offer most moms-to-be some kind of new and improved talent that sort of shapes the pregnancy. Mine was that I could remember things; not the big things, like car appointments or mortgage payments, but the minutiae of life's white noise—milk expiration dates, for example (August 26, by the way); or how many pairs of clean underwear were in Alex's top drawer (six, plus a pair of tighty-whitey backups). I couldn't remember the names of half of Robby's friends' mothers, but I could recall with certainty exactly how long each had nursed, their preferred brand of diapers, and what kind of footwear they favored (including one unfortunate bout with a crocodile stiletto). It had its allure, this superpower, I grant—but it also allowed me to remember with daunting precision the multitude of my various social missteps and embarrassments. I wish I could claim that stumbling into the numerous social gaffes that awaited me during these nine months was, in fact, another side effect of the pregnancy; however, that would be a lie. The ugly truth is that I've always been a Velcro strip for mortification. So, although pregnancy added to that, it couldn't be blamed for it entirely. I just lucked into the good fortune of being able to remember all the details of my embarrassments with an even greater clarity afterward. That was my superpower; well, that and the heroic capacity to eat tremendously large quantities of anything at all, at any time. I don't like lasagna, but if there was enough of it on a plate when I was pregnant, it became irresistible. One Snickers repelled me; however, seven in a row provided temptation that was impossible to resist.

So, while other mommies-to-be were discovering that their superpowers were things like an incredibly elevated sex drive or an inner peace that allowed them to forgive their mothers, I developed unwanted memories and insatiable hunger. My best friend's superhuman aversion to yellow food at least kept her away from fries; my cousin's pregnancy-driven power of smell, which she claimed was strong enough to detect the aromatic difference between the green and brown M&Ms, kept her off anything more heavily scented than cold cereal and applesauce for three months. Sure, I ate a lot when I was pregnant with Robby, but then, I had the compensation of the Sleepwalker Woman alter ego who burned off most of the unwanted calories when I was too unconscious to feel the torments of waking exercise. During my second time at the plate (an apt metaphor, I assure you), I had no such luck: I had only memory and an appetite with no calorie-burning penchants.

I grant, many pregnant women sit gracefully by, still able to cross their legs, glowing beatifically and caressing their growing stomachs lovingly; I just wasn't one of them. Instead, I tripped and ate my way through nine months of pregnancy and family upheaval of many varieties, because much happened during these forty weeks. (By the way, aren't forty weeks actually *ten* months? Whoever told us pregnancy lasted nine months was a dirty, low-down, lying, um, liar. That's what.) A lot of growing, forming, changing, and re-forming took place—and I'm not just talking about the baby, either.

Chapter One

*R*obby, my three-year-old, had been making the round of birthday parties for about three months. And while this may sound fun enough, especially for a three-year-old, it was not—for either of us. Because his birthday had been one of the earliest of all his playgroup buddies, he'd had his expectations raised—you know, thinking that every party he went to, he'd get to have his own cake, get to blow out his own candles, and get to take home his own million big plastic presents. So, under those false assumptions, Robby was starting to get a little impatient with these parties. And, try as I might, I just could not disabuse him of the notion that all birthday parties were for him. That other kids needed presents, too, just wasn't part of the logical, intellectual makeup of his three-year-old brain.

These parties were starting to get to him. Hell, they were getting to all of us. How many clown-frosted cupcakes or cowboy-shaped cakes or giraffe-painted cookies could a kid and his mom eat in a quarter year? And there were eleven kids in the playgroup—which meant eleven parties. And eleven tantrums for Robby—including one at his own party, when he opened a present containing a shirt instead of a toy. And even though math would dictate that those numbers averaged about one a month, the birthdays were all crammed into about a four-month period by some fluke of either nature or poor timing. Anyway, by the end of August, there were seven down, but four still loomed in front of us like booster shots.

The playgroup, just so you don't think I'm crazy right away, began with only four of us new moms: Jenn, the other Jen, Jen's sister, Betsy, and me—four of us who, until a few months earlier, had gotten to apply mascara and lipstick on a daily basis (now I use a leftover tube of Lansinoh—yes, that's the nipple cream—for both), eat at restaurants not beginning "Mc," and wear clothes with a DRY CLEAN ONLY tag. But we had given up our perky breasts and regular haircuts for the requisite sports bras and ponytails of suburban motherhood, preferred, if not actually demanded, by the residents of our small New Jersey town. So it seemed to follow logically that we would get together often enough to introduce some fun into the monotony of toddler life. And we moms, well, we were all afraid that if we didn't get some regular social contact, we'd become creepy shut-ins, ordering our clothes from the Fingerhut catalog and stockpiling canned goods in the basement. However—predictably, you may safely add— the four moms became six moms. Then six turned into eight, and soon there were just, like, random mothers and their children arriving at my, or Jenn's, or the other Jen's, doorstep. We had some kind of labyrinthine system of rotation in place for hosting these free-for-alls, but I swear it seemed as though I had this football team of a playgroup in my family room a hell of a lot more often than once every eleventh meeting. And though I can't speak for my husband, I'm pretty sure Alex would agree that the playgroup signature was being scrawled a little too indelibly on our poor unsuspecting house, given his expression upon passing the juice-stained, Cheerio-encrusted patches of residue these baby barons always left in their wake on the family room rug. But both Alex and our beagle, Chipper, were good sports about the invasions. Chipper loved it because, after emerging from under our bed upstairs, he could come down and root out enough edible shrapnel from the battlefield of my destroyed carpeting to survive a winter in Helsinki. And Alex, well, he's Alex, and he is always a good sport about toddler detritus.

So, Tuesday arrived along with party number eight. Robby pretty well knew the dance by this time, so as soon as he spotted me slipping the Elmo-bespattered gift bag out of the closet, he started whimpering that he wanted to stay home. We were going to one of the New Joiners' today, and, given how rare it was *not* to have everyone at my house, I was actually, well, kind of up for it. I mean, I wasn't dancing on a chair and lip-synching "I Will Survive" into an empty champagne bottle or anything; but I was somewhat less pissed off at all the New Joiners and their hazardous offspring. Robby, however, *was* pissed off—as much as a three-year-old who's already had his party and is tired of watching all the other kids open up eleven presents in a row can be. And, I was learning, that was pretty much a lot of pissed off. So his whimpering soon became full-fledged crying. The full-fledged crying soon became grabbing on to immovable objects affixed to the house. And, then, perhaps inevitably, the grabbing on to immovable objects became puking.

If you've never seen a three-year-old puke (and if you haven't, can I please meet you, shake your hand, and move in with you?), it defies all the laws of Newtonian physics. And Robby's was pink. I don't know, never having studied medical science, what exactly can turn kids' puke pink, but my speculation is that Robby had consumed so much frosting at these multitudinous parties that his stomach had actually been dyed from the inside out. Remember the tattoos they give out at carnivals that you lick and stick? Well, imagine what seven batches of neon-colored confections sitting in a stomach full of saliva could do to you. So Robby's puke—and who knew what other organs?—had been tinted pink, and the puke had tie-dyed my foyer.

Torn between equally strong feelings of aggravation, repulsion, and maternal concern that my son's innards had become tie-dyed into some kind of psychedelic wonderland, I navigated back to the kitchen as if passing through a minefield and called the pediatrician. I figured I had better seek out some objective advice, sage counsel, professional wisdom, or medical expertise. And above all, this doctor was hot—really hot. He had blond hair with just a touch of gel, tan hands, great shoes (never sandals), and a smile that made you remember high school. Hard to believe a guy named Dr. Herrold Hornby could be hot, but let me assure you, he made going to the doctor's fun. Even Robby liked him since he always gave out beanie-bag germs to his patients. Don't get the wrong idea; it wasn't that I was going to cut out on Alex or anything, but being pent up in a house all day with a pink-puking three-year-old wasn't exactly all that sexually arousing, or even interesting. Seriously, after a while, even the UPS guy started to look tempting—and he wore kneesocks and brown polyester. Imagine what a pair of crisp khaki pants and a stethoscope could do for you after that. And as for conversation? I love my son, but really, since quitting my job, the most intellectually stimulating daytime dialogue I've had has been with television commercials. And, in all honesty, they're not very good conversationalists.

So, I hit speed dial one. It doesn't take long to figure out that you need to put your kid's doctor as number one on speed dial, in case you're wondering. And I adjusted my voice to sound as cool as possible in case of the ridiculous potential that Dr.

Hornby—Herrold, as I referred to him in my mind—would answer. Instead, I got Michael. Michael was the receptionist; a twentysomething aspiring artist whom I'd become pretty great friends with over the past three years.

I love Michael, and I count on him. He's the kind of guy who'll tell you that the cargo pants you've been wearing for nearly a year aren't "quirky"; they're just dumpy. And, in fact, he did tell me this; but even though it was somewhat painful to hear, as when your mom tells you you're going to have to get braces, I had to admit it was true. Still, I hated having to toss those cargoes. And Michael was a pretty aggressive salesman, too: While all the moms waited for their kids in Herrold's waiting room, he always tried to sell them the paintings he'd done of his former lovers. Because I liked him so much, I actually once considered buying one of his abstracts entitled *Lars*. But after I had been staring at it for a while, a huge erection seemed to appear amid the swirls of oil paint, and I figured Alex would never go for it.

"Doctor Hornby's office," Michael snapped into the phone.

"Hi, Michael, it's Annie. How are—"

"Hello, Annie. Still wearing the Dumpsters?" I could almost hear his smirk. Maybe he was still pissed that I hadn't taken *Lars* off his hands.

"Look, I'm wearing a perfectly good pair of yoga pants today, if you must know."

"Oh, *yoga* pants. The last hurrah of youth until it sinks finally and irrevocably into the miasma of leggings. How nice for you."

This was too much. First my cargoes. Now my yoga pants? Soon I'd be forced to wear Prada and stilettos just to get Robby's temperature taken.

"Paint any rectal cavities or bulbous testicles today?" I inquired casually, trying to change the subject.

"Tee-hee. But, if you must know, I did just sell a *Peter* to Mrs. Jensen. So there."

"Barbara Jensen? Josh's mom? *She* bought a *Peter*?" I asked. Although I had never actually seen a *Peter*, I was willing to guess it was in the same vein as his other erotics-as-art paintings.

"Yes, she most certainly did," he asserted.

"But *Barbara*? I mean, she seems so . . ."—I was on the verge of saying "normal," but I didn't want to insult him—"so strait-laced," I ended lamely.

"All I had to do was tell her that the penis hanging out of the thong was a banana overflowing from a fruit bowl. After that, she was putty."

"How exquisitely commercial of you. Soon you'll be able to quit your day job—if that's not selling out too much. Now, can you take your mind off genitalia long enough to help me?"

"I aim to please. Shoot."

"My son is puking pink."

"Eww. Come on, do you have to describe it?"

You gotta love a guy who works in a pediatrician's office while maintaining a healthy aversion to children's bodily fluids.

"Look, can Hornby see us?" I tried to stay the course.

"Annie, you have to stop fabricating these gastronomical disasters just for an excuse to get out of the house. Even though, between us"—he lowered his voice to an obvious whisper—"I think Herrold's worth making up excuses for. So look, haul that bum of yours—looking ever tighter, I might add—down here stat, and we'll squeeze you in."

"Thanks, Michael! I'm on my way. But, just so you know, I think 'stat' actually means the opposite of what you intended to say. I'm pretty sure 'stat' stands for 'static.' You know, as in, not moving?" Burn. I loved besting Michael; he could be such a know-it-all sometimes.

"Oh. My. God. Please tell me you are not really this impaired! The word, or *abbreviation*," he said, drawing out the word as if to instruct me, "is *stat*, and it means to get down here *in two minutes*, or I will give your spot to Susie Kelley, who's here with her Magilla Gorilla child, and *you'll* be cleaning up pink vomit with a foot up your ass—mine."

And with that, he hung up.

Okay, so maybe I was wrong about the stat debate. That meant I now had two minutes to scrub down Robby, touch up my makeup, and—thanks to Michael—change out of the offending yoga pants and somehow find out what "stat" stood for. I just knew the bastard was going to quiz me as soon as I got there. Time was short, but I put in an emergency call to Jenn, who, luckily, picked up on the second ring.

"Jenn? It's me. What does 'stat' stand for?"

"Are you kidding? Haven't you ever watched, like, *Grey's Anatomy* or *E.R.,* or anything *ever* on television?"

"Seriously. I have to know *now*, 'cause I'm on my way to Hornby's, and Michael's gonna grill me."

"You're going to Herrold's? You really shouldn't be talking to me, then, Annie; you should be putting on mascara. And a push-up bra. *Immediately.*"

"Immediately? Really? My boobs are that bad?"

"No! Immediately is what 'stat' stands for. It's Latin or something. *Statim*—that's what it is; it's an abbreviation for *statim*."

God, how I loved this woman. Underneath her fabulous hair and gorgeous face lay the brain of an actually smart person.

"*Statim?* What the hell is that? I always thought 'stat' was short for static—which seemed weird, because everyone always uses it to mean 'right away'—whereas static, well, that kind of means not to move at all, doesn't it? I thought for a while, back in the nineties, during the *Chicago Hope* days, that it may have stood for statistic. As in, if we don't do something *stat*, this guy is going to be just another statistic. But that never really panned out upon deeper reflection. . . ."

"Annie?"

"Yeah?"

"Shut the hell up and get yourself dressed for Herrold. *Stat!*"

"Got it! Oh, and by the way, if I can't wear yoga pants, what should I wear?"

"Why can't you wear yoga pants?"

"Because Michael hates them."

"Ahh, Annie, I'm pretty sure he's gay."

"Jenn—I'm not hitting on him! But he just told me that yoga pants are to moms what leggings are to old people."

"He did? That bastard. Didn't he just write off cargo pants, too? So, what are you going to wear?"

"That's what I'm asking you!"

"So, no yoga pants, no cargoes. What do you have?"

"Shorts?"

"Too generic," she replied without a second's thought.

"A skirt?"

"You're kidding, right?" she asked, incredulous. I knew she kind of had a point, though, so I didn't bother to push it.

"Well, help me! What else is there?" I pleaded. I was beginning to hate her.

"Jeans," she answered after a moment's reflection. "And a sweater tied around your waist. I read somewhere that guys think that's cute."

"Jeans. I can do that. I think. My God, I haven't tried my jeans on in weeks. And they can be kinda moody."

"The good ones always are. See what you can do. Oh, by the way, why are you going? Everything all right?"

"Robby's throwing up. And it's the color of Kendrick's cupcake frosting."

"Eek. Gross. But I bet it's nothing; the sugar probably made him sick. Or maybe Kendrick did. I know she makes me sick. God, I hate that kid. Don't you? Did you see her drooling when she was blowing out the candles? Drooling, for crissakes!"

"How could I miss it? Oh, by the way, will you tell Laura I'm not gonna make it to Connor's party? Damn. I really wanted to see her house. But I really gotta run—I have some jeans that need squeezing into. I'll call you later on, okay?"

Generally, no matter my mood or schedule, I'm always up for a conversation about one of two things: kids I hate or the homes they live in. But I knew if I was going to make us at all presentable for Herrold, I had to cut this particular chat short, so I hung up and—in what struck me as a pretty efficient mom manner—stripped Robby, sponged him down, then re-dressed him in a top-tier outfit suitable for Herrold. In the remaining thirty seconds, I crammed myself into a pair of Sevens, making a mental note to self to thank Jenn for the invaluable suggestion of the sweater-around-the-waist idea. I mean, these jeans were so tight, you could make out the birthmark on my left hip. And even though I'd rather not have to confess this, the truth was I couldn't button the top button. But what was I going to do? I had to be at the doctor's ASAP; I had no time to rethink my fashion options. So I grabbed a sweater, tied it in a double knot (obscuring the bursting buttons), and ran out the door with Robby in tow.

Chapter Two

Once in his car seat, Robby began to settle down. I guess he could sense he'd won the battle. And he was always good in the car. When he was a baby, Alex and I used to drive around the block, spying on our neighbors in order to get him to sleep. However, unlike Robby, I was not quite so composed. For me, a typical trip to Herrold's required a good thirty minutes of personal grooming and primping, followed by a complete prewash, soak, and spin cycle for Robby. After all, I didn't want Herrold to think I was slovenly in any of my female responsibilities. But for this appointment, I had no real prep time and a kid whose guts could expose my lax cupcake policy. Plus, I was contending with the "stat" debacle. I was not, needless to say, in peak form. I just prayed that Robby wouldn't throw up pink—or, really, any other color, either—on himself or me until Herrold had the chance to see the outfits I'd selected specifically for our date. I mean, visit. Okay, appointment. Whatever.

"How ya doing, Robby? Does your tummy hurt? Do we need to stop the car?" I was ready to pull over in an instant.

"Mommy, I don't feel . . . I don't feel . . ."

Oh God, he was going to puke. *Please don't puke. Please don't puke.* I just kept repeating that to myself over and over. *Please don't puke. Please don't puke*

"You don't feel what, Robby? Are you going to get sick? Are you going to throw up?"

"Mommy . . . I don't feel . . ."

"Don't feel what, Robby?" I asked. This was starting to get to me. Even my stomach was in knots. I slowed the car down and began to pull over to the side of the road.

"I don't feel . . ."

"Honey, you don't feel what?" *Spit it out,* I thought to myself. Then, immediately, I took it back. *No, don't spit it out. Don't spit it out. Don't spit it out.*

"I don't feel . . . like going to the doctor's. Even if he does give me a beanie germ."

What a relief. A kid who didn't want to go to the doctor's I could deal with; a kid who was going to puke on the sweater that held my unbuttoned pants together was another story. Fleetingly, I imagined how everyone would be telling me breezily to "just take it off," to simply remove the puke-stained sweater, as if it were just there in case I suddenly took a chill.

"Well, we're here now," I said as I pulled into the parking lot. "So let's just let him take a quick look, okay?"

We walked hand in hand to the front door. I was too worried that Robby would puke on the sweater to say a word. I didn't want to rock the boat. *Don't puke; don't puke; don't puke,* I repeated to myself, willing him to obey. It was kind of like the séances we used to have at sleepover parties; you know, when everyone keeps saying, "Light as a feather; stiff as a board," over and over again until the girl on the floor gets levitated. I didn't expect Robby to start floating or anything; I just really, *really* didn't want him to puke on my sweater.

Swear to God, we weren't halfway into the office before I heard Michael's voice from behind the reception desk beckoning to me.

"Well? What is it short for?" he demanded from across the room.

"'*Statim*.' You know, Michael, I'm a mom, not an idiot."

"Yeah, right. Who'd you call to find out? And don't say 'Nobody,' because I called you back to tell you Herrold could see you, but your phone went straight to voice mail, which it only does when you're on the other line."

"As if! You think I go around calling people to find out what stupid abbreviations—"

"Who?" he interrupted.

"Jenn," I shamefully admitted.

"I *knew* it. I bet you don't even know what IQ stands for, do you?"

"Duh, Michael. I'm not going to take a quiz to prove I know how the English language works," I responded, adopting my most bored of tones to suggest how far above all this I was.

"I'm waiting," he said, smirking. Although his arms weren't actually crossed against his chest, they may as well have been.

"Intelligence quotient," I said as smugly as I could, waiting for his acknowledgment. But he was quiet for just long enough that I started thinking I was wrong. "Okay, wait. I mean, I mean, intellectual quotient. No, it's intelligence quantity, right?" I was starting to get nervous.

"And I cannot believe how low yours is right now," he said in between laughs. "I knew if I let you stand there long enough, you'd start doubting yourself. Really, Annie. Grow a couple grapes, would you?"

And just like that, with the mere mention of the word

"grapes," it happened. For all my praying and hoping and begging that Robby wouldn't puke, the puke happened anyway. And it was pink, too.

Only this time, it wasn't Robby. It was me.

Right there in Herrold's office, in front of Michael and about a half dozen other mothers, my digestion chose to throw itself in reverse. I hadn't even really felt it coming—just a little queasiness on the drive over. And, really, who wouldn't feel queasy after being crammed into a too-tight pair of jeans on the heels of cleaning up three gallons of pink vomit? But, boom, it hit me all at once; and next thing I knew, I was leaning over an empty Lego bucket, hoping that in this tiny room full of people whom I would certainly now be seeing everywhere I went, no one would see me.

It was bad enough when your kid's vomit was pink, but your own? In public? With a hot doctor right down the hall? I mean, I had been doing my best to look like a cool and at least moderately sexually attractive adult. And as difficult as that may have been with my pants undone and nothing but a sweater to keep that secret, let me assure you, it's even harder when you're grasping a red plastic bucket and spewing Day-Glo pink—and wearing the still-undone pants, mind you. God, how I hated that little Kendrick and her whole stinking family for forcing me to eat two and a half of their vile Barbie cupcakes.

Getting up was no real option, as every time I so much as moved, I felt a recurring wave of nausea, so I just waited for it to pass, hoping I was done with the actual hurling part of the proceedings. I started feeling really sorry for myself as I knelt there on the little gray highway- and choo-choo-patterned carpet, and I felt a further wrenching, a little deeper, in my guts. I wished Alex had been there with me. Or Jenn. Or even my mother. I must have looked almost as pathetic as I felt, kneeling there in the corner, because after a few minutes, Robby sidled over to me and offered up his coveted juice box. And Michael, in a rare burst of silence, just held my hair back and rubbed my back.

Of course, that was when Herrold chose to make his appearance in the waiting room. As the door swung open ominously, I could see from my particularly low vantage point the tailored cuffs of his pant leg and the glorious quality of the leather loafers he wore. I wanted to dive and roll against the opening door, screaming, "N-n-n-o-o-o!" like a slo-mo shot in an action movie, but he walked in so quickly, I couldn't attempt it. I was busted. Casually, he surveyed the happy little vignette before him, taking it all in with a glance, then looking down at his charts. Without missing a beat, he spoke up.

"Annie Forster? Do I have an Annie Forster who wants a beanie germ?" he asked nonchalantly.

He was covering for me, pretending I was one of the sick kids so I could jump ahead of all the rest of them! It was like the time in middle school when Stephen Fox—aptly named—let me cut in front of him in the lunch line because I'd gotten hit in the eyebrow with an icy snowball during recess. And now here I was, twenty years later, with another fox letting me cut—and this time not a single person was yelling, "No cuts! No butts! No coconuts!" like the last time. Herrold even made it seem that I was going in for a routine checkup so Robby wouldn't be scared, as if the shoes alone hadn't already convinced me what a fine choice I'd made for my son's health care. So, while Herrold went to locate our charts, I, trying to look as dignified as possible, clambered to my feet and headed toward the exam rooms. As we were leaving the waiting room, I thought I may have heard the angry undertones of someone muttering, "No cuts!" under her breath, but then the door slammed shut, and I couldn't hear anything else. Maybe it was the nausea, but I could have sworn it sounded like Kathy Smith. Ick.

As Michael let us into the office, he said, grinning, "Now sit here, and get a little R and R—oh, that stands for rest and relaxation. Got it?" He elongated each syllable and spoke loudly enough that a hearing-impaired hermit would have understood each word.

"Yeah, I got it, Mr. Smart-ass. Oh, and by the way," I added, since I was starting to feel much better, "F.U. Do you know what that stands for?" I said proudly, beating him at his own game.

"Annie—are you for real? That doesn't *stand* for anything. It's not an actual abbreviation. What do you think the *U* stands for? Umbrella? Unicorn? It's not an initial; it just sounds like the word. So, burn on you."

And with that he left, letting the door shut behind him. Damn, he'd gotten me again. This was starting to hurt my ego.

Robby seemed pretty much back to normal, and, while we waited for Herrold, he played on the scale and looked at a *Highlights*. I reapplied my lipstick and sat as still as possible; however, I began to get a little nervous that Herrold, like Michael, would start thinking I was fabricating my son's illness in order to finagle a look-see at his butt or catch a whiff of his Ralph Lauren cologne. So I focused all my attention on acting responsible and not at all interested in the distracting attractiveness of my son's physician.

A few moments passed, and then he knocked on the door and entered.

"Hey, Robby," he began. "Why don't you jump up here and let me take a look at that tummy of yours!"

He proceeded to give Robby a pretty thorough going-over,

and as he did, he asked me about a million questions. This wouldn't have been all that strange except that the questions were about my puking rather than about Robby's. I mean, looking back, I probably should have been able to guess exactly where the questions were heading, but I was so preoccupied with a) Robby's pink puke; b) my own pink puke; and c) the fact that Herrold had seen me puke pink and was now asking me about it, that I didn't really have too much attention to spare. Otherwise I would have noticed that his line of questioning was leading to one singular, unavoidable—obvious, actually—point.

"What have you eaten recently? Has your appetite been normal? Any cravings? Fatigue? Your ob-gyn is Dr. Weiss, right? And when did you last see her? When was your last period?"

And so forth. Admittedly, after that last one, I should have figured it out. Really, I'm not usually that stupid; honestly, in any—well, at least some—other circumstances, I would have caught on much more quickly. Finally, though, it hit me. And—oh my God—did it hit hard.

I was pregnant!

I, a thirty-five-year-old woman who'd already had a baby, had, without even noticing, exhibited and then admitted to every single symptom of pregnancy known to anyone who's ever seen *The Simpsons* or *Family Ties*, or, basically, any televised broadcast even remotely involving the imminent birth of a new family member. That I, a red-blooded, television-loving, child-bearing-aged American woman had managed to miss this knowledge astounded me. And that my son's hot pediatrician figured it out before me was, well, quite frankly, embarrassing—not that it wouldn't have been embarrassing if he hadn't been hot, but it certainly would have been less so.

"I'm not an obstetrician, Annie; but I really think you should see Dr. Weiss. I'll bet you that's why you puked out there," he said gently. Like a fool, I had been trying to convince myself that he hadn't actually seen me bowing before a Lego bucket filled with pink vomit, while he'd already moved beyond that and on to telling me I was pregnant.

Gradually, the concept began to take hold. Pregnant? Again? And just when my butt was getting "ever tighter" as Michael had put it. It couldn't be. I mean, Robby was still so new to me. I still carried him, sung him to sleep, bundled him after his baths. His hair was still coming in, he wore feety pajamas, and he loved jarred Gerber's food (although I wasn't particularly proud of that one). It had taken nearly a year of focused effort for us to get pregnant with Robby; how could this time be so spontaneous? I wasn't ready—not for two of them. Two would mean twice the crying, the colds, the loads of laundry, the chicken nuggets, the worrying. That would be followed in later years by the pubescent fights, the sibling rivalry, the inevitable family therapy. I was starting to panic. . . .

But then a wave of relief washed over me. *That* was why my jeans were so damn tight! And whether it was the relief, the anxiety, or the hormones, I burst into tears.

"How could this happen?" I asked out loud.

"Well, Annie, you see, mommies and daddies are built differently . . . ," Herrold began, smiling.

Then Robby started in. "*My* mommy and daddy are different, too. My mommy eats cupcakes, but my daddy eats hamburgers. But my mommy also eats cookies. And cake, too. Sometimes she gives a piece to my daddy, and he pretends to eat it, but when Mommy's not looking, he gives it to Chipper. Chipper is my dog. Sometimes I give Chipper my hot dogs if I don't want them. . . ."

And so he continued. You get, I'm sure, the embarrassingly

confessional nature of a three-year-old's strain of dialogue. My dignity was wounded once again—only this time under friendly fire. Anything any normal person would ever want to keep private was, somehow, tumbling out around me like a pair of statically charged panty hose clinging to the outside of your skirt that you then proceed to wear around all day until the static electricity is lost, at which point they drop to your feet in the hallway between Mr. Green's biology lab and Mrs. Holland's chemistry class.

However, as embarrassing as it was for a grown woman to get pregnant without knowing it and then proceed to overlook each and every warning sign of that aforementioned pregnancy, it was somewhat understandable for me. I mean, in addition to being—on only the rarest of occasions—a bit, well, clueless (okay, so I thought "stat" stood for static or, maybe, statistic—was that really so crazy, though?), the no-show period was pretty much par for the Annie Fingardt Forster course. Hell, I didn't even get my period until I was wearing white shorts (of course) in Mr. Mullen's eighth-grade homeroom. And although by freshman year of high school all my friends knew exactly which class they'd be in when theirs would come, mine was still so spotty and unpredictable that during one seven-week menstrual hiatus, I actually convinced myself I must have gotten pregnant from using a hotel bathtub after my cousin, George, when we were in the Adirondacks that summer.

I've had a lifetime of fashioning what seemed, at the time, to be quite plausible explanations for my irregular periods. I remember one excruciatingly long spell sophomore year during which I fully believed myself to have been impregnated by Rufus the Dufus, our sixteen-year-old, still-a-Boy-Scout next-door neighbor, because my mom had lent him my bike for a weekend. And, in my defense, a girl does get pretty intimate with her bike seat. So even though I wiped the seat down with Stridex pads to ensure a Rufus-free ride, it seemed likely enough back then that exactly such a catastrophe would be the inevitable result of having let a gross and just plain weird Boy Scout sit for prolonged periods of time on my absorbent Schwinn seat.

Anyhow, after Robby came, these so-called monthly visits were even more erratic, but Dr. Weiss told me herself that it wasn't that unusual for periods to be irregular after one had given birth. So I stopped worrying about it and gave a rest to the far-out, sci-fi type of justifications by which I was explaining to myself these missing periods. Now here I was, with twenty years of experience under my belt—well, under my undone jeans, anyway—still finding myself confounded by the whole thing.

Still in shock, I got Robby dressed, collected his beanie germ, and said good-bye to Herrold and Michael. In a daze, I drove to the pharmacy and bought four different pregnancy tests. While waiting for the results, I called to make an appointment with Dr. Weiss. And less than five minutes later, each and every one of the tests turned positive—a pink line; a blue plus sign; two blue lines; a filled-in heart-shaped window (my favorite).

Chapter Three

After triple-checking all the little white plastic sticks, I pulled Robby onto my lap and grabbed the phone to call Alex. His secretary, Diane, answered. I'd known Diane for three years, and never once did she make me feel weird about calling Alex at the office. She never acted as if it was an inconvenience or an imposition. And she never patronized me or made me feel bad for being at home, taking care of my kid, as do so many of the working mom Gestapo. And when Robby was a baby, she gave us a bunch of toys and books and stuff that her four sons had outgrown. In a word, she was awesome.

"Good morning, Hoffman, Berg, Share, and Tulliver. How may I help you?"

"Hi, Diane. It's Annie. Is Alex around?"

"Sure, hang on a minute; I'll get him. You doing okay? Your voice sounds a little weird."

"Does it? Well, I just got back from the doctor's office with Robby—maybe that's why."

"Mommy threw up. And it was pink," Robby yelled into the phone. I had been hit twice by my own kid—the little narc.

"Why'd you puke? You're pregnant, aren't you? You know Sally, Bill Tulliver's assistant, is due in two months. Although, between us"—she lowered her voice—"it looks more like two days. Anyhoo, you guys'll be pregnant at the same time! Hey, do you know anyone looking for temp work, by the way? Bill's going to need someone to cover for her while she's on maternity leave."

Did absolutely everyone in the world have to figure out that I was pregnant before me?

"No, sorry," I answered.

"Oh, you're not pregnant? Too bad! Not that I'm suggesting you have to have more kids; certainly, the number of children you have is up to you. Even though, personally, I've always liked a big family. . . ."

"No!" I had to interrupt her. "I said 'sorry' because I didn't know anyone for the temp job. Not because I'm not pregnant!"

"So you *are* pregnant? I knew it!"

"You, Diane, have clearly worked too long in that firm, because you sound way too much like a lawyer right now."

"Okay, okay, I get it. Change the subject. Anyway, how'd you get sick?"

"I ate a poisonous cupcake at a birthday party yesterday," I responded, trying to speak over Robby, who was kindly reminding me that I'd actually eaten *three* poisonous cupcakes at the party. "Could you put Alex on?"

"Sure. He's in his office; I'll connect you. See you. And stay away from those cupcakes! If the poison doesn't get ya, the refined sugar and flour will," she added as she transferred me to Alex's line.

"Hey, what's up?" Alex asked as he answered.

"You give your cake to Chipper?" I asked as he got on the line.

Although it was not the salient point, it was troubling to know that, when it came to our dessert life, my husband was faking it.

"What cake?"

"Any cake. You give it to him and pretend to eat it?"

"Robby told on me, didn't he?"

"Yeah, to Dr. Hornby. I can't believe you!"

"What? I never actually lied or anything. I never actually said I was eating the cake. It's not as though I was blatantly dishonest!" Alex jumped on the defense.

"No, I don't care about that! I just can't believe you don't eat cake! What kind of person doesn't eat cake! It never hurt anyone. Oh, well, except Kendrick's cupcakes, which is why Robby and I were at Dr. Hornby's to begin with. He puked pink. Then so did I."

"You guys puked? Pink? Are you all right?"

"Well, according to Dr. Hornby, Robby's fine. I, however, may be in for a couple more months of puking, particularly in the mornings. . . ." I trailed off, seeing how he'd take it.

"Huh?"

He was not on the same page yet.

"Well, not just puking," I continued. "It's puking followed by cravings and topped off by late-night runs to Peking Dragon." That was the local twenty-four-hour take-out place. When I was pregnant with Robby, I would have moved in if they hadn't kindly escorted me out the back door of their kitchen when they saw me arriving with my sleeping bag tossed over my shoulder.

"Annie, are you . . . ? What are you . . . ? Annie . . . What's . . . ?" He was slow—at least as slow as I was—in figuring it out. But I was glad to have someone else who'd failed to put two and two (or, more accurately, one and one) together.

I didn't want to tell him over the phone, but I couldn't let him stew anymore, so I asked, "Could you do me a favor? Could you come home? I have something to tell you. And four things to show you!"

He didn't say anything for a while, but when he finally did speak, I could hear his voice kind of wobbling in and out; you know, the way men sound when they're about to cry but won't admit it. It was the way he'd sounded when we found out Chipper didn't have Lyme disease, and when he'd gotten his first convertible—almost as if he were embarrassed about being so happy. He nearly dropped the phone and said he'd be right home.

I gave Robby a quick bath and cleaned myself up; then we went outside to wait for Alex to arrive. Robby, who'd recently outgrown his all-things-garbage obsession (i.e., Dumpsters, trash trucks, garbage cans, etc.), was fostering a new interest: cars. And he was getting pretty good at identifying the different models. I think he must have inherited it from Alex, who absolutely adored cars; but wherever he picked it up, it certainly wasn't from me. To me, cars were identifiable by one trait, and one trait alone: color. What kind of car did I have? A red car. What kind of car do they drive? A black one. Oh, wait, maybe dark gray. You get the idea. Anyway, cars were Robby's new fetish, and compared to garbage, let me assure you, cars were just fine. Hell, pornography probably would have been preferable. So, in order to encourage him in this nongarbage interest, we'd gotten into the habit of waiting for Alex to come home outside on the lawn, so that Robby could name the makes and models of all the cars that drove by. Finally, after what seemed like a longer trip home from the office than usual, Alex's car appeared around the corner. Robby spotted it first, and his little-kid knees started bouncing. Maybe he thought he was jumping; I don't know. Alex pulled in and stopped at the end of the driveway. When Robby ran over to him, Alex picked him up and put him on his lap as he drove into the garage, pretending Robby was driving.

When I got to the garage, and it was my turn to hug and

kiss Alex, I could see he'd been crying. It was weird: He never cried when he was sad or mad; he cried only when he was happy. Once I caught him wiping away tears in a Steve Martin movie. I'm not kidding—Steve Martin. He wrapped his arms around my waist, while there was still a waist to be found, and sort of lifted me off the ground a little. Then he hid his face in the hair above my shoulder and wept. He didn't say anything; he just rocked me side to side as if we were doing a slow dance at the prom. We stayed like that so long, I started to wonder how long he'd been lifting me. This led me to wonder how much weight I'd already gained, which led me to wonder how much I would continue to gain. And then I wondered if he'd ever be able to lift me again. And then I cried, too. I'm sure our neighbor across the street, Mrs. Kravitz (her real name was Lutz; I just couldn't resist the *Bewitched* reference), was suspicious of our PDA, but I didn't want him to let go. Even if it meant his having to have surgery to repair what would certainly be an inevitable hernia from having lifted me. But Robby, the voice of reason and social decorum, started tugging at Alex's pant leg, so we had to act like parents again.

We were about to go in, when Alex remembered something in his car, so we followed him.

"Hey, Tee, can you hit this button for me?" "Tee" was the first real sound Robby ever made, and it kind of stuck as his nickname.

This was Robby's favorite game and the highlight of his day—hitting the button on his dad's remote and unlocking the trunk. Robby pushed the little button as hard as he could until he heard the familiar click-and-whoosh sound of the trunk releasing. Then, with his most serious tough-guy face, he pushed up on the back of the car. Half of the time he did it, he was actually pushing up on the bumper, but Alex was always subtle in administering the help needed to actually spring it open, and Robby was never the wiser for his assistance.

Let me add here that when Alex first got this car, the year before Robby was born, I had to sit through more lectures than during my sophomore year in college about the ravages of shutting a door too hard, leaving fingerprints on handles, wearing dirty shoes while driving, and a whole host of other sundry pointers and how-tos. When it finally dawned on me that I was basically required to shower in bleach and wear surgical scrubs just to get a ride to the grocery store, I left the car alone. I even averted my eyes when I passed it in the garage—Lord knows, I didn't want a four-credit college course on the evils that a direct stare can wreak on a paint job. But when Robby came along the following year, it was as if all the statutes and mandates governing that half of the garage no longer applied. Maybe he just trusted Robby—being a boy and all—not to harm the precious mechanical darling; all I knew was that all bets were off. Hell, if my own son could touch the trunk without using lye and fire to clean his hands first, well, you can believe I was going to be a little more free and easy with the car, too. I used only soap, water, and a touch of Purell before I got near the car and gave just a quick pass with the chamois as I went by. That showed him.

So, with a little undetected help from Alex, Robby managed to get the trunk open; and inside was an exact replica of Alex's car, only about a quarter the size. Robby could not control his knee bouncing and gurgling in the anticipation of getting his own real car. Alex pulled it out, and Robby climbed into it immediately. Without even knowing that the battery had to charge before it could move, Robby was in metal-head paradise. Fleetingly, I glimpsed a future of mullets and concert T-shirts—just like Chad Cornett in Mr. Harper's auto shop. It wasn't pretty.

"I figure we can let him use it without the motor until he gets used to it. Plus, it's way too big for him now. He can't even really use the mirrors," Alex explained. As if I'd be able to put up any resistance to a present that gave Robby so much intense happiness.

"Wow. Our kids sure are lucky to have a dad like you." I hugged him.

"And for the mother of my second child . . ." He made me close my eyes.

"I don't think you could fit two of those little Mercedes cars in your trunk, could you?" I asked. I could just see myself, nine months pregnant, squeezed into that little car, on the road to Jenn's house.

"For you, I didn't get a car. I figure Robby can give you a lift if you need one. Hey, are you peeking?"

"Not really."

I was.

"Okay, open," he said, the tears coming back into his voice.

In his hands were a bottle of club soda that he'd stuck a cork into and a carton of egg rolls with three packets of duck sauce. That was what had kicked off my Peking Dragon addiction, and he'd remembered. And around the club soda bottle was a paper-clip chain bracelet. Auspiciously, he popped the cork. Then he removed the bracelet from the bottle top and held it up for me to admire.

"Just until we can pick up the one I ordered from Greenfeld's," he said, kissing my palm and hooking it around my left wrist.

But, truth be told, even after the diamond one arrived, I still preferred the paper clip one.

Chapter Four

As the end of summer approached and September loomed near, and I'd had enough time to get used to being pregnant again, Jenn, Jen, and I decided we had better make a go at a preschool. The first Jenn was already four and a half months pregnant with her second, and she still looked so awesome, it was almost difficult to keep being friends with her. And the other Jen had been aiming for a second for a couple of months. Once they knew I was "loaded," as they called it—a term replete, ironically, with the pleasures of college drinking binges—we disbanded the ever-growing playgroup and took on the very aren't-we-so-responsible task of seeking out institutions of learning suitable for our progeny.

I should confess here that, before Robby came on the scene, I had harbored a deep-seated hatred for those mothers who acted as though nursery schools, or "glorified babysitters" as I'd thought of them then, were the academic and intellectual equivalent of a Silicon Valley think tank. They aren't. I know that. Really. But until you're in it, you probably can't even conceive of all the different types of nursery schools that exist. Who would think? There's only one kind of elementary school, one kind of junior high, one kind of high school (okay, two kinds of high schools if you count vo-tech schools, and I guess there are also prep schools, so that's three, but you get the point). But for the toddler set, there are countless numbers of competing preschools, each with a philosophy based on the single principle that if you *really* loved your kid, you'd send him to that particular school.

So I scouted some out and narrowed it down to the two closest to our house, either of which seemed fine for the three hours a day Robby was going to be there. I mean, why shouldn't proximity be a legitimate criterion for selection? Hell, I chose my college based on the advantageous guy-to-girl ratio.

However, the day before registering Robby for the fall session, I had the misfortune of running into Kathy and Richard Smith in the express lane at the Shop 'n Save, where I learned a valuable lesson: If I *was* going to use proximity as a criterion in selecting what would someday be Robby's alma mater, I had to keep pretty quiet about it.

"What?" Kathy scoffed loudly, in response to my admission. "You can't choose a nursery school just because it's convenient for *you*!"

She smiled patronizingly at me and exchanged one of those looks with her husband—the kind of look my middle school gym teachers, Miss Miller and Miss Hardy (both, oddly enough, unmarried and in their late forties), gave each other when I couldn't climb the rope for the physical fitness test. In fact, Kathy Smith kind of reminded me of Miss Hardy: They were both pudgy, and they both had a man's haircut—you know, that kind of crew cut thing that some women adopt as their look, as though the rest of us won't notice that their hair is cross-dressing.

Then, at the same time, Kathy and Richard both exhaled a "hah" and smirked at me. It was as if they'd practiced their timing. I could just see them synchronizing their watches and mentally counting one-Mississippi, two-Mississippi before launching their insults. I swear it was like the girls' field hockey captains (Miller's and Hardy's pets) telling you that you weren't good enough to make the team—and enjoying it.

Then Richard piped up.

"So, you've chosen to attend a co-op?" he asked in a seemingly harmless way. "Because we're less than comfortable with a *cooperative* nursery school—where the primary care provider participates in the daily activities of the school."

He enunciated the "cooperative" part slowly and loudly, as though I wouldn't understand him if he'd spoken at a normal pace. And what did he mean by "primary care provider"? Was he talking about a parent? And really, did this guy honestly think I didn't even know what kind of school I was sending my own kid to? Of course, I wasn't exactly crystal clear on it, but that was beside the point entirely; I mean, it wasn't as if he knew I didn't know.

And then, taking a pause from delivering his heady lecture, he proceeded to visibly count the items in my basket to make sure I wasn't using the express lane illegitimately. Counting only nine, he was then free to pick up where he'd left off. I hated to admit it, but he had a point there. I've often found myself becoming outraged when an express cashier continues checking out items that exceed the stated limit.

"We just feel it is of paramount importance for children to learn that both parents are equally significant contributors to their evolution and development. And if one parent is seen to participate and nurture more regularly, even during school hours, then how will they be able to understand that critical concept? You see, after having Randall, I changed careers in order to be able to participate more fully in the upbringing of my children. I now run my own computer consulting firm so that I'm home during the day with them. I guess I just love my kids."

Now, while the sentiment was certainly admirable, the delivery was almost too much. Was he telling me that Alex should quit his job so we could both cut Robby's hot dogs into little pieces together? Plus, the guy was wearing a short-sleeved madras shirt. I almost started to laugh as I imagined the look on Alex's face when I told him that one. *Equally significant contributors to their evolution and development.* I repeated that line to myself so I wouldn't forget it. What was this guy? Some Darwinian scientist disguised as a dad in a minivan commercial?

"You know," I responded, "you're probably right that Robby would benefit tremendously from having both of us around all the time, but we're taking the long-term approach: preparing him for the loneliness and abandonment of adolescence."

I kind of chuckled a little just to let them know I wasn't totally serious about abandoning him, but I don't think they appreciated my levity when it came to child rearing. Or should I say "nurturing"? Kathy's eyebrow immediately arched in contempt, while Richard looked away in disgust. Much to my chagrin, however, his scornful glance happened to fall directly upon Robby, who had wandered over to the produce section where he was picnicking on the stray grapes that had rolled off the carts and onto the gritty floor beneath. It was like some Joan Crawford–type nightmare to see my own flesh and blood huddled under bountiful mounds of fresh fruits and plump vegetables, feeding like a Dickensian orphan upon the tiny dusty grapes that had shriveled beyond any discernible shape or color; but the Smiths' Super-Parent Power had rendered me helpless to take any action whatsoever. I was simply frozen to the spot. Luckily, Robby soon moved over to the lettuces, where he began replacing the torn-off brown leaves to their rightful cellophane bags.

"And look at that," I added as a sort of truce. "At least he's learned how to tidy up the Shop 'n Save. If we could hire him out, we might not need a nursery school at all."

"I suppose we also feel that a co-op doesn't encourage the children to play an active role in their own education," Kathy continued, totally ignoring every word I had spoken and just picking up right where the diatribe had been paused. Neither of them even acknowledged the intervening moments since their last comment. And while I can't be certain, I'm pretty sure they thought I was, in all earnestness, trying to get around sending my kid to nursery school. I really couldn't take much more of this. And, my God, the cashier seemed to be taking an inordinately long time—"express lane," my ass. There were still three customers to go. Thinking fast, I realized my best strategy was to shift the topic to their favorite subject—themselves.

"So, are you going to send Emily to Ascension?" I asked casually, thinking all the while that whichever school poor Emily was going to would be the one school I sure as hell would *not* be sending Robby to. I simply wouldn't be able to back the car out of the garage in the mornings if I knew I would have to endure Kathy's daily opining on teaching philosophies or contemporary politics or what kind of underwear I wear or whether my exercise program was effective. Which, by the way, it isn't, as I don't actually have one.

"Ascension? Nooooo," she answered with another smirking glance at her supercilious husband. However, neither seemed as disgusted by the school itself as by my not already knowing where they had decided to send Emily—as though there were a telephone chain to keep all of us mothers apprised of and in the know about what decisions Kathy and Richard Smith were making for the health and well-being of their family.

"Randall attended that institution and didn't seem to *flourish* as we'd hoped," Richard responded.

Flourish. I'm not kidding. He said "flourish." I couldn't help conjuring an image of Randall as a little dirt boy sprouting petunias and begonias if treated properly.

"So we're sending Emily to the Montessori," Kathy finished. It was as if they were taking turns speaking, divvying up every other sentence.

"Oh. Where's that?" I asked casually, simply marking time until the Apocalypse or my turn at the cash register came.

And I'm not sure, but I think she rolled her eyes.

"In Springwater. Near where the fireworks were held last year," Richard answered, it being his turn and all.

Now, I didn't go to the fireworks last year, but I knew that Springwater was a good forty-five minutes away. Seriously, you'd have to pass at least a baker's dozen of perfectly fine nursery schools to get there. I love Robby. I do. I don't want him squelched or suffocated or impeded or harmed in any way. I don't want him, in twenty years, staring up at the ceiling of some corduroy-wearing shrink's office. I don't want him to mount a post office flagpole and open fire on our fellow postal patrons. But there was just no way in hell or purgatory that I was going to drive an hour and a half, five days a week, in order to have him finger paint for three hours.

"It's a ways, but we feel it's best for Emily," Kathy said, continuing the couple's alternating style.

Eww. I've always hated that expression, "a ways."

"We feel that the Montessori just seemed to answer all of Em's needs." Richard fielded this one, with a particular emphasis on the "we," as if to underline just how involved with his kids he really was. "With their pedagogy, we're confident that we're making the right choice. How do you see your son fitting in with the Montessori philosophy?"

Was this joker testing me? I mean, I remember having heard the term "Montessori" in some freshman sociology class a hundred years ago, but I'd had a brutal hangover during that class. And now this Ward Cleaver alter ego wanted me to demonstrate my knowledge. I don't even think Professor McNaugh put that on the sociology final. And now, nearly twenty years later, I was supposed to whip out a number 2 pencil in the express lane at the Shop 'n Save to satisfy this plaid-wearing meddler's smug curiosity? Why couldn't Alex or Jenn be here? And why couldn't Robby sense my predicament and tear himself away from that godforsaken produce? Lord, how I hated vegetables at that moment.

I took a deep breath—which in reality does nothing to calm you down—and replied as seriously as I could. "I'd love to hear your thoughts on the Montessori, but we've really got to run. It was so nice to run into you; you've given me a lot to think about."

I smiled as convincingly as I was able to, as I threw my *legitimate* number of items in a bag and walked off to pull Robby out from under the cucumbers.

After that, I had no choice but to stick to my original plan and send Robby to the nursery school closest to us, the co-op. It had been Alex's first choice all along, anyway, and after all the research that he'd done on the subject, I knew I could trust any recommendation he made. I mean, seriously, he read *Parents Magazine* until the covers fell off; he bought eleven different books on how to select a good preschool—and read them all; under the alias of Stephanie Graf, he even joined an Internet chat group called Mothers for Excellence in School Systems. I figured if he was willing to become a MESS for the cause, his advice was probably pretty trustworthy.

The Smiths, I grant, may have been well intentioned, and certainly their kids were a huge priority for them. But the pride they took in their utter absence of a sense of either humor or style was astounding to me. Do I need Jerry Seinfeld for a best friend? I certainly do not. Tim Gunn? The answer is no. However, people with no sense of humor or style seem to suggest a lack of awareness that I find unnerving and, quite frankly, a bit creepy. And these two lacked it in spades. Were they evil? No. Annoying? Oh, sweet, dancing Jesus, yes.

Chapter Five

When we pulled into the garage, I was still kind of itchy all over from my encounter with the Smiths, so I didn't register that Alex's car was there. It was Robby who noticed it first.

"Daddy's here! Daddy's home! Daddy's car!"

It wasn't the only time Alex had come home in the middle of the day, but it was one of a select few. And it was the first time he hadn't called me first to tell me. I checked my cell phone to make sure I hadn't missed his call, but I hadn't gotten any calls at all. It gave me a weird feeling.

"Let's go see him!" I said as I scooped Robby and the two grocery bags and headed inside.

"Tee!" I heard as soon as we opened the door.

"Daddy? How comes you home?"

I couldn't have said it better myself.

"Well, Tee, it's kind of a long story; maybe you can go take a spin in your car, huh?" Alex said, looking over Robby's head and catching my eye as he unlatched the basement door and sent Robby scurrying down the steps. Then he shrugged a little in my direction and made a we've-got-to-talk face. I knew that face; every guy who'd ever dumped me had given me that face. I knew what that face meant, and what it meant was nothing good.

"You're cheating on me and you want a divorce," I blurted out as soon as Robby had disappeared into the basement to find his car.

"What? What are you talking about?" Alex asked, genuinely confused.

"Then what? You're dying. It's cancer. It's cancer, isn't it? Which one? Lung? Prostate? The butt one? Can men get breast cancer? Is it breast cancer?"

"Ah, no, Annie," Alex said, suppressing a smile while pulling out a kitchen chair for me to sit down. "But I do have to tell you something. And it's not great."

"I knew it. I swear, I knew it. You had on that face."

"What face?"

"*The* Face. You know, the eyes, the eyebrows, the mouth, the whole, you know, *Face*."

"I don't have a Face," he denied.

"Yes, you do. Everyone has a Face."

"No, they don't; not everyone has a Face," he asserted matter-of-factly. His certainty about this was not only faulty but seriously irritating as well.

"Oh yes, they do," I countered. "Everyone most certainly does have a Face. And yours, I hasten to add, is particularly brutal."

"Even if I had a Face, which I don't, it wouldn't be brutal. Come on, Annie. You have to admit I do not have a Face."

"Yes, you do, Daddy," came Robby's voice from the basement. "You's got a face. Only bad guys don't have faces. Thems wear masks, like in my superheroes."

"I rest my case," I said, rising imperiously from my chair and sauntering over to give the kitchen counter a swipe. "You have a Face."

Alex then strode into the foyer to check out his Face in the big hanging mirror. And that was that.

Until several minutes later, when I realized he had been on the verge of imparting some important information to me. I'd been too busy gloating about my victory to focus on the issue at hand. It was the same as when my parents first agreed, after suffering prolonged haranguing, to let me see an R-rated movie; getting their permission had been so hard-won that I hadn't really paid attention to the fact that what I had begged and pleaded to see was actually a Rambo movie. Really, *Rambo: First Blood Part II*. After fifteen minutes, Laura Cahill and I sneaked out and went next door to watch the rest of *Desperately Seeking Susan*, which was rated PG-13 but was far better nonetheless. So I guess I had a history of sacrificing the larger point in favor of the minutiae.

"So, what is it?" I asked as I approached him, still staring at the mirror.

"I think it's this," he said, turning to face me with a grimace that can best be described as Ward Cleaver after having ingested a medley of tequila, expired olives, and a small assortment of variously sized carpet tacks.

"No, not that," I said, anxious about getting to his news.

"So, what, this?" he inquired, reconfiguring his countenance to resemble more of a Mr. Peebles–after-discovering-more-of-Magilla-Gorilla's-antics kind of look.

"No, Alex. Not that. I mean, what were you going to tell me?"

I could tell that he was, at first, still somewhat distracted by his desire to unearth his "Face," but he pulled his eyes away from the mirror to look at me. Then he became pretty serious.

"Annie, I got sidebarred today," he said simply.

"You got what?" I asked, hearing his words but not really processing them.

"Sidebarred. Tulliver told all six of us unnamed partners today at lunch."

"But, like, but, what does it mean?"

"We're sidelined, pulled from the game, designated hitters, benchwarmers," he went on, in a weird sports-analogy-laden way, as if I were famous for my appreciation of and prowess in all things athletic. Which I am not.

"They fired you?" I asked, stunned. He'd gotten an enormous bonus the year before, so I couldn't believe they didn't want him around.

"Annie, we're a real estate firm. And with everything being what it is now, that means there just isn't enough work to go around. They're paying us a retainer to keep us around for six months, and we'll earn a consultant's fee if we do work; but, until things turn around, I'm sidebarred."

"Sidebarred," I repeated, not knowing why. Why do people always repeat things like that? And what was more, I bet I'd find myself using that word I'd never even heard before tonight in about seventeen different contexts by the end of the week. The word "potpourri" did that to me, too. I heard it for the first time in a Pier One when I was Christmas shopping with Tina Esposito in eighth grade, and then I heard it at least six more times by the end of that afternoon. Natch, that was what an easy half dozen people on my list got as their present that year. Vaguely, I wondered how many of my friends and loved ones would now be getting "sidebarred."

"Annie? You okay? You kind of drifted there for a minute. I know it's terrible timing, with the baby coming and all, but it's really not *all* that terrible. We'll still have a fair amount coming in, and I'll start looking around to see what the job market is."

"But you can't!" I jumped in. "You can't leave Hoffman, Berg! You've been there your whole career; you're next for named partner! You can't leave. You don't want to give that up!"

"Yeah, but what's the alternative? Moving cross-country to paint sidewalk murals and write folk songs outside of Boulder? I need a job, Annie."

"Why does it have to be there?" I asked, suddenly lost.

"It *doesn't* have to be there; that's what I'm saying. Hoffman, Berg's been great, but there could be even better places I don't even know about yet."

"No, I mean, why outside of Boulder?"

"I don't know; I just think of Boulder as kind of, you know, outdoor-paintingy-and-folk-songsy, as compared with the suburbs of New York City. Don't you?"

"Yeah, I do; but why *outside* of Boulder? I mean, isn't Boulder enough?"

"I guess so, but I was just trying to dramatize the point that, if times were really tough, we might have to hover on the outskirts of a city rather than live like the fat cats inside the city limits."

"I see what you mean. Robby wearing sandals and panhandling; you driving an old sixties van, maybe a VW or something; me wearing long homemade dresses and parting my hair in the middle. I get it—and I think you're right."

"Good. So I'll call a few headhunters on Monday and see what they have to say about a new job."

"No! Not right about looking for a job! I mean right about living *outside* of Boulder. It was a good, illustrative example. But as far as the job? You can't just sack it on account of the new baby. Your job means a lot to you. You have to hang in and wait to see what happens at Hoffman, Berg. In the meantime, I could try to go back to work."

And you know what? Maybe after a few years at home, it'd be a relief to actually have somewhere to be that wasn't made of plastic and primary colors.

"Annie, I love you. And I think you were and could be still and will again be a great lawyer. But going back to work now? When you're going to have a new baby in a few months? That's just not a good idea. Not right now. Robby needs you. The new baby needs you. I need you."

With that, he came in for the kill: the kiss on the lips and the hug with the arms on the outside of mine—not under mine and around my waist, but circling my whole body as if I were a totem pole he was replanting. I could never resist that kind of hug, so I knew this was important for him.

"I'm sorry about your job," I said softly into his shoulder. "I know it isn't easy, but please know I'm on your team. And we'll work together to sort it all out."

"Can you just kind of shut up here, Annie. We were having a moment," he whispered romantically in my ear.

And I knew then that, no matter what happened, we really would work together to sort it all out.

Of course, it still sucked.

Chapter Six

Luckily, our—ahem—change in circumstances didn't affect our choice of preschool for Robby. We were still sure about the co-op. I could deal with morning sickness and job loss, but add in having to deal with the Smiths on a daily basis, and there was a hat trick I'd rather not experience. So the decision was made. All that was left was for me to sign him up and convince Jenn and Jen that they should send Chris and Sarah there, too. It is true that it would have been possible for me to send Robby there without the benefit of his two best buds. I am aware of that. But the idea of his going there by himself was, well, unsettling. It was like going to the school cafeteria at lunchtime: You didn't *need* your friends there, but if they weren't there, you knew you'd feel like a loser eating your baked ziti and cling peaches among relative strangers.

The first Jenn was easy. She and her husband, Henry—who, in spite of his horrible name, was actually a really great guy—pretty much knew they could coast on any recommendation of Alex's. And if I thought Alex's research was thorough before his sidebar, well, I was simply a fool; with all the extra time he now had available, he succeeded in amassing enough information on preschool education to change his name to Dr. Spock—the baby-book-writing one, not the Vulcan played by Leonard Nimoy.

Or was it Leroy Neiman? And why didn't that dude ever smile? Although, their suits being what they were, I can imagine some serious chafing issues—not to mention the constant threat of an impending wedgie; and certainly the haircut must have lent itself to some ruthless ridicule aboard the *Enterprise* as well. Astronauts and aliens aren't really known for their fashion sense, are they? I'd have to ask Jenn about that. Ah, yes, so, speaking of Jenn, she and Henry were more than willing to give the co-op a shot.

The other Jen, though, was more of a holdout. Jenn and I suspected she'd come around eventually, but we'd both known her long enough to know she would want to appear as though she'd made her own decision on the matter. She put up a good fight, too. She was pretty convincing, actually. For a while, I really thought she was going to send Sarah to the Montessori. And even though I hated to pull out the big guns, I had to tell her about the Smiths.

"Are you aware that Crew Cut Kathy is sending Emily there?" I inquired, quite casually, when the three of us were all at the local lake together with the kids on what was one of the last days it would be open.

"I still can't believe she's not homeschooling those weird kids," the first Jenn put in.

"Well, it's supposed to be a great environment for artistic children," the other Jen added defensively. "And I think Sarah could do well there."

I guess the irony was lost on her that, at that exact moment, Sarah was not-so-artistically stomping on Chris' sand castle.

"Jen, look, I don't want to tell you what to do, but *go to the co-op*," Jenn commanded as she got up to help Chris reconstruct his upside-down-bucket sand castle. "Seriously, Jen, didn't you read Alex's treatise on the place? I swear, Henry and I hope he never goes back to work so he can research all our big decisions for us from now on. Oh, that reminds me, Annie, we have to replace our roof. Can you ask Alex whom we should use?" she asked as she strode over toward the wreckage of sand and buckets.

Jenn was more than four months pregnant; yet she still had great legs, a good butt, and a tan. When I was pregnant with Robby, I carried extra weight everywhere. I'm pretty sure even my fingernails gained weight. I was barely two months pregnant now, and already I felt fat deposits welling up in the most unseemly places. Jen and I watched her wrap herself in a floral sarong and sashay off to the water's edge.

With Jenn gone, Jen expressed her anxieties a little more fully.

"So Crew Cut's really sending Emily there? She's pretty overbearing. Kathy, I mean; not Emily, of course."

Jen was too kind and gentle to ever really light into a kid. It was one of her best traits, and the one I'd most like to have changed.

"You should have heard the lecture I received at Shop 'n Save," I answered. "And her husband was there, piping in, too. Believe me, that's where they're going."

"Then could you tell me again why Alex thinks the co-op is better?"

And with that one seemingly harmless question, I knew she was sold.

The next day, all three of us went down to enroll.

The sign-up started at ten, but I'd been on the phone with my mother. She had insisted on first telling me the "nuts and bolts," as she so quaintly put it, of my father's prostate exam, and then dissecting every aspect of Alex's sidebar, so I was later than everyone else. By the time I got there, Chris and Sarah were already playing at an easel together, while Jenn, Jen, and the other parents were sitting around a picnic table with Miss Jenkins, the teacher. I brought Robby over to where the other kids were playing, then headed back to the parents' table to join in the discussion about our responsibilities and all that. I sat down unobtrusively at the end, across from a scrawny, bare-faced, hairy-legged mom in clunky suede sandals, so that I could keep an eye on Robby, who was surveying the field.

There were, maybe, nine or ten kids strewn about the nursery school yard, two of whom he'd seen nearly every day of his life. There were kids climbing on plastic jungle gyms, kids riding tiny cars, kids painting with watercolors, kids looking at picture books. Robby could have done any of these things. He could have played with any of these kids. But where did Robby go? To Chris? To Sarah? To the cool little blond kid in the Nike sneakers? No. Robby sought out the elite company of some gangly kid, sitting all by himself in the dirt, wearing a cape. And I don't mean like a superhero cape. This kid wasn't dressed like Batman or Spider-Man or even Wonder Woman. Oh, no. This little Beau Brummel was dressed like Oscar Wilde on opening night. He was wearing a brown velvet cape, lined with satin fleur-de-lis. I couldn't believe that anyone would even let his kid behold such a garment, let alone wear it. And to his first day of school. I'd rather stroll through the Shop 'n Save in a black merry widow and a Ginger Grant wig than let any kid of mine be seen like that. And Robby, before my very eyes, was befriending this Solitary Swashbuckler. Visions of a future filled with Dungeons and Dragons, tuba lessons, chess club, and AV duties nearly blinded me with a clarity I rarely experienced. I saw him, in fifteen years' time, sneaking out in his own brown velvet cape in order to watch *Star Trek* marathons and learn Esperanto with a group of oddballs he'd call his "cronies" or something equally off-putting.

I was paralyzed with fear and anxiety for my son's welfare; I'd been through middle school and junior high—and I knew what was in store for a kid in a brown velvet cape. It wasn't good. Hell, I could protect him from scurvy, bad haircuts, and oncoming traffic, but if he was going to throw himself in the way of this kind of tragedy, I guessed I had no choice but to sit back and watch him do it. Unless . . . My thoughts raced. I could still put him in the Montessori! And just as I was weighing the merits of betraying my husband's and best friends' decisions and following Crew Cut Kathy's and Madras Richard's advice, the blond kid in Nikes ran by the Caped Kinder, pushing him over and knocking him right down on his side. It's funny—you'd think I'd have felt bad for the Victorian gadabout. Yeah, you'd think.

As soon as the Velveteen Boy realized he'd been knocked over—a reality he'd best get used to if he planned on continuing in this particular vein of haberdashery—he started to cry really loudly. He didn't pick himself up or anything. He just lay there on his side, screeching. I think maybe the cape had pinioned him to the ground. But say what you will about his sumptuary choices, the kid could howl. I'll give him that. After about five minutes, he was still screeching, so his mother got up to help him. And, lo and behold, which one was she? None other than the no-shave sitting across from me. I should have figured. I quickly surveyed the other parents in order to see if any of the others could have fit with VelviBoy, and the answer, as you probably guessed, was no. The way I looked at it, only a mom who placed such little emphasis on her own appearance would disregard all the playground politics governing her son's apparel.

So, while her son howled, still lying stiffly on his side and trapped by what he had probably formerly thought of as a rather more team-spirited, helpful sort of cape, she calmly sauntered over to him, knelt down, and began talking to him. Talking to him! I swear, she did not so much as reach out a finger to help untangle him from his Victorian vestments. Now, don't get me wrong. I'm not saying I'm a modern mom; I'm not even saying I'm a good mom. But if my kid were rolled up in a cape, tipped over sideways, fastened to the ground, and howling because a better-dressed kid knocked him down, *I'd help him up*. Call me old-fashioned. But this one? She simply squatted in front of him and tried to reason with him. I guess she just thought he wasn't thinking his way out of the cape snafu efficiently enough for a three-year-old.

Finally, Robby, who had been hovering nearby awaiting the cessation of the screams, teetered over to the prostrated kid. Very gently, he knelt down, reached out his little hand, and pushed the Velveteen Boy back upright. Then he walked over to where the blond Nike kid was playing with some trucks and joined him. I don't think I'd ever been so proud of him in all my life. He'd helped someone! A truly altruistic act! And he wasn't even three and a half yet! And better even still, he'd chosen a different friend as a result. I wouldn't have to betray Alex, Jenn, or Jen after all. We were going to the co-op!

"Now, whose little one is that?" Miss Jenkins asked as she surveyed the scene.

"That's Robby; he's mine," I answered, trying not to sound boastful. But I couldn't really help gloating. My son was the star of the class. His future now appeared to me as one long stream of Abercrombie, varsity sports, easy A's, and cute girls he'd blow off—had better blow off.

"Well, I think he needs to learn *boundaries*," she told me.

She pronounced it as *bee-youn-dreez*. "But we can work on that while he's here," she finished with a smile that reminded me of my mother's look whenever she saw me eat dessert. "If you ever want to get a decent husband," that smile seemed to say, or, in the case of Miss Jenkins' smile, "If you ever want to get a decent son." I was a bit deflated after that. I figured I'd have to keep a lid on my self-satisfaction until I could get home to tell Alex all about it. At least there was a silver lining to his having been laid off—he would always be in easy reach if a good story broke. And at this place, I had a feeling, there would be some decent tales to tell.

After maybe an hour or two more of hearing Miss *Jerk*ins (for such was how I referred to her from thereon in) drone on and on about how important it was that we all take an active role in the co-op, she finally let us out. I was heading over to the Jenns to ask if they wanted to come over for some lunch with Robby, Alex, and me. Although I was in only my second month—the time when I should rightfully be so nauseated that I was rendered unable to eat and would consequently lose five pounds—I could think of nothing except what to eat next. But my two erstwhile friends were over by the fountain, brownnosing the teacher, so I headed over to the mini–jungle gym to collect Robby instead. However, my path was thwarted by Cape of No Hope's mother. She seemed to appear out of nowhere, holding the hand of her son—who had, at this point, donned his secret identity as Regular Boy by losing the cape.

"Hello," she said cautiously. "I'm Marta Lippincott. And this is Dale." She spoke more slowly than Mrs. Kohn, my first-grade teacher. Then she looked at Dale and waited, as though he were going to pipe up with his own eloquent salutation. I half expected a deep bow with a flourish from him. A "How dost thou?" at the very least.

"Oh, hi. I hope Dale is okay after that knockdown," I said, trying to close the gap of the pause.

"Well, I'm just a little concerned about all the physical contact. I'm sure *you* know what I mean." She emphasized the "you" in a strange way I couldn't quite crack.

"I . . . I . . . I think it was just a little push. I wouldn't worry too much," I said, trying to encourage her to either forget, repress, or get used to kids knocking down her be-caped boy at every opportunity. And maybe every so often, Cape Kid would get lucky and have a Robby there to prop him back up afterward.

"Well, I know that's how *you* see it, but . . ."

Why did she keep emphasizing the "you"? And why didn't she finish her sentence? I was starting to get a bad feeling about this. Weren't we on the same side here? I mean, not that I support accessories for three-year-old boys, but our kids had actually had a moment of solidarity against an aggressor.

"I'm sure that blond boy—whoever he is—will have his fair share of knocks and bruises, too," I offered democratically. "I think it's just part of growing up. And I don't think we have to worry about it getting any worse. The kid was probably just a little hyper on the first day with all these new people, you know?"

"Well, wait. I'm sorry. But to whom are you referring? Aren't you that boy's mom?" She pointed at Robby.

"Yeah, he's mine," I said, awaiting the pursuant thanks and praise for having a son who'd save her caped son from the numerous perils that were, inevitably, waiting for him.

"Well, I'd just hate to see him get physical like that with any of the other children in the school."

Oh, my God. Ohmigod, ohmigod, ohmigod. As if Miss Jerkins weren't bad enough, now I had to deal with the mother of the very kid for whom my son risked all prospects of future normalcy and popularity to help out! I couldn't process it! Where were the Jenns? I needed some support here.

"I don't want to tell you how to raise your son, but I know that in our hate-free home, we have a no-tolerance policy toward aggression of any sort."

Yes, she said "hate-free home." And, yes, she also said "no-tolerance policy." Apparently, what I'd mistaken for a conversation about child rearing was, in actuality, a negotiation for international peace and global free trade. I don't take offense easily, for the most part, but I very nearly had tears in my eyes. I could take the slings and arrows when they were directed toward me—but Robby? Did he, too, have to suffer at the hands of this preschool Ma-poleon? This was too much, no?

"Well," I replied, my thoughts emerging slowly, as if through mud, but I continued. "Thanks for your concern. Oh, and kudos to you for dispensing with the conventions of standard attire. It's refreshing to see such individuality on the playground."

"Yes, we do try to support freedom of choice and freedom from conformity."

"You've done a good job," I said earnestly, and I meant it. Really, if their goal was to cast off the binding chains of polite society, they managed not only to loose the ties, but to melt down the links and refashion them into a giant metal middle finger directed at the rest of us.

"I don't know about you, but we feel it's important to let Dale choose his own attire," she began. "We don't limit him to traditional selections. If he wants to wear a skirt one day, we support him. Clothes are a truly random social construct, anyway, so if he picks a cape to wear, so be it."

The cape was weird and all, but it was actually her unshaven legs I had been referring to the whole time. Kids, after all, will be kids. And unless directed and encouraged along particular paths, they will certainly explore some uncharted territory—a cape here and there being part of the journey. But her, to have so brazenly dispensed with the niceties of suburban expectations was truly surprising. I mean, really, even men—straight men, at that—groomed unruly hair these days. Hair, in the new millennium, is very much a choice; where, if, when, and how much is all part of its deliberate design.

Moments later, as I backed my Volvo out of the lot, I smiled inwardly at the happy thought of my Gillette Venus, snug in the corner of my shower, awaiting my next morning's visit.

Chapter Seven

The following Saturday, we spent the day at the lake with Jenn, Henry, and Chris. It was the last weekend the lake would be open, so everyone from town seemed to be there. We were waiting for the other Jen, her husband, Tucker, and Sarah to show up before we started the barbecue. But, to be honest, I couldn't really relax and enjoy the afternoon. For several days, I'd had an uneasy feeling. One might assume that my having another baby *at the same time* as having a husband out of work was responsible for my stress. But such was not the case. I mean, it wasn't great to have our chief breadwinner out of commission, but I had known a guy in college who'd sold both his blood and his semen to medical science for a reasonable fee; so, if need be, I knew Alex, being a decent specimen, could probably command a rather tidy sum for his vital liquids. Instead, the real reason for my discontent was the whole co-op escapade. I couldn't stop wondering if our son really had been aggressive. Alex did his best to reassure me that we weren't raising a toddler psychopath, but he was Robby's dad after all, and he could have been prejudiced by his paternal investment. It was going to take a day with the Jenns to convince me that Robby should stay at the co-op. Because, frankly, I was giving serious thought to hunting for a school where creepy caped kids were *expected* to get knocked over and where, if they were lucky enough to get pushed back upright, they appreciated the kindness.

I unloaded Robby's beach toys and lathered him up with sunscreen. Even under all that grease, he still felt like a normal three-year-old; not like what you'd expect a psychopath to feel like at all. Not that I've felt many psychopaths—other than Mr. Lawrence, my chemistry teacher, who used to try to create static cling by rubbing his polyester sans-a-belt pants against the girls' acid-washed Guess jeans. Meanwhile, as I quietly seethed, Alex had dug a hole in the sand the size of a large mixing bowl and laid my towel on top of it. Proudly, he told me that I could now, in spite of the gargantuan stomach, which shamefully belied my mere two-month pregnancy, lie down on my front, a feat that had become uncomfortable as of late. Jenn started laughing and commanded Henry to do the same for her.

I was kissing Alex and seriously doubting that his genes could ever have created a monster toddler, when I saw them. There, at the water's edge, and talking to one another, were Crew Cut and Madras Smith engrossed in a conversation with Marta the Unshaven and some bearded, long-haired guy whom I could only guess was her husband.

"Al, look—right there! She's the Caped Kid's mother. Talking to the Smiths. I didn't even know they knew one another! And that guy standing next to her must be her husband. See if you can see a little kid wearing a brown velvet cape with fleur-de-lis lining."

"How many kids in capes are you expecting on this beach?" Henry asked me. "Wouldn't just the fact that he was wearing a cape—any cape at all—kind of give him away? Did you really need the added detail of the fleur-de-lis, or whatever you called it?"

Henry was always a smart-ass, giving me a hard time like an older brother. Then he and Jenn proceeded to joke about the abundance of capes of various fabrics and linings on the beach, not just the velvet and fleur-de-lis kind. Hah. Hah.

"Wait, that's her husband?" Alex whispered to me.

"I guess. I've never seen him before, but—look—eww—they're holding hands."

Really. What self-respecting couple held hands at the side of a lake, at sunset on a Saturday evening?

"Well, I think that's Lippie the Hippie," he said as he instinctively inched closer to the shore.

"What?!? That environmentalist lawyer you've told me about? You know, I think she told me her last name is Lippincott."

"Oh, yeah, that's him, all right. You know, that guy is loaded. He runs his own firm and is actually huge in environmental law. He's the one who bought up all those acres off Maple Lake Road to save them from development. And then built that humongous solar-powered house on them."

"*That's* the guy who owns that solar house?" Henry asked. "That is the ugliest house I've ever seen. And that kid's going to school with Chris? Ahh, Jenn, you've got some 'splainin' to do!" he said in his best Ricky Ricardo accent.

"Look, Henry," Jenn said, "the family's odd, but they're not evil. Just think of them like the Addams Family. Not only does the mom have Morticia's hair, but, I mean, they probably also have a butler named Lurch, a dismembered hand in a box, and a really hairy cousin."

"You mean Itt?" I asked.

"No, I don't mean it, Annie. No one keeps a hand in a box or has a butler these days. Duh. It was just an *Addams Family* reference. Don't you remember that show?"

"Yeah," I said wistfully. "You know, 'Itt' should have had a spin-off."

"Yeah," Jenn said, "a spin-off on Wednesday."

"No, a spin-off on 'Itt.'"

"I know what you said, but a spin-off on Wednesday *would* be a spin-off of it because Wednesday was the name of their daughter," Jenn answered smugly.

"A spin-off on 'Itt' would be a spin-off on it also, whether it was on Wednesdays, Mondays, or any other day of the week, because 'Itt' was the cousin. Don't you remember?"

"Oh, yeah. You're right! Cousin Itt. And Pugsley. And Endora," Jenn elaborated.

"No!" I said quickly. "Endora is from *Bewitched*. How could you not know that?"

It always irked me when people confused *Bewitched* with other shows of the "magic-sitcoms" genre. You know, *I Dream of Jeannie*, *The Munsters*, The Great Gazoo on *The Flintstones*. That sort of thing.

I could have continued discussing the Nick at Night repertoire, which, next to making fun of people who are not me, is just about my favorite topic, but I heard Robby starting to fuss about his beach toys being too sandy. I therefore decided I'd better help him out before he drew the attention of the Smiths or the Lippies, who'd think his fussing was only a prelude to spinning his head all the way around and shouting about what objects I suck in hell.

When Robby saw me, he settled down immediately; so, quietly and unsuspiciously, I gathered up the toys in a big bucket and headed down to the water to rinse them off—kind of in the general vicinity of the Smith-Lippincott summit meeting. Not for the *sole* purpose of eavesdropping, I can assure you; but, if

I happened to overhear a little of their conversation, well, I just wouldn't be able to help that. It was, after all, a public lake. I mean, people must hear one another's utterances all the time here. So, working as slowly, unobtrusively, and silently as possible, I rinsed one after another of the toys until not a single grain of sand remained on any of them. I admit it was longer than I'd spent cleaning anything ever before in my life, including Robby's bottles when he was a baby, but what the hell? I was doing espionage work. Reconnaissance. Undercover. Okay, I was just plain eavesdropping—but whatever. As I knelt down at the shore, their conversation trailed over to me in bits and pieces. I really wanted to figure out how they knew one another. Why I cared so much, I couldn't have speculated; but it was unnerving to have them buddying up—kind of like doing the favor of offering Matt York the Dork your eraser in homeroom and having his only friend, Wet-the-Bed Fred, tell you, "Shove it." Eventually, the wind blew correctly, and I could hear them.

"Seem to flourish the way I'd hoped . . ." Crew Cut Kathy's voice carried first.

That was exactly what Richard had said to me at the Shop 'n Save! It was as if they'd been testing out their new material on me, practicing for the real performance with the Hippie Lippies.

"We considered the Montessori, but we chose the co-op because we think communal cooperation is essential to every . . . ," the long hair spoke.

And as he spoke, I got a surreptitious glance at the shirt he was sporting—a gray tee bearing the witticism HEY, CAN I HAVE A PEACE? Clearly this guy must have spent the last three decades locked as a prisoner in a VW minibus on the outskirts of Woodstock.

"One boy knocked him over, and another almost equally aggressive child pushed him back up. . . ."

Marta the Unshaven was talking about Robby!

"The Montessori answered all of *our* . . ." Richard took this one, complete with the same emphasis on the "our" that he'd given me.

Then the wind changed direction, and I couldn't hear them for a while. I wanted to ask them to cease their conversation until the atmosphere was more conducive to my listening in, but I thought that might put the kibosh on my spy work, so I merely continued to rinse and dry the same shovels, pails, and buckets over and over again. When the couples started shaking hands, clearly taking their leave of each other, I started to regret not having made more of a concerted effort at overhearing them. But then, just as suddenly, the wind changed again, and I could hear them even more clearly than before.

"It does sound as if the Montessori pedagogy would better suit Dale's needs; don't you agree, Alan?" Marta asked.

"Well, I hate to think that the idea of a cooperative school won't work out," Lippie the Hippie replied, "but if others aren't willing to participate in the communal element, what other choice do we have? True communism only works when everyone takes what they need and gives what they can, so I guess there's nothing we can do. I agree; we have to send Dale to the Montessori."

"We can't, as you well know, choose a nursery school because it's good for *us* as parents, after all. We have to choose one that's right for our *children*," Crew Cut said. Once again, retreading the material she'd used on me.

"I couldn't agree more. And if Dale is going to get roughhoused because he chooses to express his individuality through his clothing, well, I think we have no choice but to remove him from that environment. We have to put him in a safe place that nurtures and fosters his individuality. Not in one that squelches it," Marta the Unshaven said.

"In the name of conformity," Lippie the Hippie added.

"Well, then I guess we'll see you next Monday! Maybe we could work out a carpool once we know who will be attending," Crew Cut said.

"I'm so looking forward to it. Thanks for really *listening* to our dilemma, Kathy," Marta the Unshaven said.

"We're always glad to help," Richard said, sneaking in those words.

He was always so damn desperate to put his two cents in when it came to that stupid nursery school. It was almost as if he owned the place.

With that, they left. I was saved! The Smiths had, inadvertently, rescued me from my nemeses, the Hippie Lippies! The hippies were going to the Montessori! I would never again have to deal with the unshaven legs or unjust observations of Marta or her husband. And to know that they would have to keep on seeing each other as long as their kids were at the same school was an adequate punishment for each. It was true justice! True relief! True catharsis! I felt like an entirely new woman. I was free!

So, with a light and happy heart, I gathered up all the plastic toys I'd been rinsing, drying, resanding, rerinsing, and redrying and headed back to home base. As I was walking back toward our stuff, I saw that the other Jen, Tucker, and Sarah had arrived. All five of the adults were struggling with a collapsible—and collapsing—beach umbrella, and Sarah was, once again, smashing Chris' sand piles. Chris sat on the edge of his blue and white cloud-patterned beach towel, watching her and whimpering about the destruction.

Robby, who'd been brushing off the sand from his towel

(what was with him and the sand?), looked up to survey the scene in front of him: Sarah, stomping and gloating in her demolition, and Chris, suffering and crying as a result. Without missing a beat, Robby walked over to Chris' toys, picked out the biggest bucket—bright green with a white loopy handle—and carried it over to Chris. Sitting down in front of him, Robby filled it with damp sand, packed it down with the back of a white shovel, and offered it to Chris. Then the two of them dumped it out together.

It wasn't a perfect sand castle. It had gaps and holes in the walls where the sand hadn't been packed hard enough. It had no suitable foundation to support its weight. It lacked ramparts and battlements and rooks and casements. And, truth be told, it toppled over under its own shoddy construction just moments after having been erected. But so what? What did that matter at all? Robby had helped a friend; a friend in need. He'd come to save the day when Chris was in trouble. I didn't care what Crew Cut Kathy, Madras Richard, Marta the Unshaven, or Lippie the Hippie had to say about it: My son was no psychopath. Robby was good. Kind. Smart. Trustworthy. Reliable. Loving. Not much of an architect. But pretty upstanding, nonetheless.

Of course, when we got home from the beach that night, he stole Chipper's dog bowl out from under him and started eating his Alpo, but Alex and I convinced ourselves that all superstars must have their quirks.

Chapter Eight

After a couple of weeks of hanging around the house, waiting for things to resume their sense of normalcy, Alex started getting antsy when they didn't. Originally, I think both of us just kind of blithely thought our old life would return before we could even get acclimated to the new one, but that was proving not to be the case. Financially, we were okay for now; we'd saved enough that with some moderate tightening of the belt (a poor choice of phrase, as it made me ponder my—ahem—*flourishing* midsection), we weren't in any real trouble. But, in spite of our fairly secure familial economy, Alex still wore the demeanor of an overwrought three-year-old at someone else's party. Rather than assuming the comfortable form of all the cumulative television programs about out-of-work husbands that I had ever seen, Alex's unemployment took an altogether different tack. No unshaven bathrobe wearer, he was instead thrust into a constant state of Weekend-Casual Alex. Up by six thirty most mornings, he would squeeze in a several-mile jog and a quick shower before donning the ageless attire of generations of English countrymen or golfers the world over. Unable, as a consequence, to fully unwind, he would then proceed to attend to his days with the focused concentration of a feudal shoemaker (assuming there were shoemakers in the Middle

Ages, and that their attention to detail merits the comparison) or Gary Legere, my first-grade desk mate, who used to hold his pencil up too high toward the eraser end, and, hence, had to strain and clench and grimace his way through any written assignments.

"So, what's the schedule for today?" were the words that greeted me for what was surely the seventeen-hundredth time in a month, as I entered the kitchen with Robby to get breakfast ready.

"Alex?" I said, nudging Robby into the family room, then turning to face my beloved husband squarely and resolutely.

"What?" he replied, already preparing a somewhat defensive tone.

"I love you. You know that, right? I love you, and I respect you. As a man, a husband, and a father. I need you to understand that right now. Because other than that love and respect, I want to kill you brutally and painfully. Twice. Or maybe even a good three or four times."

"Well, jeez," he said, donning an affronted countenance. "What's wrong with *you* today? Got up on the wrong side of the bed, or what?" Then he kind of snuffed a little, and reached past me for a coffee cup.

"No, really, Alex. I know being home day in and day out with a pregnant wife and a three-year-old wasn't how you'd planned to spend your thirty-sixth year of life. I understand this. I can see that this is stressful for you, and that you need to adjust, but with every occasion of your asking me what the schedule is, or what our plans are, or—and this is the worst—*what's on tap* for the day, I think I just may hate you a little bit more."

"You know, you don't have to be so, so, so like that. All I'm doing is trying to get a sense of what the day is going to hold."

"Look at me. Am I wearing white kneesocks and a pageboy

haircut? I am not Julie McCoy, your chirpy, coke-addled cruise director. And this is not the *Pacific Princess*. There will be no luau on the lido deck."

"So you're saying I've turned into Merrill Stubing, is that what you're saying?" Alex shot back, getting pretty worked up. "Because it sounds like that's what you're saying. That I've become a warmhearted, sexually unintimidating, morally unassailable father figure. Is that what you're saying? Because if it is, that's a pretty shitty thing to say to someone."

"No! I'm not calling you Merrill Stubing," I explained.

"Oh, what, then? Gopher? Is that it? The ship's infantilized lackey? Or worse: Doc—the horny charlatan. Where'd he go to med school? Hooters?"

"That's not it at all," I said, growing strangely impressed by all the *Love Boat* desiderata.

"Isaac? Am I Isaac? Because, well, that actually wouldn't be bad. I mean, sure, he was racially marginalized and had, like, no airtime or developed storylines, but he was pretty cool. Except for the 'stache and outsized seventies do."

"Really, Alex? Really? I say I'm not Julie McCoy, and I get a twenty-minute diatribe on you being—most emphatically—*not* one of the other staffers. That makes no sense."

"Okay, maybe you're right. I just got worked up a little. I'm a little sensitive these days, in case you couldn't tell; I realize it makes no sense. Bad analogy."

"Right. It is a bad analogy. Because if I'm Julie, then the analogy works only if you're David Birney."

"Who the hell's David Birney?"

"One of the guests. A regular on *The Love Boat*," I replied huffily, offended that someone I was married to wouldn't possess this knowledge.

"Oh, yeah. Permed hair and a tan?"

"That's the one," I answered, reaffirming my faith in my matrimonial choice.

"Host of *Win, Lose or Draw*, right?"

"As if. That was Bert Convy."

"I defy you to tell me that there's even a remote difference between those two."

"One was married to Meredith Baxter."

"Who's that?"

"The mom on *Family Ties*."

"Which one?"

"There was only ever one mom on *Family Ties*. Dads and daughters can be switched, as in *Bewitched* or *Roseanne*. Or *The Brady Bunch* reunions. But moms never get switched."

"I know who Elyse Keaton is—I meant which cheeseball was she married to."

"The one with the slightly less curly hair," I replied with a knowing sniff.

"You're kidding me, right? Tell me you cannot possibly think that would be enough to distinguish one of those polyesters from the other."

"I think we're losing sight of the larger issue here, Alex," I said, hoping he wouldn't probe further on the Birney-Convy Divide, as I had pretty much used up my store of knowledge at this point.

"You don't know the difference, do you?"

Why couldn't a phone ring or a fire start immediately? I wondered. Couldn't Robby take a fall that would require just a little maternal attention?

"All right, maybe I couldn't identify each in a police lineup, but I have very specific memories of them on *The Love Boat*.

And there is just no way that I can be the Julie McCoy here and do what she did for them to make all your plans and dreams a reality."

"I know that. Because that would be *Fantasy Island*, not *The Love Boat*."

Oddly, I laughed at this. As infuriating as he was, he always spoke my language—Aaron-Spellinglish. That was a good one, I told myself. I'd have to reuse that one—Aaron-Spellinglish.

However, as scintillating as our conversation was, it hadn't, alas, brought us any closer to a mutual understanding or meaningful resolution than we were before. This left us exactly where we were at the outset—still on each other's nerves and Robby unfed. So I grabbed the cereal boxes and proceeded to pour while returning to my original point.

"I'm sorry if I sounded mean. And I don't want to be insensitive," I began, "but it's just kind of hard to be faced every morning with questions about the day's events when, in actuality, there really aren't going to be any. Each day is pretty much the same. The biggest excitement around here is whether we're having Rice Krispies or Cheerios for breakfast." I grabbed the boxes at hand with a flourish in order to illustrate my point.

This being not only a very true statement but a very sad one, I felt myself beginning to get that buzzing in the sinuses that can only signal one thing—tears. Had I really gotten so mired in the daily functioning of life that the mere choice of breakfast cereal was the sum of my day's interest? The more I thought about it, the lower I began to feel. And then the tears made their presence known to one and all.

"You okay?" Alex asked, unsure of how to respond to the recent turn in the conversation.

"Well, it's just that it's so sad," I said, grabbing for a tissue.

"Honey, don't worry," Alex said, embracing me in a manly, protective kind of hug. "I'll get a job, and all of this will be fine. We'll be fine."

"No, not that. It's the question. I'm crying because of the question."

"All right, okay; I'll stop asking about the day, if it's important to you," Alex said, still unnerved by the sudden onset of my tears.

"No, not that question. I don't care about that question," I replied, having moved on to a far greater concern than Alex's demand for a daily itinerary.

"Then what? What is it?" Alex pursued, genuinely confused by my change of course here.

"The cereal question. Really, is that what I've been reduced to? Just a question of which cereal to eat? It's as if my life has become a commercial for breakfast cereal, only with no catchy tune or memorable mascots. Where's my triumvirate of industrious elves? Where's my singing toucan, huh? I've been reduced to a background character in an ad with real people. And no one even eats cereal that's sold in commercials with humans in them. I've become All-Bran. I'm Wilford Freakin' Brimley, for chrissakes. Only this is my real life."

"I actually liked Wilford Brimley, you know," Alex responded, attempting to cheer me up. "And I still remember that commercial of his where he told us all that we were doing the right thing by eating oatmeal. He had such credibility; I wanted to give him a low hug."

"Well, I hate Wilford Brimley. He used the word 'tasty' in that godforsaken commercial. No one uses that word, and if they do, they should have the decency to use it behind locked doors, after dark. Like pornos. Or drugs. *Tasty*. What an ass."

"Annie, no matter what else you are or may become, trust me, you're no Wilford Brimley. In fact, you're about as far from that pillar of the American screen as it's possible to get."

I knew I'd married him for a reason.

With that one comment, I felt better. I felt freer and calmer and all-around happier. I can't say for sure that I had ever actually operated under the assumption that I was, in fact, Wilford Brimley, but Alex's assertions that I wasn't really hit the spot. I found myself feeling, strangely, much sexier and younger than I had in weeks. Being told you're far from Wilford Brimley really does wonders for a girl's ego; I would have to recommend it as a pickup line to any single guy I knew. And it was empowering, too. It had given me the strength to resolve that I would, henceforth, strive to make a little bit more of each day. At some point, Alex would go back to work; Robby would get married; and even this tiny amuse-bouche-sized baby I was carrying would have its own apartment. The days went fast; it was up to me to appreciate and to maximize what I had. If breakfast detritus depressed me, too bad. I would have to move on to something that didn't.

With my equilibrium and good mood regained, I proceeded to attend to the morning's events: cereal selection, cereal consumption, cereal disposal, and the inevitable cleaning up of all cereal appurtenances. It may not have been exciting. Surely, it wasn't novel or entertaining or intellectual. But it was necessary.

So you can just bite me, Mr. Wilford Brimley.

Chapter Nine

The co-op, as it turned out, was truly a great place for Robby, and he really loved it. We went in the mornings, from nine to twelve. My job—because, at a cooperative nursery school, all the parents have one—consisted of being the go-to girl for the grubbiest, grossest, and dirtiest of the eleven kids in the class. I had to have a constant supply of prêt-à-porter ensembles for kids who'd poured, peed, puked, or painted on their own clothes, and then I got to wash and change them—"them" referring to both the kids and the clothes. I landed that work assignment after I put in a transfer from the Baker of Treats role I'd occupied during the first month of the school year.

The baking thing, *in theory*, sounded so good, Alex was astounded that anyone—let alone his cake-loving wife of nearly eight years—would want to trade it for a job that sounded so much more disgusting. I, too, at first, was fooled into thinking that the baking thing would be a pretty good gig; you know, one long parade of cookies, cupcakes, brownies, and all the excellent junk food that you—and by "you" I mean "I"—never grew out of. I couldn't understand why everyone had sat quietly with averted eyes when Miss Jenkins (whom I left off calling "Jerkins" after she let Robby have the only purple ice pop in the box) asked us who wanted to do it. It was like the algebra teacher asking for a volunteer to solve the equation on the board. I was baffled, but I didn't want to look too eager to grab what I thought at the time was, by far and away, the best job in the house. But after a few moments of awkward silence, I spoke up.

"Well, if no one else wants it—sure, I'll do it. I just make snacks for the kids each day? That's really it?" All the silence had made me start doubting whether I had missed hearing about some other part of the job. I didn't have to grow my own wheat or milk my own cows or anything, did I?

"Yes," Miss Jenkins answered calmly.

She never said "yeah" or "uh-huh" or "yep" or even "okey-dokey." Always "yes," with a little extra hang time on the *s*. It made me wonder how she must talk to her boyfriend when they were doing it, since she was so proper here in the school. Was that wrong of me?

"All you need to do," she continued in her controlled voice, "is just find out what the kids like and bring it. That's it."

Then she looked at me with one of those looks you see mothers give their sons in movies when they go off to war.

And right then, although I may have imagined it, I heard all the parents simultaneously suppress a giggle. Once, when I was about twelve and cultivating a huge crush on Mike Culligan, I went to the bathroom, where eight or nine girls were standing in front of a mirror that read *Annie wants to suck Mike* in baby pink frosty lipstick. I heard that same stifled laugh back then, too. Then, as all the other parents resumed their normal behavior, Jenn patted my back and offered up her help if I needed it—like condolences or something. The other Jen just sat, staring down at her wedding ring, biting the insides of her cheeks as if remembering a dirty joke while in church.

It wasn't fifteen minutes later the very same day when the reality hit about what a fool I'd been. My phone was already ringing when I got home, and I ran to pick it up.

"Hello? Ahh—" I dropped the phone as soon as I'd answered it because I'd run in so fast, then hit my head on the corner of the cabinet as I stood up again.

"Hi, Annie? It's Katherine-Rose from the co-op. . . ." I'd never had good luck when it came to people who had two names masquerading as one, so I was already pretty pissed off. Plus, a lump was beginning to swell into existence on the top of my head.

"Hi, what's up?" I asked, swallowing my irritation.

"Well, I don't want to be a pain, but . . ." I was old enough to know that nothing good ever followed an opener like that. "Kaitlyn can't have anything with dairy, un-kay?"

Just the way she pronounced "okay" made me want to cram a carton of lactose-full ice cream and a gallon of milk right down her throat.

"Well, thanks for the notification," I said through a clenched jaw. "But I just got home this minute, and I haven't even started to think about what I'm gonna make for tomorrow. So how's this: If I make anything with dairy *products* in it, I'll bring in something else for Kaitlyn."

God, I was tired of people using "dairy" as a noun; we'd all grown up with it as an adjective. It was just like that instant in time when our society went from calling it "Bombay" to "Mumbai"—as if we weren't supposed to notice that those names sound almost nothing alike. And speaking of that, when did "in the meantime" become just "meantime"?

"Thanks so much, hon."

Yes, she really called me "hon."

"Sure. See you tomorrow," I answered, eager to tend to my son and my lump.

I didn't want to give in to Katherine-Rose's demands, but I thought it would be victimizing the wrong culprit to poison Kaitlyn with creamery items in retaliation for her mother's irritating personality. Kaitlyn was going to have years of hard work ahead of her anyway with a mom like that, so I figured I'd lay off the dairy issue in honor of her impending psychological struggles. Then the phone rang again.

"Hello?" I still sounded moderately pissed off.

"Hi, Annie? It's Belinda, William's mother. . . ." She was waiting for me to acknowledge that I knew her, but I had a feeling I knew where this call was tending, so I let her hang. It also irked me whenever parents called their kids by their full names; I wasn't picky—Will, Billy, Liam, hell, even Sparky would be better than William. Was he going to inherit the throne or something? "You there?" She had to have it confirmed.

"Sure. What's going on?"

"I'm sorry to bug you, but . . ." Again, she paused as if I were going to ask her to continue. But I already knew what was coming, and there was no way I was going to make it any easier for her. "William is allergic to nuts. I hope it won't be too inconvenient for you if you make something without nuts in it. Or eggs." She added that last one in as if it weren't a whole separate request.

"Okay, I just got home, but I'll figure it out. Apparently Kaitlyn can't eat dairy products, so I'm trying to work some magic with, like, water, ketchup, and some old bread."

"Oh, he can't eat tomatoes, either."

"That was just a joke. Anyway, I really had better be going if I'm ever going to get my act together. So I'll see you tomorrow, okay?"

Did this woman have absolutely no sense of sarcasm or irony? I mean, really—did she honestly think I was going to feed the kids soggy condiment sandwiches? I couldn't take much more of this. And yet the phone rang again not five minutes later.

"Hello!" I yelled into the phone.

"Whoa, it's just me!" Thank God, it was Alex. His voice always sounded soft and clear, and he kind of slurred his vowels. "What's going on? You sound pissed as all hell."

"You have no idea. These mothers at the co-op think I'm gonna be their kids' personal chef and nutritionist. Is a damn snack so important that they can't bring their own? I hate them all."

"Well, let's get our priorities straight. How much time will this be taking away from the culinary preparations you'll be undertaking for my dinner? You know I need all seven courses."

"I'd love to laugh, but the reality is that they want me to whip up a dairy-free, egg-free, nut-free, tomato-free delicacy by tomorrow at nine."

"Don't you mean dairy *product* free?"

Okay, I actually laughed when he said that. I should have known he would remember my strict dairy-as-adjective policy.

"Busted." I copped to it, still smiling. "So, where are you, and why aren't you here to help me suffer?"

"Bill called this morning, and Hoffman, Berg needs my help with a few things, so I'm back here in the office for the next couple of days. It's not my old job back, but it still feels good to be doing something productive again."

I let slide the fact that what he must think of as the unproductive something he'd been doing for more than a month now was precisely what the sum of my productivity was. And he did sound happy to be back at the office.

"Good for you. Do you miss us?" I asked.

"Robby, I do. You, not so much," he said, but I could hear the smile behind his voice.

"Nice. Now maybe I won't let you taste the great oeuvre I will be presenting the toddlers tomorrow after slaving away this afternoon."

"Bet you'll change your mind if I bring pizza from Tony's home for dinner. What do you want? Pepperoni and tomatoes?"

"Yeah, or whatever you want. Just no eggs or nuts," I said, mustering a little laugh. Only Alex could get me out of a bad mood like that.

Just as I was teetering on a good mood, the phone rang again. I picked it up. Frozen in a moment of time I would never forget, I realized with blinding clarity that *I had become my mother*. My mother had never, not once, screened a phone call in her entire sixty-four years on this earth. Never. This inability to leave a ringing phone unanswered must have been a recessive gene in the Fingardt women that made itself known only after enrolling our eldest in nursery school, because I was certain that as recently as a few months ago, I was quite adept at ignoring any inconvenient device signaling its activity.

"Hello?" I could hear the suspicion in my tone.

"Annie, I'm so happy I got you?"

Even before she said her name, I could tell it was Elaine— Noah's mom—by the way she phrased everything as a question.

"Actually, so sorry, but I'm on my way out," I lied, hoping to avoid another request.

"Oh, I'll be really quick? Noah is just getting over diarrhea? So, if you could, could you avoid anything fruit based?"

Let me tell you, I hated people who made special requests for their kids' snacks. And I hated people who phrased declarative sentences as questions. I even hated people who referred specifically to their kids' bathroom issues. But I really and truly hated people who wore blue plastic glasses and smock tops. And she wore both.

"Yes," I barked. I'd never "barked" anything ever before, but it felt kind of good.

Stymied by my overly abrupt concession to her demands, she hemmed and hawed for a while. "Ahh . . . well . . . That's . . . I really appreciate it? Thank you so much? And I'll see you tomorrow?"

"I'll be there tomorrow?" I copied her intonation, so what was actually a fact sounded just like a question.

"Huh? Tomorrow's Tuesday; the kids have school just like normal." She actually answered my question, which was not a question but simply intoned like one.

"Yeah, I know? I'm just saying I'll see you there?"

"Okay, Annie. See you then. And thanks." By the end, I think she may have caught on, because she seemed to stop talking in questions herself.

After hanging up, I promptly turned off my ringer and outgoing message.

Chapter Ten

It was all well and good that I made my declarative sentence intonation point with Noah's mother, Elaine, but the last laugh was still on me, given that I now had to come up with something for a fairly large group of kids that contained:

> no dairy products
> no nuts
> no eggs
> no tomatoes
> no fruit
> no self-awareness
> no sense of humor

And I was certainly no Julia Child. I had been planning on buying some kind of mix, adding a little food coloring if I was feeling creative, sticking it in the oven, and calling it a day. But now I had nothing—except a bad mood and a hungry kid. God, how I wished I could wiggle my nose and conjure a semester's worth of snack items right then and there. Ahh, but Samantha had promised Darrin she wouldn't use magic, so she would have had to make them herself, too. And my mere mortal's nose, when I tried wiggling it, produced nothing more than an urge to sneeze and a need for a tissue.

Such were the lofty thoughts swirling through my mind when, in the middle of cutting Robby's grilled cheese in half, the doorbell unexpectedly rang.

"Oh, shit!" I screamed. "What now?"

Robby, who'd been repeating every new word he heard for the last few weeks, started in.

"Oh, stit. Oh, stit. Oh, stit," he copied, complete with the curse-word emphasis one tends to bestow upon those choice terms.

Even though he hadn't gotten the exact pronunciation right, there was no question that he was a three-year-old who was swearing at his own mother. I gave him his sandwich in the hopes that it would stifle him as I ran to the door; however, I could hear him still cursing as I opened it.

There was a man standing in front of me in a bluish gray jumpsuit with a clipboard and some kind of wire thing attached to a box he was holding.

"Hi, can I help you with something?"

"Yeah." He said it as if it rhymed with "duh." "I'm from CableView. You made this appointment. . . ."

He raised the clipboard and started scanning it, as if to verify when I'd made the appointment.

"Oh my God, I remember. I'm sorry—come in," I said in as conciliatory a tone as I could muster.

"September twenty-seventh."

I guess he didn't believe me when I'd said I remembered.

"I remember. I mean, I forgot, but now I remember again. Sorry."

"You want to add a DVR, right?"

Wow, he was right to the point. No chitchat. He didn't even respond to my apology.

"Well, I have to connect this box, so which TV do you want it on? You know, I've been trying to call since twelve fifteen, but there's no answer, no message, no nothing."

It sounded as though he was accusing me of something much worse than screening my calls.

"Sorry about that," I said contritely. It was my third apology in about six seconds. Even though, to be totally honest, I didn't really feel it was my duty to apologize for that last one—I mean, a girl's allowed to silence her own phone, isn't she?

"Well, too late now," he said.

I didn't know whether he was referring to the apology or to the DVR installation. He kind of smiled at me when he said it, though, so I figured he must not be too mad. He looked, maybe, mid- to late-twenties, which I'd only just started to realize was *not* really the same generation as mine; but he didn't seem to think I was some old or outdated freak for being at home in the middle of the day with a kid swearing at me from the kitchen.

When I first quit my job, I was so sensitive about service people finding me at home during the middle of the day and thinking, therefore, that I was idle or lazy (or both) that I always grabbed some sort of cleaning apparatus or power tool before opening the door to make it look as though I was a productive, contributing member of society. I stopped that a while ago, after inadvertently seizing a fire extinguisher I didn't even know we owned and accidentally setting it off as I opened the door for the electrician I'd called to install a dimmer switch in the dining room. But this cable guy seemed to think it the most natural thing in the world to come to a house in broad daylight and find a mom at home with a cursing three-year-old in the next room. I liked him a lot for that.

Because I thought we'd gotten off on the wrong foot, as I led the way to the family room to show him where to put the DVR, I figured I'd strike up a conversation.

"I don't usually turn my ringer off, but . . . well, I've just had a lot going on. It's been one of those days that . . ." And before I could say another word, I burst into tears, right there in front of the guy. He'd been walking toward the family room directly behind me, and I just stopped walking and started crying. "I mean, I have to cook all this stuff, and my son's taken up swearing, and I hate the way I look in these pants, and . . ." My voice choked off because I was sobbing so hard.

When I was pregnant with Robby, I had very few mood swings. Maybe it was because I was still working, and I couldn't very well waltz into the senior partner's office and start weeping about my pants becoming too tight, but I don't remember a single utterly irrational breakdown like this one. And the poor cable guy just stood there gaping at me, paralyzed by shock, fear, contempt, loathing, or hatred; I didn't know which. When he was finally able to move, he edged over to the couch and sort of lowered himself very carefully onto the very edge of the cushion. He stared straight ahead as he sank down; he didn't even tilt his chin or anything. Only his knees moved; the rest of him was stiff.

"I'm not usually like this. It's just that, well, I'm preg—" I couldn't finish because I had to blow my nose so badly. I excused myself to get a tissue, but finding none in the dispenser, I grabbed a paper towel and went back to make my apologies.

Imagine my surprise when, upon returning to the family room, I found the cable guy himself in tears. I couldn't believe it! They always say laughter is contagious, and yawning, too, of course. But I never knew that crying was as well. I didn't really know what to do, so I just ripped off half my paper towel and handed it to him. Then I sat down on the rim of the next cushion over from him, trying to sit the way he did, so he'd feel more comfortable. It felt kind of weird sitting on the edge of my own couch cushion like that, but I didn't want him to think our family sat any differently than he did. I didn't want him to think we were snobs who sat with our butts firmly planted in the middle of our cushions. I peeked quickly at the white name tag ironed to his front shirt pocket; in red script was written *Duncan*.

"Mr. Duncan, would you like a glass of water or something?" I asked as softly and calmly as I could. He nodded his head, which was hidden in his hands, as a reply.

I went to the kitchen in a state of bewilderment. There were only a few guys I'd ever seen cry—and none of them was a cable guy. Not that that mattered. I mean, cable guys are allowed to have feelings, too, right? It was just that I didn't know a lot of, or really any, cable guys. So, needless to say, I was more than a little distracted by this curious turn of events, and I wasn't really focusing when I grabbed a cup off the shelf and put some ice and water into it. Robby had finished swearing by now and had begun to eat his sandwich, so I figured he would be all right for a while. I grabbed another paper towel and headed back to the family room. I sat down on the very edge of the couch again, just like him, and handed him the cup and the paper towel.

"Here, Mr. Duncan. I'm sorry, but I couldn't find any tissues."

"No, this is good," he said, holding the whole flat paper towel against his face.

"Um, Mr. Duncan, here's some water," I said as I handed him the cup.

He was still visibly upset, but he took the cup and started to sip at it. And that was when I realized I'd brought him water in one of Robby's plastic sippy cups with the clear plastic lid on top.

His lips pursed around the little spout, and he drank—ahem, sipped—without saying a word, as if he always drank out of a royal blue toddler's cup with a lid on it. I guess he didn't want me to feel bad for serving grown-ups water in sippy cups any more than I wanted him to feel bad for sitting on only the outer edges of couches, even though it was rather unsettling to see an adult's full-grown mouth squinched around a tiny little spout built for a three-year-old. But there was no way I was going to say anything. Hell, I was trying to make him feel better. And what if he *did* always use sippy cups? What then? I would have made him feel worse by drawing attention to my thinking it unusual for a stranger to enter my house, accept a cup of water from me, and then not even remove the lid before drinking from it, so I just let him sip in peace and quiet.

"Do you want a grilled cheese, Mr. Duncan?" It was the best I could do, and we'd been sitting there, side by side, not saying anything for a while. It was kind of an icebreaker.

He shook his head. Then he lifted his chin. Then he opened his mouth. Then he spoke.

"Duncan's my first name." Then he was silent again.

God, I felt like an ass. Immediately, I began apologizing; although in actuality, I was not really sure what I was sorry about. *I* didn't give him a last name as a first name. But maybe that was what he was crying about, having grown up all those years with a last name for a first name. So then I started really *feeling* sorry, not just *saying* it.

"I'm so sorry; I didn't want you to think I thought I could just call you by your first name because you were my cable guy. I should have guessed, but I've only known one Duncan in my whole life. Although I guess there's that one in *Macbeth*, but for all I know, you never read *Macbeth*. Not because you're a cable guy or anything, but just because you may not be a Shakespeare fan. A lot of people aren't Shakespeare fans, after all. Even though there are so many movies out now of his stuff, like the one with Mel Gibson, for example."

"What was he like?"

"Oh, he was a pretty good Hamlet as I recall, but that was a while ago. Long before he hit the precipice of those drunken episodes and the public tirades. Back around the time of *Braveheart*, you know, Sexiest Man of the Year, and all that."

"No, I mean Duncan."

Now, after rambling on like that, I really started feeling ridiculous, but I honestly didn't know which Duncan he was referring to—the *Macbeth* one or the one I knew in second grade who used to write swear words in cursive and try to get us to pronounce them. I took a flyer.

"Oh, I only knew him in second grade, but he was all right. Except I caught him cheating off me on a spelling test once. 'Plateau.' That was the word."

"No, I mean the one in *Macbeth*."

This was almost too much for me to bear. I almost started crying again before recommencing my apologies for my conversational ineptitude. If Michael were here, he'd have beaten me with Dr. Hornby's stethoscope.

"Oh, sorry. I thought you meant—"

"I did. I'm just kidding you," he said with a smile, knowing how flustered I was.

Then he caught his breath a few times, the way kids do after they've had a really good cry. He picked up the wires and the box as though to resume his job, but just before getting up, he burst into tears again.

I'd probably already insulted him enough—hell, maybe I was

what was making him cry—so, as subtly as I could, I stood up, took the box and wires, and went over to the TV stand to hook them up myself. When I was comfortably buried behind the wall unit, pretending to know what I was doing, I ventured another go at it.

"Ahh, Duncan, do you want to tell me what's making you so sad?"

He nodded his head a few times and began to explain.

"I'm not . . . I'm not really . . . I'm not really a . . ." He started choking on his sobs and couldn't finish.

I busied myself with various screws and holes and metal thingies, waiting for him to continue.

"I'm not really a cable guy," he said after a few minutes, struggling with the words.

"Huh?" I couldn't really think of anything else to ask. But, to be honest, from where I was squatting (behind the console table, staring at a bunch of wires whose only discernible purpose was either to intimidate or to ridicule me), it didn't really seem all that surprising.

"I . . . I . . . I'm really a floral engineer," he finished. Then came some more choking sobs.

I paused at that one, trying to figure out what he meant. Then it hit me. "Oh! You mean you're a florist?"

"Yeah, but we prefer 'floral engineer,'" he explained, correcting me.

"So, what are you doing working for CableView?"

"Well, you may have noticed, not too many guys work in flower shops. And when I got married, I was . . . well, I was embarrassed. So I quit and started working here."

"Does your wife know you're not really a cable guy?"

"She kind of figured it out; I mean, she would come home

from work at the beauty salon, and I'd have made huge flower arrangements in vases, pots, cans, whatever we had lying around, and I would put them everywhere. So she guessed it. You know, she actually told me to go back to being a florist if I'm so unfulfilled as a cable guy; but we have two sons now. And when they're old enough to go to school . . . Well, you know, kids at school can be pretty mean if they know someone's dad's a florist." He sniffled.

"Unfortunately, Duncan, kids don't really need any reason whatsoever to pick on other kids. I mean, some kids are going to be cruel no matter what. Once, at my son's school, I saw a kid get pushed over, and his dad is a rich and powerful lawyer," I told him. And it was the truth. Apparently, kids cared way less about their dads' professions than about their peers' choice of formal wear; so, assuming Duncan's sons weren't going to don velvet capes, an assumption I felt pretty safe in making, his kids would probably have no greater chance than any others of getting picked on.

"Yeah, you're probably right," he conceded.

"Well, have you considered doing it again? Going back to working with flowers?"

"Yeah, but I don't know. It's not that this job is so bad; and I definitely need the money. It's just . . . It's just . . . Well, I miss the flowers," he said as he dropped his head into his hands.

"Look, if you're really a florist—I mean, a 'floral engineer,'" I said, covering myself, "and you want to get back to it, maybe you could do it on the weekends, part-time. You know, don't quit your day job and all that, but still be able to work with the flowers."

"I don't know. Maybe. The extra income *would* be nice."

"My friend Jen's sister, Betsy, works one day a weekend at the

Baby Boutique downtown, and she loves it. Maybe you'd be able to work out something like that."

As I was dispensing these nuggets of wisdom, I was tightening, turning, wiggling, and jiggling any piece of silver I could find in that godforsaken shelving unit. And, all at once, the static noise of the television snow was replaced with a glorious mechanical silence that could only signal my success in having brought the DVR to life. I stood to witness my victory over technology and happily observed that the system was loading.

Duncan, in the meantime, had assumed a more comfortable position on the couch, leaning back with his head resting against the back cushion. He'd even taken a couple pillows to prop himself up more, so I guessed that he was probably starting to feel at least a little better. I was also in a much better mood after realizing my latent ability to connect one piece of metal to another piece of similarly colored metal in order to alter broadcast programming according to my personal viewing schedule.

"It's none of my business, really," I continued. "And I don't want to butt in; but if you wanted, I could call a friend of mine. His friend owns a chain of flower shops."

Strangely enough, this was true. Michael had been telling me about some gorgeous new friend of his named Lucas who, as Michael explained it, had become filthily wealthy from opening a succession of flower shops.

"Your friend owns flower shops?" he asked.

"Not my friend, but my friend's friend. Maybe you've heard of them—Petal Pushers?"

"Heard of them! Everyone's heard of them! They have an excellent reputation in the business," he explained. So, I guess, in spite of maintaining his alias as a cable guy, Duncan had been keeping up with the floral trade papers or journals or seminars or whatever florists did to stay current in their field. "I can't believe you know *the* Lucas Johnson!"

"I don't know him; I just know someone who knows him. So, what do you think?"

"I'd love it! God, I wish Shelly were here so I could talk to her about it. Shelly's my wife," he said with a big smile. He was clearly feeling much better.

"You can call her if you want," I said as I replaced the extra wires and the cable tools on the table where he'd left them. "I'll give you some privacy."

"You really don't mind?" he asked as he dug his cell phone out of his pocket.

"Of course I don't mind. I'll just step into the other room; it's no big deal, letting you have your conversation in peace. I should check on my son, anyway."

"No, I mean, you don't mind talking to your friend for me?" he clarified, a big smile plastered on his face.

"Consider it done."

Chapter Eleven

*A*s Duncan began dialing, I went back to the kitchen to see how Robby was doing. I really wanted to stay in the other room with Duncan so I could hear what he was saying, but I didn't think that would be very polite. And, as it turned out, the acoustics in the kitchen weren't all that bad, anyway. From what I could gather, Shelly, his wife, seemed pretty firmly behind Duncan's attempt to return to the floral industry and suggested that he might even be able to do the floral arrangements at Clip & Curl, which, I gathered, was where she worked as a hairdresser—not that I was eavesdropping. However, I couldn't help but overhear (after positioning myself a little closer to the doorway) that he, apparently, ten years earlier, had made her the corsage she wore to the prom with him. And, I guess, ever since then, she'd wanted him to keep working with flowers. I was just beginning to reflect on my own prom, at which I drank my first bottle of champagne—Asti Spumanti, actually—and got felt up in the back of the limousine that Zach Ackerman had rented for us, when I heard the click of Duncan's cell phone snapping shut. So I started talking really loudly to Robby, pretending I hadn't just overheard a large chunk of Duncan's personal phone call.

"Well, I guess you were right," Duncan said from the doorway in between the kitchen and family room. I spun around, trying to act as if he'd caught me off guard. "Did you hear me?"

"*No*, I didn't hear you! I would never listen to a phone call between a husband and a wife. That's totally your own personal, private business. What went on in that phone call was none of my business," I said, trying to convince him.

"No, I mean just now. I said I think you were right about the whole thing. I'm gonna give it a try. I'll go tonight right after work and see if they're looking for a florist in any of the shops. I mean, 'floral engineer,'" he added with a smile.

"Yay! Good for you! So, can I assume Shelly liked your idea? Hey, wouldn't it be great if you *were* hired and could do the flowers for Clip and Curl?"

Whoops.

"Wow, would it ever!" he answered cheerfully. If he caught my blunder, he didn't let on.

"Excellent! I'll call Michael—the friend of mine who knows Lucas—and tell him about you. Your wife will be so happy! Once you get the job, you could make her a corsage just like the one you made her for the prom!"

I'd slipped up again. I'd heard of pathological liars, but I was starting to get the sense that I was a pathological truth-teller. Why couldn't I eavesdrop in peace? Why did I always trip up and reveal my dirty secret?

"Hey, how'd you know? Oh, I guess you heard me. Was I talking too loud? Shelly says I scream when I'm on the phone. Sorry."

"No, it's just that the rooms are so close, I couldn't help hearing a couple of things."

This was excellent! I eavesdropped; he apologized. He was in such a good mood about the potential to become a florist again that he probably would have apologized for the rainy summer we'd had and the parking ticket I'd gotten at the library.

"Thanks for your help. I really appreciate it," he said, trying to be serious, but he couldn't stop smiling.

"No, thank you for coming to connect the DVR," I answered. He may not have actually hooked it up himself, but he did *come* to hook it up, so I thought he still deserved some thanks.

"Oh, by the way, what are you making?" he asked on his way toward the door.

Was it the norm for cable guys to go around asking what their customers' incomes were? I didn't know. But as I thought about what I used to make before I quit and what Alex was making now, it seemed like pretty much more than what a cable guy would make, so I felt a little funny telling him. I mean, we'd become pretty good friends, and I didn't want a difference in salaries to come between us.

I guess my awkward silence tipped him off as to my confusion, because he soon added, "When I got here, you said you had to cook a bunch of stuff. So, what are you making?"

"Oh, 'making' as in baking . . ."

"What did you think I was asking?" He laughed. "If you were making a model airplane or a tree house or something?"

"No, I thought you meant money. You know, how much money did I make." I felt like a real ass, but it brought me back to the dietary dilemma I was in over the damn co-op. "I have no idea except that it can't contain eggs, milk, tomatoes, fruit, or one other thing I forget right now."

"Well, I wish I could help you, but I really have to go."

"Oh, nuts!"

"Well, I'm sorry; I'd like to stay, too; really, I would. But I have to go to Cranberry Lane to do a hookup for a new customer."

"No, nuts is the other thing."

"Oh. Hmm," he said contemplatively. "No eggs, milk, toma-toes, fruit, or nuts. Well, how about . . ." He thought about it for a while. "Popcorn balls?"

Popcorn balls! He was right! He was a genius! He'd saved me! He was my own private Dr. Bombay, a little shaky maybe on the form, but always there to help Samantha out of her predicaments.

"Duncan, that is *just* the idea I needed. Thank you!"

"No, thank you for all your help with my job! If you ever need any help with the cable or anything, I'll be there for you."

I almost felt like I should hug him or something, but instead I just showed him to the door, promised I'd put in a good word with Michael, and told him to call after his visit to Petal Push-ers. Then Robby and I waved good-bye as he backed out of the driveway.

Popcorn balls! Perfect! Good ole Duncan had saved the day! I'd show those co-op moms. I'd bring in the sweetest, stickiest, gooiest treats this side of spun sugar. If they didn't want eggs or fruit or anything that all normal kids have eaten from time im-memorial, I'd deliver something that would induce such a sugar rush that their little darlings wouldn't sleep for two weeks. So, after popping about twenty bowls of popcorn, I plunked Robby on the counter to watch, and I proceeded to mix every conceiv-able sweet thing I could get my hands on in a huge bowl: maple syrup (two kinds), honey (Robby helped squeeze it out of the honey bear container), melted light brown and dark brown sugar, chocolate syrup, hell, even molasses. I didn't know I owned mo-lasses, but there it was, hiding out behind the powdered sugar on the top shelf of my cabinet. Oh, and I added the powdered sugar, too, just for spite. Then we stirred in cupfuls of popcorn at a time and tried to form globs of the stuff.

After the trays of the numerous sticky balls were all cooled, I tried one. Then two—okay, seven, in total. They were, without a doubt, the best popcorn balls I had ever eaten in my life. What began as sheer revenge had metamorphosed into the biggest gift I would ever bestow on a bunch of undiscerning toddlers and their ingrate parents. I resented them all the more as I sampled one (two) more.

But before I either ate them all or packaged them up to take to the co-op, I filled a big bag with a dozen or so, boxed it all up, and sent the package off to Duncan at CableView. It was the least I could do, given it was his idea.

Chapter Twelve

*O*nce the popcorn balls were finished and the cleanup complete, I called Michael at Dr. Hornby's.

"Dr. Hornby's office," Michael snapped into the phone as he answered.

"Hi, Michael. It's Annie. I'm wondering—"

"What elaborate scheme have you whipped up this time, just to get some more face time with Herrold? Perhaps something a little subtler than puking into a LEGO bucket this time, huh?" he cut in.

"Well, let me see. . . . I could try to contract rabies. Or diphtheria. What about bubonic plague? I hear that's making a comeback," I answered.

"Tee-hee. So, really, what is it? Do you need to come in?"

"No. I have a favor to ask, though."

"Oh God. What is it?" he asked begrudgingly. "You don't need money, do you?"

"No, but a guy I met today does."

"What, is he a hooker or something?"

"He's a cable guy. Well, actually, he's a 'floral engineer.' "

" 'Floral engineer'? Well, la-di-da. You mean 'flower guy'?"

"They prefer 'floral engineer,'" I explained with an in-the-know kind of scoff.

"Yeah? Well, I prefer 'flower guy.'"

"Look, could you help him out? He was crying on my couch because he said he 'missed the flowers.' Couldn't you talk to your friend Lucas and see if he could use him in any of his shops? He just wants part-time, so there's no real risk. C'mon, Michael, please? Will you do it? What do you think?"

"What I think is that Annie has a crush on the cable guy. You *love* him. You want to marry him. Annie and Cable sitting in a tree, K-I-S-S-I-N-G," he started to sing. "Oh, Herrold will be so jealous," he whispered in a mock-serious tone.

"If you must know why I want to help him out, it's because he told me to make popcorn balls."

"Told you to do *what* with balls? Now I'm interested."

"To make them—popcorn balls—for Robby's school. I had to volunteer for something, so I volunteered to be the Snack Lady."

"Oh, Annie. How could you volunteer for *that*? Don't you know anything about raising kids at all? Now you're going to get ten thousand calls about kids' allergies and aversions and restrictions. 'Oh, little Joey's a vegetarian.' 'Little Suzie's kosher.' 'Little Billy thinks ice cream's too cold.' Really, Annie, what ever possessed you to take that assignment?"

"How come you know this? How is it possible that *everyone* knows this except me?"

"Because absolutely every person in the world—except you—understands that human nature is a gross, vile, selfish, and ugly thing, and that, given the chance, every person will make as many special requests as possible for the comfort and convenience of himself and his little Patsy-Pigtails and Timmy-Toughskins. So, you had to make a ball for every kid in school, huh? Did you eat any?"

"What? Why would I eat any?"

"I didn't ask *why* you'd eat them; I asked *if* you ate them."

"Just a couple."

"Annie . . ." He stretched out my name in that way my mother used to when she'd catch me trying to sneak out to the bus stop wearing eyeliner and lip gloss.

"Okay," I said contritely, "six." It was a slight understatement, tantamount to shaving a few pounds off my weight.

"What a naughty thing you are, putting those balls in your mouth. Annie, I'm ashamed of you."

"Hah. Hah. Look, I'll bring you some of the balls if you help me out. So, what do you say? Will you do it? Will you talk to Lucas for him? His name's Duncan, and he's going to Petal Pushers after work tonight. Will you please put in a good word? I mean, what's the point of having all these high connections if you're not willing to use them? I would have thought you, of all people, would have realized that."

"Oh, fine. I'll mention your Mr. Balls to Lucas."

"Thanks, Michael! And his name's Duncan."

"Okay. I'll tell Lucas to hire your Mr. Duncan."

"Ahh, Duncan's his first name."

"What? That's a last name. Haven't you ever read *Macbeth*?"

It wasn't worth explaining that I'd had this same thought process moments before.

"Yeah, but he has only one name."

"You said it was his *first* name. First implies a second, Annie," he said in that I'm-copying-you tone my cousin used to use when we were about six.

"No, Duncan in *Macbeth* had only one name," I clarified. "Like Madonna. Cher. Barry."

"Barry? The Barry Leibowitz I went to high school with? He goes by one name now?"

"I'm so sure. I'm talking about *the* Barry—Barry Manilow."

"Oh my God, there are just so many things wrong with that example, I don't know where to begin explaining. Suffice it to say, if, in the future, you're ever going to illustrate your single-name category of people, do *not*—repeat, do *not*—use Barry Manilow to do so. Promise me."

"I promise, as long as you talk to Lucas. Remember—tonight around six! And thanks, Michael. Really. I owe you," I said.

"All I request in return is that you share his sticky balls with me, okay? See ya." I could hear him laughing as he hung up.

Later that night, after Robby'd gone to bed, Alex and I were flipping around, trying to find something to watch on TV. Strangely, though, the remote control kept picking up all the premium channels. It stopped on HBO (an old Will Ferrell movie); it stopped on Showtime (vampire saga); it stopped on Starz and Encore and Cinemax. Sundance. Independent Film Channel. Even a Golf Network. We had *every channel!* Alex and I turned to each other, trying to figure out what was going on, but before he could formulate a question or I could formulate a theory, the phone rang.

"Hello?" I answered.

"Hi, Mrs. Forster?"

"Ye-es?" I replied, wondering who it was. No one called me that besides Miss Jenkins. Vaguely, I thought of my mother-in-law. Was that who this person was trying to contact?

"It's Duncan. I just wanted you to know that I stopped by

Petal Pushers on my way home from work," he said in a very dejected tone. I figured no good had come of my talking to Michael.

"And . . . ?" I asked with trepidation.

"And . . . I got the job! I got it! I'm going to be a floral engineer again! I start next weekend. I work Wednesday and Friday nights and every other Saturday. He even said I could pick up other shifts later if I wanted! I can't believe it!"

"Congratulations, Duncan! That's great news!"

"And I owe it all to you. It was your idea, your plan, your connection. Really, you're a good friend. I don't know how to thank you!"

"Well," I replied, putting two and two together, "it seems as if you may have found a way—a way that answers all my cable-viewing needs; am I right? Do we have you to thank for the Premium Gold Package?"

"That's nothing compared with what you did for me; and don't worry, the hookup's legit. We offer this kind of service to our Level One clients. And you are definitely Level One!"

"Thanks, Duncan; but that was totally unnecessary," I told him, at which point Alex started punching my leg and gesturing with that sawing motion across the neck that tells a speaker to clam up quick—or else. He must have really liked that Cameron Diaz movie he was watching.

So, after mutual thanks and mutual praise, we hung up, and I lay back against Alex's shoulder to take in and enjoy the craft and fine workmanship of Hollywood's brightest stars.

Adam Sandler had never before seemed such an artist.

Chapter Thirteen

*O*ctober seemed to pass by quickly, once I put in for the transfer of duties at the co-op. Alex was adjusting to the slower pace of daily life around the house, and although he had no intention of becoming a stay-home dad, he was filling the role graciously while it endured. But however mixed his feelings about the situation were, Robby's feelings were a constant and abundant outpouring of unadulterated joy at having his dad around during the day. And Alex's presence on the home front was timed to perfection, for, as my first trimester drew to its conclusion, I found myself so physically tired that I once—literally—fell asleep while sitting on the side of the tub, cutting Robby's nails after his bath. The extra man on deck didn't seem like a luxury at those moments; it seemed like a requirement.

We talked a lot about the new baby, in the hopes that we could prepare Robby for the arrival of someone who would surely rouse all the sinister feelings of jealousy, rage, injustice, and irritation until the years and years of therapy could diminish their impact, but I'm not sure how much Robby understood. Each night, Alex would read to Robby, and then the two of them would pick out a baby book to read to my stomach. I have no idea if Robby grasped that his soon-to-be brother or sister was underneath that mound, but he seemed to get a kick out of talking to my abdomen. Alex also loved it. I, however, was less overjoyed with this nightly ritual, as it made it increasingly unavoidable exactly how huge I was getting. But the two guys never seemed to notice, or if they did, they were too cagey to acknowledge it verbally, and that made me feel somewhat less hideous.

I'd also seen Duncan a couple of times after he started at Petal Pushers, and he always smiled to the point of laughing every time he so much as touched a stem or a bud. When Jen and I threw a baby shower for Jenn's new baby, it was Duncan who did the flower arrangements—beautiful, voluminous creations with pink, pale blue, and pastel yellow flowers cascading out of immaculate white porcelain vases. And when he came to the house to set them up, he brought me six other recipes for treats that didn't contain any of the no-no ingredients from the list that had, by that point, grown to include, but was in no way limited to, eggs, nuts, dairy products, tomatoes, fruit, food dyes of any sort, chocolate, refined sugar, refined anything, and all wheat products or products contaminated by wheat products or wheat by-products. And for Robby, he brought a little stuffed teddy bear that held a ceramic pot in its lap in which a perfectly shaped tiny Christmas tree was growing. Jenn and Jen loved Duncan, and when they told him as he was leaving that they'd never use another "florist," he didn't even correct their nomenclature. He simply beamed at them, thanked them, and offered his other services as a cable guy as well.

Halloween was also made easier by Alex's presence on the home front. Because one of us could man the doorbell while the other walked the streets trick-or-treating with Robby, I felt far more assured that we wouldn't end up with a front yard filled with eggs, wet Charmin, and our own smashed pumpkin. And, of course, all the leftover candy didn't do much to hurt the season's bounty, either. I should confess here, the *leftover* candy wasn't really so much "leftover" as it was a deliberate oversupply to begin with. I mean, we'd lived in our house for five years, and every year, we'd gone through the exact same amount of candy— three and a half bags. And toward the end of the night, I usually ended up giving kids something like seventeen candy bars each just to get rid of everything except that last prized half bag that I told myself was security against any potential late-night trick-or-treaters, but was really just stuff I wanted to eat the next day. Well, this year, I was nearly four months pregnant, and I knew damn well that four bags just wouldn't cut it, so I bought a dozen bags of candy. We used up the standard three and a half bags as predicted and were left not only with the eight and a half unopened bags, but with Robby's cache as well, because he was now officially old enough to trick-or-treat.

For the first time in his little-kid life, he could actually go and demand candy from neighbors. However, as he was discovering this astounding phenomenon, I was discovering an even greater one of my own: My own flesh-and-blood son had inherited his father's candy-indifferent gene rather than my candy-adoring gene, which, heretofore, I had always believed to be a strongly dominant gene in the DNA link. But Robby, like his father before him, remained woefully uninterested in anything of a smooth, nougat-filled nature. For Robby, trick-or-treating wasn't about the reward; it was all about the power. He liked the quest, the hunt, the triumph in getting his neighbors to drop foodstuffs into his plastic pumpkin. He just didn't have any interest in consuming the candy once the thrill of the chase was over. So, I was on my own with the equivalent of nine, maybe ten, bags of candy. "Fun-sized" my ass. What's fun about a little stump of candy bar?

I had to unwrap twelve to fourteen in one sitting to have even a modicum of fun. "Fun-sized" would have run the length of my living room. A twenty-two-foot candy bar—now, *that* would be some freakin' fun.

I ate my way through the bags I'd bought first. But when Robby's uneaten candy was still sitting in the plastic pumpkin three weeks after Halloween, I figured it was fair game. I asked him one last time if he wanted any of it, and with an absolute lack of interest, he said, "No. Ice pop, please." I figured it was a win-win: I'd steal all his candy, and he'd get the bland, frost-encrusted, good-for-you ice pop made of one hundred percent fruit juice. If you've never stolen candy from a baby, just so you know, it feels kind of weird—reaching into the kid-sized opening of his plastic pumpkin, grabbing a midsized bar, unwrapping it, and downing the thing. I mean, was he going to end up writing a book about me? Were greasy talk-show hosts going to ask him to describe how I forced him to surrender his rightful Halloween treats? Was there some Freudian theory about moms who stole candy from their sons? I wondered about these things as I continued to consume Robby's goods piece by piece. But, in my defense, Thanksgiving was rolling around, which meant that I had to put away all the Halloween stuff; and that included the candy-holding plastic pumpkin. Looked at in that light, eating his candy was actually an act of supreme self-sacrifice—you know, taking one for the team and all that, just so I could keep an orderly and seasonally decorated house. In those more providential moments, I fantasized that the book he'd write would be entitled *Home Sweet Mom* maybe, or *How My Mom Saved My Teeth: Lessons in Maternal Devotion*. Or something along those lines.

So, when the candy was all gone and my chocolate-to-real-food ratio was returning to more typical proportions, I brought up the box from the basement and started to pack away all the Halloween decorations and costumes. And, lo and behold, who knew? But as it turned out, *these* were the parts of Halloween that Robby cared about. So, to recap: After stealing all his candy, I then had to deprive him of all the ghosts and spiders and jack-o'-lanterns we'd hung all over the house. He cried to see them go—a true little-kid cry. Sitting on the floor in the family room, his little arms hanging limply by his side, he just let loose. I couldn't get mad at him; I mean, it made me wonder how I would have felt if someone tried to deprive me of the part of the holiday I liked the best. And then I started to think about Alex or Jenn or my mom or someone coming in to pack up and put away all my candy, and I started to get a little weepy, too. Was it the pregnancy? I don't know. But I did know I would miss these moments with Robby—when he was still a baby to me, with no little brother or sister to put his older-kid status into perspective. I scooped him up and rocked him. And then I promised he could keep his costume out to play with if he wanted. That made him happy enough to stop crying and run off to go find it. And just as I finished up with the packing, he came in wearing his costume.

He was still obsessed with cars—perhaps even more so since Alex's presence at home had grown to full-time. He had told me weeks earlier that he wanted to be "Daddy's 'vertible" for Halloween, but I didn't know how to transform a little boy into a trick-or-treating automobile. So, we did the next-best thing: I made him into the Mercedes emblem from Alex's car. I spray painted Robby's sneakers, mittens, sweatpants, and hooded sweatshirt silver. Then I got a hula hoop and cut it to the right size for Robby to stand in; then I spray painted that silver, too. And you know what? With his hood pulled up tight into a peak, his arms up over his head holding the top of the hula hoop, and his feet spread wide on the bottom rim, he actually looked even less like a Mercedes emblem than you might think. Most people thought he was a peace sign. Some thought—I guess because of the silver—that he was an alien.

But a few of the neighbors guessed what he was right away and got quite a laugh out of how seriously Robby was taking it. I think he thought if he played the emblem well enough, he'd actually *become* the one on Alex's hood. So, he stood with his little arms tight to the sides of his head and his silver-painted face looking very intense and angry, posing as the emblem at each door we went to. It was kind of tough for him, though, since Sarah, who was trick-or-treating with us as a fairy princess, kept hitting him with her wand and saying he was not an "unbloom" anymore; and Chris, who was a cowboy, kept galloping through Robby's hula hoop on his stick-pony and twisting him all around. Anyway, even though it was now past the middle of November, I let Robby keep the costume out to play with—it was a small sacrifice to make (though one I hoped would make it into his book) if it made the transition from Halloween to Thanksgiving any easier for the poor kid.

I only wish I'd had someone who could ease the transition for me, but no such luck. As I was down in the basement storing the Halloween stuff and retrieving the Thanksgiving stuff, the phone started to ring upstairs. Alex had taken Robby to the playground, so I knew I'd have to run back up the steps to get it myself.

"Hello?" I wheezed into the phone.

"Honey, hi. I can't talk, but I just wanted to make sure all is well with next Monday when we'll be arriving," my mother's voice chirped in the receiver.

She had a way of opening every phone conversation with the proclamation that her time was short, and therefore, I was to infer, valuable. I guess maybe she was trying to imply that I had such an abundance of time that I must be either very idle or very unimportant—maybe both.

"Of course! I can't wait to see you and Daddy! I've even already bought the turkey for Thanksgiving," I told her. And it was true. I was going to host my first Thanksgiving dinner ever, and I was actually pretty excited.

"Oh, honey, if you buy it this early, it's sure to be left over from last year. You'll just have to return it and get another. The store will let you exchange it, I'm sure. You can't buy a turkey more than a week before Thanksgiving Day. You know that! Never in all my years have I bought a turkey more than a week before Thanksgiving Day. I think Auntie Nancy did one year, but that was the year we went to your dad's side of the family. Now, *they* always buy theirs weeks before, but with the chestnut stuffing that they make, who can tell how old the bird is . . . ?"

Why my mother insisted on calling turkey "the bird" I have never in my thirty-five years known. Birds fly around outside. With feathers. Alive. Turkey is what comes sliced up and tan colored on your plate at Thanksgiving. Maybe on a sandwich occasionally.

"Mom, please call it turkey. If you must, you can call it 'a' turkey," I begged.

"And you're not going to make chestnut or oyster stuffing, right? You're just going to make the regular old kind I always make, right? Half cornbread, half Pepperidge Farm croutons, right? And about the pies . . ." She went on, disregarding my request altogether.

And so the conversation continued in this vein for twenty minutes or so. For a woman who was short on time, she sure could talk. I think she wanted to make sure I was carrying on *her* family's traditions exactly. Now that I had Robby and a second on the way, she had gotten weirder about staking her claim to the family rituals. For her, coming to my house for a holiday was the American equivalent of the Changing of the Guard at Buckingham Palace. For me, having Thanksgiving at my house was pretty much the only option: I just couldn't see myself wedged into one of those airplane miniseats with a stomach that I could almost watch grow larger in front of my very eyes alongside a three-year-old whose favorite conversational topics involved body parts and their accompanying functions. Plus, to be honest, Alex had begun to show some cracks. Although we were still solvent, he spent a lot of time thinking about and planning around our newly limited finances. He'd taken to entering all manner of numbers and figures in the Microsoft Money program that came installed in his computer, and I think he was starting to get the tiniest bit apprehensive about spending loads of money on what would surely be a trip that would put the "ache" in vacation for both of us. So, it was settled: In exactly five days, my mom and dad would be arriving at the airport. If I knew my mother, she'd have checked enough luggage to scare Alex into thinking they were staying for six months. Then, while my dad would probably sit quietly in the front seat, making occasional references to new real estate development or fancy cars that we passed en route, my mother would busy herself with cleaning the backseat of my station wagon with Handi Wipes the whole forty minutes back to our house.

But, in spite of the mild anxiety I had over their visit, I was actually really looking forward to it. It meant, in some weird way, that I had made the cut. I was now officially a grown-up. I would be cooking my own bird. Ahem. Turkey.

Chapter Fourteen

By the time the following Monday rolled around, I was prepared for The Arrival. My parents were getting in at 2:25 p.m. (not 2:30, as my mother pointed out on three different occasions), and I had everything in order. I'd also tried pretty hard to prepare Alex, who, because he was home full-time with us, now had the illustrious assignment of driving us to the airport to retrieve them.

"Just don't talk about work," I cautioned as we headed down the highway.

"Annie, first of all, they already know I've been laid off. Don't you remember that forty-five-minute conversation my ear had with your mother about using this time 'to—'"

"'To forge the bonds of home life,'" I concluded for him. "Yes, I remember."

And it was true; my mother had, in fact, discussed Alex's sidebar with him in such nauseating detail and at such profound lengths that the conversation had eluded the typical waiting period for such things and had jumped right to the front of the line of family jokes and obscure references. The expression "to forge the bonds of home life" had not only been uttered by my mother—without the slightest trace of irony, mind you—but had now been reiterated by Alex and me dozens of times in an attempt to rid the expression, through ridicule and mimicry, of its inherently processed cheesiness and embarrassingly Waltonsesque tone. "Home life"? Really, was that even a word? And why was it known by and, more important, used by anyone I was related to? And "forge the bonds"? I mean, the fact that that expression made an appearance in a conversation with my husband couldn't even bear contemplation.

"And second of all," Alex continued, "don't you think they'd notice me, say, playing with Robby in the backyard at twelve thirty in the afternoon on a weekday?"

"Yes, but they wouldn't have said anything—even if they didn't already know you'd been sidebarred. It's just the way my family is. We don't say anything."

"Really? Huh. You say nothing. Hmm. What about that twenty-minute diatribe about advertising agencies using the word 'fresh' in commercials? Or what about two nights ago when you kept me up until one forty-five discussing the way your third-grade classmate pronounced 'cookie'?"

"Look, I stand by my assertion that the word 'fresh' is a disgusting word and should be banned from all media. And it wasn't 'cookie'—it was 'cracker.' I can't help that Cindy Barr somehow managed to remove the first *r* in the word but to keep the second. How is that possible? I don't know, but she did it. Cacker. God, it makes my skin crawl to think about it."

"So, come again? You hail from a family that says nothing—is that what you're telling me?"

"No, Mommy," Robby piped in. "You says a lot. You talking to Jenn so much about Grammum's bird, me and Chris finished all our coloring."

"Grammum doesn't have a bird," I said, confused.

"Uh-huh. You said so. You told Jenn she has a bird at Thanksgiving," he explained.

Oh. I guess I had shared my turkey/bird pet peeve with Jenn the day before.

"Not a real bird, honey. And at least you got to finish coloring. What were you drawing?" I asked, hoping to shift the subject.

"The bathroom walls," he answered, matter-of-factly.

Uh-oh. When I'd collected him and our stuff after visiting with Jenn before the onslaught of my parents, I hadn't thought to check out the damage of the playdate. I guess he'd redecorated. How cool of Jenn not to call me out on it. And, knowing Jenn, she'd already had the room Magic Erasered to within an inch of its life.

"My point is simply that my parents never talk about problems or issues or unpleasantries. That's all I meant. So, as long as you don't bring it up, they'll leave the topic well enough alone."

Jeez, all I intended was to offer a little advice to my beloved husband, honed over three and a half decades with my mother, as to how to avoid another foray into conversations best left to the season finales of sitcoms that have decided to take themselves too seriously. And this was what I got.

Alex, though, never one to be flustered, just smiled as we approached the airport. In spite of all of his good qualities, Alex actually liked my mother a great deal, so I wasn't too worried about them. And I knew my dad would be a dream. I was really just anxious on my own behalf.

Having gotten there right on time, I went in with Robby to meet them, while Alex stayed in the car, circling the terminal. I saw my dad first, and I let go of Robby's hand, so he could run up to his granddad.

Then I saw my mom. She was wearing a green Prada suit with a magenta pashmina tossed around her shoulders. I didn't know a single woman who still wore a pashmina, but my own mother did. And she actually looked good wearing it. Suddenly, I regretted wearing the black maternity leggings and plain black turtleneck. It's a very sad day when a daughter looks at her sixty-plus-year-old mother with fashion envy. Her hair, as always, was streaked with bronze and blond (she called it "tinting"), and her makeup was flawless. She'd even used lip liner. On my best days, I was granted the four and a half seconds it required to apply lipstick—but never lip liner. I started to feel my face getting oily and blotchy under the absence of foundation. And the eighteen pounds I'd already gained were weighing heavily on my self-esteem.

"Hello, darling," she said as she hugged me. Then she held me at arm's length to evaluate. "Oooh, look at that tummy! No one would think you weren't pregnant," she added.

What the hell was that supposed to mean? At least on *Bewitched*, when Endora criticized anything, she was direct. Although my mom had never, to my knowledge, had an unexpressed thought, her comments were usually so enshrouded in cryptic and encoded language that I was always unsure as to what exactly she was talking about.

"Hi, Mom!" I said into her shoulder as I hugged her. She still wore Chanel No.5, and it reminded me instantly of the golden color of the liquid, the square cut of the bottle, and the cut glass tray on her vanity where she kept it. She collected perfumes— she must have had more than sixty bottles—but I only remember her wearing Chanel No.5. It was a scent distinctive enough to leave its mark (her words)—yet heavy enough to annoy all social contacts (my words). Chanel No.5 must have been to her what a lance and a shield were to knights of yore—serviceable weaponry against all and sundry potential offenders. My mom was protected by the force field of fragrance.

"Now, let me touch you," she addressed my ever-growing stomach. And she bent over and scrunched my guts between her hands and cheek. Maybe she was trying to exert her influence to get the baby to flip around, I don't know. Then my dad came up, carrying Robby in front of him on his forearm, the way men, who have no hips, carry little kids.

"Hi, sweetie!" He leaned over to kiss me. Then Robby got tangled in my hair, and I had to tear myself away from my mom's pincers. "Is Alex outside?"

"He's circling. I'll call and tell him we're here while you guys get your bags, okay?"

Robby wanted to go with his grandparents, so I waited by myself for Alex to circle back for us. Within two minutes he appeared, presumably enjoying the last private and quiet moments he'd have for the next four and a half days. He smiled at me and blew a kiss as he popped the trunk for their luggage. Then his face changed to a look of shock or confusion or sheer horror—I wasn't sure which. I turned around to see what he was looking at, and there was my mom, buried in an electric cart beneath what looked to be hundreds of bags. And they all matched—brown gusseted leather with tiny initials all over them. There were two suitcases and a garment bag, several smallish valises, a shoulder bag, a carry-on, and even one of those squarish pillboxes with the handle on top. They told me they were staying for five days—five days. I think Alex must have thought I'd asked them to move in. Truly, I don't think the accumulation of all the clothes I'd ever owned would have needed so many bags for their transportation. And that was saying something, given that my underwear had of late become the size of a small sailing vessel.

But Alex, being Alex, took it all in stride and actually started to chuckle with my dad as they loaded and pushed and wedged and crammed the bags, one by one, into the back of the wagon. We were left, in the end, with only two of the more unwieldy chunks of baggage that wouldn't fit in the far back, so we had to put them in the backseat—the backseat. With Robby's child seat squarely attached in the middle, there was room for only one other passenger back there. Well, Alex was driving, so he was out. Robby was legally required to be in the car seat, so he was out. That left my mom, my dad, and a very fattish and pregnant me. My dad had a bad hip—so there was no way he was going to navigate the terrain of the luggage-engulfed backseat. I told him to ride shotgun. So he was out. It came down to my mother or me. We started alternately eyeing each other, then the backseat, then each other again; Mexican stand-off style. There was room for only one of us. I vaguely hoped that the fact that it was all her luggage that was causing the problem might tempt her into deferring. Or the fact that I was pregnant. Or the fact that it was my car. But no. Without so much as a shiver, she slid right in beside Robby, gave him a huge kiss on the cheek, and handed him a juice box. Meanwhile, I clunked over the handles and buckles and clasps of the bags in order to assume my position atop the luggage, in the back of the wagon behind Robby. His juice box promptly exploded up behind his shoulder, staining my hair and right breast purple.

Surprisingly, the drive back home wasn't as unpleasant as I'd anticipated, sitting atop a butte of square-cornered suitcases, with Robby corralling my mother into game upon game of Bubble Gum, Bubble Gum, in a Dish, and Alex and my dad chatting manfully in the front seat about the tanking of the economy and the eruption of foreclosures in their area. My dad inquired considerately and briefly into Alex's professional circumstances, but my dad was always so kind and so forthright, there was no way to take umbrage. And even my mom evinced no concern or judgment on the matter whatsoever. Their total acceptance of all things Alex actually stirred a primal and somewhat puerile feeling akin to sibling rivalry that left me wondering why my mother couldn't just take me as I was the way she did Alex. But, I figured, it was a pretty good thing to have your parents and husband get along as well as mine did, so I manned up and enjoyed the evening.

And after dinner, my mom even presented me with a gift: a fuchsia pashmina to call my own.

Chapter Fifteen

The next day, my mom came to Robby's school with me. She had repeatedly told me she was eager to see what life was really like for the Forsters, so I figured we'd reenact the motions of a typical day. Plus, I knew that if we didn't get out of the house, I'd never hear the end of all the variations I'd made on her traditional Thanksgivings, which—by the way—I tried to duplicate as closely as possible just so I wouldn't have to listen to such critiques. I even made corn soufflé. Two and a half hours I spent, knowing that not a soul would touch it, let alone taste it. I mean, did anyone ever in the history of human existence—anyone at all—like that stuff? Oh, if so, please feel free to stop by my house the Friday following Thanksgiving, to pick one up.

So, Tuesday morning, after Alex and my dad had ventured down to the basement in all their manly glory to see if they could fix the furnace, which had taken to making creepy, special effects–types of noises in the middle of the night, the three of us—Robby, my mom, and I—packed ourselves into the wagon and drove to the co-op.

Before my mother's right pump (no kidding—actually three-inch heels) had hit the gravel parking lot of the school yard, she had already critiqued with a hawk's eye the appearance of three of the mothers. This put me in the singularly unenviable position of feeling as if I should defend them when, in actuality, I disliked all three of them myself. Each of them had put in special requests for snack time when I was manning that chore, and I had been maintaining a healthy hatred of them all as a consequence. However, in this particular instance, I had no choice but to defend them, given that they *were* at a nursery school with their three-year-olds. Who, besides my mother and possibly Michael, given his strict no-cargoes-or-yoga-pants policy, would expect them to wear anything *except* jeans and sneakers?

"But, *really*, look at her. She could do so much more with herself if she put in an extra half hour a day," my mom said as she scrutinized one poor soul who had the misfortune of having worn a sweatshirt and a ponytail that day. However, if my mother didn't remember what it was like with a little kid in the house, I wasn't going to be the one to remind her. Hell, that very morning, I was interrupted in the shower by Robby's cries for more waffles and didn't get to finish rinsing the shampoo out of my hair. At the thought, I raised my hand to touch it, and it felt kind of crisp and kind of greasy at the same time. And my mom seemed to think an *extra* half hour was all it would take to turn any one of these co-op moms into Angelina Jolie.

Not until she saw Jenn step out of her Range Rover with Chris did she stop providing commentary on the slovenliness of the hausfraus I saw—and was one of—every day. Jenn was now nearly eight months pregnant, but you'd never know it unless you looked right below her belly button. She could still wear all her rings, shoes, and regular bras. I was already up to a 38 C cup. And try as I might to overlook the fact, especially during my mother's stay, my wedding and engagement rings were already getting tight—really tight. The week before I'd actually had to grease my finger up with baby lotion just to slide them off.

"Now, *Jenn*," my mother said to me, laying particular emphasis on the name, so as to assure me that I was in a separate category entirely, "she always looks won-der-ful."

She said the word slowly and wistfully, breaking up each syllable for greater impact—a rhetorical habit she'd employed for as long as I could remember.

"Hi, Mrs. Fingardt!" Jenn ran over to us and gave my mom a big hug and kiss. "Look, I'm having my second in six weeks!" She arched her back and stuck out her tummy to provide evidence of the pregnancy that was virtually undetectable without such heuristics.

"No! That far along? Well, you have *never* looked better. So lean and healthy. You carry just the same way I did. When I was younger, my goodness gracious, I couldn't keep the weight on! The doctor told me I had to have an ice-cream sundae every night just to keep on track. And your hair! How do you get it so shiny?"

My mom stroked Jenn's hair adoringly as Jenn beamed with the attention and praise. I'd heard that G.D. ice-cream sundae story since I was twelve. And let me assure you, when you're struggling to go four and half minutes of life without putting something either deep-fried or chocolate-frosted into your mouth, hearing that your mom had to force-feed herself frozen confections doesn't really help your mood.

"Well, because of the baby, I don't want to dye it, so I've been using a henna rinse and a deep conditioner. I think I like the honey undertones. What do you think? And your hair—always impeccable, Mrs. Fingardt. Annie, you *do not know* how lucky you are to have a mother who knows and appreciates good style. I wish my mom did."

They continued chatting with each other about haircuts, designers, fall lines, and *In Style* magazine. It reminded me of the time I went out on a double date with Matt Finch, Katie Lasser, and her boyfriend, Jim Sullivan, and Matt spent the whole night trying to sit near Katie and talk to her about soccer. I don't think Katie much cared about soccer, or Matt for that matter, but it was just the point—that your own date wished he were your friend's.

I gathered Robby's and Chris' stuff together, and took them inside, while my mom and Jenn talked. They were standing side by side, shoulder to shoulder, looking down at a catalog Jenn must have had in her car. Occasionally, one or the other would point at some item; then they'd either discuss it for a while or laugh and turn the page. My jealousy was only mitigated by the fact that, in spite of it all, it was kind of cool to have your mom and your best friend like each other so much. I may not have fit in with them just then, but I liked knowing that they were hooked together through me. When I came back out to the parking lot, my mother was, once again, proffering criticism in a louder-than-speaking-voice whisper about a woman who had, presumably, just pulled in to the lot. I couldn't see who they were talking about, but I imagined that it must be yet another mom who'd been—as my mom would see it—devoid of the self-respect, conscientiousness, and discipline to take the two hours necessary to complete a decent toilette. Their conversation trickled over to me as I approached them.

"Those *shoes*! I've never seen such unfeminine, just plain ugly footwear in all my life," my mother said. Her nose was crinkled up as she spoke as if she were cutting onions.

"*I* think it's the hair. It's mousy to begin with—so she really can't afford to go with such a plain-Jane cut. She really needs some style there if she's not going to change the color. And she won't—believe me," Jenn commiserated.

"Why does she have to carry such a huge bag? It looks so . . . well . . . bohemian," my mother said, still cutting onions.

"Well, *she* thinks it's *practical*. But I've tried to tell her. Don't think I haven't tried," Jenn answered.

What had she tried? Whom did she try to tell? Whom were they talking about? And just as I reached them, Jen and Sarah emerged from behind the big wooden playhouse that had eclipsed my view. And sure enough, poor Jen was carrying a huge pink baby bag and wearing thick-soled sneakers with big white rubber crescents over the toes. Her hair, pushed back in a rolled bandanna, fell in waves onto the tops of her shoulders. Poor Jen. Maybe I should have warned her that the Soignée Sisters would be in town, and that she should probably go with cashmere, heels, and pearls in order to spare herself this kind of scrutiny.

Then, as if to add to Jen's misfortunes, Sarah ran toward my mother and Jenn, screaming, "I hate my mommy. I hate her. I want *you* to be my mommy."

Jenn picked up Sarah and walked over to the other Jen. She handed Sarah back and tucked in some of Jen's stray hair that had crept beyond the bandanna. Jen had found out a couple of weeks earlier that she was pregnant (yay!), and though less than two months along, she confessed she'd already gained ten pounds. I knew this detail would not be lost on my mother—whose tact and discretion had never prevented her from discussing my menstrual cycle or bra size with various teachers or store clerks or family members—so, I had to bust a move. I walked over to the Jenns and told Jenn that my mom wanted her stance on the age-old debate over matte vs. sheen cosmetics. Then, when I was alone with the other Jen, I walked her inside with Sarah, who'd forgiven her mom enough to hold her hand and kiss her good-bye. There, inside the safety of the nursery school, I looked around at all the other dowdy frumps who'd been once-overed and thrust aside by my mom and Jenn. It was like a reject sorority—formed by all the castoffs and also-rans, and established simply because we had the numbers, just not the good shoes—or the manicures.

And so the day proceeded. Nursery school was followed by a trip to Friendly's for lunch, where I was too self-conscious to eat anything more than a grilled cheese sandwich and half a plate of fries. Even though I'd been desperate for a sundae ever since hearing my mom mention it earlier to Jenn, I managed to refrain. Robby got his usual—a chicken fingers platter for kids with extra ketchup. And my mom got a chef's salad, no cheese, no bacon, no croutons, and dressing on the side—as if I didn't feel bad enough.

At Bloomingdale's, my mom got Robby a new outfit to wear for Thanksgiving, and she purchased some new Estée Lauder fragrance. No doubt it was fated to join the ranks of the unused and over-looked soldiery of perfumes already adorning her bureau, I thought as the scent of her Chanel wafted over to me. And I got Alex one of those electronic massage tools he'd been eyeing, in order to undo some of the tension he must have been feeling with a houseful of my mother and still no paycheck coming in. He was a pretty easy-going guy in general, but this kind of double stress would send even Ghandi running to the strong Swedish arms of the closest masseuse, so I figured shelling out for a small, unobtrusive gadget was the least I could do to secure both his sanity and our marriage (because, really, how many couples can survive the lovingly firm ministrations of some Katarina or Vendela or Johanna Swenska and her attention to—ahem—tense male anatomy?). And surprisingly enough, when we were busy shopping, my mother, too occupied doing what she loved best, didn't pause to make so much as one comment about any of the passersby. All in all, it was a very pleasant afternoon.

But for the absent sundae.

Chapter Sixteen

Later that night, after dinner, Alex and I were upstairs putting Robby to bed when I heard the phone ring. My dad was still buried in wires and tools in the basement, so my mother answered it. Strains of her side of the conversation wafted up the stairs, and I listened vaguely to see if I could tell who it was.

"Oh, Jenn! How *are* you?" She had taken to emphasizing select words in each of her sentences, as if to create extra meaning that way.

"No, she's upstairs with Robby," she continued.

Then she whispered something and started to laugh. Hmm. Very suspicious.

"Not great, but *okay*," she said. I didn't know what wasn't great but was okay, but I was pretty sure she must have been criticizing me.

"Sure, I'll tell her you called. But my God, that was an eye-opener today! Those women . . . so unkempt. So frowsy. Especially that one with the little girl. What a fright she was! She had so much to work with, and yet she had so clearly let herself go. So puffy and dowdy. And her daughter! Has she ever had a hair brushing? Or worn a dress? What a pair they were. I guess 'the apple really doesn't fall far from the tree,'" my mom said, ending with a chuckle.

And then I heard a lot of cut-off words and gasps.

"Wha? Oh . . . I . . . I . . . Oh, my . . . Well . . . Just . . . One sec . . ."

A brief pause; then, "I'm so sorry. I'll be sure to tell Annie you called."

And she concluded with, "I'm sorry. Really. Okay. Truly. I'm so sorry. All right. Good-bye."

I crept out of Robby's room and down the stairs. Clearly, something had gone wrong. A little wrong? Pretty wrong? Terribly wrong? I didn't know. But neither Jenn nor my mother would have gotten off so abruptly if nothing were wrong. Hell, they hadn't even discussed *Project Runway* or Botox yet.

"Mom? Hey, Mom!" I called on my way into the kitchen. "Is everything all right? Who was on the phone?"

As I entered the kitchen, I saw my mother corkscrewing open a bottle of chardonnay. She'd already gotten a glass out of the cabinet. She was peculiarly pale.

"Honey, don't get mad . . . ," she started slowly.

"What? What is it? Bad news?" I hated when people prolonged pain—especially when it was my pain.

"Well. Jen called," she said slowly and deliberately.

"I figured. So, what'd she want? What's wrong?"

She'd started gulping down the wine. Then she wiped off her lips—lip liner and all—with the back of her hand, Dirty Harry style. I thought she might actually say something along the lines of *and make it a double this time*, what with the way she was swigging and bracing herself against the counter.

"Mom, please, tell me what's going on. You're scaring me."

Clearly, I was going to have to beg it out of her. Like the first time I got to stay home without a babysitter when my parents went to Le Petit Oiseau with my aunt and uncle.

"Well, as I said, Jen called," she continued with remarkable equanimity for someone who had just inhaled her second glass of wine.

"*Yes* . . . You said. So what?" I was gritting my teeth with mounting terror.

"Hmm." She either cleared her throat or tried to laugh; I don't know which. "Funny thing. As it turns out, you have *two* friends named Jen."

And then it all made sense. It wasn't Jenn she was talking to; it was Jen. And when talking to the Jen she thought was Jenn, she insulted the other Jen. To that very Jen's face (or ear, I guess, since they were on the phone). It hit me in stages—the various repercussions of this gaffe that only my mother seemed capable of making. Whereas I was a living embarrassment to myself, only my mother could so swiftly and effectively mortify others—namely, me. It reminded me of the time in middle school when Daniel Tunney, who had only one friend among a whole sixth-grade world of enemies, was getting tormented by a group of popular kids; and when he was finally allowed to return to his lunch table with Justin Cobb, his only ally, I overheard Justin say to Daniel's tearstained face, "You know they're right. You are a weanus." Then Justin picked up his lunch tray and moved.

Well, here it was, some twenty-odd years later, and my own mother had, for all intents and purposes, told my good friend that she was basically a weanus.

"Mom, no! Please tell me you didn't insult her. Please. She's already feeling bad about herself as it is."

"Well, it's not as though anything I said wasn't, strictly speaking, the truth. Maybe she needed to hear it. And if *you* weren't going to tell her, well, someone had to."

Once again, she used the strange emphasis, implying that I

was remiss for not going around critiquing my friends' sartorial selections.

"Mom . . . I . . ." There were just so many things wrong with her response that I didn't know where to begin. But, judging by the fact that she—whom I hadn't seen drink so much as a sip of champagne since my cousin Gertrude's wedding eight years ago—had already poured her third glass of wine, I was pretty sure she must have felt pretty damn bad about it all, no matter how she was spinning it to me.

"Really. Her hair *is* terrible. And those *clothes*. And . . . and . . ." And then she burst into tears.

If you've never been in this position, try to understand. My mother, friend and foe for thirty-five years, had just ripped away whatever shreds of dignity were clinging to one of my best friends, and she was in tears in front of me, requiring my sympathy. Some women cry a lot. Jenn's mom cried each time she watched a rerun of *The Golden Girls*. My first boss cried at every AT&T long-distance commercial that came on TV. I had an English professor who once cried as she read a Wordsworth sonnet to the class. But my mom was not one of those women. She'd watched *Sophie's Choice* dry-eyed. At my graduations and wedding, she hadn't shed a tear. Even in the recovery room with me and a six-minute-old Robby, nothing. But this? This shook her.

I was so disconcerted that I actually poured her more wine. Then I got the Pop-Tarts and Milky Ways. The whole time I was growing up with this woman, her catchphrase was, "Oh, I couldn't eat another bite," which she'd utter after taking a taste so tiny it was almost mimed. Well, let me tell you, she sure scarfed down those sugary carbohydrates that night. Maybe she'd just never been introduced to the allure of the foil wrapper—how it yielded with just the right amount of resistance to the pressure of thumb and forefinger; how the almost inaudible sigh was released when the vacuum seal was broken; how the tiny chips and shards gathered in the creased corners. I often imagined that unwrapping a foil package provided its possessor with the same kind of titillation and prurient thrill that men who watch strippers must feel. And here was my mom, learning for the first time that same joy and satisfaction. That alone, plus the fact that she ate even more than I did, made me want to forgive her.

"Please, honey, call her. Call her back. Tell her I was kidding. Or drunk. Or senile. *Anything*. Please. I feel just awful," she said plaintively.

So, I picked up the phone. I had no idea what I was going to say to Jen. Or what she'd say to me. Or if. But she picked up on the second ring, when I was still trying to compose myself. I mean, this had never happened to Samantha and Endora; and without the sage advice and predictable format of a sitcom to guide me, I was really going commando.

"Hello?" she said. That was good—a normal opener.

"Hi, Jen," I said hesitantly. "It's me. With the pathological mother. Who's so sorry that she hurt your feelings that she got drunk and ate more candy bars than *I* did."

Jen knew all about my mother's Spartan regimen when it came to calories, so I figured this would illustrate my point.

"No, no, it's all right," Jen answered almost cheerfully. "I just never knew people saw me like that. I guess I didn't realize how far I'd let myself go."

"Jen, please, whatever you do, don't reevaluate your entire existence because of what my mother said. She doesn't know the latest styles, and she's always hated any look that was remotely informal."

My mother piped up at this, about to take offense at my

invidious characterizations of her, but I shot her a look that informed her, quite unambiguously, that if so much as a syllable passed her lips, she would be force-fed the remaining Pop-Tarts and Milky Ways until she choked on them, so she shut up.

"But I *have* felt crappy lately," Jen went on. "I wish I could look like you, Annie. Or Jenn. Or your mom. She has those sexy legs, and her boobs are always perky. . . ."

"My mother's breasts are *not* perky," I responded, a little too loudly, since both my father and Alex had entered the kitchen by this point.

"Not your mother's, you idiot," Jen explained. "Jenn's! What do you think? I analyze the sex appeal of senior citizenry?"

My mom couldn't control herself after this critique of her physical charms, and she quickly snapped out, "Well, for a woman my age, my breasts are holding their own. Pretty. Damn. Well."

Jen must have overheard her, because while I was gesticulating wildly to my mother to compel her to stop speaking, I heard a subversive chuckle from her side of the line.

"Hah, hah, hah. Tell her they might be fine for a woman *of a certain age*, but mine are fine for a woman of any age. Pregnancy *does* offer some compensations," she said with mock bravado.

I began to breathe a little more easily after that, knowing that if she was able to joke around at all, she couldn't have been too permanently injured by my mother. And after all, I figured we would be able to bond even more closely after this muddle, since Jen now knew the force I'd been alternately riding and resisting my whole life.

"Let me talk to her," my mother, quite drunk by this time, said as she lunged for the phone. "I want her to know, without all your *sarcasm*, how sorry I really am."

"Sarcasm" had long been one of my mother's favorite words, so I was rather surprised that she slurred it into something that sounded more like "Sure, kiss him" when she was drunk. And before I knew it, she had wrenched the phone out of my hands. For a brief moment, I thought of taking her down and wrestling her on the hardwood floor of the kitchen, but I'd read enough Freud in the course of my life to decide with relative certainty that a thirty-five-year-old pregnant woman who'd just made mention of her mother's breasts did not want to put herself in that circumstance. So I refrained and waited to hear what she'd say to the woman I hoped would still be my friend when she was finished.

"Hello, Jen?" It was a fairly innocuous start. What Jen said, I could only imagine, but I hoped it wouldn't be too hard to piece together their conversation from hearing only my mother's side.

"Dear, I'm really so sorry for those horrible things I said to you."

". . . No, I didn't. I had no right."

". . . No, really."

". . . No, really."

". . . No, really."

Okay, this was getting difficult—and boring.

"Don't you dare do that; you have lovely hair. Maybe it just needs some tinting."

Oh my God, she was going to embark on a whole new voyage of insulting critiques!

". . . Well, we leave on Saturday morning."

". . . Well, I'm sure I'd love to."

". . . Absolutely."

". . . Absolutely."

". . . Absolutely."

There was no way to crack this cryptic—and rather

repetitive—one-sided conversation. Was she trying to shake me, or what?

"Okay, then. One o'clock. I'll be here."

". . . Yes, you, too, dear."

". . . Okay, dear, I'll see you then."

". . . Bye-bye, dear."

Once, when I was a kid, I tried to read a Japanese newspaper that my neighbors, the Sarukis, had lying around. I thought that if I stared at it long enough, the symbols would just sort of cohere into comprehensible words. *That* was an easier undertaking than trying to fill in the blanks of the conversation I'd just overheard between my mother and one of my best friends. And my mother didn't seem to want to pony up the info any too quickly, either.

"Please, for the great love of God, tell me what she said," I begged as soon as she hung up.

"Oh, not much. I don't think she's *too* upset."

Even drunk, she was still emphasizing strange words. Why "too"? What did that mean? Really upset? Very upset? Just not *excessively* upset? What was *too* upset, anyway? And still she sat there, staring complacently at me, filled with an abundance of wine, Milky Way, and self-satisfaction.

"Mom, go on and tell me everything. Did you execute the demise of my six-year friendship? Is there hope that I may still be able to salvage it? What just happened?!?"

Three years with Robby—including the I'm-not-going-to-eat-anything-but-white-food era and the ask-why-in-response-to-every-conceivable-comment phase—had done a lot to lengthen my patience span; but my mother was severely testing those limits.

"Long story short," my mother answered, "she's coming over on Friday, so we'll have to change our plans about going to the museum."

Long story short? *Long story short!* All my life—dating back to my earliest memories of my mother recounting her bridge tournaments to me through the slats of my crib—I had yearned for a mother who could make a long story short. I craved it just as other kids craved sweet cereal or pierced ears. For thirty-five years, I dreamed of digressionless narratives that actually had a point. Of phone calls less than forty-five minutes long. Of the words "just one more thing" truly meaning *just one more thing.* Now, for the only time in my life that I could remember, I actually wanted the long story long. I wanted the whole thing. From beginning to end. With commentary, if that was what it required. And *this* was the moment she decided to be brief? *This* was the occasion she chose to make a long story short? No details, no verbiage, no nothing? Maybe it was the alcohol; however, I doubted that, since people tend to ramble on and on when they get drunk. My freshman roommate used to come home after a night of carousing and fall asleep telling me about her barroom adventures; then, periodically throughout the night, she'd wake up and pick up her story exactly where she'd left it, until she dozed off again. It figured that my mom would get drunk and reticent the one time I needed her sober and chatty. Long story short; screw that.

"Why? What's going on? What do you have planned? Does she still like me?"

But the rest of my questions had to remain unanswered, since my mother elegantly put her head, forehead first, down on the kitchen table and fell asleep there.

The next day, whether because of residual regret or a wicked hangover, take your pick, my mother was more helpful and more, well, normal, than she'd ever been. And even on Thanksgiving Day itself, her criticisms of the year-old turkey (she didn't really think I was going to return it and get another one, did she?) were kept to a minimum. And the fact that I ate nearly half an apple pie all by myself escaped with nary a comment. When Alex, Robby, and my dad went for a drive around the neighborhood to "walk" off Thanksgiving dinner, she actually did as I asked her and threw away the leftover rolls and potatoes without so much as a scoff. My mother! The woman who saved absolutely *everything*. When I was a kid, she once instructed me to save six peas that were left clinging to the side of a serving bowl after dinner was over. Six of them—I actually counted. And smears of greasy butter—well, they had to be wrapped up in more plastic wrap than an entire stick of new butter was worth.

But now she was acceding to my demands and tossing the useless leftovers with something approaching gusto. I briefly wondered if I had enough friendships that could be jeopardized by her to keep her lulled into this state of extreme cooperativeness every time she visited. If she came twice a year, pissed off one friend per trip, and spent the rest of her vacation making it up to me, was that too high a price to pay? I figured it probably was, even though it seemed awfully tempting, given her current docility and compliance.

We conversed our way first through hors d'oeuvres, during which I ate three-quarters of a pound of tapenade, then through the entire eight courses of Thanksgiving dinner, during which I ate seven different kinds of carbohydrates, and finally even dessert, during which I ate nearly a pint of ice cream along with the aforementioned half pie. And not so much as a judgmental glance or advisory comment escaped from her. Not even a single quarrel took place. This was unprecedented! But through it all, my mother remained strangely tight-lipped about the approaching day with Jen. So, I figured I had no choice but to wait.

And at exactly one o'clock Friday afternoon, Jen arrived at

my front door with Sarah, whom she made wipe her feet before entering. Jen's hair was loose, and she was carrying just about every T-shirt I'd ever seen her wear. Sarah's hair, on the other hand, was neatly clipped back in two *matching* apple-shaped barrettes. She was wearing—for what was probably the first time in her three-year-old life—a dress. It was a khaki twill little number with happy red apples embroidered on it. She was so cute without being cutesy that I barely recognized her. And the dress must have had magical powers to make her behave, because she was actually being good. She promptly skipped off to find Robby, who was playing with my dad and Alex in the family room, leaving my mom and Jen to get down to business.

"Honey, come upstairs to Annie's room," my mom directed, "and show me each of the T-shirts, one at a time, so I can get a sense of which colors look good on you. No, no, dear. Hold them up under your chin, so I can really get a good look. *That's* right."

And before either of us knew it, my mother had Jen sitting on the toilet in my master bath, stripped down to her bra and cargo pants. Since she'd become pregnant, she'd stopped dying her hair; and much as it pained me to admit it, my mother was right—it needed something. Then, as if out of thin air, my mother produced a bowl of henna that she'd mixed and began applying it to Jen's hair. After her hair was plastered with the stuff, the two of them agreed on the T-shirt that best matched her complexion (pinky red, which my mother insisted on calling "watermelon"), and, of course, it wasn't long until my makeup case was unearthed and sampled.

So *this* was what they'd planned. This was what my mother hadn't told me about. After criticizing, insulting, and demoralizing one of my best friends, my mother was now remaking her. Jen was being overhauled in front of my very eyes. Willingly. Happily. Gratefully. And you know what? My mother was actually very good at it. So good that—dare I say it?—I started to feel the rumblings of something very similar to the feeling I got in third grade when the fourth grader across the street got a green Schwinn ten-speed, while I still had my pink Barbie three-speed with the basket on the handlebars. I'd known my mother for thirty-five years; yet I was discovering talents of hers that had been hidden from me my whole life. Where were these beauty tips when I broke out in hives before my first boy-girl school dance? Where was the corrective henna rinse when I went off to college with two big blond chunks masquerading as "streaks" in the front of my hair? Where was this woman when I'd waxed off one of my eyebrows with Dianne Moulton junior year? I didn't know the answer to these eternal questions, but I did know one thing: I may have had to wait thirty-five years for initiation into this secret club, but initiated I would be.

So, *long story short*—by three o'clock Friday afternoon, Jen and I both had golden highlights, elegant cheekbones, pouty lips, and tawny complexions. And for the first time since I wet my pants in kindergarten, I clung to my mother as she was leaving the next day, knowing how much I'd miss her.

Chapter Seventeen

*I*t didn't take too long after Thanksgiving for me to realize that, in spite of my mother's cosmetological assistance, I was still in pretty deep trouble in the physical appearance department. I was now five months pregnant—which placed me dead center in the danger zone where people weren't sure whether I was pregnant or portly. I mean, in a spandex leotard or a bikini, my condition might have been more recognizable; but I figured I'd spare humanity that sight and opt for a more full-covered approach even if it meant confusion as to my suddenly, ahem, blossoming midsection. Oh, and at five months, I'd already gained all the weight that Dr. Weiss had allotted me for the whole nine months. I still had four months to go—the biggest and heaviest four.

Alex was either so blind or so grateful he didn't have to be the pregnant one that his niceness and patience grew at the same rate as my waistline. When I was pregnant with Robby, Alex would bring home lollipop bouquets, cakes with messages frosted onto them, cookies with pink and blue icing on top. This pregnancy, I begged him not to bring any gifts of an edible nature into the house for me. So, instead of foodstuffs, Alex brought scarves or perfume or bubble bath or heart-shaped boxes of soaps. And he somehow never let what I imagine must have been a really stressful situation for him affect Robby or me in any way. When he was first sidebarred, he'd imagined it might last, maybe, a couple of months; but now we were into the fourth month, and he'd been keeping his equanimity and good humor throughout. He had, much to his relief, been brought back in as a councilor and consultant for a few cases after Thanksgiving; so, he was relieved to have the semblance of his old life back during the holiday season. We weren't sure how long he'd be occupied with these cases, but he was happy to have a place to be three or four days a week that actually required, say, pants—and buttons.

One Thursday night, shortly after beginning his new assignment, he was coming home, the same as he used to before the sidebar. His recent return to the office, even though it was only part-time and temporary, had Robby reeling and sad because he had grown so accustomed to having his dad around full-time. Robby heard the garage doors go up, and he started clamoring to get to Alex. Down the stairs he flew, followed by a significantly slower, less graceful mother (remember Weebles? "Weebles wobble but they don't fall down"—that should provide a visual). But eventually, I made it down to greet them. Robby was happily ensconced in Alex's arms playing with his key chain; but I noticed amid the stack of mail that Alex had brought in with him, a familiar holly-embossed envelope among the various bills and Christmas cards.

"Uh-oh," I said as I kissed him hello.

"What's wrong? Did someone puke pink again?" he inquired as I extracted the ominous envelope. Then he saw what I was holding. "Ohhh . . . Uh-oh," he repeated.

"Uh-oh! Uh-oh!" Robby recited as Alex and I tore open the envelope. It was like the sound track to a scary movie. You know, an initial uh-oh gradually builds to a frenzied *uh-oh!* with music and volume expressing the intensity. And then a shark appears or a guy in a mask jumps out of the closet or whatever.

"Aw, man," I said as I perused the engraved lettering, "I thought because you'd been *sidebarred*, we'd be able to *sidestep* this little number."

"I wonder if I hadn't been brought in as a consultant on these cases if I'd have been invited," Alex wondered aloud.

"Is it too late to reconsider?" I asked, smiling at him.

There was just no denying it: My most dreaded event of the year was Alex's official Office Holiday Party. I'd already been through eight of these annual ordeals, and apparently the time had come for the ninth. The first five, though bad, were tolerable—but, of course, I was a lawyer back then myself, so I'm not sure you can trust that—perhaps unfairly generous— evaluation. However, since Robby had arrived on the scene, well, aside from these kinds of professional gatherings resurrecting all my insecurities about quitting my job to take care of him, these so-called parties just plain sucked. The legal profession is, in case you were under the impression that it was like *L.A. Law* or *Ally McBeal* or even *Boston Legal*, not remotely cool—distinctly not remotely cool. It is very, very, very distinctly not remotely cool. It is nothing like those shows. Lawyers, in reality, do not wear thousand-dollar ties or six-inch spandex skirts; they do not infuse every room with a smoldering sexual tension; they do not have male strippers or perky blond nymphomaniacs for clients; and— above all else—they definitely do not know how to throw a party. Hell, these parties couldn't appeal to a higher court.

"Oh, honey bunny," Alex said in his falsetto, buttering- me-up voice, trying to change the subject, "look what I got for you on my lunch break at that boutique around the corner. It's a bottle of scented lotion that smells like that hair stuff you used to use. Do you like it?"

The bottle was curvaceous and rosy, the way I wanted to believe I used to look before (and—please, God—during) the moments of conception. It smelled flowery and spicy; he was right—just like the HairSpa mask I used to use back in the days when I could shower for longer than four minutes without being interrupted by screams to find Moose the Moose or a runaway Little People. Those were the days, I thought, rubbing some on my hands and smiling at Alex.

"I love it! And it does smell just like HairSpa mask. But am I supposed to believe this lotion was purchased purely coincidentally on the very same day that the company invitation appears?" I asked suspiciously. "You're a nice guy, but you're trying to buy me off. You are! You're trying to buy me off with a bottle of HairSpa-scented lotion! You *are* trying to buy me off, aren't you?"

"Well, I *did* have to go out to lunch," he began, teasing me with his how-could-you?-I'm-so-offended voice. "And Bill and his client were in the office all morning, so I had nothing to eat *all* day until after one. But, still, I took time out of my busy schedule to walk *around* the corner—*before* going to the Chinese buffet, *before*, I tell you—just to get you this. And you malign my good intentions by—"

"Guilt . . . too . . . strong . . . Gotta . . . break . . . free," I stuttered with my hands over my ears. "I'll go; I'll go; I'll go to your damn party! Just please, lose the my-mother tactics!" It was like nails on a blackboard.

"Assuming my gift was a bribe. Really, Annie, I just don't . . . *What?*" He pronounced the "what" the way Mr. Carmichael used to on *The Lucy Show*.

He had kept on talking throughout my response, which was

a common strategy he resorted to when he knew I didn't want to do what he wanted me to do. I wasn't sure if he had picked up this strategy in Dr. Silva's Law and Language course back when we were in law school. "If you talk enough, you can always beat opposing counsel; just yack, yack, yack, until they crack, crack, crack," Silva used to tell us. Or maybe he'd modeled it on my mother's prototype, which had proven effective for the many years that she'd been manipulating me with monologues. As Alex must have figured, this was a great trait to possess if you were either an attorney, which he was, or a husband wanting his wife to do something he knew she didn't want to do, which he also was. So I figured I'd better acquiesce and calm him down right away before he started procuring evidence and referring to me as "the party of the first part."

Really, what did he think? That I would have left him to twist in the wind at his own Christmas party? And after he'd been side-barred, at that? It might not be the highlight of my life—in fact, I was already dreading it more than the coed swimming lessons I had to take before I started using tampons and had to wear Stayfrees into the pool—but if he wanted me there, I'd be there. I didn't quite know *why* or *how* he wanted me there—I was huge and moody and utterly incapable of keeping my mouth empty for more than a four- to five-minute stretch. But it was important enough for him to get all talky about, so I guessed he must have really wanted me there. And I had to admit that kind of desire went a long way toward making a girl feel pretty good about herself.

As he hugged me, whispering a gentle "Thanks" in my ear, I started to feel really great about myself. What an excellent wife I was! What a fabulous mother! I was such a good person! I gave to charities! I was a terrific friend! Hadn't I babysat Sarah just the week before, so that Jen and Tucker could go to her niece's wedding? Yay for me! Hurray for Annie Fingardt Forster!

Of course, the euphoria of juvenile self-delight was immediately replaced with panic about what I'd wear.

"Ahh, when is it?" I asked, hoping not to betray my anxiety.

"Next Friday. Do you think Alicia can sit for Robby?"

"I hope not. I mean 'so'! I hope *so*! Really! Sorry, that just slipped out. Honestly! I'll get a new outfit and try to pull myself together in a way that doesn't embarrass either of us."

I tried to sound sure as I said it, but pretty much the only thing I was sure about was the fact that with only eight days to go, I would never be able to get close to anything that even remotely approximated "pulled together." And the new outfit? Short of wearing my king-sized duvet cover as a toga, I was fresh out of ideas as to what would fit. But what could I do? So, I reached up, hugged him, and gave him a kiss. I mean, it was kind of cute that he'd gotten so worked up over it all.

Chapter Eighteen

*E*arly the next day, I put in calls to Jenn and Michael to see if they'd go shopping with me so I could leach off their fashion sense. I had only a week to find an outfit that would reveal enough to let people know I was pregnant, and yet conceal enough that they could conceivably think it was all just the bigger boobies and tummy that were making me look so huge. Yeah, right. I desperately needed their advice.

"Sure, I'll go!" Jenn answered happily when I asked. "I need something for the holidays, anyway. I'm going as Jolly Old Saint Nick this year—you know, with the gut that 'shook like a bowl full of jelly'?" She laughed. Sure, she could evince a good sense of humor about it all; she was nearly nine months pregnant and Dr. Weiss had told her she needed to drink a milk shake every day in order to take in enough calories for the baby. I don't think I could have fit into her so-called maternity clothes even before I'd conceived. I warned her this was no ordinary quest; it might even require the Knights of the Round Table to find me, Lady Gains-a-lot, a decent dress. But at least Jenn would be there—Lady of the Legs.

Then I called Michael at his house; he never worked Fridays and consequently might be willing to accompany me. I was surprised when someone whose voice I didn't recognize picked up.

"Hello?" the voice asked in a calm, unassuming way.

"Hi, this is Annie Forster. Is Michael there, please?"

"Yah, he's right here; I'll get him. But do you mind my asking—are you the Annie who knows Duncan the engineer?"

"That's me! Is this Lucas, then? How is it going with him? He told me he loves working for you as one of your floral engineers!"

"Floral engineer?" He repeated the words the way someone would pronounce "pan-flashed ahi-ahi with a merlot demiglace" if he happened to read it on a McDonald's menu. "I thought he was a *cable* engineer. Isn't that what he is? A cable technician?"

"Ahh, yeah," I said, covering—really smooth. "But I thought the guys in the floral business preferred 'floral engineer' to florist. Someone told me that once."

"Well, 'florist' is just fine with me. But you can call me whatever you want since you were the one who hooked me up with Duncan, the cable-cum-floral engineer. Honestly, I've never seen anything like his work or his enthusiasm in all the years I've been in this business. Thank you so much for sending him down to the store. I really owe you!"

And with that, he gave the phone to Michael.

"Hello, fairy godmother to unfulfilled cable guys everywhere. What can I do for you?" Michael greeted me.

"Alex's Christmas party is in a week. I need an outfit, and I need it now. Will you meet me and Jenn at the mall in, like, an hour to help?"

"Ahh, you know, I *do* have a life, Ms. Forster. This is my day off, and Lucas and I were going to go . . . um . . . go . . . Okay, well, we didn't exactly have plans, but that doesn't mean I want to spend the day with you and Jenn picking out maternity clothes for some stuffy office party. And why, if my company is so valuable to you, did you not call me first?" he inquired.

Then I heard Lucas' voice shouting in the background.

"Of course, we'll come, Annie. Michael, it's the least we can do! She's the one who sent me Duncan. *Duncan!* That man is a genius with flowers. We owe her. Plus, it'll be fun." I heard him yelling all this to Michael, while Michael, apparently, was trying to cover the mouthpiece.

"Well . . . ," Michael said begrudgingly into the receiver, "I guess we'll go. But you have to buy me lunch."

"Okay," I said with relief.

"And give me a back rub," he added.

"Okay."

"And Lucas wants some of your popcorn balls," he said.

"Fine," I agreed.

"A lot of them," Michael added.

I heard Lucas shushing him in the background.

"Anything. Name your price. I'm desperate, and I need your help," I told him. You see, as a former lawyer, I knew how to drive a hard bargain. "Please just make sure you come. And thanks!"

So, Jenn and I dropped the kids at school, then drove to Elegant Expectancy where we met Michael and Lucas at the doors. Michael introduced us to Lucas, who was not only incredibly friendly and a touch shy, but unignorably, strikingly, unbelievably good-looking. He looked like a mix between a young Harrison Ford and the guy who walks past the copy machine in that body spray commercial—hot—and this made the shyness all the more appealing. When he thanked me again for the Duncan reference, Jenn realized who he was and raved about the flowers Duncan had done for her shower. Lucas was so gracious without being the tiniest bit pretentious that I really had to hand it to Michael. I whispered to him behind their backs how impressed I was with his taste in friends. He merely smiled. Then he whispered that I must have thought very highly of myself indeed if I was including myself among that elite category. But for all his sarcasm, I could tell Lucas meant a lot to him, and he seemed pleased to hear how much other people liked him as well.

As we entered the store, I laid out my two-pronged approach to locating if not a perfect dress, at least an it-won't-embarrass-me-or-my-husband dress. The plan was fairly simple, based on two safe truisms: Black is slimming, and hence, buy black; and I'd be even bigger next week, and hence, buy large. Thank God for the keen eyes of my friends and the friends of my friends. Because before I'd even finished perusing the first rack, Michael deposited six different outfits in my arms—all black. Lucas vetoed two and took them away. And Jenn escorted me to the dressing rooms with the remaining four.

"Even if you hate it, come out and let me see it," she said as she sat down on the bench to wait.

I couldn't help but notice that she was still able to cross her legs. I wanted to hate her, but the way she was so unassumingly biting her nails and looking around at the wallpaper made me forgive her good-lookingness.

The first dress was a joke. Gaping at the square neckline where, I was willing to guess, my breasts should have fit, the fabric stretched taut across my stomach and flared in a most unflattering way right beneath my butt. I was about to slip it off undetected when I heard her yell out.

"Remember, I want to see everything!"

I was busted, so I peeked out of the door and told her the first one was a definite no. That, poor me, wasn't good enough for Jenn, who insisted on seeing anyway. When I opened the door and stood straight, we both had to laugh.

"Yeah, you're right. That's just a heinous outfit all around. I don't know what Michael was thinking!" She was trying to make me feel better by blaming the dress rather than me, but either way, the dress had to be removed.

The second was pretty good. A long straight silk skirt with a matching heavier black cashmere V-neck sweater; it was a possibility.

The third—a pantsuit—was so tight in the butt, I thought I'd rip the pants just pulling them up. Jenn and Michael both liked that one, but Lucas and I voted to reject it in light of the prospect of splitting the seams and having to wear my underwear as outerwear for the rest of the party.

The fourth was as good as it got for me. A midlength wrap dress, it had enough shirring along the sides to flatter my, we'll say *curves*, and enough light beading along the neckline to make it semiformal. Not too cutesy, it provided plenty of room in the gut to grow into over the approaching week. And it met with Jenn's, Michael's, and Lucas' approval, which meant it was a keeper.

With my outfit bought and bagged, we focused our efforts on finding an outfit for Jenn. For her, the search was more complex—sort of like the way it could be hard for really beautiful girls to get prom dates. Or so I've heard. Everything could and would look excellent on her, so she, unlike me, wasn't limited by color, shape, cut, or even length. She took armfuls of outfits into the dressing room and, because they all fit perfectly and looked excellent, she had to narrow it down by other criteria.

"This fabric is driving me crazy; what the hell is this stuff?" That was actually one of her criticisms. In my wildest dreams, if I could have looked as good as she did, the clothes could have been made of steel wool, sticky fire, and vinegar, and I'd have worn them with a smile.

Another comment: "I hate the way these cuffs flair like that."

Cuffs. Cuffs! She was criticizing cuffs. If I could have just *fit* into those cuffs, I would have worn them and nothing else. Just cuffs. But I knew she was having almost as hard a time picking out what she liked from the hundred and seventeen outfits she had chosen as I had had picking from my four, so I offered her as much help and support as I could.

Michael was having such a good time dressing Jenn that he kept dumping off new outfits at the dressing room door. Whereas Lucas limited his selections to fairly simple, elegant items, Michael was grabbing the boldest, trendiest, chicest garments he could find for her to try on and model for him.

"Tell her she absolutely must come out in this," Michael commanded when he dropped off a magenta, coral, and tangerine floral-print sarong. And again when he delivered a sapphire-colored, sequined, backless sheath dress. And again upon handing over a crimson strapless dress with flouncing layers of tulle at the hem. And he would have kept going, except that Lucas cut him off after a half hour or so.

After she'd tried on the myriad of outfits we'd all brought for her, I went into the dressing room to help her make the final decision. She was sitting on the floor, leaning against the little bench on the wall, almost falling asleep under the exhaustion of having been a living Barbie doll all morning.

"I'm too tired to decide which one," she said without lifting her head. "You pick for me. You've always had such great taste, Annie."

Me? She was talking about me?

"Ohh, honey, lean against me," I told her as I sat down next to her. "There you go. Now, let's look over these piles of clothes. You looked so good in all of them, so let's just pick the one you like the best. Okay, for starters, I've known you for six years, and

I've never seen you in anything with a print, a pattern, ruffles or pleats, so let's dump all those over there. Focus on these—the blacks, the reds, and the creams. You're pregnant, not a loser. My God, don't you hate the way maternity clothes want to make everyone look like Mother Goose or Lady Fauntleroy? I say you go sophisticated."

"You're right," she said, lifting her head and smiling once again. "Give me that one, over there. And if it looks like crap at Christmas, well, I'm prepared to go naked."

She slipped on a charcoal sheath with brocade trim and sequined straps. Without so much as a comment—let alone a discussion—all four of us knew that was the one. I wish I could have looked half so good in any dress I'd ever worn—wedding dress, prom dress, hell, even my christening gown. She couldn't have been oblivious to how excellent she looked; yet she was so normal and cool about it. She just took it off and said she'd get it. If I looked as good, I would have worn it right out of the store and every day for the rest of my life. I'd probably even shower in it. But all in all, I was pretty satisfied with my black wrap dress just the same.

So, after a quick lunch (and by "quick" I mean nothing even remotely close to what "quick" actually means), we headed over to Burbridge's. Michael wanted to get a tie and a new pair of shoes, and Lucas said he could use a new belt. Jenn and I headed straight for the cosmetics counter. Jenn knew, as if by instinct, what colors and textures looked good on her. I, on the other hand, who'd been wearing makeup for at least twenty years, had no idea. I put myself in the hands of some person named Lynzee, and pretended I was at a sorority sleepover. Thirty-five minutes later, I had a bag full of items with descriptions that read like a chemistry text written by Danielle Steel: "succulent" this, "opulent" that, "decadent" the other. And I'm pretty sure the word "luscious" made an appearance on every tube, bottle, and case in my bag. My skin felt kind of stiff, as if I were wearing a face made of a space-age polymer; but I figured it was better to look good than to feel good. Not that I looked so good, but it was the principle. And after Alex's party, I'd probably give away all this stuff, anyway.

"Hey, what do you know? You actually have a face on," Michael said when we met back up in the men's department.

"Wow! You guys look terrific," Lucas told us.

"Thanks," I answered. "And here is some cologne I picked up for you guys to say thank you," I said as I extracted it from the multitude of bags I was carrying.

"You're kidding, right?" Lucas asked me. "Annie, I cannot take that cologne. My God, what would my mom say if she knew I'd accepted a gift from someone I was just meeting for the first time?"

"Oh, shut it, Good Boy." Michael poked him. "This is Tom Ford. We're accepting this, like it or not."

"Am not." Lucas smiled.

"So am," said Michael as he grabbed the bag.

"Well, thank you, Annie. That was really nice of you," Lucas said, rolling his eyes at Michael.

"You guys saved my sanity, my dignity, and, quite possibly, my marriage, by helping me find this dress. Trust me, I owed you," I answered.

"Whatever," Michael replied. "And thanks; it's great cologne. But am I allowed to ask why you're talking like that?" Michael asked.

"Like what?"

"Like you're wearing a Halloween mask or something. Or

like you think your skin's gonna crack. You're not the Tin Man, Annie; that's just what makeup feels like. If you wore it occasionally, you might know that," Michael said. Nothing ever got by him—damn it.

"Thank you very much for the cologne, Annie," Lucas interrupted, trying to deflect. "You really shouldn't have. If anyone owes anybody anything, *I* owe *you*. But thanks again."

In spite of Lucas' smooth deflection, I had my doubts that I'd be able to pull off this charade of cosmetics and fancy clothes. Still, the makeup did make me feel like a grown-up. And I really didn't mind the dress. Maybe this party wouldn't be so bad after all.

Chapter Nineteen

As soon as I got home, I tried on the dress again. Then, when Alex got home from the park with Robby, I tried it on again, and then again every day for the next week—you know, just to make sure it still fit. And by the time the following Thursday night rolled around, it was still a go. I had done the amazing: I had bought an outfit that I managed to still fit into an entire week later. And you know what? I actually began not to dread the event. I wasn't really psyched up for it or anything, but I figured it would probably be all right. Alicia was coming at five o'clock, so I would have sufficient time to get dressed and get to Alex's office. Friday was the last day of Alex's temporary return, so he'd be at the office already, and I'd have to meet him there.

As I thought about it, it felt, well, it felt kind of as if I were working again, as if I had somewhere I had to be—and something good to wear there. Something that was actually dry-clean only. All my regular clothes were wash-and-wear. And to be honest, not even in that order. Something more like "wash-and-wear-and-wear-again-and-if-you-have-time-wash" was probably a more accurate description of my recent wardrobe. Thus, the idea of wearing grown-up clothes and department store cosmetics was exciting. It was so exciting, in fact, that I even tried out all the makeup before going to bed that night—just to make sure I would be able to do what Lynzee had done. Then I basted myself in the pink lotion Alex had brought me, hoping vaguely that it might transform me into one of those I'm-treating-myself-and-I'm-worth-it type of women I've always seen in spa ads and envied. And then, all night long, I dreamed of proms where I didn't knock the heel off my sandal, and weddings where I didn't trip on my train walking down the aisle, and office Christmas parties where I still fit into the dress I'd bought the week before—you know, visions of sugar plums and all that.

I slept better than I had since Dr. Pinault's freshman econ lectures, and woke up feeling pretty damn fine. My stomach hadn't grown to epic proportions during the night, and even though I'd gone to sleep with all my makeup on, it hadn't left much mess on the pillow. I started thinking this shindig might not be as epically terrible as I'd anticipated. Robby was rustling around quietly in his room, and Alex was still asleep next to me, so I tiptoed out of bed and into the closet just to make sure the dress was there and all was well. When I opened the double doors, my glance fell briefly over my reflection in the full-length mirror that hung there.

I screamed.

I flicked the closet lights on and stared at my image. Somehow, through some awful hoax of fate or nature or the evil spirit of cruel jokes, my skin had transformed into some kind of bumpy, plasticlike protective coating. It wasn't just bloating—my God, I was used to that—and it wasn't just an irritation. It was an inflation, like a huge red water balloon filled until the last possible moment before eruption. The makeup must have caused some kind of monumental reaction with my complexion, and now, if I turned to the side, I looked like the capital letter *B*—as huge in my face as I'd become in my torso.

When he heard my scream, Alex flew to the closet before even putting on his glasses—a good thing.

"Oh my God! What is it? Why'd you scream? Is Robby all right?" he asked as he ran over to me. "Oh, Jesus, is *that* what you screamed for? That little rash? Holy hell, I thought someone was in there with a knife or something. You scared me out of my mind. Look at my hands—they're shaking!"

His tone revealed that I was not the only one who'd woken up on the wrong side of the bed that morning.

"Alex, look at me!" I shouted. "Your party is *tonight*. How am I going to go looking like this?"

"It is not that bad. So you're a little pink. What's the big deal?" His voice was softening, and he came closer to hug me. And although to this very day, he'll deny it, I know I saw him freeze and gasp the moment his nearsighted eyes got me in focus. It was only for the briefest second, but I know I noticed it.

"Oh, my God! Even you're frightened of me. I'm gross. What's wrong with me?"

"Honey, it's noth—noth—nothing!"

And he burst out laughing. He couldn't control it. He laughed so hard and so long that he had to bend over and prop his hands on his thighs for support. He laughed until he couldn't catch his breath, until tears streamed from his eyes, until the little muscles around the corner of his mouth started convulsing. And as much as it pains me to admit it, it was kind of funny. I mean, even I started to kind of chuckle at how cartoonish I looked, and it seemed for a brief moment that it might not actually be so bad.

Then Robby walked in.

"Eeeeeergh!" He ran to Alex and grabbed hold of his shin. "Where's . . . What's Mommy being?"

And he started crying, too. But his tears were a strange admixture of terror, loathing, and that peculiar instinct in all of us that makes us want to check out nature's most accursed and disgusting phenomena as we drive by on the street.

To insure against any further damage, Alex whisked the much-shaken Robby out of the room and downstairs, where they had breakfast in peace. Yes, they could still eat—even at a time like that. Meanwhile, I put in an emergency call to Jenn.

"Jenn? It's me. Sorry to call so early, but—"

"Would you rather be fat or old?" she interrupted. She often entertained these kind of debates with Henry or me or the other Jen or whoever would partake, so the question, though apropos of nothing, didn't seem that unusual to me.

"How fat?" I asked. I mean, if I was going to weigh in with a decision, it had to be under full disclosure.

"Fat enough that you couldn't lose it until you were old," she clarified.

"Old. No, fat. No, old. Would I be ugly, too?"

"No, just old. Or just fat. But the rest of you would be you. Henry and I were up until one thirty a.m. fighting about it. So, which is it?"

"Old," I said definitively.

"Yeah, me, too. Henry picked fat. Just what a guy would say."

"Well, there are definite advantages to being . . . Wait, Jenn, I called for a reason," I interrupted myself. I'd nearly forgotten my predicament in the excitement surrounding her thought-provoking issue.

"What? Everyone all right?" I could tell from her tone that she was thinking of her answer and trying to visualize herself—maybe even in front of a mirror—alternately old and then fat.

"No! I turned into that girl from *Willie Wonka* who ate the wallpaper and turned into a blueberry!"

"She didn't *eat* the wallpaper; she just *licked* it."

"*Jenn,*" I said in exasperation, "this is an emergency! I have Alex's stupid party tonight, and I'm bright red and as swollen as a beach ball!"

"I'm pretty sure she turned blue, not red."

"Jenn! Please, take your mind off the Old versus Fat case, and listen to me!"

"Okay, I'll listen; but she *was* blue, and she *did* only lick the wallpaper."

"Look," I continued, in spite of this strange exactitude regarding *Willy Wonka.* "Alex is going to take Robby to school because my own son won't get near me. So, I'm going to try to fix myself, but I'm gonna need your help. Will you please come by after you drop off Chris?"

"Oh, sure," she said distractedly. "I'm getting jowls. I can see them already."

I knew it! I knew she was in front of her mirror the whole time!

"Jenn, do you know how much money I would give to the first person able to help me appear even remotely human? And you're staring at phantom jowls? You barely have enough flesh for eyelids, let alone jowls! Jowls? Jowls? Who gives a shit? I'd take jowls as big as cocker spaniel ears just to have my skin return to normal for one freaking night! Please—I beg of you—come and help me. But keep your big mouth shut about your nonexistent, never-were-existent, and never-will-be-existent beauty problems, all right? If I could look like you, I'd agree to be fat *and* old. And have jowls, too."

If she had been paying any attention to what I had said, I probably would have felt kind of bad about it, but I knew she was deeply engrossed in her own reflection and so had stopped listening after agreeing to come and help me out. But the important thing was that she had agreed to come.

While the guys got ready for their day, I stayed upstairs, desperately clawing through any linen cabinet, medicine chest, or random closet I could ransack in search of some miracle cure for my problem. Cortisone cream? Calamine lotion? Something called "Hello! Aloe!" that I didn't even know we owned? Maybe even Preparation H? I once read that beauty queens used that to reduce puffiness around the eye area; maybe it would reduce puffiness around the whole facial area.

When I finally ventured down to say good-bye, Alex tried unsuccessfully to swallow his renewed gales of laughter, while Robby tried unsuccessfully to endure my face getting close enough to his to kiss him. To recap: husband laughing, son disgusted, party in ten hours. Yup. Things were shaping up to be a great day.

I had no choice but to bide my time until Jenn arrived, so I sat at the kitchen table with a quart of apple juice in front of me, downing glasses of the stuff as if it were a bottle of single-malt whiskey. I even slammed the glass down and wiped my mouth with the back of my hand a couple of times for effect. Finally, I heard Jenn opening the front door. In a panic, I stood up, then froze. Did I really want her to see me? How hideous was I? Should I put a sack over my head and tour in the sideshow ("I am not an animal!")? But before I could decide what to do, she was there at the kitchen table in front of me.

"Okay, well, let's get a good look-see here." She held my chin and turned my head side to side. "This is bad, but we can make it work. There are a few tricks. With the way you sounded on the phone, I thought . . . I thought . . . Well, actually, I thought it wouldn't really be this bad. But don't worry, we'll definitely fix you up." She quickly added that last sentence so I wouldn't get too upset. But just how quickly she added it was a little suspicious.

"Please—anything. You have no idea how desperate I've become. Alex laughs when he sees me; Robby shrinks away in terror. And the party is tonight. And the saddest thing of all? I, for once, actually still fit into the outfit I bought."

It was too much. I started crying.

Jenn cradled my bloated head against her very pregnant tummy and kind of rocked me back and forth. Surprisingly, it worked. I started to feel a little less sorry for myself and a little more optimistic about my situation. Then we got to work. I took a bath in some oatmeal kind of thing she'd brought with her. I loofahed myself in the shower. I masked and exfoliated and creamed and soaked. All with products in slim, sleek silver or black bottles with Asian- or Germanic-sounding names that emerged magically from her leather bag one by one. All were products I wouldn't have known where to buy or how to use if I'd been given a comprehensive set of directions, which is basically what you needed before embarking on such a skin care regimen. I can't say for sure, but I'm fairly convinced that I went through twelve steps of facial treatment, each one containing seaweed and slug excrement. But I trusted Jenn. Jenn knew best. Jenn had known where to get them and how to use them.

And, really, what else was there for me to do?

Chapter Twenty

By five o'clock, my face, though not noticeably less bloated, was significantly less red. I don't know if the actual discoloration had faded or if we had just coated so much makeup over it that it was no longer visible to the naked eye, but whichever one it was, it was enough to convince me that I would still have to go to the party. So, while Alicia and Robby played downstairs in the family room, I put the finishing touches on my toilette—just a fancy way of saying that I sat across from the mirror, staring at the image I saw there. My hair, a month after my mother's henna rinse, was sallow and wilted. My dress—I had to be honest—felt a hell of a lot tighter than it had the day before. And my makeup . . . Well, I mean, come on—even premium gas won't make a Pinto win the Indy 500. But it was nearing six, and I had to go. Damn it, I had to go.

Alicia was holding Robby on her hip, waiting for me at the bottom of the stairs when I came down.

"Wow, you really look . . . ggrreat," Alicia said with exaggerated emphasis on the "great," just like Tony the Tiger, only without the blue box and sportif red kerchief.

"Thanks. And all it took were thirty extra pounds, a dress two sizes too small, and a recent skin allergy. It's a strict beauty regimen, I know—but not without its rewards."

"Nooo! Don't joke about it. You look terrific," she said reassuringly. "Doesn't Mommy look beautiful, Robby?"

"Why you wearing Daddy's robe?" he asked with a scowl. Oh my God. He had already made it abundantly clear what he thought of my "rosy" complexion, but now, on top of everything, I was enlightened of the fact that I looked to be cross-dressing in bedroom attire. And it was kind of true, because Alex did have, thanks to my mother one Christmas, a black cotton bathrobe that wrapped at the waist like my dress. The only time he ever wore it was when my mother was actually in our house to observe it, during their Thanksgiving visit, but Robby still remembered the damn garment. And now, apparently, I was basically wearing the same thing. So, in a flash of morbid self-pity and hatred for my son, I threw on my sunglasses and hit the road before I'd have time to reconsider the party and leave Alex stood up.

I drove slowly—really slowly—but, alas, I still managed to get there. And I wasn't even late. Damn it. I took off the sunglasses (I'm just not the I-wear-my-shades-indoors kinda girl; I mean, my future's *not* that bright), and entered the dreaded building. I used to like this place. When I had a job. And regular hair appointments. And heels on my shoes. Now I hated the place. I hated all the mature and civilized businesspeople who would, inevitably, use words like "synergy" and "incentivize" while downing trendy drinks named for cool cities I'd never heard of and would never go to. And then I started to really feel sorry for myself. I mean, I was basically an unemployed male-impersonator sporting thirty extra pounds and a bad complexion. And so, with this happy little concoction of self-loathing, despair, and seething envy for all those fortunate enough to have real employment, I made my way to the third floor where the party was being held.

On a table outside the huge conference room were about a

million place cards. And that was when yet another ice ball of reality hit me full on in the skull: This was going to be a sit-down dinner. Great. My favorite. Being captive the whole night to eight or ten complete strangers who would, no doubt, meander their way through each interminable course, talking on and on about boring deals and tiresome closings and wholly uninteresting clients, pausing only long enough to laugh at their own jokes and humiliate unsuspecting waiters. So, while I looked over the cards in search of mine and Alex's, I actually started inventing outrageous stories that I could tell at the table to kind of liven things up if things got really dull. I decided I would pretend to be hip, chic, in the know. I'd tell fabulous anecdotes of humorous though socially significant events; I'd regale them with savvy political insights; I'd entertain them with witty cultural commentary. You know, I'd lie like a hooker in the back room at a poker game, though in the forefront of my mind, I knew I couldn't even pull off lying. I mean, I hadn't read a newspaper since, well, ever; and as for television, the only shows I watched featured either characters from Nixon-era Americana or characters in colors these guys hadn't laid eyes on since the Day-Glo explosion in the eighties. And in case you're wondering, furry Day-Glo creatures don't impart many edgy social or political insights. Nor do witches, genies, or blended families from the 1960s.

So, in growing anger and dread, I searched the piles of cards; and just as I found our name tags, Alex came up to me.

"Hey, your skin looks better! What'd you do to it?" he asked as he hugged me and kissed my neck.

"Thanks. Jenn came over and worked on me. You didn't tell me this was a sit-down."

"I didn't know it until ten minutes ago. But I switched us around to table six. We have Dave, Liz, George, and Mark. Dave and Mark have been sidebarred with me, but since we're all work-ing on the temp cases together, we've all been invited. There are a couple others at our table I don't really know that well, but they seem all right. And if it sucks, we'll leave. No biggie."

No biggie? My own husband had just said that. *No biggie.* I was coming face-to-face with Businessman Alex, the suit-wearing, briefcase-toting, lame-expressions-hurling, overseas-conference-calling alter ego of the man who'd been masquerading as my hus-band for the past almost-eight years. My God, who was he? He seemed strange and foreign to me. But not in an Antonio Ban-deras sort of way—more in an Alf or E.T. sort of way. I mean, Husband Alex never used expressions like that. Especially ones from decades ago. If I'd thought it wouldn't hurt his feelings, I would have responded with a "Groovy, man" or maybe a "Totally gnarly"; but it wasn't as if he wanted to be there, either, so I just smiled and followed him in.

In the past, when I'd gone to these parties with Alex, there was no sit-down dinner to suffer through, *and* I wasn't pregnant, and therefore could get drunk. However, this year there *was* a sit-down dinner to suffer through; and I *was* pregnant, and therefore *couldn't* get drunk. In addition, Alex's position was far more tenu-ous this year than in years past. So, I kind of shifted around, once inside the reception room, with no obvious purpose of any kind. Alex had gone off in search of some sort of nonalcoholic bever-age for me; but that left just me and a bunch of people who were better dressed, better paid, and better complected than I was. It was my thirteenth birthday all over again, when my best friend, Emma, threw a surprise coed party for me in her rec room (that was what her family called the basement) and—entirely caught off guard—I had shown up in jeans and a baseball shirt. Every-one else had on skirts from The Limited and Vaccaro turtlenecks.

Even the boys looked more feminine than I did. The whole rest of the evening I obsessed about how bad I looked until Michael Umberling took me into the tool section of the basement ("rec room") and made out with me. But tonight? Well, even if I was relatively assured of scoring a home run with Alex should the mood strike, I feared it wouldn't be enough to compensate for all the evening's prior suffering. Needless to say, I didn't have as high hopes for the conclusion of tonight's festivities.

I hadn't been waiting too long when Liz came up to me. She'd worked with Alex for a few years, and I always liked seeing her at the office parties and stuff. She was smart and funny and was so happily self-deprecating, you couldn't help but love her.

"Hey, that dress is excellent! Keep it for me in case I'm ever lucky enough to be in your condition," she said as we kissed cheeks.

I thought that was pretty damn cool of her to pretend to admire my current state of matronly bloatedness. And it worked—I actually started to feel better.

"Hi, Liz! Your hair looks great; and Alex told me you're giving the keynote address tonight—that is amazing! Congratulations! Are you excited?"

"Oh, Annie, please don't mention it. Oh shit. Oh shit."

She started to look visibly paler, and she began sucking her cheeks in and out. Even before she said the inevitable, "I think I'm gonna puke," I knew she was gonna puke. You don't hang out with three-year-olds all day without picking up a thing or two.

"No, you aren't," I said as calmly as I could, kicking into mommy gear. "You are a grown-up woman wearing a suit that I would kill for, and if you puke all over it, I will, in fact, kill you. Now, sit down right here"—I ushered her over to the closest table—"and take ten deep breaths. It has to be ten. And close your eyes. No one's looking, so don't worry. And when you're done, put this in your mouth. I promise, it'll work."

I had changed purses for the occasion, but that simply meant dumping the contents of my regular bag into this only slightly smaller but satin version. So, luckily, the Children's Tylenol Meltaways I always carry for Robby were safely transferred to my evening bag. I gave Liz two of them, then grabbed the glass of seltzer from Alex as he came up to us.

"Now drink this slowly," I said, giving her the glass.

"What's up?" Alex asked. "Something wrong, Liz?"

"Ahh, not anymore," she answered with a smile. "Your wife just saved my ass."

She was starting to get her color back, and she was able to stand up.

"Why? What happened?"

"I was gonna puke because of this damn speech I have to give, and Annie fixed me. Really. I feel good as new. I can't believe it, but those little things worked! Thanks, Annie. I owe you big for this. You don't know what an idiot I would have felt like."

But I did know. And I was pretty much feeling it right then, although after ponying up the kids' Tylenol, I was starting to feel—albeit very slightly—like less of a loser. The only problem was that I really wanted the club soda that Alex had brought for me, so I left Alex and Liz to go in search of my own beverage. I headed for the bar, hoping I could twist the bartender's arm and actually get some cherries to go along with the club soda. When I finally got to the bar area, there must have been about, well, I'm no good with numbers, but I'd say ten million people waiting for alcohol. You only really realize how desperate people are to get drunk when you, yourself, are not desperate to get drunk. If I hadn't felt a little queasy myself after the Liz incident, I would never have ventured into this tumult of people in search of a good buzz. But I just wasn't ready to run the risk of, once again, puking in public, so I got in line and waited with the rest of the people whose drinks, unlike mine, would do more for them than merely quench thirst.

I couldn't have been in line more than a couple of minutes when some guy carrying nearly a dozen different glasses of wine and mixed drinks came jostling through the middle of the line. While I couldn't say for sure that all the drinks were for him, I couldn't say for sure that they weren't. And he'd already—quite obviously—gotten a jump start on those dozen as well. So, he came bobbing and weaving through the crowds, eyes half shut and glazed over; and just as he was about to pass through the throng safely, he veered, careened, lunged, and sloshed a glass of merlot all over the crisply starched white shirt front of a good-looking guy about Alex's age.

"Damn it, Jim!" the wet-shirt guy yelled at the drunk guy. "What the hell? No, don't wipe it; you'll only make it worse. Just give me the napkin," the guy said as he tried to blot his shirt front.

"Sawry. I diden't mean to do zhat," the drunk guy—Jim, I guess his name was—slurred. And with that, he wandered off, equally wobbly, but slightly less laden with alcohol.

"Umm, excuse me," I said to the guy still blotting his shirt. "This may help." I handed him another renegade mommy-item that had inadvertently been transferred to my evening bag.

"Hey, thanks. What is it?" he asked.

"It's a stain wipe. Just hold it against the splotch, and when it dries, you probably won't be able to notice anything."

"Thanks, I'll try it; I mean, it can't get worse, right?" he said as he ripped open the packet and applied the gauzy cloth to the stain. "Hey, I think it's already working." He chuckled as he blotted and peeked, blotted and peeked. "I can't believe it! How did you ever think to carry one of those with you?"

If only he knew. If only he knew.

"Thank you so much!" he continued. "I have to introduce tonight's speaker, and I would have died without this—this—wipey thing. You saved me!"

Hey, what do you know?

Chapter Twenty-one

Of course, I still had dinner and speeches to sit through with a bunch of blowhard show-offs yammering on about the great World of Professionalism of which I was no longer a citizen. So, I sauntered over to our table, where Alex and Liz were already seated. I grant, "saunter" may suggest an image slightly cooler than how I really moved—but you get the idea. Even before taking my seat, though, I noticed the floral arrangements that were being placed in the center of each of the tables as they were set for the dinner. Every table had its own design and color scheme, but they were all coordinated by their dark, rich, wintry shades and foliage. Only one person could have been responsible for such a display. And, as I looked around, admiring all the different bouquets, I heard a quiet voice behind me.

"Hi, Annie!"

I turned quickly, shocked that anyone could have recognized me looking the way I did and being there, where I knew no one besides the two people already at the table.

"Duncan! What are you doing here?" I asked as I reached up to hug him.

He kind of leaned in and, in a sort of formal hug, gently patted my back a couple of times.

"Lucas let me do the flowers, which I still can't believe. I delivered them at four, but the lady running the party said she wanted me to put them on the tables only after the cocktail hour was over, so everyone would know it was dinnertime. What do you think?" he asked sheepishly, but obviously very proud of his work. "I only wish I had smaller scissors so I could trim the ends of these ribbons." He was a true artist—perfecting his work until the last moment.

"Oh, wait a sec," I said, opening my bag. I was pretty sure I had a pair of tiny first-aid scissors that I'd never taken out of my purse since I'd brought them to Robby's first Fun-nasium class. "Yeah, here you go!"

"Thanks, Annie! How lucky to run into you," he said as he deftly clipped the ends off all the meticulously sculpted ribbons. "You're a lifesaver!"

Somehow I doubted that lending a pair of scissors to a guy who wanted to cut a superfluous half inch of satin ribbon from holiday centerpieces quite earned that distinction, but it was nice to hear, all the same.

"Duncan, these arrangements are even better than the ones for Jenn's shower! I can't believe your talent! Are you still enjoying it?" I asked with trepidation since I was the one who'd kind of pushed it on him.

"I love it. I've never in my whole life been happier. And you know what?" he started to ask with a gleam in his eye, just as Alex and Liz came over.

"Alex, this is Duncan! Liz, this is Duncan, our cable guy. No, I mean, florist. No, I mean, floral engineer," I said, catching myself quickly.

"Ahh, so you're the famous Duncan," Alex said, smiling and shaking hands. "I owe you a big thank-you for all the premium channel hookups! It's really excellent!"

"Don't tell me you did these flowers!" Liz spoke up, although it wasn't hard to guess that Duncan was responsible for the flowers, given that he had just picked up the last remaining vase to be placed on the tables.

"Well . . . I . . . Yes, I did," he said, trying to suppress a smile of pride.

"Oh my God! If I ever get married, will you do the flowers for my wedding? These are the best arrangements I've ever seen! And I don't even usually care about flowers! Great job!" Liz said with earnest enthusiasm.

"Well, it's all due to Annie; she's the one who encouraged me—and let me borrow her scissors," Duncan said humbly as he gave me back the scissors. "If it weren't for her, I wouldn't be here right now. I can guarantee you that!"

"Hey, me, too," Liz said with a smile. "Is there anything she can't do? She must secretly be magic!" She winked at Duncan, then wiggled her nose at me, *Bewitched* style, as she took her seat.

"Everyone sure seems to love your wife, Alex," Duncan said with a smile.

"Yup! They sure do!" Alex responded.

And maybe it was just the glow of the newly lit candles, but I thought I noticed a sort of gleamy brightness in his eyes as he said it. Then he stroked my hair and just kind of—well, if it weren't such a weird word, I'd say "gazed" at me before sitting down.

"You were about to say something," I said, turning back to Duncan to resume our abbreviated conversation.

"Well, yeah. I was going to tell you that I really owe you, Annie. Because of taking this job, I'm not only happier, but with the extra money . . . I mean . . . Well, I mean, now we can afford . . . Shelly's pregnant!" he finally blurted out.

"Congratulations, Duncan!" I said as I hugged him. "Good for you! I am so happy for you guys! Wow, what good news!"

"Well, I owe it all to you. I mean it—thanks," he said with feeling as he waved and walked off to finish arranging the flowers.

Running into Duncan—and hearing Liz compare me to Samantha—had really improved my mood, but I knew I was entering what would, no doubt, be the longest and worst part of the evening, so I was still wary. I sat down by Alex and was immediately flanked by another guy I was pretty sure I'd never seen before. Great. I had to sit side by side with a total stranger who, I noticed almost immediately, had this really weird habit of staring at the palm of his right hand. And when he wasn't staring at it, he was picking at it. Now, that makes for some tantalizing dinner companionship, I can assure you.

"Hey, guys," he said, looking up from his hand for a moment. His eyes were soft and friendly. He looked vaguely familiar to me.

"Hey, Mark." Alex smiled over at him. "This is my wife, Annie. Annie, this is Mark. You guys have probably met at one of these events before."

"Hi. Good to see you, Mark," I said, reaching out for a handshake.

I didn't know what the hell was wrong with his hand, but I figured I'd have to risk contracting whatever life-threatening, communicable virus he was carrying on his hand for the sake of decorum. And, to be fair, he was probably equally grossed out by my skin issues.

"Oh, sorry, I can't shake hands," he said. Briefly, I panicked that it was because he thought *I* was contagious; but then he explained. "I got a splinter this weekend working on my buddy's deck, and I can't get it out for anything. It's huge." Then he re-commenced picking.

"Is that all it is?" I asked. I feared my tone betrayed the relief I felt at his not having the life-threatening, communicable virus I'd suspected, but he seemed fine with it. "Do you want me to take a look? I have a three-year-old who gets splinters constantly."

And I began to rummage in my Wonder Bag for a pin. I might not be able to practice witchcraft, but with a purse like mine, I wasn't sure I needed to. I even wondered briefly if I should switch my role model to Felix the Cat. Good old Felix. Whenever he gets into a fix, he reaches into his bag of tricks; Felix the Cat, the wonderful, wonderful cat.

"Could you, please?" he asked in a tone that reminded me so much of Robby that I had to suppress a smile.

"Of course," I answered as I located the pin. Then I burned its tip in the candle on the table (more for show than for sterility, I must admit), and began desplintering the stranger's hand. In a couple of minutes, I had extricated the longest shard of wood I'd ever seen embedded in human flesh.

"You did it!" he yelled with relief. And a cheer went around the table—since, by then, all but one of the people assigned to our table had taken their seats. "Thanks so much! It doesn't even hurt," he continued.

Then, as everyone began recounting their own splinter sto-ries, Mark leaned in and surreptitiously asked if he could see it—just like Robby. He wanted to see, and maybe even take home to frame and hang on the wall, the foreign particle that had gotten lodged in his skin. Funny—I guess no one ever really outgrows that. So I handed it to him, along with the pin, too, just so he'd always have a souvenir.

"Hey, now I remember you!" he said once the splinter and

pin were safely encased in his wallet. "Last year's Christmas party? You weren't, you know"—he glanced at my torso—"like *this* last year, but weren't you the only one who could remember the Hokey Pokey when the boss wanted everyone to do it? Hey, remember that, guys?" he asked everyone at the table. "Last year's party with the Hokey Pokey! You must remember that, Annie!"

"Ummm, sort of," I dissembled. The fact is, I remembered that day like my own name. I not only mortified myself by admitting I knew the steps, but then Alex's boss asked me to do them on the dance floor. In front of everybody. In the circle. By myself. I think I made Alex pay for that for about two and a half months. So, in a word, *yeah*, I remembered. It's funny how something like that'll stick with a person.

"Hey, yeah, I remember that!" replied one of the newcomers to our table whom I didn't recognize.

"Yeah, me, too!" added Dave—a longtime associate of Alex's who'd also been sidebarred.

"Who could forget that? It was the funniest thing I've ever seen you do, Annie," said Wendy, another coworker of Alex's whom I'd known for years. "George, you weren't there last year, but Annie got us all—including Schaeffer—to do the Hokey Pokey. It was such a laugh!"

"That was the only time I can remember actually having fun at one of these parties. It was an awesome night." Liz laughed.

Tee-hee. I chuckled along with them—not because I thought it was so funny, but because it was dawning on me that being a mom had some pretty decent perks. And to be totally honest, it actually felt kind of, well, good. I mean, to get all these accolades. It was more credit than Robby ever gave me. And I liked it. Alex squeezed my hand under the table, and when I looked over at him, he was smiling into his glass as he sipped his wine.

Oh, and imagine my surprise at discovering, when the final member of the table came to take his seat, that it was none other than the spilled-on guy whose shirt my stain wipe had rescued from the merlot-marauder earlier that night.

"Hi, everyone," he said as he took his seat. And then, as he spotted me, he added, "Hey, you're the one who saved me tonight!"

Then—and this is the best part—in unison, the whole table responded, "You, too?" and gave me (honestly, I'm not kidding you) a round of applause. Me! Can you believe it?

It may not have resulted in a make-out session with Michael Umberling in a dark basement ("rec room"—whatever), but it was a pretty great night just the same.

Chapter Twenty-two

Alex's consultant work ended after the holidays, and although he never said as much, my guess is that he had been hoping it wouldn't end and that he'd simply be able to continue on in a seamless transition back into his full-time position. While his mood around the house never fell below cheerful, it was becoming obvious that the professional limbo he was experiencing was weighing on him. When I found him in front of the extra refrigerator we kept in the basement, reconfiguring the shelving arrangement for the fifth time, I figured something had to give.

"Honey," I began, as gently as I could.

"Yup?" he huffed in a gruff voice implying the manful effort of his task.

"Honey, we don't use that refrigerator," I informed him, as kindly as I could.

I had no idea how long he was planning on continuing at this chore, but, literally, that refrigerator had remained empty ever since we'd bought the house. We'd brought it with us from our old rental, and we'd stuck it in some obscure corner of the basement that our real estate agent had assured us would make a "fabulous caterer's kitchen" if we ever chose to finish it; however, given that the only caterer in our house was named Boyardee, a whole kitchen dedicated to this fine profession seemed a little like overkill. Hence, we had an empty refrigerator in an obscure basement corner. I wasn't even sure the thing was plugged in.

"Yeah, but the shelves in here were just really illogically placed. It's always bothered me. The top shelf didn't even have enough space for soda bottles."

"But, honey, we don't use the refrigerator. What difference does it make if the shelves aren't logical?"

"Annie, you know me, and you know I'm a firm believer in logical shelving," he replied, totally in earnest.

"I'm not saying I like illogical shelves," I replied. "And you've really done a great job reconfiguring the shelves in the upstairs fridge, but, honey, *we don't use this refrigerator.* Ever. It has never held an item, soda or otherwise. Tall or short. So what could it matter if the shelves don't make sense?"

"Look, I don't care if I'm never going to open the door. I don't care if the thing is unplugged and rendered totally useless. *I just care that the shelves make sense.* Shelves need to make sense. Shelves need to be logical. The whole purpose of a shelf is simply to provide a rational, sensible foundation for what needs to be supported. That's it. If it can't do that, it's, well, it's failed. The shelf is a failure."

Shelf, huh?

"Um, Alex," I hemmed. I had no idea how to proceed, but clearly things had derailed somewhere along the track. "Is there, like, anything else going on here?"

"What do you mean?" he asked, barely pausing from the task at hand.

"I don't want to piss you off or hurt your feelings. And if you want me to shut up, I will. But, Alex, you've been down here for two hours and forty minutes working on those shelves that we'll never use."

"So?" he responded in exactly the same tone I used to use with my mom when she'd observe that I, say, had an exam the next day, or that ice cream had a lot of calories.

"It just seems as if maybe you're a little tense. Maybe all the job stuff or the baby stuff or the home stuff is getting to you."

"Just because I want the world to be ergonomically designed doesn't mean I'm crazy, Annie. In fact, I think it means the exact opposite. I believe my desire to have well-engineered shelving space is a reflection of the clarity and acuity of my mind."

Well, what could I say to that? It seemed to me that once one's husband threw down the gauntlet of the word "acuity," one no longer had a tenable position in the discussion.

"Okay," I surrendered. "Well, Robby and I are going to go try to make an igloo out of the slush the snowplow piled up. If you change your mind, come on out, if you want."

"What kind of igloo?" he asked as he redoubled his efforts at finishing the interior architecture of the refrigerator no one would ever see.

"Huh?" I asked. What kind of igloo? The cold kind. Were there other variations?

"What kind of igloo are you going to make? Ice blocks? Packed snow? Sunken cave?"

"Please. Tell. Me. You. Are. Kidding."

"About what?"

"Okay, Alex. If that is your real name. Here it comes. I don't know who you are. I don't know where my actual husband is. If you've been cloned like that alien *Flintstones* episode, you may as well tell me now. Because the person I'm looking at right now cannot really be my husband. This person has spent the better part of a Tuesday afternoon fixated upon shelving for nonexistent, temperature-sensitive foodstuffs. And rather than jump to join in on an Eskimo party with his wife and son, he has paused to inquire about the blueprints for an igloo to be composed of nothing more than some slush and dirt clumps the plow guy left two weeks ago."

"Week and a half," he responded sulkily. "It snowed only a week and a half ago."

"Oh, well, in *that* case . . . ," I said. Seriously, was the date of the most recent plow-guy sighting really relevant to the discussion of my husband's tenuous grasp on reality?

"Fine," he said huffily.

"Fine? What's fine? Alex, this is pretty seriously far from fine, if you ask me. It's pretty much very, very not fine. Is this really what you want to be doing with your day? Really, Alex? Because I don't believe it is."

"No!" he bellowed. And Alex was not a bellower. "No! It isn't what I want to be doing with my day. What I want to be doing with my day is *working*, Annie. Working. At a job. A job that pays money. A job that provides for a family and a new baby and a freaking refrigerator with properly installed shelves. *That's* what I want to be doing with my day. And if I were sure that would ever happen again, *ever*, I would feel a lot better about simply enjoying the time I have now with you and Robby. But I'm not sure. So, in the meantime, the least I can do is make myself useful around here!"

Ah-hah. It all made sense. Alex wanted to feel significant the same way I wanted to feel significant. I got that. I understood that. I wasn't all that clear on how redesigning unused refrigerator space helped, but, somehow, all the imaginary food that would never be housed in this virgin appliance was filling the shelves of

Alex's self-esteem. And, having articulated that to myself, I began to feel better; for one, it really did provide me with the necessary insight to proceed with him, and for two, I was really quite proud of my little analogy about filling the shelves of his self-esteem, and I made a mental note to share it with Alex when his mood had picked up.

"Useful? Alex, do you not grasp how necessary you are to me and to Robby? Don't you know how much we depend on you to give our family balance, structure, sanity? Whether you're here at home or at an office, you're the one I rely on to keep me grounded and smiling. Don't you remember, just two nights ago, when I couldn't think of the name of the Brady Bunch's cousin who came to live with them? Who enabled me to stay in a perfectly warm and comfortable bed, rather than drag myself down to the computer and Google it? Who stopped me from calling Michael at eleven forty at night to ask him? Who figured out his name was Oliver? Who listened to my theory that sitcoms always jump the shark when they add a new family member? You, Alex. Only you."

"I'm still not convinced," he said. But, promisingly, he had at least risen and was backing away from the empty refrigerator.

"But it's true! You have to believe me! You're the only one who could help and support me and make me laugh and—"

"No, I'm just not convinced your theory is sound," he said, smiling at me. "*Family Ties* lasted after Andy was born, and those were some of the funniest episodes."

"Oh, come on. It's so obvious, it's not even worth talking about. *The Cosby Show, One Day at a Time, The Facts of Life, Growing Pains, Eight Is Enough.* The list is endless. It's a truism. Your exception just proves the rule."

"I've never understood that concept. How can an exception

prove a rule? If there's an exception, then doesn't it either break the rule, or mean that the rule is faulty to begin with?"

"I don't really know; I never thought about it. I've just heard people use that expression, and it seemed to fit here, so I tossed it out. But, yeah, it kind of doesn't make sense. You know what else doesn't make sense? 'Buy or beware.' What's that all about?"

"'Buyer beware' makes sense to me," Alex asserted as he packed up his toolbox. Thankfully, the afternoon's adventures in cold storage seemed to be coming to an end.

"How? Is it a threat? 'Buy this or else'? Or else what? Is some merchant going to come out from behind my closet door, swinging a chain saw, if I don't buy his stuff?"

"Huh? Annie, it isn't 'Buy or beware.' It's 'Buyer beware.' As in, if you buy this, you should be aware that it may not meet your expectations."

"Oh. Well, I guess that makes a little more sense. But still . . ." I sulked a little. I hated to be shown what a dufus I was.

He put his arm around me, and I turned in toward him for a full hug.

"I love you, Annie. And I'm sorry about all this," he whispered into my hair.

"It's just some shelves and a couple of hours. Don't give it another thought," I answered magnanimously.

"No. I mean about all of it. This. My being home, not working, just when we could most use the income."

"Alex, please listen to me," I said in an uncharacteristically serious tone. "I love you. And I know that, together, we will work this out. I don't know what will happen with your job, but I do know that we'll get through this—just as we'll get through all of life's downers. Together. If things don't happen back at Hoffman, Berg, then I can go back to work. We're two fairly intelligent people, one of us more so than the other"—here I paused to wink at him—"and this will all be fine. Maybe even better than fine."

"Hmph," he grunted skeptically.

"You never know, Alex. Maybe something really good could come of this. Shaking things up doesn't always mean the outcome will be worse. Just promise me you'll do two things."

"What are they?"

"Promise."

"Is the promise one of the two things?"

"Okay, three things. Promise, being the first."

"Fine. I promise."

"Here they are. First, believe what I've said to you today, because I meant every single word of it."

"What's the other thing?"

"Think about what you want. What you really want for your future. For our future. And once you've figured it out, let me know and we'll make that happen."

"Annie?"

"What is it, Alex?" I said, still cuddling up to him and congratulating myself over my inspirational pep talk and my being such a great wife.

"That's, like, five things."

I had to laugh.

Chapter Twenty-three

With the holidays behind us, life resumed its normal pace in the lull of the new year. I was still uplifted by the standing ovation I'd received at Alex's Christmas party and by seeing Alex return to more normal behaviors than those of an errant Maytag man on Red Bull. So, in light of these triumphs, most of the petty day-to-day inconveniences and irritations melted off me like snowflakes in the noonday sun.

The rub: It was only January, and I still had three more months to go until I was to deliver what I was increasingly hoping was going to be at least a thirty-five-pound baby. You see, at six months into this thing, I'd already gained thirty-nine pounds. And I'd love to tell you I was five foot ten and hitting one fifty for the first time in my life. Tee-hee. The reality was that at only five foot five, I was now tipping the scales at more than one sixty. Cute, huh? And now it was mid-January, and our household was still left with three and a half tins of Christmas cookies. All the best kinds, too: peanut butter with the big kisses in the middle; frosted cutouts; cinnamon shortbread; and something Alex's mom made with a foreign name that I could never pronounce, but I'm pretty sure they were globs of chocolate held together with caramel. I was doomed.

And along with my now-vanished waistline went any shred of willpower I ever possessed, which was never very much anyhow. The way I looked at it, after thirty-nine pounds, what the hell was the point of keeping track? I figured I'd just let loose and try to deal with the dismal and frightening reality of weight loss after giving birth. After all, breast-feeding is supposed to burn upward of ten million calories a day, so if worse came to worst, I could always just keep on nursing the kid until he or she left for college. That would surely give me enough time to return to—or actually find for the first time—my svelte self. I was afraid, however, that this baby, like Robby, might not ever take to the whole nursing thing and, therefore, have to be weaned after only three short weeks. But for the most part, I rode out this eating-and-gaining wave pretty gracefully.

In general, things were running remarkably smoothly on the Forster home front. This should have been my first tip-off. Alex was back to his old self and actually taking a couple of law courses in order to keep current. Robby was back at nursery school. And I had just embarked on the fast-paced and exciting track of parent-teacher liaison at the co-op—an assignment infinitely preferable to either the Snack Lady or the Cleaner of Kids. Ms. Jenkins had recommended that we parents rotate roles, so I volunteered for this new one without really knowing what I was supposed to do. But no matter what the job entailed, with a title like that, I simply had to have it. It had been more than three years since I'd held such an official-sounding position—*liaison*. I was a *liaison*. You had to admit, it had a certain ring to it. And, as it turned out, all the parent-teacher liaison had to do was send out a mass e-mail once or twice a month about upcoming events and noteworthy classroom happenings (nursery school, by the way, doesn't have a whole lot of these, in case there was any question about that). So it was pretty much excellent!

On the fourth of January, Jenn had gone into labor and given birth to Baby Brent. Both of them were now home and doing great. Robby and I—who were Chris' ride to and from the co-op—stopped in most days to lend a hand with shopping or picking up or laundry or whatever. They were all healthy, and Jenn looked so happy and beautiful, already back in her prepregnancy jeans. But to be kind of mean for a minute here . . . That name? Not that anyone asked me, but come on. Brent? What was with that? I could remember about seventy-two conversations I'd had with Jenn about the trendy Kent-Brent, Kaylie-Bailey, Kyle-Bile names that we always said we hated. And I thought we meant it. But, much to my chagrin, I was now best friends with a woman whose offspring I would forever have to refer to as if he were some 1990s nighttime soap star with a goatee and too much hair gel. But I had to admit, he was already a really cute kid—the kind of kid who would inevitably have broken my heart by making fun of my *Dukes of Hazzard* notebook in front of his friends in fifth grade. Not that I resented this two-week-old baby or anything, but you know how you can sometimes just get a feeling about someone? Well, call it my maternal instinct or female intuition or whatever you want, but I was pretty sure that if the baby I was carrying was of the female persuasion, I was going to have to set up an immediate no-tolerance policy on *Dukes of Hazzard* accessories, just to be on the safe side.

The good news was that Robby was proving daily that he was becoming quite an older-than-thou, big-brothery, protective kind of kid. He stroked Baby Brent's hair; he stuck out fingers for the baby to grab onto; and he asked repeatedly in a pleading kind of voice if he could take a turn feeding the baby—which, given that Jenn was nursing, was utterly impossible; but try explaining that to a three-year-old who fully believed his nipples to be every bit as effective as a lactating mother's. I was, all in all (breast issues aside), becoming quite convinced Robby would, indeed, make an excellent older brother.

And it was at this rather happy little juncture in our lives that the doorbell rang unexpectedly one Thursday afternoon; and, unsuspecting fool that I was, I answered it.

"Annie! Wow! You're humongous! Where's Mr. Roboto?" my wayward brother-in-law screamed in my ear as he hugged me, picked me up, and twirled me around.

"Uncle Andy! Uncle Andy! Can we play Caterpillar and pick strawberries again?" Robby screeched with joy as he ran into the foyer from the family room.

"Of course we can, Mr. Roboto!" Andy responded as he tossed Robby up and down in his usual greeting ceremony.

Andy was Alex's younger brother, and, except for the same sandy blond hair and great jawline, he was the exact opposite of Alex. Andy was a Gen-Xer nonpareil—up to and including the prerequisite Internet start-up thingamabob that made all the Gen-Xers rich for a couple of months at the end of the 1990s. The only difference for Andy was that he, unlike so many unfortunate others, timed his cash-out perfectly and had managed to keep his earnings. So, in a word, Andy was rich. Very rich. Very, very rich. He'd created a dot-com something or other, making a fortune with some kind of specialized search engine that he sold off for enough profit to spend the rest of his days in blissful freedom.

So, with no job and too much time and money on hand, he traveled around the world looking for new ways to keep himself and any number of a myriad of shaggy, free-riding friends entertained. In theory, I hated this kind of person—spoiled, immature, groundless, devoid of responsibility and hygiene; but in reality, I couldn't help but love Andy—almost as much as Robby did. I don't know; there was something kind of innocent about him—the way he could tell you that you were humongous, say, for example—that would never make you feel insulted. And he always did what you told him to—whether because he was gullible, or polite, or unaware, I never could figure out—but it was as if he trusted everyone in the world to be nice to him and take care of him. Once when Robby had threatened to run away from home, I'd asked him where he was planning on going. His response was, "To stay with Uncle Andy. He's the only one who cares about me. He's the only one who pays intention to me." I got a chuckle out of that at the time, wondering who would be paying whom the so-called *intention*; but it stuck with me because, you know, there are only a limited number of people your kid wants to get intention from, and it meant something to me that, for Robby, Andy was one of them.

"Come in, come in," I said, unable to stop smiling. "Robby, let Uncle Andy take off his coat and put down his bags first! Since when are you clean shaven and short haired?" I asked, truly surprised by his newly clean-cut appearance.

"Oh, that. Had to. Lost a bet. I was actually bald originally. Totally bald. Not even any eyebrows. But they, at least, have finally grown back."

I know, of course, I shouldn't have, but I had to ask. "What'd'ya bet on? I hope it was at least something big if you had to lose all your facial and headal hair."

"A girl in a bar dared me to eat eighteen pickles and a glass of milk. The pickles were no problem, but I puked up the milk."

So now you know why I love the guy. Who else would do that? Or admit it?

"Um, so if your stake was Nairing your entire head, what

would she have had to do if she'd lost?" I wasn't sure I wanted to know—especially with Robby standing right there, holding on to Andy's coat—but I couldn't resist. What could it have been? Her underwear? Sex? Something really kinky? At the very least, nudity of some form had to be involved—I was willing to assume that. I mean, it had to be something sexual for a single guy to go to such lengths, right?

"She'd already done seventeen pickles and kept the milk down. I was just supposed to beat her record. Then she'd have had to cut off her hair."

Oh. So that was it. But you know what? I wasn't even let down. For some reason, that answer was even better—and way more Andyish. You had to love him.

"So, are you staying? Should we put your stuff upstairs, or what? And let's call Alex, so he knows you're here. He's at class right now, but he'll be home soon," I said as I pried Andy's leather jacket out of Robby's grubby but adoring fingers.

"Yeah, I'm here for two weeks, if it's all right. Then I'm catching a flight to Kathmandu. Oh, wait, maybe it's Macao. I forget which."

When Alex and I went to Hawaii for a week a few years ago, I planned and worried and obsessed about the trip for an entire month beforehand. Now here was Andy, traveling halfway around the earth, with no luggage to speak of, no idea where he was going, and not a care in the world. If I hadn't known he'd just come back from Hungary (and Kiev, São Paulo, Edinburgh, and Fiji before that), I would have doubted that he possessed so much as a passport—or even knew he needed one, or how to get one. And then I had this fleeting memory of a cartoon I used to have hanging over my desk in high school: Two girls were in some kind of dorm room or apartment; and one—a twiggy-haired plain Jane—was cowering under a book, crouching under her desk while the other one—clearly dressed for a date—was going to answer the door. The caption read HELLO, LIFE IS HERE. I always wanted to be the gorgeous girl opening the door—and in high school, I pretended I was—but, now, with Andy around, I had to admit to myself that I was really more like the plain Jane under the desk. He was loud and messy and altogether irresponsible, but so loveable that I couldn't even resent that he was dating Life while I was hunching under inhospitable office furniture.

Oh, and he babysat, too.

Chapter Twenty-four

$\mathcal{S}$o, on the following day, I figured I'd seize the opportunity of some away-from-toddler time and meet Jen—the *other* Jen, in case you're either A) wondering or B) my mother. We met in the park for some company and convo. Jen's daughter, Sarah, had just started taking Ballet for Babies twice a week after nursery school, so with her newfound free hour and my babysitting brother-in-law, we decided to meet up, take our dogs for a walk, and hang around for a while. It was January and all, so it was kind of cold, but Jen was a good sport and said she'd come anyway. She was now in her third month and actually made me look, at the risk of sounding like either a bitch or my mother, something closer to fit than I actually was. She'd had mild toxemia throughout her pregnancy with Sarah, and now, even though she was steering clear of anything salty, had somehow already managed to pack on twenty-five pounds. But she was as good a sport about this as she was about the cold weather. Jen always took everything in stride—as if my mother hadn't tested that trait to its limit in November. And as I remembered my mom's insults and then Jen's total willingness to forgive, I had to admit that I really could learn a thing or two from Jen.

I got to the park first, and, as I was putting on Chipper's

leash, I saw Jen's van approaching with Irony's head bobbing up and down in the back window. Irony was her eleven-and-a-half-year-old West Highland terrier, who, despite the loss of virtually all her upper teeth and a substantial quantity of her coat, still imagined herself to be a puppy. Chipper pulled us toward them, and, as the dogs sniffed and pawed, Jen and I embarked on the more civilized behavior suited to a species that had been able to evolve beyond a fear of vacuum cleaners and unattractive postal employees—that more civilized behavior, of course, being gossip.

"No, not really!"

"I'm entirely serious!"

"But *her*! I mean, come on!"

"Forget *her*. What about *him*?"

And so on. I'm sure the idea of gossip is a pretty easy one to grasp.

As was our usual pattern, we hooked the dogs' leashes to the dog run, which was really just an enormous chain strung across the park that allowed dogs to get exercise without requiring the same of their owners, and grabbed a seat at the picnic table. Jen whipped out some miniboxes of sweet cereal and a couple fruit roll-ups from her baby bag, and we continued our chat, unfettered by either exercise or hunger. She regaled me with the woes of what she had dubbed her "Hellidays," spent with her parents and an older, recently divorced sister with four kids in Baltimore; and I had just begun to tell her about Andy's arrival when we heard a strange sort of whinnying or groaning coming from one of the dogs. We both simultaneously whipped our heads around in time to witness Irony in a singularly compromising position with some huge and beastly looking mutt astride her from behind. Chipper, clearly unsettled by the events unfolding before him, had headed off to the other side of the run and was sulking over his abandonment by what he'd always believed to be *his* bitch.

"Irony! No!" Jen yelled, though it wasn't really sensible to yell this at a female dog who'd done nothing untoward except to have the misfortune of having been tied to a dog run that prevented escape of any form. So, in a sense, poor Irony was just a willing victim. I mean, at eleven and a half, she wasn't getting any younger, so maybe she was willing to lower her standards. Maybe she was desperate for one last fling before old age really took hold. The ugly mutt on top of her was, I grant, aesthetically objectionable, but maybe Irony liked him. Maybe her seemingly enviable life of naps, free food, and obliviousness to weight gain wasn't so fulfilling after all. Maybe abstinence and Sarah's perpetual commands weren't enough to fill the chasm of . . . Well, I'm sure you are quite aware of just what chasm would require filling in such circumstances. And really, who among us can account for a dog's taste? After all, Chipper had been neutered when he was eight months old, so it was not as if he would have been able to satisfy her womanly needs. Consequently, that Jen was so upset actually struck me as kind of funny—that, combined with the image of the salivating hound going at it with poor Irony. I mean—God bless his little soul—he was humping for all he was worth, as if he *knew* he was going to get pulled off her in the next few seconds, and so was trying to get the most out of each vigorous little thrust.

But Jen was clearly upset, so I ran over to the lovers and began pulling and kicking and tearing the brute off little Irony, who didn't look all that ashamed or apologetic given she'd just been busted for lewd public conduct. In this respect she was just like Pee-wee Herman or George Michael, only she was unrepentant—and canine. And then, as Jen unhooked Irony from the dog run, it hit me. Irony was just assaulted! Who knew? Maybe poor old Chipper could be next. Not that he was so tempting, having been neutered and all, but I still felt a certain maternal responsibility and protectiveness. So, I started getting really irritated—you might even say pissed off. Just what kind of owner would let his mutt go free—free to jump and hump smaller and prettier house pets? There were laws, after all. Weren't there? And just as I was noting the glaring absence of any posted signs requiring dogs to be leashed, I saw Just What Kind of Owner. Coming right toward me was none other than Madras Richard Smith. Still in plaid, although now, it being January, he had exchanged the short-sleeved madras for a wool button-down under an argyle sweater. Having noticed the events before him, he kind of jog-walked over to us with what I would call a smirk pasted to his face.

"Mr. Snippets! Mr. Snippets, come here! Come here right now!" Madras Richard whined to the mutt—who clearly had absolutely no intention of obeying his so-called master. Nose in the air, the ugly thing (the dog, that is) just milled around, circling Irony and Jen as if he were corralling them; as though they were his harem girls or something. "Mr. Snippets," Richard continued, "I'm telling you to come here. *Please.*"

Then, for the first time since the whole affair started, I began to sympathize with the ugly thing (again, that's the dog I'm referring to). Who wants to go through life with the ridiculous name of "Mr. Snippets"? And who, frankly, wants to go through life with Madras Richard as a primary companion? I mean who besides Crew Cut Kathy, his wife, who, in all honesty, probably didn't have too many other alternatives. And to think this was the guy who'd made an obscenely obvious mental tally of the number of items I had in the express lane at the Shop 'n Save just a few short months earlier. This overgrown Safety Monitor, stuffed into Clark Griswold's Wally World wardrobe, had been a thorn in my side for too long. If, in fact, as it appeared, there was no leash law—I vowed I would make it my life's work to get one instituted. It would be my mission. With a blinding clarity, I knew my purpose, my quest, my raison d'être: to best Madras Richard and to get the pompous, plaid-encased Überpater back for his numerous sins against character, kindness, courtesy, and clothing. Okay, so it was no Holy Grail, but still, at least I had a calling. I would get that guy back for all his smug insinuations and self-promotion. That would be the last time that dumpy dork's mangy cur would see any action for a long, long time. I would stop at nothing. I was going to the top. I was going to city hall!

"Really, I don't understand what got into him," he kind of snorted, by way of explanation.

I was no veterinarian, but maybe it was the fact that *he was a dog*—a *horny* dog.

Jen, as always, made nice. "Well, I guess no real harm was done."

"Usually he's much better behaved than this. You see, I changed careers a couple years back so that I'd have more time at home with the children; and Mr. Snippets really responded well to my presence. My business—I run a computer consulting company—allows me the flexibility to accommodate my wife's tight schedule."

Huh? Did this guy work that piece of information into every single conversation he had? Who freaking cared about them? The only reason I even knew about them at all was because of his incessant oral autobiography; without that, I wouldn't have spent two minutes thinking about his stinking job and his pudgy wife with the man's haircut.

Since it was too difficult to endure hearing him ramble on about himself, and damn near impossible to bear observing how nice Jen was being in response, as quickly as I could, I made my departure. Jen was still talking to Madras Man, cradling Irony in her arms and comforting her—although, truth be told, it looked to me as if Irony could have used a long smoke and a dry martini more than the kind of comfort she was receiving from Jen. Meanwhile, Richard was launching into some verbose explanation of dogs' sexual appetites, so I escaped before being detected and grilled about my express lane policies or my nursery school criteria, although I'm not really sure that Madras Richard even remembered me, anyway. Not that I'm so memorable, but he *was* pretty self-absorbed.

When I got back home, Andy and Robby were outside building a snowman out of the slushy, gravelly remains of the last storm. The "man" was shorter than Robby and grayer than the unemptied ashtrays of my senior year, but I gave the two of them a lot of credit for their attempt. I hated to interrupt them, but I needed Andy's take on my newfound mission. And I needed to know if he'd take on city hall with me. You see, in the ten-minute interval of the drive home, I'd started to reconsider my quest. Maybe it was just me being stupid, vindictive, petty, and immature. Of course, turning to a guy who, sitting Indian-style on a snow patch, was trying to pull a carrot out of a three-year-old's hand while whining, "I want to put the nose on—let me have the carrot," was probably not my best option in terms of gaining an objective perspective on maturity. Deep down, I guess, I must have wanted to be talked into going through with it.

"What?" was all he could respond after I told him what had happened. He was laughing so hard that he started to choke and cough, and his eyes began tearing, at which point Robby generously gave over the prized carrot under the assumption his beloved uncle was actually crying. "The dog did *what*? Did you get

to see the whole thing? Thanks, Roboto, but you can do it, okay? Hah, hah! Hey, did you see him put it in?" he asked.

"I didn't see him actually 'put it in,' but I saw him humping her and then trying to get himself off any way he could after we'd pulled them apart," I answered.

"What the hell, Annie?" he said, laughing all over again. "I was talking about Robby! Look, he put the carrot right in the hole we'd poked out for the nose. Good job, Roboto! My God, Annie, you are such a perv! And in front of your own son!"

Then, as was inevitable, Robby picked up this new word from his favorite uncle and started repeating it ad infinitum. "Perv! Perv! Perv!" My own son had taken to calling me "perv"—an epithet I hadn't even heard since seventh grade, when the lunch lady yelled out to the cook that I wanted a "wiener," and, unfortunately for me, the entire line of middle schoolers had heard.

"Robby, it's not nice to call people names," Andy reprimanded, albeit with a huge smirk on his face. "Especially your own mom. Say you're sorry."

"Why? What's a 'perv'?" Robby asked Andy innocently.

Andy had gotten me into this, so I figured I'd let him field this one.

"A perv is a person who . . . It's a girl who . . . Well, or a boy. It's a boy or a girl who . . ."

"A girl who what?" Robby asked, all innocence and curiosity.

"Well, um, it's a girl who likes to wrestle boys," Andy replied, wrapping up the matter hastily.

"Oh! Then my mommy *is* a perv! 'Cause once when I was just little, I was scared of the dark, and I went into Mommy and Daddy's room at night, and Mommy was on top of Daddy, and she told me she was wrestling him."

And with that, Andy erupted in laughter. He struggled to

get up, but the gales of laughter and muffled gasps for air made it difficult. His jeans were so soaked across his butt and lap that it looked as if he'd wet his pants.

"Andy, get serious," I said in my most I'm-an-adult-and-this-isn't-funny voice. "I need to know if you think I should go to the town hall and try to get a leash law on the books."

He stopped laughing for a brief moment and said, "Hell, no! And prevent me and everyone else from witnessing the joy of canine sex? Are you kidding? I've waited my whole life to see that—and now you're gonna ruin my chances? Screw that!"

"I want to see candy nine sex, too, Uncle Andy. Me, too! Skwew that! Skwew that, Mommy." What a delight. My son, securely on Andy's side, was not only calling me a perv and revealing private details of my conjugal life, but he was now also telling me to "screw that" and developing a penchant for candy porn. Rather than sobering Andy up, he simply started laughing all over again at Robby's new vocabulary. But he must have felt at least a little guilty about introducing such a little kid to the concept of procreation—or at least *rec*reation—because he backed down and agreed to help me in my civic duty.

Chapter Twenty-five

I had never embarked on anything quite like this before, so I didn't really know how to proceed. Thank God for Andy. The guy didn't know how to make chocolate milk (I'm not kidding—he had to ask Robby for help), but you could always count on him to possess the more obscure knowledge of life.

"Look, just call the town hall and ask who's in charge of city ordinances. Or pet control. Or leash laws. Whatever. They'll know who you want to talk to," he told me while downing the chocolate milk. He'd put so much Quik mix in the glass that it left a thick, sludgy brown stripe up the side of the glass and across the top of his lip. I swear, he was more of a three-year-old than Robby, but I took his advice and dialed.

"Hello; with whom may I speak regarding pet control and containment policies?" I asked the town clerk who'd answered.

I heard Andy chuckling over my shoulder and mimicking my "grown-up" syntax and diction. Then I heard Robby start in on me, too. Needless to say, I couldn't really hear the response over their giggles, but I was pretty sure she'd told me to see "two boys."

"Two boys?" I asked. "Which two boys? Are they on the town council or something?"

"Not *two boys*," said the voice on the other end, laughing.

"*Dubois*. Like dew-boys. D-U-B-O-I-S. She's the one you need to talk to. And she's in her office today until five o'clock. Come down to town hall, second floor, room 219, and see her. We have an open-door policy on Thursdays, so you can just walk in. Oh, and, ahh, good luck."

I didn't get the "good luck" comment, but I thought at the time she must have meant to wish me well on my quest to get back at Madras Richard. It didn't really sink in until much later that she didn't even know my name, let alone my personal vendettas against portly plaid-wearers. But I appreciated her sentiment, thanked her, and headed to town hall. I was actually getting pretty stoked up about it. In fact, the only wrinkle in the lap of my happiness was that we lived in a small suburban town, and somehow "taking on town hall" seemed to lack the same firepower as "taking on city hall." In spite of that, however, it still felt good to have a job to do. I was, I hate to admit, actually even a little bit nervous about it. I was afraid I'd forget her name, so I kept repeating it—*Dubois, Dubois, Dubois*—over and over again to myself on the way there, while Andy taught Robby all the different words for throwing up. And I don't know if they were doing it deliberately to calm me down or not, but it really did the trick; hearing my own three-year-old kid attempting to pronounce words like "porcelain" and "Technicolor" worked wonders for my nerves. By the time I pulled into the parking lot, I was feeling remarkably composed.

"Good luck, Annie! Go get 'em!" Andy laughed as he took Robby's hand and headed over to the playground in the school yard next door. "We'll meet you up there when we're done with the monkey bars." His use, by the way, of the plural "we" in his sentence was not just for Robby's benefit; I'd seen him on no fewer than seven different occasions swinging himself across those bars with his knees bent up in front of him so that his feet wouldn't drag on the ground underneath.

With the two of them gone, my jitters returned; but I had to go through with it. I just had to. I took a deep breath, swung open the glass door, and entered. All the office doors were open; they must have really taken that open-door policy literally, I thought to myself. After climbing the stairs (sixteen—I counted on the way up), I found Ms. Dubois' office. Doo-boyz office? Doo-boyz-ez office? I wondered which she'd prefer, so I opted for the safest route and left off the possessive altogether.

"Hello, Ms. Dubois?" I asked as I tapped on the open door and stepped timidly into her office. She was wearing a pink suit with thick black piping and a full set of bulbous pearls around her neck.

"That's 'Doo-*bwa*,'" she snapped at me without raising her eyes from the tidy pile of papers on her mahogany desk. "Doo-*bwa*! Why can't anyone say it properly?" she asked the stack of papers in front of her. And shaking her head with disgust and annoyance, she slowly lifted her eyes to give me a rather obvious once-over. I felt a little underdressed in my black maternity pants and oversized charcoal turtleneck; but what the hell? I was hardly expecting Coco Chanel to be holding court at my local town hall.

"Well," she began, "what do you wish to speak to me about? I have only a few minutes—I'm catching a flight in the morning and have to leave work early today." And with that, she rose from her burgundy leather chair, turned her back to me, and started to file some papers in a tall cabinet.

It was remarkable—astounding, really—the lightning-flash speed with which I realized I hated her. She was not only witheringly rude, but she was younger than I was, better dressed than

I was, had a bigger office than I'd had, and—what really pissed me off—she had a smaller ass than I had—or ever did have. But, ironically, my courage seemed to rise with her attempt to squash me, so I continued on.

"I'm here to inquire about leash laws and pet control ordinances. Does the town currently have a leash law? Because just a few hours ago, a dog was assaulted by another dog at the—"

"No." She cut me off. "There is no formal leash law. It was discussed several months ago at a town meeting, but no one seemed to want it—or even care about it, for that matter—so we dropped it. Is that all?" Without so much as turning her head, she was dismissing me. It was cheerleading tryouts all over again, and here was Heather Williams rolling her eyes at my cartwheel/round-off combination.

"Well, I'd like to propose that we enact some kind of formal containment policy; I don't want another dog to have to suffer what happened today. And, to be honest, it was pretty gross for the people who had to see it, too. What do you think? Will you do it?" I asked, trying to be as direct and efficient as possible.

"Look, I'm on my way out. And I don't think I would be able to help you, anyway. People just don't seem to care about laws governing pets. Frankly, they have better things to think about."

No kidding—she really said that to me, as if I had nothing in my life to concern me other than inconveniencing busy town employees with trivial issues of domesticated animals. Even though that may have been the case, it was still kind of rude, you have to admit.

"Ms. Doo-*bwaah*," I responded, heavy on the "proper" accent. "It's not only distasteful to see two dogs doing it in a public park, but there are health issues and safety factors to consider as well. I assume the town doesn't want to be sued if and when some little kid sucking on a lollipop gets run down by a pack of leash-free canine delinquents. So, please, give it some thought."

Overall, I was fairly pleased with my closing argument.

"That scenario is *highly* improbable. I really don't believe anyone is going to *sue* the town over some *leash* law," she said without so much as an attempt to veil her contempt for me.

With that, she began packing some folders into the gorgeous leather briefcase lying on her desk—all but telling me to beat it. The briefcase was positioned precariously on the front left corner, and with each new folder she added, the chances of it remaining on top of the desk seemed to diminish. And, surely enough, as was inevitable, it happened. Crash. Bang. The briefcase tumbled gracelessly to the floor, unfashionably spilling its contents as it fell. I started to laugh, but she seemed so upset that I checked myself and knelt down to help her reassemble the order. I grabbed randomly at the toppled papers and pamphlets and anything I could get my hands on, and, seeing a book that had fallen under the desk, I reached under and retrieved it.

And lo and behold, there in my hand was none other than a tattered copy of *Dumped and Desperate: A Single Woman's Guide to Getting Her Man*. And it was brimming over with printouts from Match.com and eHarmony.com. That poor little paperback was nearly bursting with online dating service résumés.

"I'll take that, thank you very much," she said, stuffing it quickly and unceremoniously in her briefcase. "And I can do this myself. Thank you for stopping by," she finished curtly. Then she stood up—presumably to make sure I would leave that very instant.

Hah! So Little Miss Perfect—Ms. Doo-*bwa*—was on the prowl for some unsuspecting SWM, nonsmoker, twenties or early thirties, no pets, professional a must, looking for long-term commitment only. Hah, hah, hah. I had my very own husband, and here she was, struggling even to get a date! And as I looked at her, standing in front of me with her good haircut and her bad attitude, her ass grew three sizes under that Chanel skirt.

Feeling something akin to triumph but knowing I hadn't completely satisfied my quest, I kept my equanimity, thanked her for her time, and turned to leave; however, just as I stepped out of her door, Robby and Andy appeared at the other end of the hall, covered from the hips down in thick playground mud. I tried to play it cool—you know, look straight ahead, keep on walking, and pretend you don't see anyone in your peripheral vision kind of thing. Granted, that works only when you're in, for instance, eighth grade, and John Berg, of the feathered blond hair and Adidas Sambas, walks past you and Theresa Silvestri; ignores you in spite of your overly nervous and loud giggling; and succeeds in making you die of shame and lust for the rest of the semester in Mr. Quarlton's history class where he sits behind you and continues to take absolutely no notice of you whatsoever. And so ended my suave, in-control getaway.

Smooth exits have never been my forte, anyway; I always end up forgetting my purse and having to slink back in, or slamming my coat in the door, or tripping over some invisible obstacle or something. Growing up on a steady diet of soap operas— daytime, as well as the mandatory *Melrose Place* and *Beverly Hills, 90210*—I had full faith in the one hundred percent success rate of the dramatic final exit; real life, though, made no such guarantees. And here, once again, I was being offered proof of that.

Rather than fight the inevitable any longer, I simply scooped up a very muddy Robby and listened while he regaled me with his little-kid ecstasies of adventure and filth with his best buddy, Andy—a real live grown-up, willing to play in the mud alongside him.

"Oh, Mommy, it was awesome," he squealed with delight, using what was clearly a new word straight from Andy's lexicon. "Uncle Andy did the slide with me. At the same time!" He was so excited to share the news of Andy's participation that he cupped my cheeks in his red-and-blue-mittened hands to make sure I heard every word. He had actual tears in his eyes as he laughed and squirmed in my arms.

"Yeah, Annie, it was awesome! You should have come! I can't remember the last time I was on a slide that good," Andy added. I wondered briefly how many slides he must have been on recently in order to have the basis for comparison. Probably a fair number, was my conclusion.

"Can we come back later? Do we have to go home now? I really, really want to stay so bad," pleaded Robby.

And just as I was starting to shake off my irritation with the SWF in the office behind us, she appeared in her doorway, looking very disapprovingly at the scene.

"Ahh, excuse me, but this building will be closing in half an hour. And as I mentioned, I'm on my way out now. So, if you would, please . . . ," she said, sort of glancing-nodding toward the stairwell where, presumably, she wanted us to go.

"We're on our way," I said, trying to remain somewhat civil. It was tough, though; I really wanted to bite her, or have her dog get humped in front of her. So, I put Robby down, took his hand, and marched off down the hallway, down the sixteen stairs, and out the doors to the parking lot. Only once we were outside in the fading sun of the approaching evening did I realize that Andy was nowhere to be found.

"Mommy? Where's Uncle Andy?" Robby asked timidly, more than a little afraid of having lost his prized relative the way he'd lost the Matchbox Mercedes I'd bought him at the Shop 'n Save last week. Fleetingly, the image of Aunt Esmeralda and her erratic disappearing and reappearing crossed my memory. I kind of thought I knew what Samantha must have felt at those times.

"I guess he's back inside. Let's go find him," I said calmly; but in actuality I was panicked to think what havoc he could be wreaking in front of my fellow townspeople. And even though I hadn't made much (any) headway with the *Dumped and Desperate* SWF, I feared to think of how my Get-Even-with-Madras-Richard campaign would be jeopardized if Andy had tried to be friendly to the Great Mizz Doo-*bwa*. So we quickly retraced our steps back inside and up the sixteen stairs to locate and reclaim our Andy.

As we reached the top of the stairs, I heard his voice floating down the hall from one of the many open doorways. He was laughing and speaking in his loud, kind of husky drawl, and every so often a female's high-pitched giggle punctuated the conversation. I didn't want to interrupt (that's a lie), but I did want to find out whom he was talking to, so I kept on walking, glancing in at the open doors as I passed them. Slowly but surely, I was drawing nearer and nearer to the dreaded room 219, and his voice was getting clearer and clearer. No, he wouldn't. He shouldn't! He *couldn't*.

He did. Sure enough, as I looked into Dubois' office, there was Andy—leaning cavalierly against the windowsill, while Dubois sat flirtatiously on the edge of her desk, crossing and recrossing her legs and flipping her freshly cut hair first behind her shoulder, then in front, then again behind. He looked up when we walked past.

"Annie! Annie, I'm coming! Hey, Mr. Roboto, wait up," he shouted. Even while smoothing this ice queen, he was the same old Andy he always was—no pretense, no games, just being himself in his muddy (now crusty) jeans and scruffy hair, and yelling out to my three-year-old as if they were total peers. I forgave his betrayal on the spot.

"So, I guess I'll see you later tonight, then," Andy said to SWF as he headed toward her door.

"Okay." She beamed in return. She pronounced it like uh-*kayyy*. "I'll see you, then. Can't wait," she ticked out gleefully. She even added a giddy "G'-bye" to me and Robby as well. What was with her? Two minutes before, she'd been stiff, curt, and bitchy; now, after a few short words with Andy, the girl was as loose as change. If I'd known all it took was a suitor to woo her into a more pleasant and malleable mood, I'd have tried hitting on her myself. That was how badly I would have worked to avenge myself of Madras Richard. But having Andy do the job for me made my work all the easier. Though I have to add that I was more than a little worried for Andy's sake.

Once in the car, I asked in my most mature, motherly, concerned voice, "Are you freakin' crazy? What are you thinking?"

"What?" he answered casually.

"Do you or do you not have a date with that woman?"

"Well, yeah." He grinned goofily. "Can you believe someone like her is *available*?"

Ahh, in a word, yes. I could. I'd seen the proof. But I kept my mouth shut and instead asked, "Do you mind my asking, why her?"

"I thought she was hot. And it turns out, she's pretty cool, too," he answered, still smiling.

"Leave her temperature out of this. And please—just tell me you're not doing this for me and my Burn Richard campaign." I knew it sounded egomaniacal, and I didn't mean it to, but I just had to make sure he wasn't taking one—especially one this big— for the Forster team.

"Annie, it may surprise you, but some people in the world make decisions without consulting with or thinking about you first," he said, grinning at me.

"I know. And I know you have way better things to think about than me and my stupid dog-sex laws, but I just had to ask. Forgive me?"

"Under one condition," he said, pretending to be serious. "Can I borrow your car tonight?"

I had to trust that he knew what he was doing, and I said yes.

Well, to cut to the chase, a week later when Jen and I went back to the park, there was a huge yellow and black sign at the entrance to the park:

REQUIRED:
LEASHES FOR ALL DOGS
Town Ordinance #PC16427A.

So I'm guessing they must have hit it off.

Chapter Twenty-six

*H*aving had Andy around had not only been a nonstop carnival for Robby and welcome comic relief for me, but it had gone a long way toward helping Alex feel more optimistic about his life's pattern as well. Something about a wayward, independently wealthy nomad in search of good times and new friends can do a surprising lot for a suburban out-of-work lawyer, and Alex was not one to pass up this fine offering.

In fact, one night toward the end of Andy's stay, I heard the two of them at the kitchen table after dinner with what must have been a bottle of something alcoholic between them. I was putting Robby to bed, but I couldn't help catching bits of their conversation as it drifted up the stairs.

"You're so lucky, man," said Andy's voice.

"Huh? What are you talking about, dude?" It was Alex's voice. Of course, I could only evaluate this on pitch and tone, rather than diction and usage, as the word "dude" did not typically figure into the conversations of my middle-aged, nonsurfing husband.

"You, man," continued Andy. Followed by a *whump* of bottle (I guessed) hitting the table. "I mean, look at this. Look at all this."

"Yeah, right," Alex answered. A *whump* sounded again; this time a little more gently. "Just what I always wanted—to be an unemployed loser with a wife and two kids I can't afford."

"Don't be a dick, bro." It was Andy's voice, sterner and louder; no *whump* this time. "Don't you get it? Don't you see?"

"See what? House payments? Taxes? A shitty job that I didn't even like in the first place—and now I don't even have that? Exactly what am I supposed to see here, bro?"

I never knew Alex felt that way. I had never known he hadn't liked his job. I strained to hear more, fearing that what he shared with Andy would be stuff that I should know, but never *would know* if it was left to Alex to share it with me directly. That he knew I was in the house, just up the stairs, gave me the license and the resolve to continue listening without feeling sneaky about it. I couldn't have eavesdropped on such a conversation, but I could, with impunity, sit on my son's bed as he fell asleep and listen.

"You're such an asshole, Alex," Andy said, accompanied by the *whump* of the bottle. "You've got Robby, who's, like, the best kid I've ever even seen in my whole life. I'd kill to have a kid one-quarter as good. And you have Annie, who's about the coolest wife in the universe and still manages to look like that hot older sister in that show we used to watch on Wednesdays when we were kids."

"I know," Alex said in a softer tone. "I've told her that, but she thinks it's not true."

"Well, she's wrong. But that's beside the point. The point is, you have the two of them, and I have, like, jack. So screw you if you start feeling all sorry for yourself, you asshole. Because I don't; I don't feel sorry for you for one freakin' minute. From where I stand, you have a pretty freakin' great setup here."

"Andy, I have no job. *No job.* And unlike you, some of us actually have to work to pay for stuff. Like food. Clothing. Shelter."

"If you need money, bro . . ."

Whump. "Screw you, man." Alex raised his voice to a distinctly un-Alex-like level.

"Fine, I'll shut the hell up. But seriously, man, you should know how lucky you are to have what you have. Don't shit it away because one part of it—the least important part—isn't going your way. So freakin' what if your job situation sucks? Change it, then. Do something different. Whatever. But don't lose sight of the fact that your life is pretty freakin' awesome. Especially for a loser like you who had to be Aquaman, like, eight years in a row for Halloween just because you freakin' had blond hair."

"Beat the shit out of Peter Pan," Alex replied, slurring his vowels just slightly enough that I knew full-fledged drunkenness was not far off.

"That was one year! And I was, like, four," Andy scoffed. "You were Aquaman until you, like, went off to college."

"At least Aquaman could kick Peter Pan's ass," Alex offered with an uncharacteristic swagger.

"Yeah, but I was Rambo when I was ten. Who could kick whose ass then, huh? Aquaman would be squashed like a freakin' minnow by Rambo. 'Member that gun Mom let me have?"

"I was, like, in high school by then, but I was still jealous of that gun. Where is it now? That was an awesome weapon."

"I still have it in my stuff at Mom's. Want it? Want to give it to Robby?"

"I think Annie'd kill me first," good old Alex replied.

"Good woman, that," Andy said. A *whump* followed.

"I know. That's why I feel so shitty about all this. I don't want to let her down."

"Dude, you see the way she looks at you? She looks at you as if you're a freakin' superhero—and not a shitty little Aquaman, but a real superhero. Superman or Spider-Man or Iron Man. One of the good ones."

"Really?"

"Really?" Andy said, mimicking Alex. "Yes, really, you loser. You don't deserve her, but you got her, so don't screw it up, bro."

"I know. That's why I have to get my job back. Get the house back in order. Get everything in line before this baby comes."

"Dude, I don't want to be a downer, but what happens if your job doesn't *come* back? And even if it does, do you really want it to?"

"I don't know, man," Alex answered, with a soft *whump* to follow. "I don't know. I don't know if I want to go back. Hoffman, Berg was okay, but, man, being home has shown me that there's more out there. There's, I don't know, there's just more out there. You know?"

"Freakin' kidding me? Yuh, I think I know that. It's what I've been running all over the world for—to find what you have right here. Right freaking here. A job's just a job, but your family, man . . . ? That's the main thing."

"When'd you get so deep, loser?" Alex teased.

"Not deep, just right," Andy replied. "Now give me that and quit Bogarting."

I heard the sound of the bottle being slid across the table, then *whump*—a loud one.

"So, what's the answer, genius boy?" Alex slurred in a louder-than-usual voice.

"Don't know. Would you even listen if I did know?"

"Probably not," Alex replied, firmly planted in the nonsober garden by this point.

"Do what's going to make you happy. You and your family. That's what matters," Andy proffered, sounding sane, rational, and very undrunk, comparatively.

"What I want is to see my freakin' kids. I don't want to miss everything that happens to them during the day. You know, I didn't even know until I was laid off that Robby's favorite color was dark gray. Dark gray, dude. You know how cool that is? And you know why? He said because it was the color of the inside of my car and Iron Man's first suit."

"That rocks, bro. That's the shit," Andy concurred.

I didn't know that, and I'd been home with Robby every day of his whole life. Since when did any offspring of mine cultivate such an artist's eye for hue, shade, and tone? I thought kids fell into one of two groups: those who liked pink best, and those who liked blue best. Maybe a red or an occasional yellow to mix things up a bit, but dark gray? That was only marginally less weird than a preference for magenta or that shade of green in all the Frances books that I grew up calling, inexplicably, Winnie-the-Pooh green. Still, it was pretty interesting information to have at hand.

"But how can I do both? I can't. I can't work and be home, dude. So, I have to be a man and quit waiting around for something to happen that isn't going to happen."

"You tell Annie any of this?" Andy asked reasonably.

"Naw, man. Didn't even know I was thinking it until right now. Never really thought about it all, about my job or whether I liked it. I just did it, and it wasn't so bad, so I kept on doing it."

"So, that's why now you should try and do something different. Do something you like better."

"Shuh, right. Why don't I be a baseball player? Oh, wait, no, a rock star. That's what I'll be. How's that sound?"

"Except that you sucked at the guitar. I remember Jimmy

Hogarty coming over, and we listened to you in the basement with Mike What's-his-face from up the street and that fat kid, Kevin. You guys totally thought you rocked, but you sucked."

"You're so full of shit—you and Jimmy actually paid us five bucks to come in and listen. If Mom hadn't made us give it back to you, we could have charged you and all your little asshole friends to hear us. We kicked ass with 'Smoke on the Water'; that's how good we were."

Who was this man, I recall asking myself at this point. And why was I partaking in child rearing with him?

"You blew. So you'd better have a plan B in that guitar case of yours, asshole," Andy said, laughing.

"Okay, okay," continued Alex, undaunted. "I'll be an astronaut. How about that?"

"No, I was the astronaut. For, like, ten years, I wanted to be that. You can't steal it now."

"Cowboy? Inventor? I mean, if I'm gonna change careers, I may as well go for the gold, right? Oh, what about Olympic shot-putter?"

"No, hurling. Even, like, eighty-year-olds can do that. It's basically shuffleboard on ice."

"No, it's curling."

"Hurling, dude."

"Curling, trust me."

"Whatever the shitty sport's called, do that. You're old, but you may still have a season or two in you to compete."

"How d'ya train for that? Think those guys actually have to work out?"

"Pshyeah, right. It's like a steady diet of organ meats, beer, and potatoes, then straight to bed after a couple of smokes and a *Matlock* rerun."

"Then maybe I *could* do it," Alex said, far too contemplatively for my peace of mind.

"Keep hope alive, bro. Keep hope alive. But for real, what do you want to do?"

"For real?" Alex answered. "I don't know. Law is the only thing I know, and, to be honest, I do it pretty well. I don't have any idea what else I could do."

"Dude, I'm about to pass out right here in this chair, so I'm going to take myself upstairs before your wife finds me in a pool of my own saliva. But, in closing, may I just say that you should give some serious thought to what you can do to get yourself back on track at this junction."

"At this *juncture*, you freakin' idiot," Alex interrupted.

"Right. At this junction, you need to decide what's right for you."

"Juncture. It's *juncture*. At this juncture," Alex corrected, ever the big brother.

"Juncture, junction. Whatev, bro. 'Conjunction junction, what's your function?'" Andy began singing as the scrape of chair legs signified his removal from the table. "'Hookin' up words and phrases and clauses . . .'"

When Alex entered our bedroom, where I'd taken up shelter after tucking in Robby, he was humming the "Conjunction Junction" song and walking on his tippy toes—two signs, if ever there were, that he was both drunk and happy. I didn't want to pry, and I was entirely unsure of the coherence of any response I'd get, so I didn't ask anything about his conversation with Andy. I figured he'd share what he wanted with me when he was ready. Instead, I just cuddled up to him in bed.

"What's the one about adverbs?" he asked me, apropos of the humming, which he knew I'd recognize.

"'Lolly, Lolly, Lolly, get your adverbs here; Lolly, Lolly, Lolly, get your adverbs here . . . ,'" I replied. I was always a sucker for the *Schoolhouse Rock* jingles.

"Oh, yeah. Well, I have an 'Interjection!' for you here," he whispered. "*Hey!* I love you!"

"Aw, I love you, too," I countered with one of the interjections from the jingle.

"I was talking with Andy," Alex said, still slurring as he spoke into my hair.

"Anything good?" I asked, noncommittally.

"I'm gonna be a rock star when I grow up," he said.

"That's nice, honey," I answered as he fell into the deep and still sleep of the drunken.

But I knew, as I lay there with his arm draped across me and his nose buried in my hair, that he wasn't the only one who was going to have to start thinking about our future. I was going to have to make some decisions, too. After all, he wasn't alone in this. I was his conjunction junction, wasn't I? As I drifted off to sleep, I recalled the closing bars of that fine song: "Conjunction Junction, what's your function? I'm going to get you there if you're very careful." Was there no question too great for Saturday morning cartoons?

Chapter Twenty-seven

With Andy gone but his late-night conversation with Alex still looming large in my mind, I couldn't help but contemplate the shape and form of my life. Their discussion, along with my little victory at city (ahem, town) hall, really got me thinking about the future. Alex was on his way to figuring out what he wanted; now I had to figure the same for myself. I was almost ashamed to admit just how long it had been since I'd done anything that had an impact beyond my own front door—a good three years, at least. And seeing that leash law posted up there for all to obey—including (especially) Madras Richard—made me feel as if I'd really accomplished something. I know, I know; it was small, and it probably had nothing to do with me, anyway, given that Mizz Doo-*bwa* was trying to reel in my brother-in-law; but I don't have too much dignity to prevent me from taking credit for it, anyway. I'm hardly an activist, so I had to look for my triumphs wherever I could find them. I mean, I'm not really very socially conscious and, to be honest, I don't really care as much as I should about saving trees or boycotting animal products or banning anything that makes my life more convenient or comfortable in any way. Although, to be more accurate, it's not so much that I don't care as much as I should, as much as that I don't care to investigate whether I should care more than I do—if that makes sense. Because I don't want to be thought of as some evil, greedy, selfish person. Because I'm definitely not evil. Or greedy, for that matter. For all I know, there may really be an activist hidden somewhere deep down inside me just waiting to expose all the social injustices on the planet. It's just that I kind of hope this hidden activist doesn't emerge while I'm out to dinner or sleeping or watching a really good sitcom—you know, that kind of thing.

So, having "spearheaded the grassroots movement for the protection and enjoyment of park denizens" (that was how I imagined it would read on my next résumé), I felt a surge of excitement. I mean, I evened the score with Madras Richard, ensured the chastity of generations of dogs to come, and, what the hell, I even set up "Dumped and Desperate" Dubois with my brother-in-law. That wasn't, I know, so much my doing as the chance hand of fate and hormones, but I'm okay with that, too. And, though it was now more than a month later, she and Andy were still going strong. Once Aimee (that, my friends, if you can believe it, was not only Ms. Dubois' first name but how she *spelled* it as well) returned from her weekend away, they were inseparable until Andy went to Calcutta. (Note: He was mistaken about both Kathmandu *and* Macao.) Even this Calcutta trip he'd delayed by a week so he could keep seeing her.

But, as his postcards assured us, he was due back in a few weeks; at which time, he indicated, he'd be staying with Aimee for a while. This he underlined and followed with a drawing of a mini smiley face and six exclamation marks. Of course, the real irony was that, once paired up with a guy as genuinely likeable and low-key as Andy, Aimee had become infinitely more likeable and low-key herself. In fact, she became pretty all-around decent. She even taught Robby how to do "Miss Mary Mack" when I couldn't remember it. And she never cared about Andy's money; she made him return a pair of diamond earrings he'd bought her before leaving; and when he replaced them with a simple kite and a bubble-blowing kit with a huge ring to blow giant bubbles, she seemed really happy. Then they took them to the park with Robby and me, and we took turns posing for photos in front of "our" new sign. No kidding, it was actually a lot of fun. Maybe it was just sexual frustration and dealing with all those dog issues that had made her act kind of like a bitch before.

As I entered my third trimester, I was fully and assuredly out of the danger zone of the is-she-or-isn't-she phase. Everyone felt free to ask when I was due, and some even reached out to touch me. Seriously. People who six months earlier would no sooner have spit on me were now extending their hands to my midregion as if those hands were plants growing toward the sun. And, like the sun, I seemed to possess the power of making things grow—namely, the forty-pound baby I was carrying and myself. And grow we did. Although I had almost three months left until Baby Number Two came, I was weighing in at forty-four pounds over where I'd begun. The surprising thing was that it didn't seem to bug me quite as much as I would have thought—or as much as it did my mother.

Her phone calls, bidaily now, were a constant monitoring device on my appetite and willpower. These were inversely proportional, by the way, like intelligence and Keanu Reeves appreciation; or humor and fame in comedians—you can have one or the other; you just can't have both. My dear mother had now even taken to dispensing with the formal "hellos" and "how are yous" and went right for the jugular. Or the esophagus, I guess, would be a more apt metaphor.

"Did you make sure to skip the bread and just eat the baked chicken, as I told you?"

"Yes, Mom."

"Now, if you're drinking all that fruit juice, you're going to have to make up for those extra calories somewhere. Fruit juice is loaded with every kind of sugar, you know."

"Yes, Mom."

"And you're exercising daily, right, honey?"

"Yes, Mom."

"The doctor is aware of how you're growing and developing?"

"Yes, Mom."

"Hey, what's that crunching? *Are you eating something right now?*"

"Yes, Mom."

You get the idea, I'm sure. The thing that bugged me most, though, wasn't the daily weigh-ins, but the constant ringing of the phone. If she'd e-mailed, or sent telegrams, or even yelled it really, really loudly all the way from South Carolina, I could have endured it with equanimity. If she'd spontaneously appeared in my kitchen, wearing cat-eye makeup and a lavender and lime green cape after casting a spell on my husband and calling him Derwood, it would have been less unsettling. It was the phone itself that drove me crazy.

So, while I was getting Robby ready for school one really cold morning in February, the phone rang at the usual a.m. check-in time. Irritated at her already because I knew she would make me confess to having had three waffles that morning, I snatched up the phone, ready to do battle.

"Hello?"

"Annie, it's Michael. Gee, I'm guessing from your tone that you're not a morning person?"

"Oh, sorry," I said in a flood of relief, "I thought I was going to have to atone for eating three waffles."

"*Three?* Come on, Annie. You'll never get back your tight butt if you keep eating like that. Did you use syrup and butter?"

"Just syrup."

"Well, I guess that's marginally better than both, but really! Haven't you heard of, like, an apple or fat-free yogurt? You're really gonna pork up if you don't cut it out."

"Oh my God, you're even worse than my mother. I wish she *had* called; at least she doesn't make references to my butt. Well, very often. So, to change the subject, what do *you* want?"

"A favor."

"No, I mean for breakfast."

"Oh, I never eat breakfast. But I guess an egg white omelet with shitakes and pancetta would be all right."

"Sounds good. What is it?"

"They're mushrooms, you idiot. And Italian uncured bacon."

"The *favor*, Michael. I'm talking about the favor. Do you really think I don't know what pretentious fungi and twenty-dollar-a-pound ham are?"

"Tee-hee. But, look, the reason I called is . . . Well, you know what a good guy Lucas is, right?"

"Of course. He's not only nice, but did you ever notice how much he looks like a cross between a young Harrison Ford and that guy from the body spray commercial?"

"Yeah, but it's not Harrison Ford; it's Kurt Russell."

"Hey, you know, you're right! He does kind of look like Kurt Russell. From *Jagged Edge* days."

"That's Jeff Bridges."

"Oh. Then *Baker Boys* days."

"Bridges, again. Do you even know who Kurt Russell is?"

"Uh, *Gladiator?*"

"Annie, that is Russell Crowe. Will you please get out and see a movie every decade. Or at least read *In Style* more often. He's the one with Goldie Hawn."

"Ohhh, yeah!" It dawned on me. *Tequila Sunrise* and some Western or other. Usually I'm not this bad; I mean, paying attention to Hollywood and watching E! Entertainment Television are just about the only hobbies I have. But, to defend myself, he's not really all that memorable as an actor. Although to look at him—another story entirely.

"He's getting sued," Michael said matter-of-factly.

"By Goldie Hawn?"

"Lucas, you idiot!"

"Lucas is suing Kurt Russell?" Really, that made no sense.

"Annie, you are too much," he said, laughing at me. "*Lucas* is getting sued. And before you say anything—no, it's not by Kurt Russell."

I was glad he saved me the embarrassment—because that was exactly what I was thinking. Maybe for copyright infringement on his trademark face or something. I hadn't gotten as far as the reason.

"Michael, that is totally unfair. I did not for a minute think Kurt Russell was suing Lucas. They don't even know each other, do they?"

"No. Now, can we please end the whole Kurt Russell thing?"

"Of course. Tell me about Lucas. Who's suing him? And for what? Does he have a lawyer yet?"

"Well, you won't believe this, but he's getting sued for donating a ton of playground equipment to the Busy Bee Montessori. Annie, you've got to help us. Can you come over ASAP to discuss it with us? Oh, and in case you don't know, 'ASAP' means, like, *now*."

Even when asking for favors, he couldn't resist ridiculing me. You had to respect that kind of integrity.

"Tee-hee. And yes, of course I'll come. In spite of your sarcasm. Let me just ask Alex to drop Robby off at the co-op, and then I'll be right over. My *ETA* is approximately nine thirty," I added smugly—you know, quid pro quo and all that. "Oh, and in case you don't know, 'ETA' means 'Exact Time of Arrival,' " I added in a superior-than-thou tone of voice.

"You really are such a moron, Annie. 'ETA' means '*Estimated* Time of Arrival.' So you really don't need to say your ETA is 'approximately' anything." He was laughing so hard, he choked on his own "Good-bye."

Damn, once again, I'd been burned by those stupid acronyms. Or were they just initials? If it didn't spell out a real word, could you call it an acronym? Well, whatever the answer was, I resolved, let me assure you, to avoid abbreviations of all varieties when speaking to Michael in the future.

But, as I kissed Alex and Robby good-bye and got into my car, I had a feeling of purpose and fulfillment I hadn't had since the town hall episode, and I recognized it immediately as a very satisfying feeling indeed. I had no idea what I could possibly offer to the situation, but I was eager to find out.

Chapter Twenty-eight

So, off I went, moving as quickly as possible (not quickly at all) and, just over forty-five minutes later, I pulled into Michael's condo's parking lot with a TA of exactly 9:37 a.m. In spite of his merciless teasing, I could tell Michael was truly worried about Lucas, so I was glad I made it there in such good time. His door was opened promptly by Lucas, who, though I'd spent an entire day with him a few weeks back, was even better looking than I'd originally thought. And he did look like Kurt Russell. I think. Or else, maybe like the guy in *Dirty Dancing*.

"Hi, Annie," he said softly, stepping back out of the doorway so I could enter. "I guess Michael told you I'm getting sued. I'm really glad you could come over."

"Hi, Lucas. It's really nice to see you again. I'm just sorry it's under these conditions," I said as we shook hands and kissed cheeks. His hand, like his voice, was dry and soft; a good hand. And though I wasn't sure, his cheek felt a little damp, as though maybe he'd been crying before I'd gotten there. Once again, I made a mental note to tell Michael how happy I was that he'd found someone like Lucas.

"Annie, is that you?" Michael yelled from the kitchen. "I'll be right there. I'm making herbal tea and coffee cake—not that you need it. Go sit in the living room."

So, we went and sat in the corner of Michael's huge beige chenille sectional and began discussing Lucas' problem.

"Well, the thing is this," he answered, after I asked him to explain the situation. "I had a nephew who went to the Busy Bee Montessori a year ago, and this coming fall, his little sister, my niece, Alexa, will be starting there. So, I thought it would be, well, nice"—he shyly looked down at his lap—"to give the school something. I mean, I don't have any kids of my own, but Alexa and Jeremy seem about as close to it as you can get. So, I looked into it and talked with the teachers, and everyone at the Busy Bee thought it would be a good thing for the kids to have playground equipment. You know, a climber, jungle gym, swings, sandbox. That kind of thing. So I ordered it all back when Jeremy was still going there—back in November, a year and a half ago."

"Wow, I can't believe you did all that! It was so great of you. So generous. The Busy Bee sure is lucky," I replied. Really, Lucas was turning out to be even nicer than he was great-looking. And, I thought to myself, I bet Kurt Russell or Jeff Bridges, or whoever it was, would be an absolute a-hole in comparison.

"Well, I was really doing it for my niece and nephew. It was selfish of me, really," he said with total and humble sincerity. "Anyhow," he continued, "some of the stuff was available immediately—the sandbox and the jungle gym. But the tree house, swings, and climber section were sold out and back-ordered for a year. They weren't going to be available until this past November. I told them I still wanted the whole thing, but to deliver the available stuff to my house instead of the school, and after all the pieces were ready, then we'd deliver it all in one piece to the Busy Bee. That way my niece and nephew could play with it in my backyard while we waited."

"And did they do it?" I asked.

"Oh yeah," he answered. "The company who made the stuff was really cool. They even said they'd relocate it from my house to the school for free because of the delay. So, in, like, early January last year, the sandbox and gym were delivered to my house. No problem. Alexa and Jeremy loved them and played with them all spring and summer. Then, finally, this November, the rest of the stuff became available; KiddieCare came and picked up the sandbox and jungle gym that had been at my house, and everything was delivered and assembled at the school in one piece, just as promised. And for about two weeks, everything seemed fine; but then the parent of one of the kids started complaining. The teachers, Miss Kerry and Miss Barbara, told me not to worry, that they loved the stuff and that the kids did, too. But still, this guy kept on complaining."

"About what? Was it misassembled or something?"

"No. I made sure of that. I'd even hired an independent inspector to come and double-check everything. There was no problem there. It was just that . . ."

"What?" I asked. He seemed to be embarrassed about continuing.

"Well, I guess the sand in the sandbox is from some protected wetlands not far from here. I'm not really sure about the details; but that's why he's suing me."

Michael appeared in the doorway. "Can you freakin' believe that!?! What nerve that asshole must have. Annie, you're a lawyer—you've got to help us. This is ridiculous. No one can sue you for doing a good deed, can they?"

"Michael, I haven't practiced law in more than three years.

But in my experience, a person can sue any*one* for any*thing* as long as they're willing to go to court. This case, though, sounds unbelievable. Can you tell me the rest?"

"Okay, well, for a while, I heard nothing about it, so I started thinking it was a done deal—you know, he'd forgiven me—"

"Forgiven!?! For what? Giving his friggin' brats a playground to play on? Screw him!" Michael interjected. I could tell he felt as protective of Lucas as I was starting to.

"Well, forgiven or whatever," Lucas responded, looking gratefully at Michael for those protective instincts. "But, then, out of nowhere, I get *this*—registered mail!" He handed me a thick document containing what I knew would be the legal restrictions, ordinances, and procedures.

"You're the best lawyer we know, Annie; you have to take his case," Michael added as he put down the tray he'd brought in from the kitchen.

"Look, I don't know. . . . I mean, I haven't worked in so long; I don't know if I'm your best bet. I'll talk to David Ferber at Walker, Cain, and Finch—that's my old firm; I'm sure someone there could help you a whole lot more than I could. And, by the way, Michael, you don't know any other lawyers."

"Well, that may be the case, but we still want you! Plus, the whole pregnancy thing is bound to work in our favor if we have to go to court," Michael said, smirking. "I've watched enough *Law & Order* to know how juries dig pregnant chicks."

"Guys, you know I want to help you out, but I'm just not sure I'd be any good at it. Who's the guy suing you?" I asked them as Michael flipped through the disorganized documents to find the plaintiff's name. "I mean, it's been more than three years, guys; I'm afraid I'd be out of the loop. Really, this isn't even my field of expertise; I used to practice—"

"Alan Lippincott," Michael yelled out as soon as he'd found it.

"I'll do it," I said immediately.

It may not have been rational or sane; it may not have been the best reason or the soundest logic; but, by God, fueled with the seething hatred I'd harbored for Lippie the Hippie ever since that Labor Day on the beach, I knew I'd give more to this case than any other lawyer they could possibly hire. Hell, I was the Jack McCoy of Hate-Lippie law. I didn't just want to see him go down; I *needed* to see him go down. Lippie the Freakin' Hippie—of all people! I should have guessed—who else would have the nerve or the cash to trump up this kind of lawsuit?

Oh, I'd be taking this case.

Later that night, when I told Alex about it, he nearly died of the shock.

"Annie, I don't think you understand just how critical it is that you win this thing," he said after he was able to speak again.

"What do you mean? Because I haven't practiced in three years, all my colleagues will be watching me—and judging? Or because it's so important to Michael and Lucas? Or because of the social statement it would make to those considering bringing nuisance lawsuits against people doing good deeds?"

"No!" he said emphatically. "Because I hate that guy!"

I burst out laughing. Only Alex could do that to me. I had been feeling mounting stress about agreeing to take the case, and within two seconds of talking to Alex, I felt total relief. Of course, knowing I'd be doing this for Team Forster added a little anxiety to my return to the professional world, but it still felt pretty good to be going back to work—even just for this brief time—with the full support of my family.

"So, you *really* think I should do it?"

"You know how you felt about Madras Richard and town hall? Well, now you know how I feel. I don't think you *should* do it—I think you *must* do it!"

"Do what?" Robby asked as he entered the kitchen with some new cars he wanted to show Alex.

"Mommy's gonna be a lawyer again. About a sandbox!" Alex said as he scooped him up and put him on the kitchen counter.

I could see his lip start quivering. Then his little blond eyebrow furrowed. "But . . . but . . . who's gonna take care of me? Who's gonna play with me and push me in the swings? Who's gonna pick me up from school? Only Mommy makes the best grilled cheese for me."

I could see tears welling up. Maybe I hadn't thought this through very well.

"Oh my God, Alex. Why did I agree to this? I can't do it. I can't do it."

"You're doing it, Annie. You have to. Just leave this to me. Look, Robby, remember that I'm home, too, now. I'll be here to make your breakfast and your lunch. And if my grilled cheese isn't as good as Mommy's, then I'll tell you what: We'll go to McDonald's for cheeseburgers. How's that sound? And if Mommy has to go to court and talk to the judge, then I'll take you there to see her. What do you say to that?"

"Who will read me *Mr. Duck's Wild Ride* at nap time?"

"I will, honey," I answered, figuring I should jump in with an assist. "Most of the time, I'll still be home; I'll be doing most of my work on the computer, so I'll still be here."

"Who will give me my bath at night?"

"Oh, Robby! Mommy and Daddy will still do that together!" Alex explained.

"Who will take me to tumbling class and play cars with me

and pour my juice and put this"—he pulled up his sleeve to expose a newly banged-up elbow—"Band-Aid on me? And kiss it, too?"

I could tell he was pretty worked up about all this. Apart from the appallingly limited catalog of domestic duties that he enumerated, I could see just how huge a role I played in his little-kid life, and it touched me—deeply. In fact, I had to turn around and grab a paper towel because I'd started tearing up myself. I mean, he was so cute, so small, so worried. And Alex was such a good husband, and so cute himself. And, truth be told, mixed in with all the weepy feelings, I felt a surge of horniness right then, as inappropriate as it may have been; I made a mental note to jump him as soon as Robby was in bed. Which I did. Excellent, by the way.

Alex knew, as I did, how anxious Robby was about this, so he put his hands down on either side of Robby, and looked him right in the eye for a man-to-man. "Robby, Mommy will still be here to take care of both of us. And by the time the new baby comes, this case will be over. It will be over by then, right, Annie?" he asked over his shoulder.

"Absolutely! In the files Lucas gave me, the court date was set for four weeks from yesterday. So, even if we do have to go to court, which I doubt, it will only be a month. One month."

"So, what do you say, Robby? You'll be at school most of the time she's working, and maybe you could even help her out when you get home. Would you like that?"

"It's about a sandbox?" Robby inquired hesitantly.

"Yes, it is. And you know some things about sandboxes, don't you?"

"Yeah. When I was at Chris' house, I played with his. He has green pails to dig with. And one has a turtle on it and one has a froggy on it, and Chris wouldn't let me play with the turtle one, but I played with the froggy one, and it was better because I could bury his cars with it." He went on in this vein for a while, cheering himself up with the recollection and diversion.

"Then, Robby," Alex responded once Robby was finished, "what do you say we tell Mommy 'Good luck' and 'Go get that poseur Hippie!'"

"Mommy," Robby said in his most contrite tone. I turned and stood in front of him at the counter. He reached up and stroked my cheeks with both his hands. "Mommy, good luck! And go get us a possum hippo!" Then he doubled over with laughter as Alex picked him up and hugged him.

So, with my menfolk fully in my corner, I decided I'd go for the KO.

Chapter Twenty-nine

The next morning, I gave the old gang at Walker, Cain, and Finch a call. I didn't know exactly how they'd respond to my news, but they were amazingly supportive; David Ferber even offered to be cocounsel. For some mysterious reason, this case was bringing out the best in everyone I talked to—Robby, Ferber, even Michael. It was as if the world knew what I knew and agreed with me: Lippie the Hippie had to go down. David suggested that we put in for a continuance in order to have more time to prepare, but time was really of the essence, since I was getting larger by the minute. And unless I wanted Lippie the Hippie's hands up my skirt, delivering this baby (which I most decidedly did not), the case simply had to be wrapped up in the four weeks allotted.

This meant that I had a ton of work to do: reading their files and depositions, researching past cases and precedents; familiarizing myself with recent laws governing protected lands, Green Acres, and wetlands; writing up our prospective angle; and conducting an investigation into the discovery of an outfit that I could wear without disgracing myself. Did pregnant lawyers, outside of television, actually wear suits? I was very unsure, so I put in a quick phone call to Jenn to address the critical issue. She wasn't a lawyer, and, in fact, never had been, but if anyone knew what pregnant lawyers wear both in and out of court, on and off TV, it was Jenn.

"Hey, Jenn. Do pregnant women wear suits?"

"Why do you need to wear a suit?"

"Michael's friend Lucas is getting sued, and I have to look good for him."

"Ahh, Annie, I'm pretty sure he's gay."

"Come on! I'm not asking *for me* for me. I'm asking because I'm going to be his lawyer for the next few weeks. Well, just co-counsel, really. But I don't know what to wear."

"You're going back to work? Are you mental? You're due in, like, two and a half months. What are you gonna do with the baby, carry it around in a briefcase? Stick it in a file cabinet? Or are you getting a live-in? You're getting a live-in, aren't you? Oh, you'll be all glamorous and professional, and I'll still be stuck at home all by myself. This sucks. It's totally unfair—"

"No, really, Jenn, it's nothing. I'm just doing this one case because it's for Michael. And because Alex hates Alan Lippincott."

"Who's he?"

"That hippie lawyer we saw on the beach with the Unshaven Wife on Labor Day. He's suing Lucas because of his swing set."

"That is so closed-minded. And homophobic, too."

"What are you talking about?" I asked, fully confused.

"Don't act so shocked; I know people who swing. I may not be a hotshot lawyer, but I know people, Annie. And some of them are, in fact, swingers."

"Not a set of swingers, Jenn. A *swing set*. You know, jungle gyms, sandboxes, kid stuff. And who do you know who swings? The Carletons? I always kind of suspected them. Am I right? I'm right, aren't I? The Carletons swing, don't they?"

"No. Well, I mean, I don't know. I was just making it all up. I lied; I don't know any swingers. I just wanted to sound contemporary. You know, fit in with you and the cool crowd. I mean, I haven't been out of this house since, well, long before swinging became fashionable again."

"So, do they?"

"I already said *no*; I barely know the Carletons, anyway. Although they are kind of creepy."

"No, I mean do pregnant women wear suits?"

"Not really. Imagine what a jacket would look like wrapped around a pregnant midsection. Very Hercule Poirot."

"The fat guy from that mystery show?"

"Exactly."

"He's enormous. What show is that?"

"*Sherlock Holmes*, or something. The point is that that guy solves, like, every mystery. He's dashing; he's clever; he's suave and sophisticated. But what's the first thing people think of when they think of him? That he's a fat man stuffed into a too-tight suit. Do you want to be Hercule Poirot?"

"No, Agatha Christie!"

"Yeah, I agree. Better to be Agatha Christie. She may have been old, but she was a great dresser. And rather slim, as I recall."

"No, *Agatha Christie's Poirot* is the mystery show with Hercule Poirot," I replied. "And how do you know how Agatha Christie dressed?"

"WE did a retrospective on female authors a while back. She and Dorothy Parker. Great style."

"Who are 'we'? Did you go back to work, too?" I asked, confused. Had she gone back to work and not told me?

"WE TV. Women's Entertainment Network. If you tell me

you haven't heard of it, I don't think I'll be able to remain friends with you, Annie. I live for WE."

"That's called 'WE'? I've always called it 'Double-u, ee.'" Although, now that I thought about it, I was pretty sure I'd never actually uttered the name of that station aloud.

"No, it's 'WE,'" she said in the decisive tone of one who, should she choose to return to work, would be doing so as a corporate executive for that fine network.

"Great movies, WE," I answered, remembering back to a story I'd seen on stylish suffragettes a while back.

"How about a knee-length wrap dress? That'd look good," Jenn replied as I reflected vaguely on what those brave and snazzy early feminists had worn.

"For suffragettes?" I asked, confused again.

"No, for you. Unless that's what we're calling pregnant female lawyers these days."

"Is it suffragettes or suffragists?" I pursued, curious to get to the bottom of this long-standing question.

"Suffragette, suffragist, suffer my wrath if you don't start focusing here. A wrap dress. And go all out on expensive accessories, so they know to take you seriously. You want to borrow my Louboutin boots?"

And so, once again, Jenn saved me from disgracing myself sartorially in yet another social context. I swear, she was the Mac-Gyver of fashion. Give her a cell phone battery and a baby wipe, and she could spin out an ensemble to make even my mother weak in the knees. Not only that, though, but she offered to pick up Robby from school and bring him back to her house for a playdate with Chris the following Thursday so that I could schedule and attend my first meeting guilt-free and Alex wouldn't have to miss his class. How nice was that? You know, it was almost understandable that my own mother wanted to be her friend more than mine; Jenn was cool, awesome, and, in the end, a pretty damn good person.

Alex really came through for me, too. If I'd ever forgotten why I loved him—and why Robby loved him—so much, this week brought it all back for me. He fed Robby, played with Robby, chauffeured Robby, and even cleaned Robby up from a particularly unfortunate encounter with Taco Bell (fine establishment though it may be). I don't claim to be the ultimate in responsibility or maturity, but I had to admit I would have had a tough time surrendering my parenting role to anyone less invested in the outcome than Alex. And, if I were forced to be totally honest, in terms of responsibility and maturity, Alex had me beat. He was, in a word, the perfect stand-in—so perfect, in fact, that Robby didn't even seem to notice my lessened presence.

So, with my outfits taken care of, Robby's mornings and afternoons organized, and my nerves in decent check, I spent each of the next eight days researching the case and studying up on all the prior cases that could impact us. Two weeks earlier, I couldn't have told you the difference between a wetland and a water park; but after this weeklong cram session, I could make the EPA look like the NRA. I knew more than I would ever want or need to know about endangered species, eroding beaches, national watersheds, and public *and* private conservation lands. Me! Who'd never read a newspaper except the front page headlines as I was throwing it out rather than recycling it and wasting, I may now add, no fewer than two and a half trees per toss. Me, who wouldn't have noticed a bald eagle if it came to my front door wearing a comb-over. Me, who used disposable diapers, Styrofoam cups, and, back in the eighties (and, truth be told, even a little of the nineties), enough aerosol hair spray to keep a family of four held firmly in place in spite of humidity, rain, or wind. Now I was not just informed; I was armed. Lippie the Hippie would not best the Forsters. At ten thirty, Thursday morning, he was gonna go down—and hard.

He was, wasn't he?

Chapter Thirty

Michael, Lucas, David, and I had gotten together several times throughout the previous week, so we were all up to speed and pretty well-informed; however, I couldn't sleep more than four minutes in a row the night before the big meeting with Lippie. It had been so long since I'd negotiated and handled cases—I mean, whom did I think I was fooling? I was a three-year-old's mother with another baby due in just over two months. I was a fraud. I was a fool. I was panicked.

At five thirty in the morning, I figured the pursuit of sleep was fruitless, so I got out of bed. Though bone-tired and irritable, I just couldn't see the point in staying in bed any longer when there was, clearly, no sleep in store for me and, into the mix, a third-trimester baby kicking my guts so hard that, if I hadn't known better, I would have thought he or she was a paid witness for Lippie. This kid wasn't even born yet, and already I could tell he—or she—was pissed off that I'd gone back to work. I would certainly be hearing about this decision come the teen years; I could feel it in my bones (and bladder and spleen and even the tonsils I had removed in third grade). But, it was too late to back out, and, knowing how much Alex and Michael were counting on me, I had to go. And Lucas—whom I'd gotten to know pretty well through all this—turned out to be just as good a guy as I'd thought he was when he helped me pick out my Christmas outfit. And he'd hired Duncan. So, I really felt I owed it to him to stick with it. And he sure was good to look at, too.

Because I'd gotten up so early, I was ready to go with two hours to spare. This was only the first of two scheduled meetings with Lippie and his posse, but I had a feeling that this meeting was all or nothing. This meeting was the one that was going to make or break us. I was as prepared as I could possibly be, but I was still praying we wouldn't have to go to court on the twenty-third. I was angling for a settlement of some sort. I'd been a lawyer long enough to know that settlements, if they didn't occur in the first meeting, rarely occurred subsequently. My God, how I hated Lippie and lawsuits and courts and judges at that moment. But, I must say, after catching a glimpse of myself in the full-length mirror, I felt a little better. Jenn's suggestions were exactly what I'd needed; and, feeling generous and grateful, I made a mental note to forgive her for her excellent wardrobe and physical gorgeousness.

I didn't want to be late, so I left an hour and fifteen minutes to travel the thirty-two minutes it used to take me to get to my old office in the pre-Robby days. Needless to say, I arrived with almost a half hour to spare, having to pee as badly as I'd ever needed and freaking out more than slightly at the very real possibility that I wouldn't be able to make it through the entire meeting without having to excuse myself and make a run for the ladies' room. It reminded me of this kid from Mrs. Threadwaite's fourth-grade class—Glenn Atchinson. He was one of those kids who was always getting into trouble for something—writing in textbooks, making fun of Paul Goldberg, putting thumbtacks on the toilet seats—that sort of stuff. Then one day he asked Mrs. T.—that was what we called her—if he could get a pass to go to the bathroom. Because he'd put a Stayfree in the boys' urinal the week before (big stuff if you were a fourth grader), she said no. A half hour and a half dozen repeated requests later, Glenn darted from his desk to the door, a huge wet stain spreading across the seat of his pants. I still remember the tan jeans and the long-sleeved green polo shirt he was wearing at the time. God, I hoped I'd be able to last through the meeting. I mean, the outfit I had on was far more expensive than a pair of 6x-sized Toughskins and a Garanimals top, so I really didn't want to risk ruining it. Plus, unlike Mrs. T.'s, the chairs in the conference room were leather—a material far more susceptible to leakage than the nearly-impervious molded plastic of the standard fourth-grade classroom.

I was, of course, the first one to enter the conference room, so I laid out all my files and spent a few minutes reviewing the important names, places, and dates. And just as I heard familiar voices coming down the hallway, I stumbled onto the most remarkable discovery. It was incredible! I don't know how I could have overlooked it! It was so simple but brilliant. I was positively beaming when David, Lucas, and Michael entered the room.

"Hey, Annie. What's with the smile?" Michael asked as he kissed my cheek. "And damn, woman, did you spend the night here, or what? Because you obviously were nowhere near a bed, judging by those Hefty SteelSaks under your eyes. Haven't you heard of cucumber slices or tea bags? Or how about a scalpel?"

"I think you look great, Annie," Lucas added apologetically. "Is that sweater cashmere? It's gorgeous. And I love the Louboutins."

"Gosh, it's good to be working with you again, Annie," David said as he shook my hand. "You guys really got one of the best lawyers around when you got Annie Fingardt. Any chance of your coming back? No, I guess probably not," he added as he glanced down at my stomach. Thank God the baby had stopped kicking by then, or I'd have been afraid he would have noticed the weird bulges of a stray arm or leg as it swam across my insides.

I was bursting with the good news of my discovery, and I could barely wait to tell them, so I quickly greeted them all and was just about to inform them of what I'd discovered, when Lippie the Hippie and no fewer than three other attorneys arrived at the door. He was wearing (I'm honestly not kidding) a ragg wool cardigan over a tie-dyed T-shirt that proudly displayed the motto GREEN *WITHOUT* ENVY. I couldn't wait to tell Alex that one. Of course, his pants were wide-wale corduroy, and I swear to all that is holy, he was wearing Birkenstocks with socks underneath. Really. Truly. I couldn't make this stuff up. He was, like, a walking parody of his own self-image. He took his seat at the farthest end of the table. Did he think he was king or something? All he needed was a drumstick—tofurkystick, excuse me—to throw over his shoulder. And after his three henchmen flanked him on both sides, we began introducing ourselves. Very civilly on our part, I might add, given his pompous demeanor throughout.

"Hello, I'm Anne Fingardt Forster," I said as I rose to shake hands.

"I'm David Ferber, cocounsel; and these gentlemen are Lucas Johnson and Michael Schaeffer."

"Greetings, one and all." Yes, he actually said those words. "I'm Alan Lippincott. And this is my lead attorney, Jean-Thomas St. Michel, and cocounselors William Donaghue and Peter Anderson."

"So, John's the lead attorney?" Michael asked, seemingly in earnest.

"I am not called John! Eet eez Jean-Thomas—you see? J-E-

A-N." The guy spoke up with a heavy French accent, spelling out his name in what, I could only guess, were supposed to be English letters.

It seemed quite important to him, and perhaps indeed to all his countrymen, that we Americans learn to say "Jean-Thomas" correctly. You know, with the "Jean" part kind of rhyming with the "unhhh" you say at the dentist's when his hands are down your throat, and with the "Thomas" sounding more like "toe-*moss*." Very French.

"Oh, *Jean*," Michael said, pronouncing it like the denim fabric, and wearing a smirk I recognized all too well.

"No, not 'Jean' like zee Levi's, eet's Jean—Jean-Thomas. You comprehend, no?" The guy was starting to lose his cool.

"Ohh! *Thomas*, did you say it was? Do you mind if we call you Tom, then?" Michael continued. He was relentless.

"Look, my name eez Jean-Thomas. Just like zat. *Jean-Thomas*. If zat is too deefficult, call me St. Michel."

"Ahh, just so you know, 'Michelle' is a girl's name in America," Michael offered.

"Let's just get zis started, shall we?" he said, struggling to regain his equanimity—and pretty damn well, I might add, for a Frenchman who'd been bested by a smart-ass Yankee.

"Sure," Michael responded. "But I'd just like to know one thing: We *are* all aware, aren't we, that in this very room there are currently a John-Thomas, a Willie, a Peter, and a Johnson? The only one missing is Dick!"

"Why eez eet wee need a Dick? And how do wee get ahold of one?"

Well, that did it. Even Lippie had to laugh at that. The room erupted in a peal of laughter. Not nervous, tittering kind of laughter, but full-out, bend-over, oh-shit-I-might-wet-my-pants laughter. Michael was ruthless, but he was funny. And for once it wasn't at my expense. Well, at least I thought so until Lippie spoke up in a grim tone.

"Well, that little exchange is going to cost you. These gentlemen and I charge six hundred dollars an hour; and you just wasted fifteen minutes of each of our time. I've made a note of that, and you will be responsible for shouldering the cost," Lippie began.

Oh, please. As if he weren't laughing right along with it. He was the type who would try to get his money back for seeing a movie he didn't like.

"Gentlemen, let's leave discussions of remuneration and compensation until the end." I spoke up in my most serious voice. "I think if we examine the facts of this case, it will become increasingly obvious that our clients won't be 'shouldering' the costs of any of this."

Now it was my turn. And with Michael's antics having eradicated all my anxiety, I was as collected as my grandmother's Cryin' Angel figurines.

"Ah, excuse me?" Jean-Thomas interjected. "'Ow do you figure? Your client 'ad a sandbox filled wiz zee illegal sand. Eet is protected sand from zee protected wetlands on zee Clapham coast! Did you not read zee federal ordinance? We sent eet to your client several weeks ago. I would 'ave thought zat you would 'ave read it."

Sarcasm? From a guy named after a penis? Now I was getting pissed off, but I continued to act the part of a mature adult and proceeded to make the point I had just discovered half an hour earlier that had escaped all our notice until then.

"Well, sirs, if you would turn to page seven of the writ in front of you, second paragraph, you will see your error," I con-

tinued. "As my client and KiddieCare—the makers and install-
ers of the equipment—can attest, and as the receipts on record
will show, the sandbox was filled with sand collected in *December*,
fourteen and a half months ago. Do we all concur on that point?"

After a brief huddle, Lippie, Frenchman & Henchmen all
nodded in agreement.

"I fail to see how this bears on zee case at hand. What deef-
ference?" He pronounced "difference" the way you'd say *"Vive la
différence"* if you'd just bought a baguette and a red beret. "Zee
sand is sand zat needs to remain in zee dunes for the preservation
of zee coast. Do you not see zat?"

"Well, whether I see 'zat' is not the salient point at the moment," I continued. I heard a snicker from Michael, but I didn't
dare look at him. "The point *is*, this was not declared a protected
wetland until January—*thirteen months ago*. Until then, if private
corporations were willing to pay for the removal of sand from any
of the public lands in Clapham, all they needed was cash and the
mayor's approval. Which, by the way, my client received the prior
month, and which is duly noted on page eight, third paragraph. *I
would have thought you would have read that*," I concluded, yearn-
ing to have put on a phony accent while saying it.

They stammered around for a little while, flipping pages and
reexamining their files, but they were finished, and they knew it.
After several minutes, they looked up.

"In summary, gentlemen," I spoke up, "your case is unten-
able. You have needlessly harassed my client—a kind man who
made a kind gesture for the good of your children, Mr. Lippincott. And this is how you repay him?"

"Oh, no," David spoke up. "*This* isn't how he repays him.
This is how he repays him." And for effect, David whipped out
his checkbook. "Gentlemen, we'll need to confer with our cli-

ent about just how he wants to settle this nuisance lawsuit. But I hope you're very good at drawing circles, because there will be a lot of them on any check you send to our client."

"Oh, but what was it you guys were going to charge us for the delay we caused by laughing?" Michael interjected, in a bitingly sarcastic tone. "I just want to find out, so we know how much to charge you for the delay you just caused us now, looking through all your little papers. Oh, what the hell," he added, "I'm feeling generous. How about we call it even, huh?" And he looked away in disgust.

"Well, for what it's worth, I'm awfully sorry to have inconvenienced you, Mr. Johnson," Lippie said as he stood up and collected his things. "I just hope you know, honestly, that I didn't bring this suit against you to offend you. I did it because, well, because I just believe the world should be a greener place."

And, you know what? I really think he meant it.

Only after the door shut behind the four of them could I muster the courage to look at Michael. I figured he'd have some kind of sarcastic comment about my argument or my professionalism, or, hell, my hairstyle, for that matter. But when I turned to him, he said nothing. With tears in his eyes, he just hugged me. Then I heard him whisper in my ear.

"Thank you, Annie. You saved Lucas' ass."

Only after that hug did I realize how very much I'd missed my job. And it gave me a whole lot more to think about.

A week and a half later, after the settlement was reached, a huge truck pulled into the co-op parking lot. Out of the back, two men in KiddieCare coveralls unloaded the entire line of Kiddie-Care playground equipment. Robby and the other kids watched in joyous disbelief as the men installed it all before their very eyes.

And as they laid the sandbox and began to fill it, one of the men handed me a note:

> Since you wouldn't accept money,
> we're making this small donation
> to Robby's school.
> And please notify all parents:
> The sand is
> synthetic and anti-bacterial!
> Thanks for everything,
> M and L

As I looked at Robby's face—wide-eyed and openmouthed—I wondered how much a guy must love sand to be able to sue after seeing his kids get this kind of windfall. Poor Lippie; it must have been a whole lot.

Chapter Thirty-one

March. Just over one month left. I could no longer pick Robby up; my entire wardrobe consisted of men's work shirts and the verboten yoga pants; and the only sustenance that *didn't* appeal to me was, as of yet, undiscovered. Surprisingly, however, I was up only forty-eight pounds—somehow, I guess because of all the excitement surrounding the lawsuit, I'd managed to gain only four measly pounds in an entire month. And being up forty-eight wasn't really so much after all; I mean, assuming my math was correct, the baby would have to weigh only thirty to thirty-five pounds (give or take) at birth in order for me to be right on track. It'd have to be a C-section, I was wagering; but, what the hell, that was an accommodation I was willing to make.

Alex—who, amazingly enough, seemed to have a blind spot the size of a gargantuan pregnant woman's abdomen when it came to seeing me objectively at this stage of the game—was so thrilled with the news of the Lippie the Hippie settlement that he called the local paper and gave them what he kept calling "an exclusive interview." And they actually printed it on the very front page! A whole article—two and half columns—all about the case. There was even a picture, much to my chagrin, of me taken outside my old office building. This proved the theory I'd been fleshing out for a while that you're seen and/or photographed only at the precise moments you least wish it. But, hey, I'd defeated my husband's nemesis and won a complete KiddieCare playground for my son in the process, so who really cared about a big waist and a bad photo? I mean, of course, besides my mother. Because, in spite of the fashion wasteland I was inhabiting and the psychological anxiety of anticipating future dieting, I was—really and truly—feeling great.

It was well-timed, I might add, because Alex and I were about to celebrate our eighth anniversary, and I wanted to make it fun—and memorable. You know, the kind of thing we'd look back on in years to come and say, "Ahh, now, *that* anniversary was fun—and memorable." With his career still on hold and his patience wearing thin, this was a pretty important year to make special. He'd had a few temporary returns to his firm as a consultant, but it was really beginning to look as if things at the Hoffman, Berg well were drying up. The law courses he'd been taking had gone a long way toward preparing for a potential shift in his field of legal expertise, but he had told himself and his old firm that he would give it until the baby's arrival to make a decision about his career. As of mid-spring, he'd be either back at Hoffman, Berg full-time, or he would get a new job.

That kind of pressure doesn't do much to cheer a husband up as his eighth anniversary approaches, so I figured I'd better do some due diligence in the spreading-sunshine-around department. And I was fairly confident that I would succeed. I already knew what I was going to give him: lessons at the racetrack and father-son tickets to the Mid-Atlantic Auto Show and Race. He'd wanted to do it for so long, and I figured if he didn't do it during the final weeks of this pregnancy, he might very well miss his opportunity for the next eighteen or so years. Carpe diem, and all. I had the whole thing planned out—our anniversary was, by chance, on a Friday, so, after his classes got out, Alex could take Robby to his Soccer Tots class in the afternoon while I made a fabulous dinner; Jenn had already agreed to have Robby sleep over, so Alex and I would have the house to ourselves for the whole night; and I'd even bought new lingerie—maternity wear and not very sexy, but black and lacy, nonetheless. The only detail that remained was picking up a pair of driving gloves and a racing helmet so he'd have something to open. And for the first time in my entire life, I kept my plans a surprise. It almost killed me not to confess—well, brag really—about what a great wife I was and what great gifts I'd gotten him, but I didn't. It was harder than having to face Mr. Wilkes' sixth-grade English class after he overheard me trying to convince Kelly Bartell that *The Red Badge of Courage* was about a girl who got her period, but somehow, I managed to keep my mouth shut about it all.

By the time Friday rolled around, I had my plan in gear. While Robby was at school, I'd go to the grocery store, the bakery, and the tailor's. I had to have my dress let out. Duh. Then, after picking Robby up, while Alex was still in his class, I'd make a fast dash to the mall to pick up the gloves and helmet for him. Then, when Alex and Robby were at soccer, I'd get my hair done and start on dinner. It was all timed to perfection. If I'd done a dry run, it would have taken four hours, tops—including the salon. And I had from nine in the morning until six thirty at night! Piece of cake. Right?

Hmm.

All morning, my plan worked like a charm. I completed the errands on the list in an orderly and timely way; I was organized and efficient; I was militarily precise in my scheduling. Everything was going according to plan.

And then I picked up Robby for a fast dash to the mall.

You'd figure I'd been a mother long enough to know that when you're sporting a three-year-old, bursting the seams of your maternity pants, and carrying an extra forty-eight pounds of "water weight" (that was how I liked to think of it, I mean, beyond the thirty-five-pound-baby scenario, which probably wasn't all that realistic), a "fast dash" to the mall passed like football time. But, somehow, that gem of motherhood had not yet crystallized for me. I blame the mall, really. I mean, just the thought of it whisked me back to the days when I used to have a job. You know, a *real* job. The kind of job that lets you sleep until the indulgent hour of seven thirty, wake to the dulcet tones of Lionel Ritchie on the alarm, and then choose from a half dozen different shades of taupe panty hose waiting patiently in their little plastic eggshells for you. Ahh, yes, the mall always took me back to the days when every shower afforded the luxury of both legs shaved. And when I used to use conditioner—John Frieda. My God, how I loved that sleek creamy bottle. Now I used Pert—one lousy green bottle that did everything hair could ever need, short of cutting out the wads of gum and chewed grilled cheese sandwiches that inevitably found their way onto my scalp.

Usually, for me, a trip to the mall meant even more prep time and outfit changing than a trip to Herrold's (excuse me, Dr. Hornby's); but given that I knew what I was going to buy and where it was displayed in the store, I figured I'd just keep my head low, walk quickly, and dodge anyone I recognized. That way, no one would spot me in the mammoth black yoga pants with dried rivulets of the soy milk Kendra spilled down my leg at the co-op that morning; the no-longer-white Keds filled with sand from Michael and Lucas' sandbox; and Alex's work shirt, which I had draped over an industrial-strength sports bra and which was splotched across the left breast with the apple juice that exploded out of Sammy Jordan's juice box when I punctured it with the straw for him at snack time. Since I was going to the salon that afternoon, I had just thrown my hair up in a messy ponytail—utterly devoid of any of the stylish dishabille of, say, a Megan Fox or a Gwyneth Paltrow—and hit the road.

Well, how stupid could I have been? Did not the lesson of the local paper's photograph teach me anything? I had even fleshed out that whole theory about moments in the spotlight—so how could I have been such a fool? Because, seriously, I wasn't even to Burbridge's front door when I saw Tiffany Sparkings. I swear to God that really was her name. She had lived across the hall from me my freshman year of college, and we used to have to share a bathroom. Put it this way: She used to hand wash her silk lingerie—and who, by the way, even had lingerie in college?—in the sink because the fabric was so delicate, the machine would tear it. Her mother used to send care packages to her every month. And they were not filled with the Dial soap, Suave shampoo, and Chips Ahoy! cookies that everyone else's moms sent. Oh, no—hers were filled with Ralph Lauren jackets, Laura Ashley skirts, Benetton sweaters, and Calvin Klein pants. You name it. I swear to you, that is what the girl received on a monthly basis. God, I hated that bitch.

And now, years later, here she was. When the only restaurant I'd been to in three years was a McDonald's, and the only stiff drink I'd had was the frozen grape juice ice pops I made with Robby last summer, she had to show up in her Prada suit and Louboutin pumps, tossing her flirtily businesslike blond head (bleached, by the way—she was brunette in college) and fresh haircut without so much as a trace of urine or strained peas anywhere on her. I still hated her. Needless to say, I pretended not to see her, slowed my pace, and was only mildly unsettled by the narrowness of my escape.

Of course, it was at that moment that Robby chose to plunk himself down on the curb outside the mall's entrance and begin serving himself up a wholesome lunch of cigarette butts and already-been-chewed gum from off the road in front of him. I tried to be reasonable, but in the interest of avoiding a scene that would, inevitably, attract Tiffany's attention, I actually considered letting him continue on with his buffet, but I was too grossed out to let him. So, I bent down to begin negotiations—which was hard enough given my size—while trying to balance the immense baby bag slung over my right shoulder that carried Robby's juice boxes, snacks, toys, books, discs, change of clothing, and anything else necessary to take a three-year-old to either the South Seas for six months or the mall for fifteen minutes.

Anyway, I leaned over, and as I leaned, a column of Ritz Crackers made a break for it and vaulted, javelin style, right into Robby's elbow. Now, I've never actually been assaulted by a stack of Ritz myself, but there was no way that it could've hurt as much as he made it sound, because, let me tell you, this kid let out a wail the likes of which I hadn't heard in the entirety of his three years. Although, for all I know, maybe he was simply stunned by having been the victim of a guerrilla attack by what he had come to think of as such a friendly cracker. But for whatever reason, he yelled—loud and long. He yelled so loud and so long that not only Tiffany turned to look, but people as far as three towns over had to close their windows. Robby had blown my cover. He'd screwed me. My own flesh and blood! I guess, in the back of my mind, I always knew he'd grow up, go to the prom, get married, and leave me. I just never thought the stab in the back would come so early in his little-kid life. But it was done; it was too late.

Because I'd seen Tiffany, Tiffany had seen me, she had seen me see her, and I had seen her see me see her.

"Annie! Annie Fingardt! Ohmigod! You look . . . Well, what have you been up to?"

"Tiff! I don't believe it! Still looking fabulous! Do you work around here? What are you doing now?" We began talking at the same time, but the way she cut herself off after the "You look . . ." comment didn't go unnoticed by me. And, coupled with the air kisses she blew somewhere in the vicinity of my left cheek, my hatred grew deeper.

"Yesss, I work across town. I'm doing nearly all the trial work for Lippincott, Bindler, Schwaab, Smith, and—soon to be—Sparkings! Can you believe it? I'm becoming a named partner next month!" Oh God, how I hated her. And that was before I'd even known she worked with Lippie. I hadn't thought it was possible to hate her any more than I had. I was wrong.

"Wow! Fabulous!" Why I was using that word so often I had no idea. "Congratulations! We'd all be so proud of you in East Hall!"

"Gosh, that seems a hundred years ago. Well, what have you been up to?"

The way she tried to make me feel like a loser for bringing up our college dorm as though I'd never gotten over leaving the place really pissed me off. What a bitch.

"Well, I worked for a while doing corporate law. Then quit to have Robby here, whom I've done such a good job raising that he's already addicted to cigarettes at the age of three." I figured I'd make light of the fact that he'd had a fistful of butts when she first laid eyes on him.

"Hmm. That's a shame. I guess he'll grow out of it," she said distractedly while admiring her flawless manicure. My good God, she actually took my cigarette comment seriously. I hated her. "Well, I have to run," she continued. "I just came in to pick up a bikini—I'm on my way to St. Croix tonight. You know how it is, squeezing in a week of vacation before . . . *the tourists.*" She pronounced the word as if it implied a truck full of toothless inbreds from an Appalachian trailer park.

"Well, that sounds like a fabulous trip! Have fun. And it was great to see you," I lied.

"Bye, love! We'll talk when I get back, 'kay?"

She twinkled her fingers at me and blew me a kiss—really, she did, the phony bitch—and skipped off to her car. I dove into the Burbridge's vestibule so I could spy on her unobserved. She sashayed over to a champagne-colored Jaguar and smoothly opened the door. My legs went weak in a flash of prepubescent jealousy as I glimpsed the buttery leather interior, the backseat free of baby carriers of any kind, the shiny newness of all the unfingerprinted metal and chrome.

And then I saw it, as she sexily lowered herself to enter the front seat. A run! A run in her smoke-colored hose! It started at the side of her knee and slithered up under the hem of her skirt. And as I went in to purchase the gloves and helmet, I laughed out loud. Tiffany Sparkings had a run in her hose! Tiffany Sparkings had a run in her hose! The refrain repeated itself in my mind like a prayer or a song, and by God, I was so happy, I didn't even mind that Robby was peeing into the brass ashtray in the corner.

Chapter Thirty-two

*A*n hour and a half later, when I was at Jenn's dropping off Robby, I told her about the encounter. Jenn and I had gone to college together, and although she didn't have the benefit of sharing a bathroom with Tiffany, she still knew her well enough to partake of my hatred. Hell, at our college, everyone knew Tiffany—and if you didn't want to sleep with her, you hated her. And, according to Jeff Mancini and the guys at Alpha Alpha Delta, even the ones who wanted to sleep with her still hated her. So I figured Jenn would appreciate the run-in-the-hose story nearly as much as I did. And did she ever.

"Tell me again. Start from the beginning. Give all the details." She was practically giddy with the news. "Not now, Chris. I'll play Candy Land with both of you after Annie leaves. Right now I'm too busy."

So, I indulged her with a second (and then a third) retelling of the events before she could be satisfied that Tiffany had been bested by a pregnant mom in a stained shirt and elastic hair band. But, as time was of the essence and I had an appointment at the salon awaiting, I had to take off after we'd fully dissected the issue for the fourth time.

"Oh, by the way, do you have any olives? It's the only thing I forgot at the store this morning," I asked as I was leaving.

"Olives? What do you need olives for?"

"It's for our dinner tonight. I'm making martinis."

"You're having martinis? For dinner? Ahh, Annie, maybe you should borrow a frozen pizza or something instead. You want a box of macaroni and cheese?"

"They're not *for* dinner; they're for, you know, the cocktail hour," I explained. I was trying to be suave, as though we always had cocktails with edible accessories floating in them.

"You're gonna have martinis? Yeah, right. You barely drink when you're *not* pregnant."

"They're for Alex. I'm having virgin-tinis. In other words, Poland Spring in a cool glass."

"Oh. You know, that actually sounds kind of fun. But let me see." She reached up onto her highest shelf. "Can you see? Is this a jar of olives?"

"I think so—but I can't really see. Don't you ever use olives? Why are they banished to the Siberia of kitchen cabinetry; the top shelf?"

"Because I haven't had a martini since before Brent was conceived. But I should start. You know, martinis and olives are making a comeback. Trendy. Very *Mad Men*. All the rage nowadays. You're so cutting-edge serving these. Especially if you have a retro shaker. You want to borrow mine?"

Fearing an irreversible slide into the advertising world of the sixties (*Bewitched*, of course, primarily, but, okay, maybe a little *Mad Men* tossed in, too), I declined the shaker, thanked her for the (trendy) olives, kissed Robby good-bye, and left for the salon.

Maybe I should have known to interpret Tiffany's presence as a harbinger of evil, but I was so blinded by my happiness at discovering the run in her hose that I didn't stop and think of all the bad luck she could portend. Certainly she was a jinx, and certainly she was to blame for the fact that Marianne, the stylist appointed to do my hair, was running very late. I arrived at my scheduled time, but, apologizing profusely, she told me it would be a half hour. Well, an hour and a half later, I was still waiting. But, I figured, as long as I was home by five thirty, I'd have enough time to get dressed and get dinner started, so, I wasn't too worried. In fact, it was actually kind of nice, hanging out in the salon. They served me herbal tea, let me sit in their reclining chair, and even gave me a complimentary manicure for waiting so long. And I got to read—actually read—about a dozen grown-up magazines. No *Highlights* or *Humpty Dumpty*. Real magazines. Glossy pictures with samples of perfumes stuck in the pages. Articles about sex and cosmetics and sixteen ways to eat desserts and not gain weight, and just every good thing. The only glitch was that about halfway through the wait, I became peckish. Then hungry. Then ravenous. Then so pathologically determined to fill my mouth with something that I actually contemplated tasting their citrus shampoo.

And then I remembered . . . the olives! I'd stuck them in my purse when I left Jenn's, and they were in there waiting patiently for me. Normally, just so you know, I don't like olives. And normally, just so you know, if I don't like something, I don't eat it—or a lot of it, anyway. But after the initial shock of how bad those salty little bastards tasted, I grew kind of used to them. And after the sixth or seventh one, my mouth was so puckered from the brine and vinegar that I couldn't really taste them anyway. So, as you've probably imagined, six or seven led to ten or twelve, and long story short, I finished the jar. And what do you know? As I swallowed the very last one, Marianne called me to her station.

Finally, about an hour later, my hair was done, and even though it meant nearly three hours in the salon, I have to say it was worth it. I hadn't felt this good about a cut or a rinse in years. If only I'd had it done before I'd seen Tiffany. Damn it. The only nagging problem was that it was after five thirty, and I still had myself and dinner to get ready. I felt myself cramping up under the anxiety of getting everything ready for the surprise, so I hurried home, reassuring myself that it would all get done. By the time I got back, it was after six and my stomach was in knots with the tension. I always knew I was no good at keeping secrets: Now I had physical proof of what harm they wreaked on my body. As I hobbled up the stairs to the bedroom, I vowed that in the future I would reveal any and all secrets with which I was entrusted and confess any and all surprises long before they could officially qualify as such. I mean really, as I saw myself in the full-length mirror, doubled over and clutching my distended abdomen, I determined that no unexpressed thought was worth this agony. I would, henceforth, become the very blabbermouth that in sixth grade we had all teased Katrina Hoffstater for being because she'd told the boys which girls had gotten their periods.

I was, however, determined that my plans for the night would succeed, so I proceeded as though the gut-wrenching pain would cease and desist once it learned it couldn't stop me. I grabbed my dress and tried, after removing it from the cellophane wrapping, to put it on. And that was when it hit me. Considering the way they rippled from the front around to the small of my back; the way they shot down the backs of my thighs; the way they made me feel fiery hot, then freezing cold in turn, these were not just ordinary stomach cramps. Hoah, no. This was no ordinary stomachache. This was something entirely different. And just as this reality was washing over me, I heard Alex open the door.

"Hey, Annie—hey, where are you?"

"Alex, come here. I'm stuck in the closet," I called down to him.

"What? Are you all right? Is Robby at Jenn's?" I could hear him taking the steps two or three at a time.

"Al . . . Oh, happy anniversary," I said as I saw him at the bedroom door.

He had a huge bouquet of cookies made to look like flowers in his hands. He threw them onto the bed and bent over to help me up. He looked perplexed and more than a little concerned.

"How come you're naked in the closet?"

"Well, Robby's at Jenn's for the night. And I was going to surprise you with an especially memorable night. But, ahh, things have changed a little." And here, I doubled over again, grabbing my stomach. "I'm in labor!"

"What! No, you're not!"

"Alex, I've been in labor before, and I'm in labor now."

"No. No. You have a month left. Oh my God. Annie, Dr. Weiss said so at your last appointment. You have another month. We have another month. *Another month!*" Okay, he was starting to get hysterical.

"Calm down, Alex. It's fine. Just call Dr. Weiss and tell her to meet us at the hospital. I'll call Jenn from the road so she'll know where we are if Robby needs anything."

Alex had plopped onto the bedroom floor and was searching all around him for something to fix his eyes on. Finding a stray car of Robby's partially under the bed, he picked it up and started peeling the numbers off its little metal door.

"But Annie, I'm almost positive we have a month left. It just can't be. Dr. Weiss told us. *She told us.* She said we weren't due until April fourteenth. *April fourteenth.* It's only March, Annie. *March*, I tell you!" He was really starting to lose it.

It was always a bad sign with Alex when he started repeating things—or when he tried to debate me out of going into labor. I guess he was a little slow to realize that, although *I* might be a very rational person, capable of counting to a full nine months, the little (thirty-five-pound?) baby inside me had yet to master such intellectual achievements and, hence, was in all probability incapable of responding to his logic.

"Alex, look, don't take it so personally. This kid is coming. And he or she is coming now. So either you can drive us to the hospital or you can start boiling some water and tearing up sheets. Either way, this kid is coming."

I think the fear that he would have to deliver the baby himself shook him out of his stupor, and he kicked into Alex gear. Within minutes, the necessary phone calls were made, Chipper was fed, my bags were packed, and we were backing out of the driveway.

"Oh! Did you pack my new lingerie?" I asked as we were about to pull into the road.

"What new lingerie?"

"The black nightie and robe from my dresser. I got it for . . . for . . . tonight," and with that, I burst into tears.

Alex, still struggling to come to terms with the shoddy math of the gestational period, didn't know what to make of these tears. He stopped the car, threw it into reverse, and ran back in to get the sleepwear. I sat waiting for him in tears, crying alternately for the upheaval of the only surprise I'd ever carried to fruition and for the agony of the cramps that seemed to have increased in length and intensity.

"Is this it?" Alex asked as he jumped back into the front seat.

"Oh, thank you. Thank you." I wept on his shoulder. Why I was so emotional about oversized black silk loungewear was anyone's guess. "This was for our special night. I had everything planned, and it was gonna be a surprise," I cried.

"Well, Annie, you may not have planned this, but it is definitely a surprise! And you still get to wear your new lingerie. Just think—your mom will think you always wear that kind of stuff!"

Alex always knew just what to say to make me feel better. And he was right. When I had Robby and my mom came to the hospital, I was wearing white flannel Brooks Brothers men's pajamas; she ran out to Bloomingdale's that very afternoon in order to buy me a scarlet peignoir set. "More people will see you in your lingerie today, dear, than any other day of your life; you may as well make the most of it," she'd whispered.

With this baby, I would be armed and ready, black lingerie and all.

Chapter Thirty-three

By the time we'd reached the hospital, the cramps were so intense, I honestly didn't think I'd be able to walk to the entrance. Luckily, Dr. Weiss met us at the curb and called for a wheelchair. I have to admit, I felt like a real dufus, but my legs had gotten so shaky, I really thought I wouldn't be able to make it more than a few steps. She stayed by my side the whole way up to the room, and, once we were there, she did a pretty thorough exam and asked me about a million questions. And, just as her inquiries were winding down, my cramps started to become significantly less pronounced.

"What is it, Dr. Weiss? Did you give me some kind of drugs or epidural or something? Because the labor pains are definitely not so bad now. Is everything all right?"

"Oh, the baby's entirely fine. In fact, better than fine. But, ahh, Annie, Alex, you're not in labor. You're not dilated; your water hasn't broken; your hormone levels are normal; the baby hasn't even moved toward the birth canal. And the fetal monitor would have picked it up right away. So, yes, the baby's fine; your digestive tract, however . . . Well, there's the rub. You see, what you have isn't so much labor pain as gastrointestinal pain. Caused, in all likelihood, by whatever it is you ate earlier today. The technical name for it is 'a stomachache.'" She pronounced it really deliberately, as if giving me some Latin-derived, twenty-syllable term from an obscure fourth-year med school textbook, and then she started laughing at her own joke.

"A stomachache! But I haven't eaten anything since, well, sneaking a few bites of Robby's grilled cheese. You see, it's our anniversary, and I was going to make dinner, but . . ." I started babbling on, trying to explain myself, when—from the back of my mind—came an image of the olives. "Umm, Alex, could you hand me my bag, please?"

"Yeah, why?"

I rooted around until I found it. The empty olive jar. And there, in fine print, but clear as day, marked in magenta ink across the cap was the happy little phrase BEST IF USED BY 11-21-09.

"Oops," I ventured.

"Why on earth would you eat a jar of expired olives?" Dr. Weiss asked. Alex, who was still absorbing the fact that his precious math in regard to our child's gestation had not, indeed, abandoned or failed him, was silent.

"It's Jenn's fault; she gave them to me. Although it's also Alex's fault—he was supposed to have them in his martinis." I was singing out names like a canary, hoping to lessen my responsibility by blaming everybody else. I guess my resolve to tattle and blab Katrina Hoffstater–style had really taken hold. "Maybe she gave them to me on purpose!"

"Jenn gave you expired olives to poison your husband with? Does she dislike him that much?" Dr. Weiss asked, smiling and glancing over to Alex, who was also smirking at the joke.

"Well, I don't know. Maybe she does." I felt I had to justify my theory. "They did argue about coffee once. And Jenn liked *Titanic*—that always bothered Alex. I think they fought about Leonardo DiCaprio a couple of other times, too, come to think of it. So, it's very likely, in fact, that she may have been seeking some kind of retaliation."

"And her plan would have gone off without a hitch," added in Alex, now roused from his silent contemplations, "if you hadn't foiled it by 'taking the bait' yourself. Falling on the sword, as it were. And all to protect me. My hero," he finished.

"Go on, you two, and get out of here! Go celebrate your anniversary. Call me in the morning to let me know how everything goes, okay?"

"Doc, it's our anniversary. . . . How do you think it's gonna go?" I asked.

"Annie, I was talking about your recuperation!"

"Oh, sorry! But I think whatever I had is gone. Really. I feel fine now. The cramps are totally gone. Am I normal again?"

"Annie, I've been married to you for eight years now. . . . You were never 'normal,'" Alex said with a smile as he helped me put on my coat.

"Well, enjoy the rest of the night, you two," Dr. Weiss said as we were leaving. "And I'll see you next month for the real thing. After this dress rehearsal, you guys'll be pros!"

Alex and I thanked her and headed out to the car. In the parking lot, I stopped and turned to face him.

"What is it? Tell me it's not labor pains!" he nearly screamed. "Do you want to go back in?"

"No, I'm fine. Really. I just feel—well, I feel . . ." I turned and hugged Alex just as I started to cry. "I'm sorry I ruined our anniversary by eating rancid olives."

"Hey, you didn't ruin it—you made it memorable! You said you wanted 'memorable,' and that is definitely what we got! The only thing is—well, I thought you hated olives—even of the nonrancid variety."

"I did. I do. But after a half dozen or so, I kind of forgot."

I could hear him laughing as he helped me into the passenger seat.

At around ten, we got home to our empty house. The stuff for that night's dinner had been sitting out on the counter for all those hours, and, to be honest, after my olive scare, neither of us wanted to risk further digestive bacterial warfare. We decided to play it safe and order pizza. My beautiful hair had lost all its shape; my newly tailored dress was lying in wrinkles on the floor of my bedroom closet; my lingerie was packed inside an overnight bag in Alex's backseat; and the special dinner was uncooked and decomposing on the kitchen counter. But when the pizza came and we sat on the floor of the family room with a bottle of club soda and toasted to our family, nothing had ever seemed more perfect.

"There is one part of my master plan that wasn't entirely ruined," I said as we were finishing dinner. "I got you something to say 'thank you' for these eight years!" I handed him the box.

"What is it?" he said, looking just like Robby, as he ripped into it. "Oh my God! Annie! Is this what I . . . ? I've always wanted to . . . I can't believe you did this! The helmet, the gloves, the lessons, the tickets. It's too much! Oh, Annie, thank . . ." Suddenly his voice sank.

"Oh, Alex, you hate it! You hate it, don't you? I can exchange it and return everything. I'll get you something you do like."

"No!" he said as he clung to the gifts with a tightened grip. "No! I love them! The problem is just, well, it's just that . . . With only two tickets, I'll have to take either you *or* Robby. How will I ever be able to pick just one of you?"

I didn't want to hurt his feelings, but that decision was a whole lot easier to make than he thought it was. You see, Robby loved racetracks; I, on the other hand, couldn't care about them enough even to hate them.

"I got the tickets for you and Robby! It'll be a father-son thing. I wouldn't dream of displacing him, no matter how tempting!" Boy, he didn't know the half of it.

"Oh, Annie! You are the best. The absolute best! Thanks!" And with that and a kiss, he handed me a box wrapped in silver paper.

"When did you get this?" I asked.

Even though there hadn't been an episode of *Bewitched* in which Darrin had forgotten his anniversary, I'd watched enough other television shows over the years that I was always somehow expecting my husband to forget our anniversary. Or repeatedly trip over small items of furniture. Or use expressions like, "Doesn't take a Jack Frost to recognize a snow job." Alex, I should have known, was quite different.

"A while ago. Open it," he said, smiling.

It was big and flat. Definitely not jewelry. Or electronics—phew. Or clothing. But what? And as I was wondering, I pulled out an elegant, gilded frame. And engraved on the parchment inside was the following:

Annie Fingardt Forster
Provider of and for Babies
Chooser of Schools
Installer of Cable
Cooker of Thanksgiving
Savior of Christmas Parties
Setter-Upper of Brothers
Protector of Canines
Fighter of Hippies
Lover of Alex

There was also a pair of diamond earrings taped to the bottom of the glass that Alex had to point out to me, but to be honest, they didn't mean anything compared to the words in that frame. I had never, in all my life, been so proud as when I read those lines. I had screwed up the entire night's celebration, but somehow it just didn't matter.

Not bad for an Eater of Expired Olives.

Chapter Thirty-four

*T*hings returned to some version of normal after the false-labor incident, which was how I had come to describe it. While I am fully aware that it was not, actually, false labor in any sense of that diagnosis, the expression just seemed to provide a much tidier and quaint pictorial than what really occurred. So, I was willing to forgo the accuracy and precision of medical terminology in order to preserve my ever-dwindling self-respect. However, having things return to "normal" doesn't really mean all that much when your husband's job is hanging in the balance, your mother's thrice-daily check-ins result in more calorie-intake monitoring than Sue Wheeler's tenth-grade diet of lemon wedges and nicotine, and your son is giving serious consideration to a future in auto-shop and asphalt removal and/or application after his weekend at the track with his dad. In fact, having things return to "somewhat strange" or "eerily out of the ordinary" or "effing bizarre" would have been rather comforting at this stage of the game.

With Alex's self-imposed deadline for his career move looming near, he was increasingly preoccupied and more than a little stressed out. I had done my best not to interfere with any decision he was arriving at, trusting him to make a choice right for him, but it was difficult to watch him struggling and not be able to help in a more direct way. It was so difficult, indeed, that, one would-otherwise-have-been-cheerful Thursday morning, I decided I couldn't sit by and do nothing any longer. After all, Alex hadn't been the only one contemplating his future over the last eight months.

"Alex?" I asked as casually as I could, entering the kitchen after having dropped Robby off at school.

"Cramps? Labor?" he replied, jumping down the stairs, exactly as he'd been replying to any utterance I'd made for the last week or so.

"No, no. I'm fine. I just, well, I just wanted to talk to you for a minute while we had some time to ourselves. I mean, with a new baby, who knows how long it'll be until we can really talk to each other again."

"Um, Annie, it's not like the Berlin Wall or anything. It's just a baby. We'll still be living in the same house together. I think we can manage a conversation every once in a while," he said, smiling. "We'll just have to do it to the tune of 'Sweet Baby James.'"

That was the song we'd sung to Robby when he was a newborn. "Sweet Baby James," over and over and over again. God bless James Taylor. I couldn't quite remember having had conversations to its tune, but it was entirely likely, given that Robby wasn't much of a sleeper early on, so I remembered precious little of those first couple of months. How like Alex to think of that now. I really loved him, I was horrified to find myself thinking—I mean, it didn't get much more Kraft American Singles than reflecting nostalgically upon how deep your conjugal love was after the arrival of your beloved offspring. It was so awful and so WE TV that I nearly shuddered with self-loathing and Hallmark shame. Next thing, I'd be hanging posters of baby seals and kittens in bibs on the back of my bedroom door.

"I really love you, Alex," I heard myself proclaiming. What was happening to me? Was I in a field of flowers or on a rocky beach wearing flowing clothes with my hair blowing out behind me in the wind? I felt myself inching one step closer to collecting Thomas Kincaid artwork and porcelain gnomes I'd have to name and pose on shelving units in the living room. Who was this woman I was dangerously close to becoming—admitting to loving my husband out loud during the final month of pregnancy? I was embarrassed for her.

"Hey, I love you, too. Is that it? Because I've almost finished recaulking the tub in Robby's bath and I have to get back up there."

While my nesting instincts took on the form of gazing at the tiny baby clothes in the aisles of Target, Alex's had prompted him to undertake—and complete—any number of unsavory household tasks that had gone unnoticed for the entirety of our time living in the hallowed walls of our family homestead.

"Well, not exactly. I kind of wanted to talk to you about, um, something, kind of, else."

"What? Oh, I know. You want me to fix the latch on the baby's closet door, right? I know, I know. It's next on my list. And then I think the room will be ready. Let me think: paint, curtains, carpet, crib's installed, the electrician did the lighting last week. So, yeah, I think that's it."

"No, that's not it, either. You've actually done an awesome job getting everything ready. I really think you've done it all. But there's just one thing I think we sort of need to talk about."

"Aw, hell, Annie, I know what it is. I know what you're talking about. And I know I was supposed to let you know my decision by now. It's just, well, I was kind of hoping you'd decide."

"Me? But it's not my decision to make. And certainly not alone," I answered. Had he gone crazy and not told me? Did he really expect me to render the final decision on a career that would, in all likelihood, last for more than three decades?

"Well, you're the one doing the work, right? Shouldn't you get the choice?"

"So, then, you're okay if I go back to work?" I asked, surprised by how smoothly it had gone, and quickly, too.

"What?" he asked, staring, openmouthed, at me. "What are you talking about?"

"Going back to work," I answered, nonplussed by his reaction. "Isn't that what you were talking about, too?"

"I was talking about baby names," he answered. "Baby names! I was supposed to give you my list of preferences by now!"

"Oh, yeah!" I answered, now curious to find out his names. "So, what are they?"

"You want to go back to work?" Alex said, no doubt trying to take the heat off himself for having forgotten to make his list.

"Honestly, I think I do," I said. "But I want to know your thoughts."

"I think your going back to work is a huge decision—especially now, with a new baby coming," he answered seriously.

"No, I mean your thoughts on baby names," I corrected.

"I like classic. You know, nothing weird. Sorry, Annie, but 'Baird' and 'Gunner'—they just suck as names. Face it."

"It was 'Laird' that I liked, not 'Baird.' Shuh! As if. You know I can't do any *K* or *B* names," I answered, outraged that he'd forgotten my policy regarding those initials and the Theory of Nighttime Soap Opera Character Names, Circa 1995.

"Ah, yes: *K* and *B* names lead inevitably toward excessive hair product use and creative facial hair patterning, if I remember your theory correctly. And, by the way, the name 'Laird' sucks, too. Good names are ones such as William, Charles, Madison. That kind of thing."

"They sound like the names of law firms. No excitement. Boring."

"At least you can't make fun of them," he replied.

"Oh, whether it's a kid's name *or* a law firm, people can find a way to make fun if they want to. Trust me," I responded with a knowing sniff.

For, in my vast experience, it was *always* possible to find something to make fun of a law firm about. Once, I actually spent two billable hours ridiculing McGovern, Stiller, and Walsh for the golden crest, which sat pompously atop their letterhead. Really, who would have the gall to adorn their professional stationery with a monarch's emblem? I went so far as to create a mock-up of my own letterhead to show David Ferber (and bring home for Alex) with the Frito-Lay insignia intertwined with the M&M Mars logo, underlined with the Diet Coke swirl resting above my name. So I considered myself quite an authority on the topic of name ridicule.

"So, law firms, huh? Is that what you meant by going back to work? Would you want to practice law again?" he asked, redirecting the conversation to its rightful origins.

"Yes," I said honestly. "Working with Michael and Lucas made me see what I've been missing. It felt good. And it made me realize that I really want to go back. It just seems like the best decision for all of us right now."

"Annie Fingardt Forster, you never, ever cease to amaze me," he said with a smile.

"Okay, then, to sum up," I replied, giving him a little hug around the middle. "Number one: Names beginning with the letters *K* and *B* are the intellectual property of the Great and Good Aaron Spelling, and anyone bearing such monikers should, rightfully, pay royalties to his estate for their use—provided all funds generated go to his grandchildren and not his spouse or offspring. And, number two: You're okay with my going back to work?"

"Annie, I don't know about that arrangement," he answered solemnly.

"Well, it's just that his grandkids seem okay and kind of cute; whereas Candy, Tori, and her brother have kind of besmirched the Spelling legacy."

"Not that arrangement; the other one," he said, humoring me with a patience that must, by this point, have worn rather thin.

"Well, it's just that, Alex, I kind of actually want to go back to work. And I know you weren't thrilled at Hoffman, Berg. I thought you were, but then I heard you talking with Andy that night, and I realized you weren't. I'm sorry I didn't know that. But now I know it, I can't unknow it. So, I was thinking you could take some time off for real. Get a sense of what you want to do. In the meantime, I could work. It seems fair. It seems right. What do you think, Alex?"

"I think you're pretty freakin' amazing for suggesting it, Annie. But you have a month left until we have this baby. Probably less. There's no way—repeat, no way—I'm going to let you have that kind of stress when we're this close to the finish line here. Can't we discuss this in a few months or something? And anyway, I've been working on a few things myself—things I haven't really talked too much about because, well, I guess I didn't want to jinx anything. Or stress you out. But it looks as if things could start happening here. So, in short, the alternative to my leaving Hoffman doesn't have to be your hitting the pavement."

"I know that. And I know that, if we decide to continue doing things the way we were doing them before the sidebar, everything would be fine. But, Alex, don't you want *better* than fine?

Don't you want a life where we're not just the stars, but the writers, the directors, the producers, and the gaffers, too?"

I wasn't sure what a "gaffer" was, but it came to me from having read so many television show credits, so I figured I'd use it—that or "best boy." But I was even less sure of what that was, and it sounded kind of porno, so I went with "gaffer."

"I do want that, Annie. That's why I've been talking to some people and taking those classes. And, well, I may as well say it, it seems as if this would be an ideal time to open my own practice in general law. I could help people navigate mortgage stuff, foreclosures, unemployment terms, severance deals, that sort of thing. According to Mark Santorini and Eric Wahler, down at the university, now's the time to do it. I want to be the craft services, the key grip, and the best boy of your life, Annie."

"You are definitely the best boy in my life," I said, throwing myself into his arms. "But I have one question for you."

"No, I don't know what any of those jobs are. I just always read them at the end of TV shows. That *is* what you were going to ask me, right?"

"No," I answered, although I was vaguely wondering it.

"What is it, then?" he asked, bending down over my head, still encircling me in his arms.

"Will you consider taking on an associate with a newborn who hasn't done anything but some pro bono work in over three years?"

"Will she sexually harass me?"

"Often and mercilessly; I guarantee it."

"Then yes," he answered.

And with that, the new firm of Forster and Forster was conceived. If only naming *all* the things conceived by the two of us were as easy as that. I mean, Laird wasn't that terrible a name. Was it?

Chapter Thirty-five

*H*aving answered the call heard by both of us on the career front, Alex and I relaxed into the final weeks of the pregnancy. We decided that he would begin looking for office space for us, and I would start work creating a letterhead that would make us proud and thwart all attempts at mockery by competitors. The interlocking *F*s I had originally envisioned conjured the swear word bearing this fine initial to such an extent that I had to admit defeat and come up with a few alternate designs, but it was actually an enjoyable and somewhat productive way to spend a couple of weeks during which I wasn't, let's be honest, going to be running marathons—or even any errands. Alex already had a list of several interested clients, so he was eager to get up and running; for me, I was a little less sure, so we decided I'd go back part-time when the baby was three months old. That way, I could ease in, arrange for a sitter for a couple of hours a day, and discover how productive I could be while working out of my home office during Robby's school- and nap time. So, all that really remained unfinished was the pregnancy.

Maybe it's just me, but the best pregnancies are kind of like the worst books. They are entirely predictable, with no irony whatsoever, and totally anticlimactic—unless you're watching a soap opera, which is the only place in America where a doctor can still spring a "Twins!" on an unsuspecting mother. But really, in this day and age of ultrasounds, amnios, chorionic villus sampling, and that creepy guy on daytime talk shows who claims to be psychic, who doesn't know precisely how many babies they are going to have? Even that woman who had eight of them knew there were eight of them. So, the only surprise in store for the Forster household was the gender, as we'd never been a read-the-last-page-of-the-book-to-find-out-what-happens kind of family. I couldn't even maintain my hopes that this baby was going to be nearly forty pounds at birth; Dr. Weiss took such precise measurements at my last sonogram that we knew the baby was hovering around the eight-pound mark. Still, that last month was a pretty exciting time for us nonetheless.

After the false alarm at our anniversary, I, and just about everyone else, had become rather skeptical about my ability to predict and identify labor pains. Seriously, because of that one measly event, I had turned into a live version of *The Boy Who Cried Wolf—The Pregnant Woman Who Cried Baby*. So no one really believed me anymore—about anything. Such as when I told Jenn that I'd gained nearly sixty pounds, which was entirely true. She just laughed and said, "Yeah, right." Similarly, when I told my mom that I'd gotten new lingerie, her reaction was, "Sure, you did. But all kidding aside, I mailed you a couple silk peignoir sets, so when you go into labor *for real*, you'll have something nice to wear." You know, emphasizing the "for real" as if to scold me for lying about it last time. And even Robby started giving me this kind of "Oh, right, I'm so sure, Mom" look when I told him he wouldn't get dessert until he ate his green beans. Put it like this: My credibility was worth less than a pair of Urkel suspenders on eBay, *Waterworld* on VHS, and Britney's opinion on Middle Eastern politics—combined.

So, when my water broke in the middle of aisle seven (cereal, bread, prepared foods) of the Shop 'n Save, we were all pretty surprised. Luckily, Alex was there; and while the frozen foods guy called 911, Alex began delivering the baby. Everyone stood around staring at me, except for Madras Richard, who, just happening to be there, ran off to collect boiling water and some towels from aisle two (housewares, paper products, sundries). And by the time the EMT guys and paramedics showed up, I'd already delivered a perfectly healthy, clean, dry baby.

Yeah, right. Any time I even attempted to tell someone that story, they rolled their eyes in obvious disbelief, snorting an "Oh sure, Annie." My credibility really was worth nothing—less than a Chevy Citation; less than parachute pants. But, really, who could believe such a scenario? I mean, no one has babies like that! Really, I can't remember a time I was ever even in an elevator with a pregnant lady, let alone with one who went into labor just as the elevator got stuck. How many people have ever seen a pregnant woman so much as hail a cab, let alone deliver in the backseat? It just doesn't happen. I'd love to tell some exciting escapade about having my baby, but that stuff only happens on *I Love Lucy*. It didn't even happen on *Bewitched*. I figured I should stop trying to embellish and just tell people what happened, which was a very by-the-book—boring, actually—delivery.

Bottom line: I was induced. Because I'd started swelling south of my knees (seriously, I could push my finger into my ankle, and a dent would stay there for the entire length of a sitcom segment), Dr. Weiss thought it best not to let this linger on into a potential full-out Stretch Armstrong mode. Not even the date and time were a surprise to me. I not only knew when I was going in, but I'd packed my suitcase with my best lingerie, a new robe, and even one peignoir set from my mom; I'd gotten myself a manicure; and, never one for waxing, I'd taken care of any and all shaving needs with the five blades of a new Venus Embrace. I'd even called my mom two weeks in advance, so she and my dad could fly in and watch Robby for us. I wasn't really sure about that last step—I really deliberated over whether to clue her in. I mean, my mom wasn't exactly the rock a girl needs when she's delivering what she hopes will, in the end, turn out to be a forty-five-pound baby. But, ultimately, I figured I needed someone there who would not only take care of Robby, but who would shame me publicly if I didn't somehow manage to stop eating for two. I knew Michael alone just wasn't going to cut it. And, for all her exactitude and—ahem—peculiarities, I loved her. You know, there are just times when you need your mom there with you. And I think having a baby ranks right up there with getting your first training bra and being zipped into the "corset" (okay, girdle) you wore under your wedding dress.

I was due to go in on April 8, so I was angling to have my parents arrive on April 7. Late. At night. Maybe even on the morning of the eighth. No such luck. She booked a flight for April 2, so she'd be there just in case I "happened to go into labor *for real* before then." She was still emphasizing the "for real." At first, I thought about performing my own cesarean section on the thirty-first, just to cut the prenatal visit short; but then I found out that Andy was coming to stay with us for six days while Aimee was at a conference in Washington. He and Aimee were not only still going out, but they'd just moved in together and had scheduled the housepainters to come while she was traveling. So he was going to be staying with us. And because I was curious to see how my mother and he would interact, I put off my plans for self-surgery and decided to enjoy the show as it unfolded before me.

And it was worth it. I never really knew what "synergy"

meant before; Mr. Waslowski, my eighth-grade science teacher, told us it meant one plus one equals three; and, as an example, he said it was like peanut butter and jelly, which are much better together than separate. He said. But, you see, I've always hated peanut butter, and the only jelly I like lives inside powdered sugar doughnuts, so I never really got the analogy. But when I saw my mom and Andy together, it all made perfect sense.

My mom, having arrived a day before Andy, greeted him warmly at the door when he showed up; but before Andy had even crossed the threshold, she began her critique.

"What the . . . ? Is this your hair? Oh, Andy! You used to have such lovely hair," she said wistfully as she ran her hand over the fuzzy clumps he'd started to grow when he was in Calcutta. "What a shame, Andy. Really." She spoke in the tone she'd used with me when I got caught doing a ding-dong-ditch to Old Man Farber when I was ten.

"Hey, Mrs. Fingardt!" Andy said as he hugged her and twirled her around. "Wow, you're still as light as a feather! So, you don't like my braids? I was gonna grow some dreads!"

"They are perfectly awful," my mother said, suppressing a smile at having been compared to a feather. I imagined a fine little white floaty thing, like the one at the end of *Forrest Gump*, and then out of spite turned it into a big ole turkey buzzard's feather. Then *I* had to suppress a smile.

"Well, if you don't like them, Mrs. F., then let's fix 'em," Andy said with a big smile. "I'm in your hands!"

And right there, in the middle of the foyer, he dropped his bags, rooted out an electric shaver, and handed it over to her. What was it about my mother that made all my friends put their trust so completely in her hands, whereas I didn't even want her picking out my nightgowns?

"Thank God!" my mother responded, and took his hand to lead him into the bathroom where she could do a proper job on him.

"Just remember, Mrs. F.," Andy said as he followed (did he think he was the Fonz, or something?), "I learned a little bit about karma when I was in Calcutta, and if you don't stop focusing on people's outsides—you know, what they look like and how they dress—then you're destined to be reincarnated as a warty, flabby, zitty, scale-encrusted hose bag with awful teeth and bad shoes."

And here's the surprising thing: Somehow, although my mom doesn't even like to borrow clothes, let alone other people's souls, Andy's philosophy of the hand-me-down human spirit made sense to her. Or maybe when it came to bad shoes, she just didn't want to tempt fate. But, for whatever reason, my mom became noticeably less critical after that. In fact, she became so tolerant and accepting that when I finished off Robby's Chicken McNuggets after downing my own Big Mac, she didn't say a word. It was as though she hadn't even noticed. And this woman had noticed every item of sustenance that had passed my lips since I'd stolen two Nutter Butters from the Abruzzis' cookie jar when I was pet-sitting in third grade. I didn't think it was right not to show my appreciation for her silence, so I told her I thought that, in light of her spiritual evolution, she'd probably be able to come back in her next life as Coco Chanel. You know, we got along a lot better after I said that.

So, Andy and my mom, against all odds and common sense, had become thick as thieves. This meant I got a brother-in-law with no Nirvana-wannabe facial scruff and a decent haircut, and a mom who smiled upon all that I ate. Now, *that's* synergy. You know, like how two king-sized candy bars are about ten times better than one. Or like the Kardashians' fame. Get it?

And Alex, who was usually so uptight whenever we had a houseful of people (or just my mother), and who would have been so nervous during the final countdown, was remarkably collected. He didn't repeat himself and he didn't resort to math; and only once did I catch him trying to debate with the baby about his or her arrival date. Pretty good, huh? I guess that would be another example of "synergy," come to think of it.

Chapter Thirty-six

$\mathcal{S}$o, with very little fanfare, the morning of April 6 rolled around, and I found myself getting into the car as though I were going to the Shop 'n Save or something. I mean, that's the thing they never tell you on TV. I don't mean to malign my favorite invention of all time, but really, I think television shows want us to believe that every birth is fraught with excitement and surprises from beginning to end. The truth is, though, there's actually a lot of downtime when you're having a baby. And that's the biggest surprise of all. Really. I walked out to the car, strapped myself into the passenger seat, and Alex and I drove off to meet Dr. Weiss without so much as a forgotten suitcase or speeding ticket. No pains, no water breaking, no screams, no en-route delivery. Just a pleasant drive (it was a nice day) to the front door of the hospital, where Alex dropped me off, while he went to park. I didn't even go in the Emergency entrance. So you see, all those cop shows and sitcoms have it all wrong. That was why I always liked *Bewitched*—the only thing they got wrong was that Samantha was the same exact size before and after having each of her kids. But I was willing to overlook that because I can guarantee you that if I were a witch—even if I'd promised my husband I wouldn't use magic—I'd wiggle my nose until it fell off in order to get a body like hers. So, for that, I could suspend my disbelief.

Just as Alex was walking through the electric doors into the vestibule, Dr. Weiss arrived. She gestured for us to stand back and said in a hushed tone that she'd take care of admitting me. Maybe, after seeing my huge size, she was starting to think I'd need a cesarean after all.

She went up to the front desk and started talking to the host or concierge or orderly or whatever the hell you call the guy who checks you in. Her back was turned toward me, so I couldn't hear her too well; but she gesticulated in my direction a few times, so I assumed she was telling him where I was going. Then I heard the guy respond in a booming voice.

"On here"—he nodded toward the red Plexiglas clipboard in front of him—"says she's scheduled for ten twenty. Room Ob12-A. That right?" He clipped off all the extra words from his sentences, as though words weren't free.

"Yeah, Marshall," Dr. Weiss said, raising her voice enough for me to be able to hear her now. "But I'm going to make one change, if I can. Instead of 12-A, I'm putting her in room 3."

"Hey, you can't do that," Marshall—I figured that must be his name—said suspiciously.

"Yes, actually, I can. If I see the need," she explained calmly and rationally, not letting him contradict her. "And, in this case, I do."

"Why? Why does she need it?"

I didn't know what it was I needed, but from the way they were talking, I was willing to guess that I wanted it. I mean, it was like an Eggo commercial, each actor commanding the other to leggo first. It made me miss those commercials; they should never have changed them. Was there anyone who could even recognize, let alone remember, an Eggo waffle commercial of today? Highly unlikely. And it all got me thinking: I could really go for some Eggo waffles. And Mrs. Butterworth's. Now, there was an ad campaign that had stood the test of time; there was an icon with some staying power, some legs. Sadly, as I thought that, I smiled at my own joke—"legs" because the bottle was shaped like a woman. That's kind of what I'm trying to explain; that there really is a lot of downtime surrounding birth and delivery. And I was using mine to recall consumer product shills.

My attention was redirected when Dr. Weiss lowered her voice again and leaned in toward Marshall to whisper something—something, evidently, that made him look up promptly, give me a once-over, then kind of smirk at Dr. Weiss. I couldn't tell what that smirk meant.

"Yeah, I guess you're right," Marshall said. Right about what? Was he making fun of me? And just as I was about to push Alex up there to defend my honor, Dr. Weiss turned around, winked at us, and broke out in a big smile.

"What?" I asked.

"You'll see," she said mysteriously as she wheeled me—she'd made me get into a wheelchair—into the elevator.

The doors opened on the third floor, Obstetrics, and I held Alex's hand as Dr. Weiss pushed me down the long hallway where the recovery rooms were. There must have been twenty-four of them in total, since that was the number on the first door we passed; and each had an A and a B alongside the room number to indicate which of the two beds the patient was in. When I'd had Robby, I was in 16-B; and my roommate, 16-A, who'd just had her sixth, stayed up all night crying the first night, then fought with her husband the whole next day—loudly. It really freaked me out. We had tried, both with Robby and the new baby, to reserve one of the private rooms in advance, but, both times, we were assured that those rooms were fully booked and that the likelihood of our scoring one rivaled that of Mel Gibson presiding as keynote speaker at Wellesley College's commencement ceremonies. I wasn't holding my breath for either to happen. But, as we passed down the hallway, I hoped room 3 would bring me better luck and a better roommate this time around.

When we passed 12-A, the room I was supposed to have, I peeked in to see what I'd be missing. Not much, was the answer. The bed closest to the open door—which would have been mine— was empty, but behind a half-closed curtain was a scary woman with obscenely gigantic breasts in bed with a newborn, flanked by two surly teenagers who were yelling at her that she was too old to have had another kid, to which she wittily replied that they could "just cram it up their asses." Delightful, really. Norman Rockwell all over.

And just as I was starting to get really nervous, wondering what kind of roommate I'd have this time, Dr. Weiss steered me into a large room with two windows and just one bed. The bed and the room were empty.

"Here you go, Annie," Dr. Weiss said as she helped me to my feet.

"What do you mean?" I asked, confused. "Where's my roommate? All the private rooms were booked solid!"

"Is there a problem, Dr. Weiss? Why do we need this special room?" Alex asked, his voice betraying his panic.

"No, there's absolutely no problem; you and the baby are totally fine. And you're right—all the private rooms are taken. But this isn't a 'room'; it's a 'suite.' There's a difference. We keep these on reserve for VIPs. There are a couple on each floor of the hospital. It just so happened that this one belongs to you!"

"Huh?" Alex and I asked in unison.

"Private suite?" Alex then said.

"Why us?" I added.

"You guys know Aimee Dubois?" Dr. Weiss said, still smiling. How did she know Andy's Aimee? Town hall Aimee? *Dumped and Desperate* Aimee? I knew I should pretend not to remember that anymore, given how cool she turned out to be.

"Of course! We actually know her pretty well; she's dating my brother," Alex answered. I was still too confused by the connection to speak.

"Well," she continued, "she's my sister!"

"What?!?" Alex and I screamed, once again in unison.

"Aimee Dubois is your sister?" Alex continued. "But she's my brother's girlfriend!"

"Not anymore, she isn't," Dr. Weiss said cryptically.

"Oh, hell, she dumped him. She broke his heart. Oh, poor Andy," I blurted out.

"He dumped her—that bastard. I really liked her, too," Alex blurted out at the same time.

"No, no, no one broke up! It's just that she's his *fiancée* now," Dr. Weiss corrected.

"What?!?" Alex and I screamed, once again at the same time.

We were starting to sound like the kind of couple who owns his and hers coffee mugs and matching Hawaiian shirts, which, thankfully, we don't.

"Yep! She called me this morning from Connecticut. They're getting married in September!"

"Ahh!" I screamed with joy. And with a little bit of pain, too, because just then, Dr. Weiss stuck the IV in my arm and began strapping a monitor around my midsection. "But wait, I thought you told me you kept your name after you'd gotten married, so how come you two don't have the same last name?" I asked.

"Well, it's kind of a ridiculous reason," Dr. Weiss explained, lowering her voice. "Neither of you can say anything or else the suite is off! She changed her name from Amy, spelled with a *y*, Weiss to A-I-M-E-E Dubois when she went to France her junior year of college. She was never going to reveal it to anyone. But then she decided to confess to Andy, because, as I'm sure you guys know, he came back from India calling himself 'Surhesh Ramaswami.'"

Alex and I just looked at each other. It must have been rather obvious that neither of us had been informed of Andy's new name, but it didn't surprise either of us.

"Wait, a Weiss-Dubois is going to marry a Forster-Ramen-noodle-whatchacallit? Oh, this is priceless." Alex laughed.

"So, we'll be kind of like sisters-in-law!" I said, smiling at Dr. Weiss.

"Yep! And since you're not only family now, but you're the one, as Aimee told me, who set them up, I figured a nicer room was the least I could do! Just remember, if the nurses or orderlies ask, tell them you've had a difficult pregnancy and that you're big anonymous donors to the hospital. Okay, I'll be back in a while to see how much you've dilated and all that good stuff!"

"Thanks, Dr. Weiss!" Alex smiled as he stretched out on the couch that furnished the room. There were a couple of chairs, too. And a table. And a nice wall unit. It was better than the honeymoon suite where Alex and I spent our wedding night. It was a realization that made me feel just plain weird—to have a nicer room in a hospital than on your honeymoon in Bermuda, but a fact's a fact.

And there was no way I was going to say anything against this sweet setup.

Chapter Thirty-seven

So, even though I was there to have a baby—and this is what I keep trying to explain to people is the weird part—Alex and I just hung around talking about what kind of wedding Surhesh and Mademoiselle Dubois would have. Would she take his name? Aimee Ramaswami? Would they name their children Pierre and Etienne, and make them wear sportif red neckerchiefs and bad attitudes? Or maybe Gupta and Lateesh, and make them wear gauze pants and great tans? Alex and I talked and talked, and then we started to laugh. And the harder I laughed, the harder my stomach hurt. But I couldn't stop. Alex was wiping away tears from his eyes after a particularly humorous speculation as to what kind of cake they would serve at their reception, when I realized I was going into labor.

"Call Dr. Weiss, Alex. I think I'm in labor," I said, although I was still laughing.

"She said she'd be back. I think we should wait for her," Alex responded, just beginning to catch his breath.

"Huh?" I asked. Was he telling me to wait until the labor better suited the doctor's schedule? "Al, I'm having the baby. Now. Could you please call her?"

"Honey, *she's* the doctor. I think we should wait for her," he repeated.

Uh-oh, that was a bad sign. Either I was still a boy crying wolf, or he'd spontaneously slipped into panic mode.

"Lovie, darling, sweetheart, sunshine of my life—get Dr. Weiss and get her *now*, please. Because, in simple terms, the deal is this: I can have this baby now and *you* can deliver it; or I can have this baby now and *she* can deliver it. And, I'm quoting here—'Honey, *she's* the doctor.' Either way, this kid's coming, so it's your choice."

Well, after hearing that, he flew out of that room and down that hall faster than a Saturday afternoon. I can still hear his cries for Dr. Weiss echoing in my head.

And, sure enough, when she returned, she checked me and told me the baby's head was already crowning. Very calmly, she addressed me with, "Okay, Annie, do you want to push with the next contraction?"

And I, very calmly, replied, "No; I think I'm good." Truth be told, I was feeling some last-minute—well, does "jitters" give the idea?

"Um, Annie, allow me to rephrase. With the next contraction, *push*."

Well, I guess that settled it. I looked up at Alex, who was standing by the side of my bed.

"I'm scared, Alex," I said.

"I'm right here," he answered. "You're gonna do great."

He didn't even repeat anything, so I felt much better.

For some reason, I remember that particular moment more clearly than anything else. I remember how his sandy blond hair fell down across his forehead, and one piece brushed against his eyebrow. I remember the thin blue and white stripes of his shirt and how, when he moved, they got all twisty in a way that, if he were going on television, would clash with the lines of resolution on a hi-def screen. You know how that phenomenon can occur sometimes? It used to happen to Johnny Carson a lot for some reason. Everyone must have been afraid to tell such a big star what to wear or not to wear on TV. You know, it was his own show after all; I probably wouldn't have said anything. I mean, he was Johnny Carson. You couldn't just walk up to him and tell him that his neckties looked as if they were made out of aluminum foil whenever he was on the air. I guess Dave and Jay and even Conan must have learned, though, because they almost always wore solids. This led me to wonder if the three of them always wore stripes or really loud patterns on the weekends in order to make up for not getting to wear them through the week. Then I started thinking about this kid named Matt Rantacki I knew in ninth grade who used to wear shirts that looked like murals. Seascapes, landscapes, abstracts—once, he even came in with the *Last Supper* around his torso. Jesus was on his sternum, and if he spun around, you could see all the disciples and the tops of their wineglasses. Their plates and food and stuff must have been tucked into his pants. It made you wonder what they must have been eating—you know, a last supper and all. I'd choose Cheez Doodles, Vinny's deep-dish pizza, and a box of Cap'n Crunch. Oh, and a cinnamon Danish. But thinking about Matt's shirts reminded me of this one day, when Nick Franco told Mrs. Kupp, the art teacher, that if the class was going on a field trip, all we needed to do was drive over to Matt's closet. Matt stopped wearing those fancy shirts after that. And that's the moment I remember most clearly in the whole labor and delivery process.

Anyhoo, then the nurse yanked my right leg up to my shoulder and told Alex to grab hold of the other one, so all my deep reflections ended right there, with Matt Rantacki and late-night television talk-show hosts. I don't really know why I thought of all that stuff, or how I remembered it so clearly, but I suppose that during life's most significant moments, I still thought a lot about TV. You'd think that a woman on her way to have a baby would have better things to think about than which shirts or ties people choose, but, you know, go figure.

Another nurse joined us shortly to relieve Alex of the leg he'd been holding, and she started telling the first nurse that there were free doughnuts on the second floor and she should get one before someone named "Snyder" touched them all. Then a third nurse entered, chewing the last of what, evidently, had been a powdered sugar doughnut, because she had a thin white rim around her lips. My God, how I wanted a powdered sugar doughnut at that moment. I would even have settled for a glazed; just not a plain. I prefer my baked goods to be wearing sugar, generally. Then she turned to a huge metal sink and washed her hands up to the elbow. I watched her as she rubbed the soap all over her forearms, and I was hoping that it was all just for show—you know, as on *House* or *Grey's Anatomy*—or that it was a purely cautionary measure, because a woman who's in advanced labor doesn't really want to think about the fact that her nurse may have a need to have arms sanitized up to the elbows, if you know what I mean. And then I felt, well, as though if I didn't push *right now*, this baby was going to launch itself out through any other available aperture it could find.

"Whhhooaaa!" she yelled to me as I pushed. "This baby's determined! This kid is coming!"

So much for a smooth bedside manner.

"Oh my God, Alex. The baby's here," I said, as though he needed an interpreter. I guess he did, because after he'd been downsized from his job as leg holder, he had just been hanging out on an orange-rust-colored vinyl chair at the side of the bed.

Once I spoke up, though, he jumped up so quickly, he seemed to be doing an impression of how a dad-to-be is supposed to react when his wife tells him the baby's on its way.

"Oh, Annie, this is it! This is it, Annie! Annie, this is it!" He repeated it three times—a terrible sign. But he didn't faint or anything; he just squeezed my hand so hard that it left a kind of whitish ridge in between two deep red indentations when he finally let go. Then I puked, and that was the last thing I remember really clearly. But even if I had perfect recall of the birth process, I'm guessing no one would want to hear all the rather gross details, anyway. Plus, I'm fairly sure that most everyone I knew had already seen the after-school special *My Mom's Having a Baby*, so I figured I could spare people the description of the next couple hours—which, entirely predictably, contained the screaming, sweating, panting, and cursing that we've all grown so accustomed to recognizing as the glorious sounds of a husband in labor. And things weren't so different for me, either.

However, less than half an hour later, it was all over. Alex was hugging me, and I was hugging our new baby. It was a girl! Robby had a little sister! And this baby girl had the very family I'd always wanted to grow up in: a good-looking dad, an incredibly put-together mother (ahem), and an awesome older brother who'd have cool friends she could flirt with when she was old enough. My baby had it all! And, looking down at her, I wanted to give her everything. She was wrapped in a pale pink blanket and, aside from her nose having gotten smushed to the left during her delivery, she was beautiful. And she already had a tiny bit of Alex-colored hair, which curled gently toward her forehead, and long fingernails, of which my mother would most certainly approve.

We stayed there, just the three of us, huddled on the bed for a few minutes more. I wiped Alex's tears away as he gently felt the hair on her tiny head. Then I guess I must have fallen asleep, because when I looked up next, Alex had moved off the bed and was napping in the orange-rust-colored chair next to me. He had something on his shirt, a towel or something; and when I reached out to touch it, I realized it was our baby. So tiny, she looked like a cloth draped over his shoulder. I cried for a little while as I watched them—already such good buddies.

I knew my mother and father and Robby would be dying to come in and see us, so when Alex nodded himself awake, I asked him if he would go get them. They'd been in the waiting room since Alex had called to tell them I was in labor, and I was starting to get nervous that my mother might kill a candy striper or something in her eagerness to meet the new baby.

"Mommy!" Robby screamed as he flew into the room and tried to jump up on the bed with me. "What. Is. That?" He slowly backed away as he saw the pink blanket.

"Robby," I said as my mother and father filed in through the narrow doorway, "come and meet your new baby sister!"

"Oh, I knew it was a girl!" my mother screeched, coming over to kiss me and the baby.

"Congratulations, honey," my dad said, still kind of lurking in the shadows, too afraid of disrupting someone or something to come any closer.

"A *girl*! Yuck! I told you to have a boy!" Robby said petulantly. "Now who am I gonna play with?"

"Well, when she gets older, you can play with her. But for right now, I think she needs her big brother to protect her and take care of her and pay lots of attention to her. And Robby, I just want you to know that having another baby doesn't change how much I love you. I will always love you so much, and anytime you need me to hug and kiss you or make you a grilled cheese, I promise I will do it. Okay?" I explained.

I'd read enough books to know about sibling rivalry and feeling displaced and all that, so I figured I'd give it to him straight. I would address his concerns at the outset and let him know he could count on me to be there for him—that sort of thing.

Looking down at the baby I was holding out to him, he started to smile. Then he leaned over and gave her the softest kiss I'd ever seen him give.

Then, laughing and looking up at me, he said, "I know you love me best. You've had me since I was a little kid, but you only just got her. But don't worry, Mommy. Even though she's teeny-weeny now, she'll start to grow soon like Baby Brent. But I'll always be bigger!"

And as weird as it sounds, that made me feel better about the whole sibling rivalry issue. Maybe Robby'd write a self-help book someday—*Bros Before Woes*, maybe. Or how about *I Will Turn This Car Around!: Navigating Sibling Relationships*. Something catchy enough to land him a spot on *Jon Stewart*, fingers crossed; and, as he launched his nationwide book tour, I would be there in the wings to support him (and meet Jon Stewart), smiling beneficently and in a matronly manner, but looking superhot, too. Natch.

Chapter Thirty-eight

*A*fter everyone met and hugged and kissed the tiny new person, my dad took Robby down to the cafeteria for some dinner, while I was wheeled back to my *private suite* with my daughter. My mom and Alex were already there waiting for us, calling everyone we knew to let them know.

"She is just gorgeous," my mother said, gloating. "Such hair, and those tiny little fingernails. So delicate. She takes after me, don't you think?" I guess if she'd been an ugly baby, my mother would have said she took after me. "What are you going to name her, honey?"

Oh. Dear. God. I looked at Alex in a panic. And his eyes locked on mine in terror. We had no idea. We'd had a couple notable discussions about baby names, but they'd all gone horribly off-track; so, the only thing we had decided for sure was that, if it was a boy, we weren't going to name him Morton. Morton Forster. That was out. Other than that, we had no consensus. In fact, I wasn't even fully convinced that he subscribed to my *K* and *B* Theory of the Nineties Nighttime Soap Operas, truth be told. Somehow, though, I just couldn't bring myself to tell my mother that we had totally overlooked that part of the having-a-baby job; she would never have let me forget it for two minutes together.

So, I looked at Alex and ventured forth with the first name that came into my brain. "Uhhh, Elizabeth?"

Alex sighed a tremendous sigh of relief, so he must have liked it. And he knew my mother well enough to know that if we hadn't acted as though this was a conclusion we'd arrived at months ago, then every conversation for the rest of our lives would contain the words, "Well, what did you expect? She was born without a name. . . ." So, given that alternative, I guess "Elizabeth" was fine with him.

"Yeah, Elizabeth," Alex said in his best yeah-what-she-said tone of voice. "Elizabeth, ahh, Sarah Forster." I didn't really love the name "Sarah," but what the hell? He'd let me pick the first name.

"Ohhhh," my mom squealed as she hugged Alex. "You named her after my mother!" And only after she'd said that did I remember that my grandmother's name had been Elizabeth. In my defense, however, I should hasten to add that I had never met this grandmother, as she had passed before I was born. But all indications suggested she had been a pretty awesome woman (a pediatrician, which was really something, for a woman of her era)—so I was fine with the unintentional namesake.

"Ye-esss!" Alex agreed haltingly. "Of *course* we did!"

"Although . . . ," she said ponderously, "didn't I meet an aunt of yours also named Elizabeth at Robby's first birthday party?" She posed the question to Alex. She was on to us.

"Oh, yeah!" Alex said, his voice betraying his surprise. Now it was his turn to be shocked at the realization that he, too, had a relative by the very name we'd inadvertently chosen for our daughter. "Hey, I do! You're right! I mean, well, yes, we were thinking of both those Elizabeths when we chose the name." And he looked over my mom's shoulder as she hugged him again and gave me a "Whew!" face and shrugged.

*   *   *

The next day, I woke up early and, after feeding Elizabeth, primped and prepped for nearly an hour for any visitors who might perchance stop by. I washed up, did my hair, and put on my new lingerie—a white linen camisole and matching bottoms. My mom was the first to arrive.

"Honey, get ready! People will be stopping by, and you'll want to look nice, won't you?"

Blame it on postpartum nerves, stupidity, or trace drugs still floating in my system after the epidural, but I just sat there limply, while she went to work on me. She not only redid my hair (which, without Robby around, I had been able to spend ten full minutes working on), washed my face, and reapplied my makeup (I'd actually applied two coats of mascara). She even re-dressed me in a new silk peignoir set she'd bought the night before on her way home from the hospital. It was petal pink with tiny covered buttons down the chemise and a robe trimmed with ivory ribbon. It took twenty minutes just to button up the nightie. Once I went home, I would never have enough time to button all those buttons—forty-eight of them. I counted. Lying in a hospital bed does afford a girl a few moments of time for peaceful reflection, after all. Hell, with two kids, I'd probably barely have time to throw on one of those pull-away Velcro suits they use on TV—but, still, it felt really nice to be able to wear the impractical little number in here at least.

Almost immediately after my mom finished with me, Michael appeared at the door with Lucas.

"What happened to *you*?" Michael said as he walked over to give me a kiss.

"Ahh, you may have heard? I just had a baby. And women who've just endured eighteen hours of labor," I said, exaggerating just a little, "often look slightly worse for wear."

"Yeah, but you actually look *good*. For once," he said with a humph at the end.

"Thank you!" my mother piped up in agreement. "I keep telling her that it takes only a couple minutes a day to pull herself together." She, by the way, had been working on me for an hour and five minutes.

"Michael, Lucas, meet my mother," I said begrudgingly. My mother and Michael together in the same room could prove to be a deadly duo. Their image sprang to mind: superheroes in matching Prada leotards and Michael Kors capes, wearing Louboutin boots, and flying all over the world and solving crimes against fashion under their assumed identities, Haute and Couture.

"Wow, I love your scarf," Michael said, as though they'd known each other for centuries. "Pucci?"

"Why, yes! Vintage," she added with a small wink. "And your jacket! To die for! Zegna?"

And so on. Not that I even knew who Zegna and his poochie were, but I guess it was kind of nice that they were getting along so well. Until they took themselves off to the couch (did I mention I had a *private suite*?), where they proceeded to lower their voices enough to rouse my suspicion that they were talking about me. They probably were. Then I heard the terms "spring line" and "fashionistas," so I figured they had discovered they had far more important things to discuss than a hausfrau and her new baby.

Lucas, rolling his eyes, came over to the bed and handed me the gift they'd brought: an immense pink basket filled with every baby accessory imaginable—in pink. It was so much more than kind, I didn't know what to say. With tears in my eyes, I began to thank him. And just then, Jenn showed up at the door.

"Nooooo!" she screamed as she ran across the room. "Don't

cry! Whatever you do, don't cry!" She must have thought something was really wrong.

"Jenn, I'm fine. It's just that Lucas and Michael brought . . . ," I said as I started tearing up again.

"I know you're fine," she said as though it were obvious. "I was screaming because if you start to cry, your mascara will run. And I saw from the door just how great you look right now. It would be a shame to waste it."

Great, three of them now.

"What do you think I've been trying to tell her her whole life?" my mother said as she rose to hug and kiss Jenn as though she'd somehow been vindicated.

"Hear, hear," was all Michael said, still sitting on the couch.

"So, where's the baby?" Jenn said as she kissed me. "I want to see her! And what did you name her?"

"Come with me! We'll go get 'Baby Elizabeth' from the nursery and bring her back here. You know, they named her after my mother," my mother whispered to Jenn as the two of them walked out, holding each other's arms and giggling. Seriously, it was just like fifth grade when Colleen McDonough and Julie Simon wouldn't let anyone sit with them at recess because they were the only ones who wore bras.

"So, you named her Elizabeth? My sister's named Elizabeth," Lucas said in his soft voice. "I've always loved that name," he added as an afterthought.

"Elizabeth. Elizabeth. Not a bad name . . . No, not bad at all. Did you name her after Queen Elizabeth?" Michael asked.

This was a tough one. I mean, I'd had to be reminded that my own grandmother had been named Elizabeth, and then Alex had forgotten he had an aunt with that name, so I didn't really want to take the credit for carrying on a family name when I hadn't even thought of it. And now I was being asked if I'd named my daughter for a famous monarch of the same name. How to play it?

However, the hard, cold reality of it was that I named my Elizabeth after the great American actress who'd enraptured audiences of all ages with her riveting portrayal of Samantha Stephens—television's most beloved witch—Elizabeth Montgomery. And, to be quite honest, I wasn't even really sure which queen Queen Elizabeth was, anyway; so, no, I hadn't named my daughter after Queen Elizabeth.

"Yes, I did!" I answered with false enthusiasm, hoping the subject would drop there.

"Really?" he pursued, perhaps smelling my trepidation. "Queen Elizabeth the First or the Second?"

Now I was in real trouble. How the hell was I supposed to know which one? I hadn't named her after either. Then, in a flash, I remembered that movie with Helen Mirren that Jen had dragged me to a few years back, all about the current Queen Elizabeth, who was this kind of looming, unstylish presence throughout the film, wearing odd hats and frumpy suits and giving everyone the creeps. And, as I recalled, she wasn't particularly nice to her own grandsons, either, and they were super good-looking. I knew then that no daughter of mine would be named after a woman who could be so indifferent to hot guys. Or fashion. So I took a stab at it.

"Ahh, the First?" I said, immediately regretting not having asserted it with more certainty. God, how I hoped that would end it.

"Of course!" Lucas spoke up, probably trying to deflect attention away from what he could tell was a really lame fabrication on my part. "I mean, she was such a great queen. So cultured and intelligent—a real patron of the arts and the written word. Not to mention the sciences."

"Oh, yeah!" I responded, as it dawned on me which queen I

was supposed to have named my baby after. "Dickens. Kipling. All that Darwin stuff," I said, desperate to change the subject to something—anything—else.

"That's *Victoria*!" Michael said, scoffing at me. "Don't you even know who you're naming your daughter for? You sure you weren't thinking of Cleopatra—the Queen of the Nile? Or Queen Latifah—former queen of the rap music industry? Or how about Glinda—the Good Queen of the North?"

"Everyone knows that Glinda isn't a queen. She's a witch," I said, trying to defend myself.

"Oh my God," he said, as if a light were just switched on. "That's it, isn't it?!? You didn't name your daughter after any queen; you named her after *Bewitched*! You did, didn't you? Elizabeth McGovern! Admit it!" Damn, he knew me well.

"Elizabeth McGovern was not in *Bewitched*. She was the one in *The Bedroom Window*, with Steve Guttenberg. And that *Women and Men* thing on HBO with Beau Bridges. By the way, Lucas, did you know you look like him?" I thought a compliment was the least I could give under the circumstances.

"Beau Bridges? You're saying Lucas looks like *him*? I thought you said he looked like *Jeff* Bridges!"

"Oops! That's who I meant—sorry about that," I said to Lucas, who, admittedly, looked pretty relieved. "You know, *Tequila Sunrise* and *Overboard* with Goldie Hawn."

"That is Kurt Russell. *Kurt Russell*. Do. You. Understand? They are *not* the same person!" Michael said, acting exasperated. "And, by the way, it's Kurt Russell you look like, not Jeff Bridges," he added, addressing Lucas. Either way, I was happy because it seemed we'd moved off the *Bewitched* topic.

"Well, whichever one it is, I meant it as a compliment. Because the one I'm thinking of is really good-looking," I said by way of an apology for the whole Beau Bridges debacle. And I was feeling generous, thinking I was in the clear.

"So?" Michael continued pointedly. "What *is* Bewitched's name? It's Elizabeth something. Oh, Elizabeth Perkins, right?"

"Elizabeth Perkins was Wilma Flintstone in the movie with John Goodman. And she did *Big* with Tom Hanks," I said smugly. Who looked foolish now?!? We'd entered upon Annie Territory; and here, *I* was queen.

"Well, it's not Elizabeth Taylor. So, who played *Bewitched*? Who *did* you name her after?" he asked with the air of a sleuth.

"Elizabeth Montgomery," I said as superciliously as possible, enunciating each syllable.

"I knew it!" He burst out laughing. "You named her after a character who, with a flip of her ponytail, can perform magic! That is too much!" he said, gasping for breaths in between the words.

"She doesn't flip her ponytail," I said testily. "That's Jeannie. And I hate Jeannie. Samantha twinkles her nose. Duh." God, it pissed me off how everyone confused those two.

"So, you do admit it, right? You did name her after *Bewitched*, didn't you?"

"Well . . . I . . . You . . . What . . . Ahh. *All right!*" I finally erupted. "Yes! Yes, I did. I confess! And I'm proud of it. She was clever, kind, crafty, smart, beautiful, and entertaining. And she was very devoted to her family. Endora, Esmeralda, Sabrina, Dr. Bombay, even Paul Lynde, the warlock. I hope my Elizabeth will take after her in a lot of ways. So there!"

Oh God, it felt so good to confess it.

"Well, it's a good thing, nonetheless, that there are a couple famous Elizabeths kicking around in the history books so that your daughter need never admit her true namesake come grade school."

That wasn't wholly unsound logic.

Chapter Thirty-nine

*L*uckily, we'd just concluded the namesake discussion as my mother and Jenn returned with my baby. And they'd met the other Jen in the hallway on the way in. The room quickly filled with the sound of laughter and baby talk as everyone was introduced to the new kid. And just as the chatter was quieting down, who appeared at the door, but Duncan!

"Uhh, hi, everyone!" he said as he entered the room. He was carrying the most exquisite arrangement of flowers I had ever seen, and all in shades of pink—no green stuff, no white fillers, just the largest, most beautiful pink blossoms imaginable. It was like art. My mother actually caressed it. Jenn gasped. Lucas just beamed.

"Everyone, this is Duncan," I said after all the oohs and ahhs went round. "Duncan, this is my mother, Jenn, and Jen."

At which point my mother leaned into him and whispered loudly, "There are *two* Jenns; just so you know."

"Congratulations, Annie," Duncan said after he greeted everyone. "These are from the gang at Petal Pushers." Then he gave a grateful glance toward Lucas. "And this is something from Shelly and me, to say thanks for all you've done for us," he added in a hoarse whisper. He bent down to Elizabeth and placed in front of her a handmade dollhouse—exactly like our real house, only tiny. And in the family room was a mommy doll hunching over a tiny TV set with teensy-weensy wires and pliers in her hand. Me! I loved it, and I assured Duncan that Elizabeth would, too, once she was old enough to know what TV was. Given she was my daughter, that probably wouldn't be too far off.

With so many people in the room, it was just like the party I always wished I could throw. The only difference was that at this gathering, I was allowed to wear pajamas—which, by the way, was excellent. It kind of gave me this insouciant Hugh Hefner *je ne sais quoi.* I half expected Alex to show up wearing a cotton tail and a black bustier. But when he arrived, about fifteen minutes later, I was relieved to discover he was dressed in a blue button-down and flat-front khakis. Whew. And in with Alex came Andy and Aimee.

"Congratulations!" everyone yelled to Alex as he entered the room. Then, while my mom and the Jenns were kissing him hello, I introduced Andy and Aimee to everyone else there.

"Hey, awesome room," Andy said as he plopped onto the side of the bed and started bouncing. "How'd you manage this?"

"Well, apparently, we have you to thank for it," I said, eyeing him suspiciously, to see if he'd crack and confess to his engagement. I glanced knowingly at Aimee, who was talking to Dr. Weiss in the hallway.

"Me? What'd I do?" he said nervously. Then Aimee came back in and, sitting beside Andy on the bed, rubbed his shoulder. You could tell how much she liked him from the way she smiled at him even when he wasn't watching.

She leaned over to me and kissed my cheek. "Annie, we'd like to keep *this* quiet for a while," she said as she laid her left hand on my lap, displaying a ring with an enormous emerald-cut diamond in the center. "Today is *your* day—and Elizabeth's. I just wanted you to know since you kind of brought us together. And I can't think of anyone I'd rather have for a sister-in-law. But for right now let's give the attention to my soon-to-be niece!"

As she got up to go see her, I wondered how I could have hated her so much at first. Although it did still bug me that her butt was so small. Then, feeling forgiving and gracious, I wondered if it was possible that I might ever stop hating the Smiths and the Lippincotts. No, I quickly concluded. It wasn't.

"So, what is it? What did I do?" Andy asked again.

I thought I should respect Aimee's request and keep their secret, so I just smiled at him and said, "Nothing. Nothing at all, Surhesh." Then he blushed scarlet and burst out laughing.

"I guess you must know everything, then, huh?" he asked. "Who knows, maybe Robby and Elizabeth will have cousins someday, after all!" He looked across at Alex, who gave him a knowing smile and a thumbs-up. I guess that's all it takes for guys. Then he looked over at Aimee, who was holding Elizabeth. His face got soft and serious; he must have felt about her the way I felt about Alex.

When my dad arrived with Robby, the party was fully under way. My mom had even called him to ask him to bring some essentials, so he showed up laden with half a dozen boxes of pizza, a case of soda, and a huge pink cake with lots of roses on top (my favorite part). It was even better than my sweet-sixteen party when I made out with Kevin Dugan on my back porch and he called me a PYT. As a proud owner of the *Thriller* album, I knew that stood for "Pretty Young Thing." Really, I was having a great time.

Until Crew Cut Kathy and Marta the Unshaven showed up at the door. What on earth they were doing there, I had no idea. But I was willing to wager it wasn't good.

"Ahh, excuse us," Crew Cut said as she knocked on the already open door. She had stuffed herself into a horizontally-striped T-shirt that even I could recognize as unflattering; she looked more aggressive than the last time I'd seen her and had even shorter hair.

"Greetings, one and all," Marta said, her words sounding familiar to me. As I tried to place them, I caught Michael's eye, and, in a flash, I remembered that was the exact same opener her husband, Lippie the Hippie, had used during our non-wetland-sand negotiations. What, did they practice it or something? Then she continued. "We're here, making rounds to congratulate all the new mothers on the floor, and to ask that you sign—"

"Well, it's rather crowded in here," Crew Cut interjected, cutting off her unshaven buddy.

Good God, it was only April, but Marta was already wearing a sleeveless shirt. Tie-dyed (predictably). And seeing those arms in a tank top was like finding a hornets' hive in the eaves of your roof—a little bit of gross and a whole lot of scary. I couldn't resist a quick glance at Michael, who looked as though he'd just tasted warm champagne—or bad milk.

"We'd like to talk to the new mother briefly, please," Marta addressed the room imperiously.

"If we can fit," Crew Cut added under her breath.

But Michael must have heard her, because he let out a huge "Hah!" And when I looked over at him, he was gesturing to my mother for her to look at the width of Kathy's girth, crammed into that too-tight T-shirt.

Marta, taking the lead, kind of nudged through the crowd toward the bed and offered me a tannish-brown-colored pamphlet. "We're here to say 'congratulations,' but we also have a little business."

Ahh, here was the catch. I mean, these two were hardly the

Welcome Wagon type, going around as mere well-wishers. I looked down at the pamphlet as Marta continued talking.

"As the pamphlet explains, just one disposable diaper takes fifty-three years to biodegrade. And during that time, it is emitting harmful toxins into the air we breathe and the water we drink. Last year alone, there were enough disposable diapers thrown away to reach to the moon and back seventeen hundred times. So, you can see, it's a real problem." And just as I was wondering when she was going to shut up, she stopped to catch her breath. Then Crew Cut immediately piped up to relieve her.

"We're trying to convince all the new mothers in the ward to agree to use cloth diapers for just six months. And after that time, we're sure you'll be convinced they're not only better for the environment, but they're more comfortable for baby."

God, I hated when people said "baby" without an "a" or a "the" or a "your" in front of it. Still, I appreciated how she cut right to the chase.

Marta chimed in then, as though they'd choreographed it for the stage, and waved a clipboard under my nose. "So, if you would, would you just put your John Hancock right here on this contract, and we'll enroll you in the local diaper service—effective immediately."

John Hancock? Did anyone say that anymore? I mean, anyone who wasn't either eighty years old or else a fourth-grade schoolteacher giving a lesson about the Thirteen Colonies.

Of course, there was no way in hell I was going to sign anything. And there was no way I was going to use cloth diapers again. I'd tried with Robby, but it was too gross for me—as I said, I'm no activist. But when I looked up at Crew Cut and saw her scanning the room, tallying up how many visitors I had—well, I'd sooner have used my own hair for Elizabeth's diapers. It was just like her husband, counting my items in the express lane at the Shop 'n Save.

"I'm sorry," I began, trying to be nice, "but I've tried cloth in the past, and they're not for me. I wish you luck in your recruit, though!"

Really, that was civil of me, right?

Well, Crew Cut stormed out of the room, leaving Marta there to collect all their stuff, and began yelling to a nurse in the hallway. Even though she was screaming loudly enough to attract the attention of several other nurses and doctors, everyone in our room fell completely silent.

"That room is overcrowded," she screeched at the nurses; we all heard her. "There are eleven people in there. *Eleven!* Not including the mother and baby. Thirteen people! When I had my daughter here, I could have only two people at a time. I want them *out!* Get them out of there! *Now!*"

And the longer she screamed, the louder and more worked up she got. Marta, who'd gathered the pamphlets and contracts and clipboards, sneered at us all through slitted eyes and went to join her friend.

Calmly, Marta took over, addressing the unsuspecting nurse in her turn. "I believe there are statutes and hospital policies that room is not observing. It's bad for the hospital if these rules and standards are broken. Please clear the room and forbid it from occurring again."

Although I couldn't see what was happening from where I was on the bed, I heard Dr. Weiss' clear, firm voice respond. "Excuse me, ladies. We, at the hospital, agreed to let you visit the rooms in the maternity ward in order to advance your cause and raise awareness, but we did not agree to let you disturb the patients or cause a commotion—"

Crew Cut screamed right over her. "There are too many people in there. I know you can have only two. *Two at a time!* Get them out! I'll sue! I *am* a lawyer, you know!"

Crew Cut was a lawyer, too? Figured. Even though I was one, I couldn't pretend not to be aware of the bad reputation we carried as a profession.

When Crew Cut was finished screaming, Dr. Weiss, in a voice of total command, replied promptly, "*That*, ladies, is a private suite. In a *private suite*, the number of guests is not restricted unless the doctor believes it is necessary to do so for the welfare of the patient. And I, as this woman's doctor, can assure you I do not. Now please remove yourselves from the premises."

With that, she stepped into our room and closed the door behind her.

Chapter Forty

"Friends of yours?" Dr. Weiss asked as the room erupted in laughter and applause. She blushed slightly, then laughed herself. Then we all had to quiet down again, because we heard their voices still echoing in the hall outside our room.

"I'm going to sue," screamed one of them. I guessed it was Marta; I mean, with Lippie the Litigious Hippie as a husband, they'd probably already begun the suit.

"I *hate* her," said the other one. I wondered who the "her" was. Me, I was willing to guess.

"Well, I'm glad we're moving," said the first one.

Huh? Moving?

"And did you see the grandmother? The scarf, the makeup, the hair—does she think she's Candice Bergen or something?"

They were making fun of my mother! Oh my God! I'd spent my whole life waiting for this moment! But they'd ruined it for me. I had always envisioned it as, like, me and a couple cool friends (obviously neither Jenn nor Michael, given their loyalties to the better dressed of the two Fingardt women), lounging around what looks suspiciously like the *Oprah* set, while I regale them with the tortures I've endured at my mother's hand. Or eye. Or, better yet, tongue. Then they sympathize and tell me their nightmarish stories about their own mothers, and they tell me how much cooler and better dressed I am than my mother. In the end, we all hug, and then fancy coffees with lots of foam appear in front of us in those giant teacups.

Well, it was quite a different scenario to have my two biggest enemies making fun of her. I couldn't enjoy it for even a second—I just wanted to kick their asses. I started to get up from the bed to do just that, when I heard the other voice respond.

"Well, what about that guy in the suede jacket, sneering at us the whole time? What a gay 'bee-yatch'!" Then I heard their laughter floating down the hall.

This was too much—first my own flesh and blood, and now Michael! I needed to do or say something, but as soon as my foot hit the floor, I saw my mother and Michael already opening the door. Hah! Crew Cut and Unshaven had chosen the wrong duo to mess with. Haute and Couture were going to prêt some serious porter.

"Hey, you! Sarge and Janice Joplin, there!" Michael yelled down to them. His voice resounded, ricocheting off the walls, as my mother and he stepped out to address them.

"Excuse me, young lady, but simply having a soldier's haircut doesn't mean you're a colonel, so you can abort your mission to command *these* troops." That was my mother! Wasn't she great?

Then Michael spoke up. "And *you!*" He must have been addressing the Great Unshaven. "First of all, Woodstock actually ended, okay? It hasn't continued nonstop for forty years, so you can commence shaving anytime you want. And secondly, if you are going to go campaigning or petitioning or proselytizing—or whatever it is you call this—trying to convert people to your side, well, then maybe you should tell your husband and his second-rate law firm not to bring nuisance lawsuits against law-abiding citizens. Oh, and thirdly, I don't know what you two seem to have against shampoo, but don't worry, *it's biodegradable*."

And with that, my mother and Michael returned to the room, slammed the door, and gave each other air kisses on both cheeks—very Continental. Even under fire, these two could keep suave. I had to respect that.

"Yay, Mommy!" I said, feeling so much pride and love for her. She came over and sat next to me on the bed. I broke through the Chanel No.5 force field and gave her a tight and long hug. She stroked my hair while I held her. She was my mom!

Michael was venting his anger and disgust to the whole room, replaying the entire scene, when we all heard the door begin to open. Everyone—even Robby—instantaneously became stone silent. Was it those two again? Were they returning with a good comeback? With a subpoena? With a *knife*?!? I mean, if someone called me dirty or hairy, I'd probably kill. I thought maybe it should even be grounds for "justifiable homicide." You know, self-defense and all that. No one in the room seemed even to be breathing; we all just sat, unmoving, while staring at the metal door handle like a scene in an eighties horror movie. Then the door flew open.

There was a collective gasp, and then a collective sigh was heaved as Henry, Tucker, and the kids, Chris, Sarah, and Baby Brent, appeared in the doorway. The Jenns went over to greet their respective husbands and children, and I explained to everyone who the newcomers were.

After they congratulated Alex and me and met Elizabeth, who was in my mother's arms, Henry came over to me and stood by the side of the bed.

"Hey, Annie, a guy downstairs gave this to me," he said, a look of confusion on his face, as he pulled out a postcard with a business card stapled in the lower corner. "He looked kind of familiar, and the name sort of rings a bell, but I can't place it. Anyhow, he was here with another guy—kind of a fat guy in a plaid shirt—and they were picking up their wives. They were no lookers, I can assure you. But I think they were talking about you as they got into the car, so I thought maybe you'd know them."

I looked at the postcard. I looked at the business card. I looked at the room full of my friends. Then I let out a huge cheer.

"Lippie the Hippie is moving! The whole firm is relocating! They're moving to New Haven! We'll never have to see the likes of Alan Lippincott again!"

A huge cheer erupted spontaneously in the room. Never doubt that "common enemy" theory, by the way, because nothing, in my vast experience with enemies, helps you forge alliances quite like one. My God, I'd never have to get sued by Lippie; I'd never have to look into the darkness of the Unshaven One's soul (or pits); and I'd never have to endure criticisms of my son or daughter—or mom— from them ever again. It was a real relief. It filled me with the same feeling of utter and complete satisfaction as did a really good mocha shake from Jake and Happy's. I leaned back, snuggling deeper into the pillows, then read the whole postcard from start to finish.

Greetings, one and all!
In order to better serve both our Boston
and NYC clients,
we are moving to New Haven.
Please be advised that, as of May 1,
we will be located at the address above.
Please attend our office-warming reception
May 15, 5:00 p.m.–8:30 p.m.
Hope to see you there! Until then:
Keep it clean, and keep it green.

I flipped it over, and there, on the front, was the new address and the full five-partner name of the firm. I glanced over the list briefly.

Alan Lippincott
Joseph Bindler
Matthew Schwaab
Kathy Smith
Tiffany Sparkings

It hit me in stages—I mean the magnitude of this information. First, I was relieved to be rid of the Hippies. Then I remembered Tiffany (I still hated her) bragging that she was becoming a named partner this month. I guess in a firm of hippies and long-hairs, they needed one attorney who could appear in court with hand-washed silk lingerie and Prada shoes from her mom's care packages. Needless to say, I was happy to be reminded of her imminent departure. But Smith?!? Crew Cut Kathy was a lawyer? A partner? A named partner, at that?!? I mean, I'd seen the firm name often enough, but there were so many Smiths around that I never for a minute thought it could be the same one! I knew Madras Richard ran some kind of computer-consulting business from his home—he was always quick to brag about this momentous career move that enabled him "to participate more fully in the rearing and nurturing of the children." Puke. But Crew Cut! I didn't even know she had a job. I thought she was totally lying to Dr. Weiss about being a lawyer—you know, to add some weight to her threat. I mean, who'd have thought a woman who used the word "flourish" and had a man's haircut would ever in a million years actually be hired to do anything other than teach gym? Let alone become a named partner in a pretty well-known law firm?

It was too good to be true, wasn't it? Lippie the Hippie, Marta the Unshaven, Madras Richard, Crew Cut Kathy, and even Tiffany "Boob-job" Sparkings were all associated with the same law firm? Was it possible that such a convergence of evil forces, such a veritable vortex of malignancy, could even exist? I mean, the firm must have been some sort of conduit to the fiery nether regions. No normal law firm could contain such a concatenation of diabolical energies; I was convinced they must have made a deal with Satan. They were lawyers, after all.

And now, in one clean, environmentally friendly, ecologically responsible sweep, fate had cleared them away. They were all going, and I was staying! I'd run them out of town—well, I guess I couldn't actually take credit for their departure, but still, I was the last man standing! I'd won! Our new firm of Forster and Forster would be able to practice in peace and fair play. We wouldn't have to deal with the continual dubiousness of their legal practices. This made our plan even more exciting!

I folded the postcard carefully, trying to collect myself. Quietly, I stuck it in my bag so I'd always have a memento of this day. Alex—knowing and sharing my feelings without saying a word—came over with Elizabeth in his arms, and they stretched out on the bed with me. Robby, seeing us together, immediately ran over to join us and jumped up onto the bed to snuggle in between us. My eyes met Alex's over the heads of our kids, and we smiled at each other; with a quick and subtle gesture, he wiped away a tear that had crept down to his cheek and began to stroke Elizabeth's fair hair. I lay back against the pillows with Robby cuddled to my chest and looked around at all our friends and family, talking and laughing together in the hospital room. I couldn't suppress my joy anymore, and a private little giggle escaped from me.

It was better than any *Bewitched* episode. And the best part was that it was real life. Quite shocking, actually—my very own real life was even better than TV. And what, really, had I done to deserve it? Nothing more than just sit back and take it like a mom!

Photo by Eric Stiles

Stephanie Stiles is a professor of English at Dominican College in New York, where she chairs the department and directs the creative writing program. Her prize-winning poetry, fiction, and nonfiction have appeared in various contemporary anthologies and journals. She received her doctorate in nineteenth-century British literature from New York University, and she now lives with her husband, son, and baby daughter in northern New Jersey.